INT.

THE TITLE OF THIS BOOK ORIGINATES FROM MOSLEM ISLAMIC JIHADIST EXTREMISTS TRYING TO KILL AMERICANS AND AN OVER CENTRALIZED RESENTED WASHINGTON KILLING AMERICA.

THIS BOOK IS FOR ANYONE WHO HAS FANTASIZED THE KING FOR A DAY SCENARIO. WHAT WOULD I DO IF GIVEN A CHANCE TO LEAD AMERICA WITH KING LIKE AUTHORITY? WHAT KIND OF BACKGROUND AND PERSONALITY WOULD BE REQUIRED IN A LEADER? WHO WOULD HE OR SHE SELECT AS A TEAM OF INDIVIDUALS TO PURSUE GOALS AND OBJECTIVES FOR AMERICA TO THEIR SUCCESSFUL CONCLUSION.

THE AUTHOR ARRANGES A FANTASY SCENARIO IN AN EXCITING STORY LINE THAT PUTS HIM IN THIS SITUATION AND WHAT HE WOULD DO TO RESOLVE THE MOSLEM ISLAMIC JIHADIST THREAT, FOREIGN-POLICY AND AMERICA'S DOMESTIC PROBLEMS IN AN ORDERLY LOGICAL WAY TO PLACE AMERICA BACK INTO THE DYNAMIC 1980'S SITUATION AND IMPROVING ON IT.

YOUNG AMERICANS THAT WERE 18 SIX YEARS AGO THAT HAVE ONLY EXPERIENCED THE PRESENT CONDITIONS AND ARE NOW 24 OR EVEN SOME 30 YEAR OLDS DON'T HAVE A CLUE WHAT A VIBRANT FREE ECONOMY IS LIKE AND A LEADER THAT DEFENDS AMERICA'S INTERESTS. THEY ARE TRYING TO BE SOLD THAT THE PRESENT MALAISE IS NORMAL AND THEY NEED A STRONGER CENTRAL GOVERNMENT TO HELP THEM. NOTHING COULD BE FURTHER THAN THE TRUTH. THE BASIC INGREDIENTS ARE STILL THERE IN AMERICA. ALL IT TAKES IS LEADERSHIP.

THIS BOOK IS UNIQUE IN THAT IT CONTAINS PRECISE TIMELINES RUNNING FROM OCTOBER 2014 THROUGH TO JANUARY 2017. THE UNEDITED VERSION OF THIS BOOK WAS WRITTEN BETWEEN MARCH 2014 AND OCTOBER 2014. SINCE OCTOBER 2014 THERE HAVE BEEN JUST A FEW ADDITIONS.

THE CONTENTS HAVE SOME ROMANCE, ACTION, DRAMA, HUMOR, POLITICS, POLICY AND EMOTION.

ENJOY

DAVID HAYNES

Copyright: © G Investments Ltd 2015

Editor: Robyn Bryant Assistant Editor: Carrie Aronson

Computer Consultant: Normand Degre'

Cover: Robbin VanHemel

Special thanks to nearly life-long friends Robyn Bryant and the real John McFarland. John for his encouragement, counsel and support. John wrote the speech to the Commerce Association that appears in the book. And Robyn I thank for her professional contribution to structure and editing, even when she did not agree with content. It would have been a mess without her.

All rights reserved. No part of this publication may be reproduced, distributed, or transmitted in any form or by any means, including photocopying, recording, or other electronic or mechanical methods, without the prior written permission of the author, except in the case of brief quotations embodied in critical reviews and certain other noncommercial uses permitted by copyright law.
For permission requests, visit www.killwashington.com
This book is a work of fiction. Names, characters, places, and incidents either are the product of the authors' imagination or are used fictitiously, and any resemblance to actual persons, living or dead, business establishments, events, or locale is entirely coincidental.

ISBN: 1511867124
ISBN 13: 9781511867122

KILL WASHINGTON

a novel by David Haynes

Contents

	Prologue: Crisis in Washington	vii
Chapter 1	The American-Canadian Connection	1
Chapter 2	A Strange Invitation	21
Chapter 3	Love Interrupted	25
Chapter 4	Flight to Washington	32
Chapter 5	The Early Years	36
Chapter 6	Baldor, Arkansas, and the Road to Success	45
Chapter 7	Arriving in Washington	59
Chapter 8	The Presentation	63
Chapter 9	The Planning Meeting; A New Direction For America	81
Chapter 10	The Problem in the Middle East	91
Chapter 11	Picking the Right People	96
Chapter 12	Reassuring the Markets	109
Chapter 13	Preparing the Press Conference	128
Chapter 14	The First White House Evening	134
Chapter 15	The Press Conference	137
Chapter 16	The Mexico Problem	146
Chapter 17	Camp David and the Kurds	154
Chapter 18	Russia Rears its Head	163
Chapter 19	Report From the Mideast and other Hotspots	174

Chapter 20	Black Conservative Night	189
Chapter 21	The New Tax Plan	194
Chapter 22	The Kidnapping	204
Chapter 23	Public Perceptions Abroad and at Home	213
Chapter 24	Taking on the Jihadists and other Threats	232
Chapter 25	A Surprise for the Administrator - And for the President	250
Chapter 26	Wrapping Up the Afc and Cuba as Well	265
Chapter 27	The Administration's Last Acts	277

Prologue: Crisis in Washington

WEDNESDAY, October 15, 2014 – Washington

It was one month before the 2014 midterm elections, and FBI Director Bill Simmons was staring out the window of his office in Washington. He loved and valued his job, so what he was currently contemplating was gut-wrenching.

He was not exactly a wealthy individual, and he relied on a steady income to maintain his lifestyle. Yet Bill was a staunch patriot who believed in the law and the Constitution, and now his investigations were being stymied by what he perceived as a lawless Attorney General and the AG's boss, President Chambers. He had recently been asked in an indirect way by staffers at the AG's office to keep quiet about his findings regarding the cover-up of the Renrazi investigation conducted by Congress. Muslim jihadists had assassinated an American ambassador and three of his guards after a lengthy stand-off in a compound in Renrazi, North Africa on September 11, 2012. Subsequently, a Congressional investigation was launched to find out what had happened and why no one had come to their aid. Now the investigations had advanced into a cover-up. The staffers did not know exactly what information had been uncovered by the investigation, but Simmons did. He had access to the files, was getting daily updates, and also had documents that had been subpoenaed by the Congressional committees. The subpoenas had been directed toward the White House and not the FBI, but nonetheless, the situation made him very uncomfortable. Simmons had been appointed by a Democratic president, but he was no ideologue. His gut told him it was just a matter of time before everything came unglued and every lower-level person was going to take a hit, as always happened in Washington.

He remembered what his father had told him when he was younger and hanging around with some dubious characters. "You hang around with crap like that," his father had said, "and you are going to get some of it on you." Those words resonated with him now.

The straw that broke the camel's back for Simmons was that for months he had been warning the administration and everyone else involved with the security of the nation about the growing Muslim jihadist threat from within the United States itself. Simmons had been trying to draw their attention to the jihadist training camps, of which there were more than 20 across the US. The administration's refusal to act on his information was based on what Simmons considered legal moronics: the fact that the individuals training were American citizens, were operating on private property, and weapons were legal anyway.

Simmons was utterly frustrated that he could not get anyone to take the internal threat more seriously. Worse, if this was allowed to continue unchecked, it was only a matter of time before the US took another terrorist hit. And this time the fingers would be pointing at him.

Standing in front of his window, Simmons made his decision. He would be proactive and resign tomorrow, in front of a hastily-called news conference. He realized his timing was not ideal so close to the midterm elections, but he knew that he needed to be out of office as soon as possible to avoid being personally caught up in an investigation. His reputation and credibility were paramount.

He went back to his desk, called in his secretary, and told her to make two copies of everything in those files, including the ones no one knew he had.

He decided to call Bob Rails, vice president and director of Fox News. He knew that Fox would do a responsible job of reporting, unlike the liberal mainstream media, which protected the Chambers administration by reporting exclusively good news and not reporting bad news. While

Simmons knew that a deceitful press was one of the most dangerous enemies to a free society, he was well aware of his own lack of media savvy, and he needed advice on how to handle the news conference.

Bob Rails picked up his phone almost immediately. "Good morning, Mr. Director! What can I do for you?"

"Well, sir, I need some advice about calling a news conference tomorrow afternoon. I am asking you because I know I can count on your discretion. I want to do this outside of the FBI building and thought you could set something up for me for tomorrow around 2 p.m."

A veteran newsman, Rails sensed something big, so he decided to test the waters. "Maybe the Watergate Hotel would be appropriate."

Simmons laughed. "That would be a little conspicuous, don't you think? How about the Hilton on 16th Street?"

"May I ask the nature of this conference?" Rails asked, curious as to the importance of the call and excited because this was not the kind of phone call you get every day.

"I assure you it will be highly newsworthy, but I can't disclose the content. You are the first call I have made. Right now I need you to set up the location and make sure other networks are notified only that there will be a news conference tomorrow at 2 o'clock, no details."

"What makes you think I can do that?"

"Because you know all the important people at the media outlets and I want to make sure the appropriate people turn up," Simmons replied.

Rails chuckled. "And what are we getting?"

"A great news story."

"Okay," Rails said. "I'll get back to you soon."

"I hope real soon. And do I have your word not to disclose to anyone that it is me who will be at the news conference?"

"You have my word. I'll call you back this afternoon," Rails said.

Now Simmons had a dilemma. He knew what he wanted to do, but he needed to do it in a way that would not get him into legal trouble. He had to get the documents into the hands of the Chairman of the Renrazi investigation, and he didn't want to risk a leak by using an intermediary.

All of a sudden, the word 'subpoena' flew into his head. All he had to do was ask the Chairman to send him a subpoena at the FBI offices. That way, he would be handing over the documents in response to a legal subpoena.

But how to contact Chairman Essa without third parties asking why the director of the FBI was trying to contact him? He wanted to be sure that only Essa knew Simmons had asked to be subpoenaed. He decided to make a call to Essa's office himself. He might just catch him there. He told the person that answered that he was Bob Rails calling from Fox News.

Essa picked up his phone and said, "Good morning Bob, what can I do for you?"

"Sorry for the deception, Mr. Chairman, but this is Simmons, Director of the FBI. If you want to verify, you can call me back at this number, extension 323, can you do that?"

"Yes, I can do that," Essa said.

Simmons' phone rang a minute later. He had already advised his secretary that he would be answering his own phone for the next 15 minutes.

"Okay, what's going on?" Essa asked.

"I need to talk to you but I don't want anyone to know about it, not now and not it the future. We need to meet where we won't be seen. You know the parking garage behind Union Station? Meet me on the top level. There aren't any cameras up there."

"What is this all about?" Essa asked.

"You will find out when you get there. I will be alone. Can you be there in an hour?"

Essa was swamped with work, but this sounded like something important so he agreed.

By now, Simmons' secretary had copied the documents and stacked them in two neat piles, each one just large enough to fit into a large envelope. Thirty minutes later Simmons grabbed a ticket from the automatic dispenser at the parking lot, found a space and waited for Essa. Simmons spotted him and headed over while Essa was getting out of his car. "Mr. Chairman," said Simmons, "I have documents in my office related to the information that you subpoenaed from the White House. I need you to send a subpoena for any documents I have connected to the Renrazi investigation before noon tomorrow."

Essa said, "This cloak and dagger stuff is extremely unusual."

"Maybe so, but it is not unusual for you to issue subpoenas."

"What is the purpose?" Essa asked.

"I can't tell you right now but you will know by 2 o'clock tomorrow. I'll need that subpoena in my office before noon. That's all I can say for now. Will you do it?"

"Well, if it's going to help our investigation, why not?" Essa said.

Simmons said, "I need your word that you will not tell anyone about our meeting or how the subpoena was activated. Just tell someone on your staff to get it done and not ask questions."

"Okay, I'll make sure you have it by noon," Essa said.

"And please use cash to pay the parking attendant. You don't need credit card proof that you were here."

Essa said, "Actually, in all the excitement about leaving the office I forgot to bring money." Simmons reached in his pocket and gave Essa a $20 bill.

"Do you have a hat or something in your car so you won't be recognized on the way out?"

Essa found a Nats baseball cap and pulled it down over his brow. At that moment a car drove by them slowly. The driver appeared to be staring at them and both men immediately turned away, hoping they had not been recognized. It was time for them to leave.

When Simmons got back to his office, he found a message from Bob Rails. Simmons called right back, hoping for positive progress.

It was all set up, Rails assured him, and added, "I hope I'm going to get something out of this, like an interview after your news conference."

Simmons considered for a moment. He would need a job after tomorrow so he might as well take advantage of the situation. "Well, maybe once the dust settles after tomorrow you can make me a Fox News contributor, and then I can do all the interviews you want."

Rails laughed and said, "You've been pretty articulate up until now. That could be a possibility!"

—w—

White House communications director Casey Rines was sitting in his West Wing office when his phone rang. It was George Dicky, better known in the news business as 'Thrill up his Leg.' Years earlier he had described a speech given by President Chambers about his relationship with Chicago's Rev. Bright as giving him a 'thrill up his leg' on a TV program and the name stuck. Dicky said, "Some of our people have been asked to attend a news conference at the Capital Hilton on 16th Street tomorrow at 2 o'clock. Do you know anything about it? It's kind of weird that no one seems to know what it's all about."

Rines said, "I don't have a clue, but let me know if you find anything out."

THURSDAY, October 16, 2014 – Washington

Early the following morning, Simmons called his secretary Linda in and started dictating his letter to the President. When he got to the word 'resign,' Linda's pen jumped off the paper and she looked at him in shock. "My god!" she said, "I had no idea that you were even considering that!"

"I didn't want anyone to know," he said. "Would you arrange a meeting with key staffers for 11 o'clock this morning so that I may say goodbye, because by this afternoon, the White House will not want me here for another minute."

Her eyes watered up and she left the office to type up his resignation. Ten minutes later she walked back in and said, "There's a bailiff from the Congressional offices here with a subpoena for the Renrazi files."

"Linda, please bring me a large envelope and the subpoena."

Simmons stuffed one of the stacks of documents into the envelope, and reviewed the subpoena. "Everything looks to be in order, please give this to the bailiff."

He put the second set of copies into his briefcase, then packed his few personal effects into a box and asked one of the clerks to have it put in his car. He asked Linda to have his letter of resignation sent by priority courier to the White House Chief of Staff.

After a last look around his office, Simmons accompanied Linda to the conference room on the second floor. A large group of staff he had worked with for years had gathered to say goodbye. He shook hands with everyone and delivered a short statement thanking everyone for their service, gave Linda big hug, and left the building for the last time.

Then he drove to the Hilton. He was early, so he sat in the small cafeteria on the ground floor and made a few notes on what he wanted to say.

THURSDAY, October 16, 2014 – The White House

News in Washington travels like wildfire, and the news of the director's resignation had already reached the office of Casey Rines at the White House. "Maybe that's what the news conference at the Hilton is all about," he said to his caller before he hung up.

When Simmons approached the room where the news conference was to be held, he could see that Bob Rails had done a superb job of preparation. He was greeted by Washington White House correspondent Dirk Penry, who said, "Look, Mr. Director, we went to a lot of trouble to set this up. Can you give me a head's up?"

"I'm resigning," Simmons said.

Penry looked surprised, "Why?"

"Look, Dirk, please let me just do the news conference and maybe afterwards we can have a little off the record conversation."

By 2 p.m. the conference room was filled with reporters. Simmons valued punctuality and stepped up to the microphone promptly on the hour. There was no point in making useless preliminary statements so he got right to it. "Ladies and gentlemen, this morning I submitted my resignation to the President, effective immediately. As of now, I am no longer Director of the FBI."

One of the reporters called out the obvious question. "What is the reason behind your resignation, Mr. Director?"

Simmons was prepared with the answer. "I think that most of you in the mainstream media are going to understand this. Ever since President Chambers launched his original primary campaign, he was your guy and anybody who opposed him was not. You report the positives about him enthusiastically. Negatives have, for the most part, not been reported or if they were, they were covered very briefly on TV or radio and could be found only in the back pages of newspapers. This sort of media coverage undermines freedom and liberty, allowing the people in power to think they can do anything they want, knowing that for the most part it won't get reported. In my opinion, this corruption has now crept into the political arena where people in power think they can bypass the Constitution and bypass the law, implementing only the laws that suit their purposes and using government agencies to punish American citizens who oppose their policies. This kind of atmosphere is contrary to my values and my reputation. I believe in the laws of this country and the Constitution."

Another reporter asked, "What specifically triggered your resignation?"

Simmons said, "I have been warning the administration for years that there are Muslim jihadist training camps operating in states all across this country, right under our noses. I don't need to tell you that this represents an enormous danger to the security of all Americans. And yet this administration has refused to heed my warnings or take any steps to thwart this threat. Now I think I've said enough. Thank you ladies and gentlemen for your time."

Reporters were still yelling questions as he walked off the stage. Dirk Penry was waiting for him, anxious to have the conversation Simmons had promised, so they ducked into an empty room just down the corridor. Penry said, "So if you've been warning about the training camps for years, what just happened exactly to push you to retire today?"

Simmons said. "I've been getting phone calls suggesting that we may want to overlook certain things in our investigations. That sort of thing, suggests that we didn't need to investigate this or that. The implication was that if we didn't comply, there were going to be problems. What I was hearing, although not directly stated, was that we had become too independent in pursuing certain matters. I can't point to any specific thing, but my gut told me there was something in the air, so I figured I'd better leave now, and preserve my integrity and my reputation; because in the end that's all we have. I figured I was going to get my ass fired sooner or later anyway, so I thought I would be proactive.

"And I'm going to tell you one more thing, just between you and me. Based on the intelligence we have acquired, it's not a question of IF we're going take a jihadist hit, it's WHEN. And you know how this town works, Dirk. If I'm still Director, they'll put the blame on me."

"Please thank Bob for doing this. Please tell him I was serious about being a Fox contributor because I think I'm going to need a job."

Both men slipped out through a side door, unobserved. Simmons went home to watch himself on the news. As he predicted, the mainstream media outlets featured very brief segments about his departure at the end of their newscasts. Fox News focused on it nonstop until almost 11 o'clock.

Simmons felt very alone that evening. What he didn't realize was that he was not the only serious player in America that felt as he did. He also didn't know that he, along with every other serious player, especially in Washington, was being monitored and followed. And he didn't know that the driver in the parking lot had taken a picture of him with Chairman Essa.

Chairman Essa watched the newscast too, and was briefly shocked before concluding that Simmons had probably had enough of the whole Washington environment. Essa had already gone through the documents from Simmons' office and realized that although some of them might lead to new areas of investigation, there was one smoking gun – an email from White House advisor Casey Rines' people outlining the talking points concerning the Renrazi tragedy. The email advised everyone to say that a spontaneous demonstration of people inflamed by an anti-Muslim video had resulted in an attack on the four Americans, when in fact it was a planned and organized attack by Islamic terrorists. The Chambers campaign needed to portray the President as a strong leader who had decimated Al Qaeda. As this attack would hurt his image and could be damaging to his re-election, the campaign decided to deceive the American people. There was a Congressional investigation to challenge White House assertions that this was not a terrorist attack. Among the media, Fox News was practically the only one to challenge this view. Since then, the Congressional committee led by Essa proved that it was, in fact, a terrorist attack and that the White House had tried to cover it up.

At this point Essa's committee was investigating the cover-up of the cover-up. And now the chairman had evidence that put one foot into the White House. The committee now knew who had instructed emissaries of the administration to deceive the media and the American people.

Essa decided to wait a couple of days before releasing the new documents. Due to his recent resignation, a premature release might leave a trail straight to Simmons.

CHAPTER 1

THE AMERICAN - CANADIAN CONNECTION

—⋘—

THURSDAY, October 16, 2014 – Canada, near the Vermont border

70-YEAR-OLD RETIRED CANADIAN BUSINESSMAN DAVID Haynes was watching the Fox News Channel showing Simmons' 2 p.m. news conference. What Simmons was saying about the media and the Washington environment only reinforced his already strongly held opinions and he suspected that there was more to the story than Simmons was prepared to reveal. Haynes didn't watch most of the mainstream media anyway, including CNN and CSNBC on the cable networks. When he did it was usually just to compare their coverage to Fox's. Once, when a serious event threatened Chambers' image, he switched the channel over to CNN to see a reporter talking about a sinkhole somewhere in America. He just laughed and switched back over to Fox.

David Haynes was absolutely fascinated by America, Americans, American politics, and American history. He had the complete volumes by Shelby Foote on the American Civil War, and was particularly impressed that Foote had written the entire manuscript by hand. He had watched countless documentaries on American history, American characters such as Benjamin Franklin, and the founders of the American Constitution. He didn't know why he was so fascinated with all this stuff. Maybe it was because he was brought up, and still lived in, the town of Knowlton in the Eastern Townships of the province of Quebec, just 15 miles north of the Vermont border.

When he was growing up, Canadians and Americans were constantly crossing the border back and forth and were in frequent contact. Still today, a lot of people have relatives and friends living on both sides; there is even a building in Stanstead, Quebec, which sits partly in Canada and partly in the USA.

Despite the fact that the province of Quebec is almost 80% French-speaking, people living along the Canadian-American border have their own unique culture and history. During the American Revolution, British loyalists fled the American colonies and reestablished themselves in the Eastern Townships, just north of the northern states of Vermont, New Hampshire, and Maine, resulting in most of the towns in the Eastern Townships of Quebec, southeast of Montreal, having English names.

In the early 1960s, the drive-in theater located just a mile over the border in Richford, Vermont, was one of the Townshippers' – and David's – favorite destinations. Early every Saturday evening, there would be a lineup of cars, god knows how long, at the border crossing. You didn't even need a passport or a driver's license then, you would just say, "I'm so-and-so from Knowlton going to the drive-in," and away you went.

When the movie was over, everybody rushed to get out so they wouldn't wait in the long line heading home. Quebec didn't have any drive-in theaters back then; the Catholic Church was so powerful in the early 60s in Quebec that they had the government ban drive-ins. Perhaps they figured there would be too much hanky-panky going on in the cars.

Quebecers often crossed the border to get things they couldn't yet buy in Canada, like soft-serve ice cream that swirled out of a machine. Country music and country bands were the order of the day in the early 60s. There were great country bars and dance halls all over the place on both sides of the border and it was common for Americans and Canadians to cross the border to spend an evening dancing and drinking at some of these joints. It was easy to see people on both sides of this section of the border had a common culture.

Another reason for Haynes' great love of the US was that he attributed his business success almost exclusively to Americans. He had been given opportunities by Americans not granted to him by fellow Canadians. He met many other American business people, many of them still great friends of his to this day. He didn't know why, but he had a special affinity with his associates from the South, who became friends. It was probably because of their rural cultural similarities.

Haynes needed to know what was going on in the world, especially in the US. This stemmed from an experience in his early 20s during one of his frequent visits to Toe Blake's Tavern, on the corner of Guy and St. Catherine streets in Montreal, named after the revered coach of the Montreal Canadian hockey team. In those days, only men were permitted in Quebec taverns. As he couldn't afford to go anywhere else, Haynes frequently stopped in to get a steak or a couple of draft beers for a little more than a dollar.

The place was a hangout for salesmen, Bell Telephone personnel, and Canadian Broadcasting Corporation employees. On one of his visits an argument about the virtues of the Vietnam War broke out. Some guys were talking like they knew Asian history and saying that Communist aggression had to be stopped. Then a Bell Telephone guy gave a half an hour treatise on Vietnam, its history, and why the French got their asses kicked before the Americans arrived. On his way home, Haynes said to himself, "I'm never again going to shoot my mouth off on something I know nothing about." It had been a good lesson.

From that point on, he started to read everything about the US he could get his hands on. After he read a wonderful book by William Manchester called *American Caesar*, which to Haynes seemed like an appropriate title given MacArthur's occupation of Japan, Gen. Douglas MacArthur became one of his favorite American characters.

If there ever was a great example of a good dictator, it was MacArthur. Contrary to contemporary beliefs, MacArthur was not just a great military commander. On the other side of his personality lived a great democratic thinker who believed in freedom and democratic institutions. He was a great political strategist capable of adapting methods of communication that suited the Japanese style and culture. MacArthur is still revered in Japan. He had absolute power, and yet only wielded it when he felt it was necessary. He instructed all the Armed Forces to be courteous to the Japanese and anyone who wasn't got their ass kicked. He let Hirohito sit in his palace while he introduced changes into the Japanese culture at a rapid pace. He allowed the Japanese to write a constitution, making adjustments from time to time. Hirohito was finally obliged to make the first move and meet MacArthur. MacArthur didn't go to the emperor, the emperor was coming to him. MacArthur, a tall man, made certain he would have his picture taken with Hirohito before the emperor left. He ensured the picture was published in Japanese newspapers. When the Japanese people saw MacArthur towering over the emperor it sent a message: Hirohito is not the god you think he is. The people are just as important as the emperor, practical power is no longer in the hands of royalty, kings, and their surrogates. Power is now in the hands of the voters.

In Haynes' view, the feudal Japanese system was not significantly different than some of the present-day Muslim countries. Women were second class citizens. MacArthur wouldn't let that continue and insisted that all Japanese women would get the vote. In fact, after some elections results poured in, one of his officers told him that a prostitute had been elected in a Tokyo district. MacArthur answered, "She must be popular with her clientele."

Douglas MacArthur brought Japan into the 20th century and as a result of the freedoms he installed, Japan became an industrial force in the world.

Haynes was fascinated by this concept and fantasized from time to time about what he would do if given the privilege of being a dictator in America for four years. He started keeping notes on the subject for fun. He called it THE LIST.

MONDAY, November 10, 2014 - Washington

It was now becoming clear to most Americans that they had been deceived on many levels; from the IRS' politically targeted debacle and Renrazi and its subsequent cover-up to a fast and furious weapons scandal and the Affordable Health Care Act, deceit was in the air. Slowly but surely, the truth was emerging, and the American people reacted by electing a majority of Republicans to the Senate and increasing the already existing Republican majority in the House.

This all culminated in a bombshell dropped on the 9 o'clock segment of The Kelly File, a news broadcast on Fox, although it was something that had been on the internet for quite some time if anyone had bothered to look for it. The report featured a videotape of one of the architects of the Affordable Health Care Act, recorded at a 2013 academic conference. The man's name was Jonathan Gruber, Professor of Economics at the Massachusetts Institute of Technology. The Fox report quoted one part of the recording:

"This bill was written in a tortured way to make sure the Congressional Budget Office did not score the mandate as taxes. If the CBO scored the mandate as taxes, the bill dies. Okay? So it's written to do that. In terms of risk – rated subsidies, if you had a law which said healthy people were going to pay in and sick people get money it would not have passed. Okay? Lack of transparency is a huge political advantage and basically call it the stupidity of the American voter or whatever, but basically that was really really critical to get the thing to pass. I wish we could make it all transparent, but I'd rather have this law than not."

MONDAY, November 10, 2014 – Knowlton, Quebec

Haynes watched the tape and made some observations.

1. This overeducated pinhead deliberately deceived the American people from the start and some individuals in Congress and the administration went along.
2. Up until this point, the people's perception was that this was just a messed up bill. Now it was obvious that the lies and deception went right back to the start.
3. Prof. Gruber called the American people stupid.
4. These academics speak a form of English which is non-discernible to average Americans. They seem to be in an exclusive club where the more complicated and lofty the lingo, the more superior they appear among their peers.

5. His body language while making his points were that of elevated superiority and arrogance.
6. He appeared to be so wrapped up in his own self-importance, and so absorbed in trying to impress his peers at the conference, that part of his brain malfunctioned. He spilled the beans about trying to deceive the American people, and fueling the fire, he called them stupid. If this guy was so brilliant why would he do a stupid thing like that?!? His friends at the White House had paid him a serious sum of money as a consultant and had touted him as a genius, and were probably going ballistic now. Gruber had just committed the number one political sin. He had just exposed them all. Now they were all running for cover. After Gruber made approximately 19 visits to the White House, some were saying they had never met him. Their efforts were to no avail. Every time they did the 'Peter denying Jesus three times' routine, Fox would show previous videotape of those same politicians extolling Gruber's genius-like virtues. They were flat-out lying. Haynes figured they thought the American people were stupid and would not believe their own eyes and ears. Fox News was, yet again, practically the only network to report this. If this had happened under Bush or Reagan it would have been all over the mainstream media. They were still trying to protect their boy.
7. The working citizens of America were going to work every day, doing their jobs, and coming home to parent their children. They didn't have time to read and watch the news in-depth every day. They expected the people they elected and the advisors that serve them to do their jobs well. On November 4th, the American people sensed that this was not the case, and fired politicians who permitted people like Professor Gruber to write stupid legislation which was unjust, unworkable, and unsustainable.

TV commentator Francis Mills said that while with CSNBC she had questioned the financial numbers aired concerning the Affordable Health

Care Act. She disclosed that she was informed by management that her doubt was inappropriate and that she was insulting the President of the United States. She no longer works there.

"I guess the American people are not as stupid as they thought they were," Haynes concluded. "America has come a long way down from when they had a President who trusted the collective judgment of the American people."

TUESDAY, November 11, 2014 - Knowlton Quebec

The Congressional elections were over, and the Republicans had won a majority in the Senate and had maintained their majority in Congress. It was now obvious that Americans were pissed off with this President. Haynes was still in Quebec, watching the US news from his summer home. He was usually at his rental house in Florida by November, but he had some loose ends to tie up.

The news reports were that Russia was bringing tanks and military equipment close to the eastern Ukraine border. As far as Haynes was concerned, this was a result of Russia's perception that America was weak. He thought the military and political establishment in the United States must be highly anxious and concerned. He sighed, switched off the TV, and went into the kitchen to make some juice.

Haynes had been big on juicing for years. Every morning he would throw an orange, apple, banana, blueberries, and strawberries into a juicer. That was normally his meal for the day. Sometimes he would have a mid-afternoon snack, but he would certainly enjoy dinner with some good wine. Haynes was in good shape for his age. He was about 6'1," 220 pounds, with a 36" waist. In his younger years he had played football and hockey. He even got a tryout with the Canadian Football League's Montreal Allouettes but was cut after an exhibition game. He was an expert skier, but now, since he had retired, he preferred to play golf during the winter in the South. He still skied from time to time, but hardly as much as he used to. He had skied practically every major ski area in North America and some in Europe he had traveled extensively during his business career.

He was also a private pilot with a license to fly twin airplanes. At one time he owned a 421 Cessna.

Once, on a clear fall day, he was flying to Ashville, North Carolina, via a customs stop in Harrisburg, Pennsylvania. He was starting his descent into Harrisburg and already down to around 8000 feet when he smelled a familiar odor – the smell of burning electrical wires. Suddenly, smoke started coming out of the vents between the windscreen and the top of the instrument panel. A pilot's worst fear was coming to life: an electrical fire had sprung up underneath the instrument panel.

Flying an airplane from A to B is one thing. Any licensed pilot can do that. Experienced pilots are measured by their ability to avoid potential problems. But what proves a skilled pilot is how they handle emergencies. Haynes' training kicked into gear. He immediately shut off the electrical master supplying power to the burning wires and most of the electrical systems. Now only the engines were functioning. He managed to keep one hand on the wheel while he unclipped the fire extinguisher and sprayed underneath the panel. The cockpit was now full of smoke, and he was struggling to see the turn and bank indicator through the fumes to keep his airplane level and under control. He thought about opening the small panel window on his left but decided not to because it might add oxygen to the fire.

The smoke slowly started to dissipate, clearing his view out of the front windscreen. Due to the chaos of the fire, he was no longer sure of his exact position. He remembered the words of his flight instructor Roger: "When faced with an emergency, don't contemplate your navel, get the aircraft on the ground NOW."

His girlfriend Lynn, sitting in the co-pilot seat, had said barely a word throughout the ordeal; she was probably scared shitless. He spotted a major highway off to his left on the horizon. He figured this was in the general direction of the airport. In his mind flashed a passage from R. L. Qualls' little book on leadership: "Get the herd headed roughly west, the rest will take care of itself." Haynes put the nose down at an angle, just steep enough to avoid to putting the speed of the aircraft into yellow section of the speed indicator, which would exceed the plane's structural speed. His objective was to get the aircraft down low enough over the highway so that, in the event of another problem, he could put it down there or on the grass in between the lanes. He needed to reduce power slowly, and in increments, so as to not damage the engines. On piston-driven, turbocharged engines, any sudden reduction in power cools the engines too quickly, resulting in severe internal engine damage.

Finally he leveled off about 1,000 feet above the highway. Unfortunately, his forward view was limited. However, the advantage was that from this altitude he could get on the ground relatively quickly in the event of another catastrophe. He preferred the latter.

He needed to get the Harrisburg approach and tower frequencies off his charts so that he could talk to the controllers. The problem was that to do that, he would have to engage the autopilot to free up his hands, but that would mean turning the electrical master switch back on, which would refuel the electrical wires; not an option if he wanted to stay flame-free. He decided to stay on his heading and attempt to locate the airport, which he knew was somewhere on his forward horizon next to the river. He would fly over the center of the active runway and make two left turns or right turns into the runway, depending on the wind direction. That way the tower would spot him, and he would have time to spot any incoming traffic. Hopefully he would not see any, and could land without contacting the tower – just like old time flying. He gave Lynn a soft pat on the leg and said, "We're okay now." The smell of burnt electrical wire was everywhere. All of a sudden he felt a rush of adrenaline. He had just remembered that the week before, by luck or divine providence, he had purchased a battery operated portable radio. "Finally a break," he thought. He asked Lynn to find the radio in the small duffel bag. She turned it on, and looked in the airport data book to find the frequencies for Harrisburg. When she had it, Haynes took the radio from her, set the frequency and pushed the button. "Harrisburg approach, this is Charlie Foxtrot Golf Delta Uniform."

When Haynes had turned off the power to his instrument panel the transponder was also turned off, meaning he had disappeared off the controller's screen. The controller said, "What happened? We lost you."

Haynes explained that an electrical fire underneath the panel had forced him to shut off the electrical master.

"Do you want to declare an emergency?" the controller asked.

Haynes said, "No."

"Do you have the airport in sight?" the controller asked.

"Negative," said Haynes, "but I can see the river and I will head in that direction. I'm sure I'll see the airport soon."

"Advise when you have the airport in sight," said Harrisburg approach, "and we will switch you to the tower frequency."

"We will advise when airport is in sight," said Haynes. He had the airplane flying at a manageable speed, but how was he going to get the gear out? If he cranked it down manually he would have no way of knowing if they were locked because the gear lights were part of the electrical system. If he wanted to get the gear out the usual way he would have to turn on the electrical master again. Either option wasn't all that inviting. Again he remembered Roger's advice years ago – "Get the plane on the ground now!" He now had the airport in sight and advised Harrisburg approach. Approach gave him the tower frequency and said there was no traffic in the area and he was clear to land.

Haynes had made his decision. About a half a mile from the end of the runway he would turn on his electrical master just long enough to drop the gear switch down and allow the gear to extend. Hopefully the gear would drop and he could ask the tower if his gear was out. Then he would turn the electrical switch back off. He flipped on the electrical switch, dropped the gear handle down, and heard the whining of the gear system.

All of a sudden there was a huge bang. It felt like the wheels had fallen off. He immediately shut off the electrical switch. He could smell the increased intensity of the electrical fire and thought to himself, "To hell with it. I am getting this thing on the ground even if I have to land it on its belly."

He asked the tower to confirm his gear was out. "It looks extended," came the reply. Haynes was approaching the end of the runway at the slowest speed possible without stalling the airplane. Now he was over the runway and he pulled the power back, nose up slightly, heard the wonderful sound of the two main wheels touching the runway, followed an instant later by the nose gear touching down. Then the dreaded happened: the right side started to collapse and Lynn said, 'What's happening?"

"Hang on, we're going for a slide," he said. He was praying that all the wheels would collapse, since that was the only way to keep the airplane straight. If only one main gear collapsed and not the other, they would do a very dangerous whirly in the middle of the runway.

Fortunately all the wheels collapsed. The props were pounding on the runway and getting a nice perm, while the belly was scraping along sounding like metal fingers down a chalkboard. Finally the aircraft came to a stop. Haynes looked at Lynn and yelled, "Get out!"

Lynn had always had trouble opening the door at the back, but this time she was out of the plane faster than a speeding bullet. She banged her head on the exit door on the way out. Luckily this was the only injury. Haynes told the tower he was exiting just as the emergency trucks began arriving. Lynn had a slight mark on her head. Haynes knew that the airplane would be a total loss but Lynn was okay and so was he, so all in all, it was a good day's work.

The FAA inspector eventually showed up and stuck his nose into the plane entrance. He took one whiff, then looked at Haynes and said, "Good job you got it on the ground."

Later, after filling out the accident report, they rented a car and drove the rest of the way to Asheville, stopping to have a round of golf before they got there.

TUESDAY, November 11, 2014 - Knowlton Quebec, 4:00 p.m.

Haynes had been cleaning out his desk and had come across the insurance report on the plane accident. Glancing at the date, he found it hard to believe how the ten years had flown by so quickly. So many things had changed. And he'd met the woman he hoped would remain the love of his life. He was wondering how she would react in a similar emergency when he suddenly realized it was 4 p.m. and time to check the stock market closing reports on the Fox Business Channel. He loved listening to stock tips from Charles Layne. Haynes had used some of Layne's tips to make a little bit of money on the stock market from time to time, and thought the man was a brilliant investor.

As often happens, the screen flashed a Fox alert and on came Dirk Penry stating that an emergency news conference was about to start. Military officers accompanied a group of former officials from previous administrations into a large briefing room at the Pentagon.

Haynes watched as people started to file in, led by four generals - one from the Army, one from the Navy, one from the Air Force, and one from the Marine Corps. There were at least sixty officials standing behind the four generals, including former secretaries of defense, former directors of the CIA, and more. One thing that got Haynes' attention was that in the middle stood Bill Simmons, recently resigned director of the FBI. Haynes flew into the living room from the kitchen and stood mesmerized. He had seen Fox alerts flash on the screen before, but never anything like this. "What the hell is going on?" he thought.

The room on the screen was buzzing with voices. Then the Army General stepped up to the microphone and waited a few seconds for the room to go quiet. He was not wearing any kind of headgear but otherwise was in full military garb. Haynes felt like he had met him somewhere, but couldn't place when. The officer at the microphone paused for a brief moment to look out over the crowd of reporters. Then he began.

"Ladies and gentlemen, we have taken over the government. We are suspending the Constitution until the next election is held, as scheduled, for 2016. The President and the Vice President are under military house arrest in locations that will not be disclosed at this point. The Attorney General has been arrested and will be criminally charged with lying to Congress under oath, among other offenses. Stock markets have agreed to close until next Tuesday, November 18th. By that time we should have a new team installed in the executive branch. They will be introduced to the American public by Monday of next week. Americans have recently elected a new Senate and a new Congress. These will continue to operate. We ask for their cooperation in executing reforms needed to get our country back on track. We are looking to install a temporary administrator to take the place of the President until a new president is elected in 2016.

"I want Americans to listen very carefully to what I'm about to say. This is only a temporary measure. Elections will certainly take place in 2016. In the meantime, we have work to do. We ask the nation to stay calm and assure you that Congress and the Senate will continue their work as normal. We feel that the country has fallen into disarray; we are witnessing a president violating the constitution and ignoring laws passed by Congress, while under the protection of an Attorney General who selectively enforces the law. Secondly, national security has dramatically declined to dangerous levels. We, as military officers, have sworn to defend and protect the American people and the Constitution of the United States. That is what we are doing: we are protecting America from a dangerous, imperial president. Between now and the next presidential election in 2016, we will be installing mechanisms to prevent a relapse of this critical situation. We view this as an opportunity to establish new methods of government function, a process which would be unattainable under present circumstances. We will hold a news conference shortly to announce who will be running the new administration. Americans can expect continued normalcy, and that American laws will be abided by. We ask all Americans to trust our leadership and to continue to engage in normal daily routines. We are not going to take any questions now. In a few days we will return to announce who and how the administration will be run."

The cameras were panning the room and suddenly settled on another face that Haynes recognized. Then it clicked, and his jaw dropped nearly to his knees. "God dammit, that's that guy Peter!" And now it all came flooding back to him. The officer at the microphone was Jim McCormick, and Haynes had met the two of them a few years earlier in Boca Raton at Ronald Stamp's golf club. No wonder Jim McCormick's phrase rang true about America having an opportunity to establish a new method of governing! It was exactly what they had discussed that day over a round of golf and dinner.

He was still standing in the living room and looking at the TV dumbfounded when his phone rang. "Guess everybody's calling everybody," he thought as he picked it up.

"This is Ronald Stamp," the voice said.

It was pretty well the last person Haynes expected to hear from.

SUNDAY, February 12, 2012 - South Florida

Stamp was a high profile American real estate investor, and a billionaire. They had met by chance in Boca Raton, Florida, at a party after Haynes retired and started spending most of the winter in Florida. After learning Haynes was from Canada, Stamp peppered him with questions about his background and interests. Naturally, the conversation turned to politics.

Stamp was about six feet tall, well groomed and well dressed, dark-skinned with jet black hair slightly long in the back. Haynes was familiar with Stamp's opinions – from his view that the government was allowing the Chinese to screw America to his heavily negative opinions of the Chambers administration. Stamp often expressed his views on Haynes' favorite TV programs. Their first interaction had been coincidental; Haynes had been brought to a gala at the club by a friend. He had been to numerous parties and gala receptions before, but had never seen anything quite like this one. Champagne accompanied unbelievable food, the outdoor facility was magnificent, and actors and TV personalities made up the crowd. Haynes caught a glimpse of actor George Rambleton enjoying himself with some woman half his age in one of the little cabanas by the pool, and several other faces he recognized from TV.

Stamp and Haynes commiserated over the state of the US government over cocktails by the pool. Haynes went right to the point, stating that neither Congress nor the President was exclusively at fault for the general mess the US was in. "The federal government is too cumbersome and too big," Haynes said. He explained that while he thought the framers had overcompensated when writing the Constitution to protect against an imperial president, they got one anyway. "When you have a mainstream media protecting their guy in the Oval Office, combined with an Attorney General who refuses to execute the law or investigate any illegalities that may damage their interest, you've got yourself an imperial president. The unfortunate part is that too many Americans don't have a clue about what's really going on," he said.

"So, what the hell would you do?" Stamp asked.

"Well, I'd amend some sections of the Constitution and add some new items, but that's almost impossible under the present system of government. What I do have, Mr. Stamp, is this list of things I would do if I had absolute power. I do it just for fun; I call it THE LIST."

Stamp said, "Well, what are some of your suggestions?"

"For example, one of them is that the Congress, not the Senate, would have the right to veto an attorney general selected by the president. If so desired, they would have the power to select their own independent attorney general. Decentralize federal power and defer it to state level, bring power closer to the people. The federal government is out of control, it is just too big."

Stamp asked, "What else?"

"I think the rest of the list is too long to discuss on this particular occasion," Haynes said with a grin.

"Would you mind sending it to me?" Stamp asked.

"Well it's just a bunch of scribbling for now but I guess I could formalize it and send you a copy."

Stamp said, "I think it would be very interesting."

Haynes found it flattering that someone with Stamp's success record and status would be interested in something he wrote. The thing Haynes found so impressive about Stamp, something which many Americans did not know, was that first and foremost he was a master builder and a great businessman second. He was a creative building artist. Creative people normally don't make good business people, however Stamp had managed to dovetail his creative brilliance with business. Haynes believed this was the reason for his immense success. Haynes appreciated Stamp's creative side because he had done many renovations of his own. This guy knew every plumbing fixture, electrical system, and the nuts and bolts of every building. Not very many people knew this about him, but Haynes did, and told him so.

Stamp was impressed that the Canadian had watched and read about him, and he told Haynes so. Not only was Haynes flattered, he was very impressed with Stamp's down-to-earth approach, and the fact that they seemed to like each other.

Haynes enjoyed himself at the gala, but eventually had to return to reality at his rental place in Pompano Beach. That week, he managed to formalize his list and send it to Stamp. But he never expected anything to come of it.

So he was extremely surprised when Stamp called him a week later at his Pompano rental condo and asked him if he was interested in playing a round of golf at his Boca Raton club. Haynes was excited at the prospect of a round at a top-drawer golf course. "Great, I'll be there Saturday," he said. Tee-time was set for 1:05 p.m. Stamp asked Haynes to be at the club early to join him and two associates for lunch.

Stamp said, "When you get there tell them who you are and they will take care of your car and the clubs. You will find us in the dining area."

That Saturday morning, Haynes arranged his golf gear and clubs and headed up I-95 to Boca. On the highway, he was wondering what the hell a guy like Stamp wanted with him. He was driving his '70 Ford Torino, hardly the type of vehicle which one would drive into a high-end golf course such as Stamp's. Haynes really didn't give a damn about what people thought about him. He kind of enjoyed driving into valet parking lots behind Jags and Rolls-Royces with his old car, and getting a look from some of the tight-ass people in South Florida.

One night he was leaving a restaurant with a couple of ladies he had met and invited out to a party. When the valet brought his car around, the two women looked at it, and decided that they wouldn't be coming to the party after all. Haynes didn't give a damn and got in his car and drove away laughing to himself, thinking, "This buggy is a good way to get rid of gold diggers."

When Haynes finally drove through the golf course gate and up to the entrance, there were two people waiting to greet him. They looked at his car and then they looked at him. Probably thinking he was at the wrong place. "What can we do for you, sir?"

"My name is David Haynes."

Their eyes popped out; obviously Stamp had given them a heads up. They said, "Yes sir, we'll take care of your clubs and car. Your keys will be waiting at the desk when you leave. Mr. Stamp is waiting for you in the dining area. Have a great day, Mr. Haynes."

The place was a little opulent, but was in good taste. Stamp's places usually were. Haynes strolled through an area with pillars reaching up to a high ceiling and found the sign to the dining room. Stamp was sitting in the corner with two other men. Stamp saw him coming, stood up and greeted him before introducing his two associates, who he said were visiting from Washington. He introduced them simply by their first names, Peter and Jim. All three were wearing golf shirts and shorts. Haynes had arrived in long pants and a golf shirt, being unsure of the dress code. He found strict dress codes excessive, but as a guest he respected the rules.

Peter and Jim both had short haircuts and looked like disciplined people. Haynes guessed they were in their late 40s or early 50s. Jim was about six foot three and lean. Peter was chunky on top and a little shorter at about five eleven. Haynes had a gut feeling that it probably would not be appropriate for him to ask too many probing questions.

Stamp, like Haynes, was a serious sports fan, so the conversation naturally led to football and some of the old athletes that they remembered. Haynes was surprised that Stamp knew a lot about hockey and recognized some of the players' names. He even remembered the famous Canada-Russia series! Canada had won in the last game in Moscow in the last minute on a goal by Paul Henderson, assisted by his friend Yvan Cournoyer.

They ordered some food. All four had the lobster bisque, followed by a salad. Nobody had anything to drink - Haynes sensed that these guys were competitive, and didn't want to compromise their swing.

The conversation abruptly turned to another subject. "I hope you don't mind, David, but I showed your list to these two gentlemen," Stamp said. "They have some questions they would like to ask you, especially about your concept of 'The American Functional Charter'."

Haynes explained his concept for almost half an hour, with hardly any interruptions. Haynes talked with a deliberate confidence and displayed his knowledge of the subject matter. He could see from their faces that they were surprised that this Canadian guy knew so much about American government and politics, even identifying key players, present and past. He even knew the names of relevant senators and governors and the parties they were from.

After lunch, they headed to the first hole in carts that looked like they just rolled out of the showroom. Haynes was relieved to see his clubs and Stamps' on the same cart. He was happy to be riding with him around the course because he found it difficult to make conversation with the other two guys. Stamp asked them for their handicaps and figured out shots to be given on each hole. They agreed to play for five dollars a hole. They all got off to a good start, hitting drives down the middle of the fairway. Haynes was not a big hitter so he was the furthest back. Yet his second shot ended up near the hole, making a birdie. Stamp made 4 and the other two made 5. On the way off the first green, Stamp made a sarcastic comment about Haynes being some kind of a hustler because he had made birdie on the first hole. Haynes' game went downhill from there on, so Stamp didn't have to repeat his comments.

By the end of the round Haynes was losing badly. Fortunately, it was only five dollars a hole. Stamp was gracious to not make it too expensive. Peter and Jim lightened up enough to make the rest of the round of golf enjoyable, yet Haynes sensed they were not comfortable being with a stranger. After the 18th hole they settled their bets. Stamp said that he had an engagement and Haynes, Jim, and Peter thanked him for a great round of golf. Haynes would normally have offered to pay his own green fees but in this case he thought it might just embarrass Stamp.

www.killwashington.com

Then just as Stamp was leaving, he said, "David, why don't you join Peter and Jim for a few drinks and an early dinner?" His body language indicated to Haynes that this wasn't optional.

The three of them made their way into the restaurant bar of the clubhouse. Jim picked a table in a corner somewhat out-of-the-way. Conversation was casual, with jokes concerning the round of golf that was just had. Haynes was throwing out indirect questions, trying to deduce who the two guys were and what they did. Finally it came out that they were military officers on a short vacation.

Jim went back to the subject of Haynes' list. He asked him to elaborate on his American Functional Charter. "It was the fundamental item that the constitutional framers overlooked," Haynes said. "However, who could blame them? How could anybody have known that we would be flying across the Atlantic Ocean in 5 to 6 hours? How could they have foreseen that new agencies such as the FAA would be required? And critically, what levels of government would administer these agencies? If they had anticipated these things, they would have known that there would be a power struggle between the States and the federal government as to who would be responsible for these agencies." Haynes went on to describe and justify the separation of powers required under his charter, with great detail on how this should be accomplished.

"How would you make this reality?" Jim asked.

"A constitutional amendment would be required. That would be practically impossible in present and future political circumstances, considering the existing political gridlock. The country has been moving, and appears to be continuing to move, to the left. We are undergoing what Churchill described as 'creeping socialism'. Socialists like centralized power because it creates dependency on the part of a large segment of the population. This is what screwed up Europe. Liberals and socialists are slowly hijacking what America prides itself on. It's called freedom. They are slowly removing the free enterprise and strong military required to protect our country from the little Hitlers of the world like Putin.

"One of the ways that they are accomplishing this is really interesting. In the past, the Democratic Party, especially in the South, was conservative. But slowly over the years a lot of Democratic politicians in the South have camouflaged themselves as conservative wolves in liberal sheep's clothes. They campaign on balanced budgets etcetera, but if you check their voting records, it's completely the opposite. The problem is that a lot of voters haven't caught onto this yet. They did in Arkansas in the last election by electing Tom Cotton to the Senate."

As Haynes slumped back in his chair looking very relaxed, Jim asked, as if it was some kind of a fun question, **"Well David, what would you do if you were President of the United States?"**

Haynes went into a 45 minute dissertation on what he would do. He was interrupted by a few questions, but mostly the two of them listened intently. Then Jim asked who would be in his cabinet. Haynes rattled off a list of names.

The conversation continued well into the evening until they all concluded it was time to leave. Haynes found the conversation engaging and felt that he had established a good rapport with these men.

Haynes found the same two greeters at the entrance as when he arrived. He figured they needed to be lightened up so he said, "Would you mind bringing my shit box around?"

It took a moment, but they both laughed. When his car arrived he gave them a good tip and went on his way back to Pompano. He enjoyed Stamp's company and the golf course but it had been kind of a weird day.

CHAPTER 2

A STRANGE INVITATION

—⚓—

TUESDAY, November 11, 2014 - Knowlton, Quebec

HAYNES STILL HAD ONE EYE on the television, where the talking heads were now busy trying to make sense of the day's events. "Are you calling about what is going on on television?" he asked Stamp.

"What do you think?" Stamp replied.

"My god, those are the two guys that we played golf with at your course."

"You recognized them did you? Where are you, anyway?"

"Sure I did," Haynes said. "I'm at my home in Knowlton, Quebec."

"Where the hell is that?"

"It's about 55 miles south-east of Montreal, just north of the Vermont border."

"Is there an airport there?" Stamp asked.

"Yeah, about 20 minutes away with a 5,000 foot strip. Why?"

"Some people need you in Washington ASAP."

"Ronald, are you talking about those guys I just saw on TV?"

"Yes."

"What the hell do they want me in Washington for?"

"They want to talk about your List."

"We already did that in Florida at your golf course."

"Yeah but there's a lot more people involved that need to be filled in," Stamp said. "Look David, after that golf game in Florida, certain people undertook to find out everything about you. They know about your successful business background, they know who your friends are, they know where you like to eat and they know who you're banging. They even flew to Fort Smith, Arkansas to interview people you know there. Your friends probably never said anything to you about that because they were told not to discuss it. They did the same thing with your old friend Kenneth Dever in Nashville."

"Jesus, Ronald, it sounds like I am applying for a damn job! What the hell do they need to know all this shit about me for?"

"Look, we haven't got all day to talk about this. There will be an airplane at your airport in a couple of hours."

"Jesus, Ronald, this is crazy!"

Stamp said, "Look these people need your help. Anyway it might be a great opportunity for you to turn some of that fantasy list into reality. Please, we need you to do this."

"Okay," Haynes said.

"Now I need the coordinates for that airport."

Haynes said, "The name of the airport is Bromont, Quebec, the airport symbol is CZBM; it's about 80 miles northeast of Burlington Vermont, it is a Unicom airport. There's no tower. The pilots can find the DME frequency and the airport frequency on their charts. They will need to contact Canadian customs to come in there."

Stamp said, "Don't worry about that; that can be arranged."

Haynes said, "How long do you expect me to be there for?"

Stamp said, "I don't know but bring some clothes and your cell phone."

Haynes said, "Well, you're going to need the number."

Stamp said, "They already have the number. They know everything about you, remember?"

"Jesus."

Stamp said, "One last thing, we never had this conversation, right?"

"Okay."

"Okay David, you better start getting ready and don't forget the List. See ya."

Haynes put his phone down and tried to gather himself, thinking this was one of the most bizarre days of his life. Anyway, he had made a commitment to Stamp and had better start packing the basic necessities; time was awasting. He ran upstairs and threw some things in a bag, grabbed his passport, drivers license, Canadian Medicare card, cell phone and his old, reliable 1980 vintage Casio Boss computer. There were some things about new technology that Haynes did not like. It changed too fast, and so you have to keep constantly learning new technology. Haynes did not have time for that.

As he was about to head out of the door, he stopped off at his desk to pick up the LIST, along with some documents which he had a feeling he'd be needing.

Things were moving so fast that he had forgotten to ask Stamp if anyone else was going to contact him. Just then his phone rang again. Haynes picked up and a voice said, "Is this David Haynes?"

"Yes sir."

"This is Captain Rob Daul of the United States Air Force. We understand that we are to pick you up in Bromont. Is everything okay?"

Haynes replied, "Yes sir, I'm just packing a few things."

"Fine," Daul said. "We just need to review the coordinates, frequencies and so on." Once that was done, Daul confirmed Haynes' cell phone number.

It was now after 4.30 p.m. Haynes did not want to leave his car at the airport because he did not know how long he would be gone, so he called his friend Derek in the village, and asked if he would drive him.

Derek said, "I can be there in about half an hour. But what the hell is going on? And where are you going in such a rush?"

Haynes said, "Washington. Haven't you been watching television? It seems that there has been a military takeover of the American government."

Derrick said, "You're kidding, it must be some kind of a joke. But what the hell does that have to do with you? Why would you go to Washington with all that shit happening?"

"I'll explain to you in the car."

Haynes had a little time so he re-checked his travel list to make sure he had the basic things that he needed. Then he sat down and wondered whether he should call someone and then he realized that his girlfriend Sonja Martinez who lived in Miami was coming to Montreal on Thursday. He had to call her and ask her to delay her flight. But should he tell her why? Was this whole deal like some kind of a secret mission? He decided the hell with it, they had been together almost constantly for over a year. He needed to let her know what was going on.

CHAPTER 3

LOVE INTERRUPTED

—⁂—

FRIDAY, March 15, 2013 – South Florida

Since he'd retired, Haynes had spent the winters in south Florida, golfing and puttering around. He liked to travel around his south Florida area on his bicycle, and often used it instead of his car to get around. One particular evening he decided to go into a little place that had jazz music. He pulled up in front and tied his bike lock around a light pole. There were people sitting at tables out on the sidewalk and he could hear the music coming from inside. It wasn't a very big place. It had a long, oval bar that stretched almost completely across the front, with just enough space on each side to squeeze past if you wanted to get to the sit-down tables in the back. The tables circled a small dance floor, with a stage for musicians behind it. There were a couple of single guys sitting in that area because they knew that the women would have to go to the bathroom sooner or later. It was just a lazy way to check inventory.

He felt like having a pizza, and this place had good pizza and the music was usually very good. He stopped at the bar for a drink, but had to stand because the bar chairs were all filled. The bartenders were busy so he glanced around the place until his eyes reached the far corner of the bar, where they came to a dead stop. He thought to himself, this is a very unusual looking woman.

She looked just mature enough. She was dressed casually but elegantly. Her clothes were reasonably tight but not too tight. Just enough to show off her wares but not enough to make her look cheap. Her hair was kind of a curly strawberry blonde, long enough but not too long. She was turned sideways to him, talking to another woman. She used a lot of hand motion when talking, so Haynes assumed that she was either French or Latin, either way would've been fine with him. He could see that she had long fingers and feminine hands and from the side view she looked like she had a great body. Not too thin, not too heavy. Her friend turned and looked his way. She knew he was looking at her friend and said something to the striking woman.

The blond turned her head his way and their eyes locked. She was unusual looking but gorgeous; her face was full and so were her lips.

Haynes' feet started to function before his brain kicked into gear. He found his way around the back corner of the bar, slipped sideways by a few people and said without even introducing himself, "Would you like to dance?" She smiled and nodded without a word. He took her hand and she slid off the barstool and they found their way through some folks to the dance floor. He put his arm around her waist and her hands landed on his upper shoulder. The whole thing just fits too well, thought Haynes. He was usually comfortable with himself and laid back but now he was feeling nervous. This whole thing has gone too smoothly.

She was very gracious and did not make him feel uncomfortable. Over the years Haynes had had more rejection bullet holes than Dick Tracy but that had never deterred him. He was always impressed with men or women that made him feel comfortable. This, for the moment at least, was the case. They were separated somewhat on the dance floor and he looked at her and said, "Hi, my name is David."

"My name is Sonja." Her voice was slightly high pitched but not offensive.

Haynes said, "Sounds like a Latin name."

"Yes, Cuba originally. My family came here when I was eight years old. Where are you from?"

Haynes said, "Canada, not far from Montreal."

"Oh," she said, "You don't look like a Canadian."

Haynes said, "I don't really know what a Canadian is supposed to look like. Just like the USA, we have some variety."

She said. "Probably, but you do look American."

Haynes said, "Well I hope that's a compliment."

And she said, "Why not?" and that's when the band stopped.

They had caught half the song. Their bodies turned to face the band and all of a sudden Haynes realized these two strangers were standing there holding hands. It did not feel awkward or uncomfortable. The band started to play another slow one and this time they were dancing closer, hardly saying a word. He could smell her body odor through a light perfume. It agreed highly with his senses.

He was suddenly reminded of an interview he'd once seen with Mellina Mancoura, the famous Greek actress. She had kind of a raspy voice and her face was so sensually unusual. It said 'make love to me now.' She had played a nymphomaniac in a film He remembered her famous line, the interviewer asking her what she liked about men and she had looked into the camera with that face of hers and with that raspy voice said, "I have to like the way the man smells."

Haynes loved the way this woman smelled. The band finished their set and they started to make their way back to the bar. Haynes put his hands on both sides of her waist and more or less guided their way back to her seat, thinking, "What a great set of hips. If this woman doesn't turn into some bipolar whack job she's probably a complete package." He was smitten.

He shared conversation with her and her girlfriend for a little over an hour, all very comfortable and pleasant. They found out a little bit more about each other but not enough. It was time to leave because she lived in Miami, a half hour drive. On their way out they stopped on the sidewalk and Haynes asked her for her phone number. She took out her purse and pen and wrote down a number and gave it to him. Haynes said, "Is it okay if I call you tomorrow?"

"No" she said, "I'm going to a play with a friend."

He almost asked her if she was married but didn't. Then, almost like she knew what he was thinking she said, "But you can call me on Sunday."

Haynes thought, "Jesus, I don't know if I can wait that long." but he said, "Okay" and took his pen and wrote down his phone number, knowing if there was a screw-up with numbers he probably wouldn't see her again. He took her hands and kissed her on both cheeks then grabbed one hand softly between his two hands and said good night.

"Are you driving?" she asked.

"No, I'm riding that bike over there."

She smiled and said, "Talk to you Sunday," which made him feel even more comfortable. The feeling lingered as he rode his bike back home.

Sunday morning, Haynes picked up his cell phone and called the number that Sonja had given him.

"This is David from Friday night," he said when she answered.

She said, "Yes I remember, how are you?"

Haynes said, "I will be better if you agree to join me for dinner this evening."

She said, "Oh, I think that can be arranged. Where would you like to go?"

Haynes said, "Well where do you live?"

She said, "I live down in Miami on the beach."

Haynes said, "Well I don't know that area very well so maybe you can recommend a nice place to go."

She said, "What kind of food do you like?"

Haynes said, "Italian or traditional American is fine."

She said, "Okay, I know a place."

Haynes said, "What time would you like me to pick you up?"

Sonja said, "Is 7:30 okay with you?"

"Perfect."

At 7 p.m. Haynes was headed south from Pompano Beach toward Hallandale on the A1A with the ocean on his left, always a pleasant drive. The only problem was the detour around the 17th Street bridge where all the cruise ships are, and then the airport.

Haynes was a punctual person and thought that being on time was a good value to have in life. As he was passing Hollywood Boulevard he phoned Sonja to tell her that he would be at her place in about 10 minutes. When he pulled up she was standing outside the front door waiting for him. She looked great. Haynes stopped and leaned over toward the passenger door to open it. She slid into the passenger seat and said, "Nice to see you."

Haynes said, "Likewise. Where are we going?" She directed him north to a place called Billy's. She said they had good seafood. Inside, they had to take a small elevator to the upper floor, which struck him as kind of unusual. When the elevator door opened he found himself staring at a wonderful view over the intercoastal waterway.

The place had a great atmosphere. Haynes hoped that the food was going to match the ambience. The maître d' escorted them to a table on the lower level beside a window overlooking the view. Haynes asked her, "How did you know this was a place that would suit my tastes?"

She said, "I guess it was just instinct."

Haynes said, "Things like that can be dangerous."

She looked at him and smiled.

Haynes opened up the wine list and noticed that there was a Red Diamond merlot on the menu, one of his favorite wines, reasonably priced but very good with an unusual flavor more like a Pinot Noir. Haynes was fed up with wine companies that started out with a great, reasonably priced wine, but boosted the price when it got popular so only wine snobs ended up buying it. In his view, the successful approach for wineries with large inventories should be to market a great wine at a reasonable price. Restaurants would buy more of it, and it would help their margins. The wine snobs would come around sooner or later. Maybe they should take the same wine, relabel it, double the price and sell it to that market who would not be caught dead with a $10 bottle of wine in their rack. He was also annoyed that he could not buy this wine in his own province at any price and if you could, you are guaranteed to pay more than double the price.

When people from Québec visit the USA they are blown away by wine and liquor prices. This is where people start to understand that the Québec government owned liquor board is a communist entity in a socialist state.

The government controls the wine and liquor distribution in Québec through its liquor board. It owns the warehouses, the retail stores, it decides prices (most of it being excessive tax), it decides which brands of wine are on the shelves and the employees are, of course, unionized. They charge restaurants more for their wine. Restaurants have to put a special label on their wine to prove that it is government approved for sale in their establishments. Haynes was shocked one Saturday evening in his favorite country restaurant full of diners at peak hour when two state police officers came barging into the middle of the customers dining, walked up to the bar like they owned the place and started to examine the bottles for government approved labels. It gave him a glimpse of what 1939 Gestapo Germany must have looked like. Not only that, but what could the customers have been thinking? Would they ever return? Or were they thinking that the owner was maybe some kind of a criminal? At the very least you would think that they could have done this before the customers arrived or after they had left, but those who instructed them to do this don't give a damn because there is not a conservative person in sight in that province to restrain these people. He thought to himself this is where America is headed if voters are not careful who they vote for.

They both ordered soup and the stone crab and while they waited for their first course, Haynes asked Sonja a little more about her Cuban background. She told him that she had come to the United States with her mother and father and her two sisters. Her father was a professional engineer in Cuba and that they were well off but not wealthy. She said that Castro had confiscated her father's property and they had decided to come to the United States. She described how her father, due to his limited English, had at first had to take any job he could get to make a living. But that he eventually ended up running his own business as a contractor and being very successful in America. Haynes could relate to this because he had had to start his own business too, not for the same reasons but because of his limited education.

She described many other Cubans that suffered the same fate under Castro's communist socialist regime and were now living in America. She hated communists and socialists and Haynes figured she had a right to because she had seen firsthand what it had done to the Cuban people.

He was impressed with Sonja's impeccable English, elegant slang and a slight and appealing Spanish accent. He was surprised to find out later that her family, for the most part, communicated in English. Their conversation was relaxed and he was thoroughly enjoying himself. She told him that she had been recently divorced and was very adamant in expressing that she was a professional business person and very self-sufficient. Haynes pondered this for a moment, wondering how to verify her claim. Then he asked her if her divorce was ugly; if the answer was yes it would probably mean that she was not quite as independent as she claimed. She said it was not and that she only wanted out and that the money was not that big a factor, so the divorce was quite smooth.

They left the restaurant and headed back to her condo. He accepted her invitation to come up for a drink. Sonja gave him the tour of her relatively large two bedroom apartment while she described to him how she had completely renovated the place, working as her own contractor. Haynes had done a few renos himself and could tell she had done a first class job. It was clear that she was just as independent as she had said. They poured themselves a couple of drinks and went out onto the balcony to enjoy the evening view of the ocean and the lights of Miami.

They talked into the late hours of the evening, when Haynes felt it was time for him to leave. He knew this was not the evening to push his luck. She escorted him to the door, and they looked at each other, their heads slowly arching toward each other until they embraced in some passionate kissing for a minute or so. Then Sonja took her finger and touched his nose and said, "I think you better go now."

"Will we see each other tomorrow night?"

"Call me tomorrow," she replied.

He did, and they have hardly ever been apart since.

CHAPTER 4

FLIGHT TO WASHINGTON

—⚞—

TUESDAY, November 11 - 2014

Haynes dialed Sonja's number in Miami, wondering how exactly he was going to break the news that her visit was off. "Hello baby," she said when she picked up the phone. "I thought you might call. Have you been watching TV? It's unbelievable. What do you think is going to happen?"

Haynes said, "Maybe they're going to form an interim government or something like that, I don't know. But I'm sorry, there is going to have to be a change of plans, you're going to have to cancel your trip to Montreal."

"Why?" she asked.

He said, "Because I have to go to Washington today."

"Why do you have to go to Washington?"

Haynes said, "I can't really tell you that right now, but I promise that I will call you this evening when I get there."

"David," she said, "you always tell me everything. What is going on? Does this have anything to do with what's been on the news?"

"Yes, but I can't tell you any more than that for now other than I have to go there to see some people, and as I promised, I will call you this evening. I just don't know what time. I'm sorry sweetheart, but I don't know much more myself. Okay?"

"Okay," she said, but she sounded a little hesitant.

At 5:15 p.m., Derek pulled into the drive and Haynes tossed his two bags into the back of his Explorer. On the way to the airport, he told Derek that he was going to be picked up by a private jet and flown to Washington to meet some important people. Derek looked sideways at him with half a smirk and said, "Are you kidding me?"

"No Derek, I'm not."

"What the hell do these people want to talk to you for?"

"Derek, I can't tell you anything right now. I'll bring you up to date later when it's appropriate."

Derek said, "Yeah, okay," and nothing much else was said until they got to the airport. Derek's brain must been racing in the silence. When they arrived there was a jet parked beside the fuel depot with U.S. Air Force lettering on it. Haynes said, "Shit, they're here already."

Derek said, "Dammit, David that's an Air Force jet. Is that the one you are going on?"

"It's gotta be because you don't see US Air Force jets around here as a rule."

They pulled up to the main terminal building. Haynes said, "I'd better go in there by myself."

"You know David, sometimes watching your life is like watching a damn movie."

"Thanks for the ride. I'll call you to bring you up to-date when I can. And I would appreciate it if you keep this to yourself until I do. You know how that damn village is. Tell one person and the whole town knows in 24 hours."

"Okay," said Derek, "give me a call."

"I will as soon as I can."

Haynes opened the car door, grabbed the two bags and headed into the small terminal building. He looked down the long corridor toward the door to the aircraft parking. There was a man in military garb who seemed to be passing a credit card, probably to pay the fuel for the aircraft. Haynes knew that this aircraft required two pilots by regulation so he assumed that this was either Daul or the co-pilot. As Haynes approached, the man turned and said, "You must be Haynes? Thank you for being early."

Haynes said, "I am, and you must be Daul? How did you get here so quickly?"

Daul replied, "We got the call in the air just north of New York City to divert to come get you. Can I see your passport?"

Daul looked at the picture and then at Haynes and said, "Thanks. Are you ready to go?"

Haynes said, "Yep! But I would like to sit in the jump seat on the way down if you don't mind, at least for takeoff and landing."

"That would be okay, but I'm afraid we'll have to go through your luggage and do a body search."

Out on the tarmac, Daul introduced him to the co-pilot, Jerry Richards, who asked Haynes to pass his bags through the door of the plane. Richards swiftly checked the bags and said, "Okay, everything seems to be in order. Would you mind coming on board?"

Richards stopped Haynes just inside the door. "Sorry, I've got to do a body search."

Haynes raised his arms and Richards patted him down. Haynes was quietly thinking, "This is the way life is since those Jihadist bastards blew up those buildings in New York." When he finally bent to shift his bags, he spotted Derek leaning over his steering wheel in the parking lot, watching this whole scene through the cabin door. Haynes knew that Derek was the kind of guy who if he thought his buddy was in trouble, might want to jump over the fence and take these two on, so Haynes stuck his head at the door gave him a thumbs up. Derek raised his thumb in return.

Richards was already in the right-hand seat. And after Daul had sealed the door, he ducked through the little opening into the cockpit and took the pilot's seat. He nodded to Haynes to pull down the jump seat from the wall just behind and in between the two pilots. Haynes was excited. He hadn't had many opportunities to fly in private jets since he retired. "Are you taking the Albany, Philadelphia or Washington route?" he asked Daul, trying to confirm their destination in a delicate way.

Daul said, "That's pretty close. We're going to Andrews Air Force Base. Maybe you can save me some time looking and give me a frequency to open up a flight plan."

Haynes said, "That would be Montreal radio on 134.15."

Daul smiled and punched in 134.15 on his switchover frequency. Haynes figured maybe it was his way of confirming he was who he said he was, because this was a Unicom airport with no tower, and only a pilot would know that pilots were in fact their own controllers, and had to communicate with each other on the local frequency. Out of habit, Haynes glanced up at the left and right frequencies on the radio communicator and saw that the Unicom frequency was correct for the airport.

Daul had fired up both engines on the tail and was taxiing out. Just before the turn Haynes glanced out the left side window and saw Derek still leaning over his steering wheel. Daul stopped the plane just before the entrance of the westbound runway and checked for approaching air traffic. Then he announced on the airport frequency that he was ready for takeoff to notify any pilots in the area. He turned the plane left onto the runway, applied the throttles slowly to the wall and they started down the 5,000 foot strip. He pulled the wheels off the ground at about 110 mph and they climbed steeply up to 29,000 feet.

It was a nice clear evening and from that altitude he could see the lights bordering Lake Champlain to the south and almost down to Albany. It was now about 6:10 p.m. Once the autopilot was on, Haynes tried to find out a little about Daul and Richards. Haynes liked to learn people's backgrounds and he loved to hear success stories, big or small. He especially liked hearing about the people who had made an impact on their lives. Daul never brought up Washington or asked why Haynes was going there, and Haynes got the feeling they were relieved he didn't bring it up either, or mention the events in Washington. It kind of went without saying that most military people didn't like the President anyway.

Eventually, the conversation drifted off and Haynes left them to fly the airplane while he thought back on the events in his own life that had brought him to this point.

CHAPTER 5

THE EARLY YEARS

—⚇—

1943 - 1970, Canada

David's father was 51 when he was born, and his mother was 46. Having a child at that age was in those days far from a common event. And David often reflected that his life had been a bit of a mistake. None of his classmates had a father who was born in 1892 and a mother born in 1897. Or had a father who had crawled around the trenches at Vimy Ridge in the First World War, and managed to survive.

His father used to drive him to the train station in Cowansville to pick up aunts and uncles visiting for the weekends and holidays from Montreal. These folks were all from the old school, with different values than today. Haynes' parents were huge gardeners and grew some unusual things like grapevines, apple trees, huge squashes and more. His dad even had beehives in the garden. His father also taught him how to build and fix things. He had helped his dad build their house.

Haynes was not able to talk to his father about what he was doing or much of anything else. He didn't know his father's real first name, Otto, or that he had been going by his middle name Irwin since landing in Canada. He actually didn't know much at all about his father's background.

Irwin Haynes kept his thoughts mostly to himself but he led by example and David learned by watching what he did and how he interacted with other people. Although his dad was not much of a communicator, when he did say something, it was short and direct and David paid attention. So when his father suggested he join the army, David did; which was how he ended up, while still in high school, in the Canadian army reserves, in the 27th field artillery.

One time, during summer boot camp at Valcartier, he and his new friend Walter Cannon, the brother of Joe Cannon, the famous Montreal broadcaster, had gone AWOL and got a lift from the cook working on the base into Quebec city to see a couple of girls. On their return, they crawled under the fence early in the morning and made a dash for the barracks. When they entered, Staff Sgt. Walsh was standing near the barracks doorway slapping his baton in his hand. Sgt. Walsh screamed Attention! Haynes and Cannon came to a stiff attention side-by-side. Sgt. Walsh started walking around behind the two of them, still slapping his baton in his hand. "Where have you two assholes been?"

"Quebec City," said Cannon.

"What were you doing there?"

"We were meeting some friends," said Cannon.

"Bullshit!" said Walsh. "You were chasing pussy. You two have 15 minutes to get out of your civvies and into full military garb."

Fifteen minutes later the two of them were doing double-time down to Captain Dolan's office. Neither of them knew what was going to happen next. Haynes was taxied into Capt. Dolan's office standing at attention.

"I understand you went to Quebec City," Dolan said.

"Yes sir!"

"What were you doing there?"

There was no point in saying 'friends' again, so Haynes said, "We went to see a couple of girls, sir!"

"How did you get there?"

Haynes did not want to get the cook into trouble so he said, "We hitchhiked."

"Who picked you up?"

Haynes let his imagination run wild and said, "A Cadillac."

"What did the guy look like?"

"He was bald with a pot," said Haynes. The questions and answers continued for a few minutes then Haynes was released. On his way out he passed Cannon and was desperately waving his thumb, thinking that Canon would get it if he was asked how they got to Quebec City.

Cannon didn't pick up the signal, and so when Capt. Dolan asked Cannon the same question, Cannon told him, "We took the bus."

Cannon got four days in the brig and Haynes got seven for lying. Haynes figured if he had been second into Dolan's office he would've got four days.

All he remembered of boot camp after that was being in constant motion from morning to night, running around parade squares with a rifle over his head. Then it was back to washing floors with a toothbrush. The worst part of it was in the morning, before double time to breakfast, standing nude with his hands over his head on the wall and his legs spread open while the MPs inspected every square inch of his cell. He knew that if it did not meet their expectations, he was going to pay. Sometimes he would get a little baton tap on the inside of the knee. It was very hard not to move knowing that stick was in close proximity to his balls. That week was an experience Haynes did not want to repeat.

When Haynes finished technical school as a machinist and draftsman, he headed off to the Montreal Institute of Technology. The days involved a half-day of shop as a tool and die maker followed by a half day in theory. Unfortunately he had no aptitude for mathematics, and when he realized he would not pass the theory component, he decided to drop out rather than waste his father's money.

He would never forget how disappointed his father had been, and years later always suspected that his dad had died without understanding his motives for dropping out. He had wanted at least one of his two sons to graduate from university, but it wasn't to be.

So that weekend, Haynes' father said, "Well it's time for you to hit the road. I've taken this program as far as it can go. I've done my job now it's time to do yours. After you've found a job you can come back home on the weekends anytime you want." Haynes was 18 years old. His dad gave him $100 to get started and took the bus for Montreal on Sunday night. He remembered his mother waving goodbye with tears in her eyes.

Haynes had a room in a rooming house on St. Matthew Street in Montreal that was about 12 feet long and eight feet wide, with one washroom down the hallway shared by four rooms. It was costing him eight dollars a week and you could get a decent dinner for a dollar and a half at the time, so his hundred dollars gave him enough grace to find some kind of a job.

He got his first job at Canadian Aviation Electronics out near the airport for a grand total of $265 a month before taxes. It took him an hour and three buses back and forth each day but he wanted to live downtown where all the action was and there was plenty of it in 1961 Montreal. The city had great night life in those days and that suited his personality. And now that he had a job, he could go home on the weekends.

At CAE, Haynes started in the machine shop but it turned out that one of the managers in the production office had been his high school football coach, so Haynes managed to get himself promoted to an office job expediting parts for the flight simulators being built for the F104 fighter aircraft. He supplemented his income selling sports equipment, mainly skis, at Morgan's department store downtown on Thursday and Friday nights and Saturdays.

He also dabbled in selling knives and forks door-to-door for Zytco. He was trained by a colorful character called Ray McPeak, who wore a pair of thick glasses and was built like Hoss on Bonanza, but somehow he managed to maneuver himself inside houses and give a presentation on knives and forks. Haynes remembered McPeak waving a knife above his head in front of a canary cage, and the homeowners looking nervous and rapidly placing an order as if to get him out of the house as fast as possible.

Then he did a brief stint working for a couple of characters selling death packages door to door. Sometimes people listening to the sales presentation on death and dying would break into tears. Haynes quit because he thought it was a bit of a con job, and actually only realized later, when his father died, that those packages were a good deal and saved families a lot of problems when a death occurred, because everything was prearranged and paid for in advance.

After two years, he decided he wanted to be an industrial salesman and after many applications, he landed a job as an inside telephone salesman with the Tamper Division of Canada Iron, an electrical motor manufacturer. There, he met and worked for two of his many great mentors. One was Mike Parent, the sales manager for the division, and a flashy high-energy and talented salesperson. Mike's assistant Roy McVicki was a brilliant and well organized technician. Haynes learned sales skills by watching Mike, and organization from Roy.

At one point a Quebec company got a large turnkey contract from the Russian government to supply and build an asbestos plant in Russia just after Haynes was transferred to another division in the same company. The company got the subcontract to build the electric motors, some of which were unusual. The packaging was also complex and the boxes had to be identified in the Russian language, which led Haynes on a week-long safari looking for a printer with a set of Russian stencils. Haynes caught hell for taking so long. He was pissed after so much running around and said, "I'll tell you what. I won't tell you how and where I found these stencils, so why don't you assholes go out and try. I guarantee you it will take a month if you find them at all."

One day, he met a guy name Ray Pedley hanging outside the general sales manager's office. Pedley had a heavy British cockney accent and introduced himself as coordinating expeditor for the subcontractors on the Russian asbestos plant project. When he found out Haynes was single and lived downtown, Pedley said, "So you must know all the good spots?"

Haynes said, "Well yeah, that's why I live downtown. I can just walk to most of them."

Just then Haynes' boss John Kirkwood came out to ask Pedley into the conference room to discuss coordination of the project with management, and Pedley said "See you later." Kirkwood gave Haynes a look that indicated he should get back to work.

About a half an hour later Haynes spotted Kirkwood walking faster than normal down the hallway back towards him. "What the hell did you say to Pedley?" he barked.

Haynes replied, "Well he started talking to me first. Did you want me to just stand there and look like an idiot?"

Kirkwood seemed taken aback by the aggressive reaction from the normally good-natured young man and decided to calm down. Then he said, "Well damn it, he says he wants you to coordinate our part of the project. and he wants you in the meeting," and they proceeded back down the corridor to the conference room. Haynes walked in and most of the tight ass company brass were there in those stripe suits trying to look professional. Haynes was wearing a simple shirt and tie and sensed that they were pissed at the turn of events and they were probably blaming Kirkwood and that's why Kirkwood was pissed at him. They probably thought Haynes was way below their pay grade and didn't belong in the meeting. Then Haynes looked over at Pedley sitting at the end of the table looking satisfactorily smug because he was in charge of this project and that all these suits knew they had to kiss his ass because it was one of their biggest contracts ever.

By some fate of chemistry, even though their conversation had been short, he and Pedley had bonded, and were thick as thieves after that. Haynes' eyes contacted Pedley's and he had to look away immediately because if he didn't he and Pedley would have broken out in hysterical laughter because they were the only people in the room who got it. Pedley was no intellectual but he had great people skills and "street smarts". Pedley knowing that he had caused David to be in an uncomfortable situation said "David there is an empty seat right next to me." Haynes proceeded to the other side the room without hesitation and took a seat beside Pedley and the meeting continued. It was apparent from the facial expressions on the other people in the meeting that they were not pleased that Haynes was present.

But Pedley looked out for him and kept him under his wings. Haynes soon realized that his job was secure at least until the contract with Pedley's company was completed.

This event taught Haynes one of the most important lessons of his life: Any company that does not perceive its customers as first is doomed to mediocrity.

After the meeting Haynes found himself in Kirkwood's office. He realized that the day's events had not made his general sales manager look good, so he apologized. Kirkwood said, "Well let's turn lemons in to lemonade. You're only a young guy and wet behind the ears. Pedley is a party animal and he knows you know your way around town. Besides, I think he likes you, but you don't know diddly squat about how to organize this project, so it will be my job to teach you how. So you better listen up and do what I tell so we don't screw this up because my ass is on the line. Do you understand?"

"Yes sir, I do," Haynes replied. He got a good education from Kirkwood as to how to organize a large project and how to bypass company structures in unusual circumstances to get things done.

Canada Iron had a great line of products, but it had really no leadership, and the company eventually closed its doors. Later in life, Haynes had a chance to compare it with the company he ultimately ended up representing years later, the Baldor Electric Company in Fort Smith Arkansas. That same year, in 1964, Roland S. Boreham Jr. was completing his first year as VP of sales at Baldor. Fred Balman, the founder's son, was running the company at the time and didn't know much about sales and marketing so hired Boreham to turn things around. When Boreham arrived, the company was doing about $5 million in sales and sliding. By the time Boreham retired in 2004, Baldor was a publicly traded company generating close to 1 billion in sales. That was evidence of great leadership. And as Haynes realized later, the contrast between how the two companies had fared had everything to do with leadership.

Haynes often found himself out in the evenings with Pedley, usually late into the morning. Pedley was a party animal and had an expense account that would choke a horse. Sometimes Kirkwood would get angry when Haynes showed up late for work in the morning after one of those soirées with Pedley.

Those were the days of the Cold War and when the Russian project inspectors showed up, the RCMP was not far behind. The last day of the project, Haynes and Pedley went down to the Montreal docks to make sure all the items were loaded on the ship. The Russian captain and a character Haynes suspected was KGB invited the two on board the ship afterwards for a celebratory drink, but they couldn't board until they'd gotten clearance from the RCMP guys standing around nearby. Of course Haynes and Pedley drank far too much and had to hang onto the wires lining the gangplank for dear life as they watched the current of the St. Lawrence River roll by between the ship and the dock below them.

By 1966 Haynes had taken a new job with the Motor Starter Company in Montreal and worked there until 1969, alongside another great salesman named Dan Depaoli. He and Dan became great friends. He would often go to Dan's place at Christmas with his wife and his three children and hang out with a guy named Peter Biller who had come to Canada after crawling under a fence into Austria after the Hungarian Revolution. Unfortunately, Dan was killed in a head-on collision in a Mini Cooper on September 20, 1975. He left a wife and three young children behind.

Haynes was earning a reputation in the industry and in 1969 received a great offer to go to work for a competitor named Telemecanique, a French company with an operation in Montreal. The president, Bernie Marcoux, hired Haynes for $12,500 a year, which was good money for a 26-year-old at the time. Marcoux gave Haynes a territory where there had hardly been any sales and within six months, Haynes had sold a half a million of product. In late 1969, Marcoux transferred him to Toronto as general manager. He was now making himself more than $16,000 a year.

The only problem was Haynes hated Toronto. Toronto was, even then, the business center of Canada and business was all anyone there could talk about. No one had ever heard of work life balance, or knew what 5 o'clock was.

Moving there from Montreal was a culture shock. Even the women in Toronto were social climbers. Their standard question after some useless small talk was, "What do you do?" In other words if you weren't a career seeker or not perceived as being successful, in most cases they would move on.

As far as Haynes was concerned, the best part of Toronto was the 401 Highway to Montreal. In just a little over a year of being there, he spent probably only four weekends there.

By November 1971 the French management in Europe fired Bernie Marcoux. As one of Marcoux's guys, Haynes knew his time was limited. He saw firsthand how European socialist attitudes had penetrated European corporations when the company sent one of their men to Toronto. The Frenchman spent almost the whole day asking him a series of questions, some of them the same as he'd asked hours earlier. He came in the next morning and started the same old questions over again. Haynes had had enough, and asked the Frenchman what time his air ticket back to Montreal was.

The Frenchman said, "5 o'clock."

It was only 11:30 a.m., so Haynes walked out to his secretary's desk and told her to call CP airlines and make a reservation for the Frenchman for 1 p.m. Then he called Bill in the back and told him to bring his car around to drive the Frenchman to the airport. Haynes walked back into his office and said, "Mr. Clement, we have arranged for you to catch the 1 o'clock fight for Montreal, this gentleman in the doorway is going to drive you to the airport."

Clement said, "But I'm not finished yet."

"You may not be finished with me but I am finished with you. The last time I looked I was still the general manager of this office, and I am done answering your stupid questions and you, sir, are going to the airport now." Haynes had his hand firmly on Clement's back, helping him out of the office and into the car. So out he went, and out went Haynes two weeks later, in late November. He was fired by the new president on a Friday during one of his weekend jaunts to Montreal. Haynes had referred to him as "Inspector Clousseau," because he reminded Haynes of that French inspector in the Pink Panther movies.

Three days later, Haynes left to spend a few weeks in Barbados.

CHAPTER 6

BALDOR, ARKANSAS, AND THE ROAD TO SUCCESS

―⚏―

SATURDAY, December 11, 1971 - Montreal

By late 1971, Haynes had finally returned to his beloved city of Montreal and managed to get a room a little bigger than the last one in the same rooming house on St. Matthew Street. He had gone full circle and was embarking on a new life with his own sales agency. And since he was still single it would be a lot easier without family financial pressures. Only now there was no salary, no car and no expense account. He had been enjoying life a little too much and was practically busted.

By January 1972, Haynes had himself a couple of product lines to sell, but he had not got any orders yet and was living on financial fumes. He was down to one meal a day along with some juice in the morning but still managed to go out once in a while. He could go over to the Stork Club on Guy Street, order a beer and pretend to drink it, but leave it in the bottle so he wouldn't have to order another one. Ironically it didn't bother him that much. He was a man with a lot of faith and somehow it would all work out.

By January his life was about to take a major turn. Later, when he reflected backed, it seemed almost as if everything had happened by divine providence. He had suddenly remembered an engineer called Alan Day that he had met a few years earlier when he was calling on people in the asbestos business. Day had mentioned something about a small electric motor company out of Fort Smith, Arkansas. Haynes called the US consulate in Montreal and got the company address and telephone number.

His room on St. Matthew Street had a bay window facing the street, with a window seat under it. He had cut a piece of plywood to fit on the window ledges so that it was just the right height for a desk. He had his phone, a bed, a small television and a couple of chairs. The bathroom was still down the hallway. He picked up the phone and dialed the number of the Baldor Electric Company in Fort Smith. The switchboard answered and Haynes asked for the person in charge of the sales division. She told him that would be Mr. Boreham. Haynes heard the second ring and then someone said simply, "Hello."

Haynes said, "Are you Mr. Boreham?"

"That would be me."

"My name is David Haynes and I'm calling you from Montreal, Canada. I have a sales agency here and your product line could interest me." In the middle of that sentence Haynes, realized, "Jesus, I don't even have a name yet for the damn company."

Boreham explained to Haynes that they only sold their products through independent representatives in strategic locations in North America and that he did not yet have someone representing them in Haynes' area. While Boreham was talking, Haynes was doodling on his notepaper and the light went on. He said to himself, "I'll just spell electric backwards." It came out as Cirtcele. Pronounced phonetically it would sound like 'sirt sel.' He thought since electronics were now merging with electrics in the industry, he could give the name a little pizzazz so he added tronic onto the word Cirtcele to come out as Cirtcele-tronic.

This guy Boreham sounded cool. He was already addressing Haynes by his first name and had said that his first name was Rollie. He said that he was the vice president of sales and that since he had joined the company, he had turned five million in sales annually into close to 30 million, which Haynes knew was not a lot of sales for a company in that line of business. There were some powerful competing companies, like General Electric, Westinghouse and many others. It was a very competitive business.

Haynes also learned that Baldor's product line was much broader than he had thought, which made it sound even more interesting. Then

Boreham said, "Why don't we start with you dropping us a line with your background, etcetera. What is the name of your company again?"

"Cirtcele-tronic."

Boreham said, "Where did that come from?"

Haynes said, "It's electric spelled backwards."

Boreham chuckled and said, "I'll be damned. I assume we will hear from you soon."

"Yes sir, thanks for your time."

Little did Haynes know that he had just talked to the person who would be his greatest mentor and friend and put his life into a direction that at the time he could not foresee.

In those days mail was still a big deal. Haynes had just invented his company name but had no letterheads, cards or envelopes. To get all these would place a major hole in his budget but at the same time he had to send a letter to the Baldor Electric Company. So he sat down and designed a logo around the name he had just invented and went to a printer. Less than a week later he sent a letter off to Mr. Boreham, asking to acquire the rights to sell Baldor products in his area.

By early February there was still no response to his letter so he picked up the phone again and called Baldor and asked for Rollie.

Haynes said, "This is David Haynes calling and I was wondering why I have not got a response to my letter sent to you in January."

"Yes," Rollie said, "I've been kind of busy but my problem is that you Canadian guys never want to come down here and visit us."

Haynes jumped on this and said, "I will be down there next Tuesday."

Rollie sounded a little taken back by this fast response but said, "Okay."

Haynes said, "What is the best way to get there?"

"These days" said Rollie, "the best way I know is through Chicago, then St. Louis then you take a stagecoach airplane that makes a couple of stops to Fort Smith, Arkansas."

Haynes said, "I will let you know how I expect to be arriving in Fort Smith on Tuesday." Then he phoned the airline to make his reservation, which in those days you could make before paying.

After a weekend of skiing and frolicking he returned to Montreal on Sunday evening. By Monday morning he realized that he did not have enough money to pay for his airline reservation. He started making calls to try and borrow a few dollars from someone, but by Monday night he was having no success. If you were self employed you couldn't even think about banks or even high-interest-rate finance companies loaning you money. He figured he'd get up early Tuesday morning and go to the airport, that way if someone came up with some funds at the last minute he wouldn't miss his airplane.

By the time he had made it to the departure floor of the Montreal airport, his anxiety level was high. He was making some last-ditch phone calls on the pay phone when he felt a finger tapping several times on his shoulder. He turned and there was Wilma Kimsey. He and Wilma had attended school together and now she was a ground hostess with Air Canada.

Wilma had a voluptuous build and thick brown hair combed straight back. Her friendly face was consistent with her personality. She was very popular in school but yet somewhat reserved.

She looked at Haynes and said, "You look very distracted."

Haynes apologized and explained his dilemma to her. It was now 10:30 in the morning and his flight was leaving for Chicago at 12:15 p.m. She put her hand inside his arm and led him to the Air Canada ticket counter. Wilma knew the lady working there and she pulled out a Chargex card and said, "This man has a reservation to go to Fort Smith Arkansas, please use my credit card to give him the ticket."

Haynes was dumbfounded. He was not good at receiving but on this occasion he really had no choice. The ticket was for $323.23 Canadian. "I don't know what to say," he said.

Wilma said, "Your reputation precedes you David, I know you'll take care of this. Sorry but I've got to get back to work, you have a good trip and let me know how it works out."

Haynes stepped forward and gave her a big hug and whispered in her ear, "Thank you so much." His eyes started to well up. "My god, more divine providence, I'm so blessed."

He had already phoned Rollie to confirm that he would be arriving in Fort Smith early evening and now he was operating on blind faith. He had just under $30 in his pocket and he spent a little to get a sandwich and a drink in Chicago.

After hop-scotching his way from St. Louis to Fort Smith via Fayetteville and some other 'villes,' he arrived in Fort Smith early evening. He entered the small main terminal building to discover there were not very many people about. He noticed a man in a plaid shirt and a pair of jeans approaching him. "Are you David?"

Haynes said, "Yes are you Rollie?"

"That would be me."

They smiled and shook hands. Rollie was about 5 foot 10, medium build, hair thinned on top, a mustache and a pair of glasses with lenses that were a little thick and made his eyes look bigger than normal. He asked Haynes, "Can I take your bag?"

Haynes said, "Thank you but I'm a little younger than you." Haynes was 29, and Rollie at the time was 46.

They both laughed and proceeded to the parking lot. Rollie's car was a 1960s four-door Ford. They went to a steakhouse close by. When they got to the table there were two other gentlemen waiting. One was Ron Clark, who was Rollie's sales manager, and the other was Fred Atkinson, owner of an independent advertising agency out of St. Louis. Atkinson looked to be in his mid-40s. Haynes was to find out later that although Atkinson owned his own company, he was considered part of the Baldor management team. Haynes, Clark and Boreham were dressed casually but Fred was dressed like a typical advertising man in a blue suit, a vest, red tie, handkerchief in his lapel and a very clean white shirt. Ron Clark had a chunky build, thinning blondish hair and an easy-going manner.

Atkinson was drinking something that looked like scotch on the rocks. Clark was drinking beer. Rollie asked Haynes what he would like to drink.

He thought a beer would be appropriate so Rollie ordered a couple more beers. They talked about Haynes' background, Canada and some philosophy and Rollie was especially impressed with Haynes' knowledge of America and American history. Rollie had served in the military in the Pacific. Then Rollie went into a lengthy dialogue on the North American motor market. He even knew the size of the market in Canada.

By now they had all had a lot to drink. Haynes later found out that it was Baldor's truth serum, a way to find out where people were really coming from. Fortunately Haynes' personality and demeanor didn't change much even after he had drunk a lot. He just got a little more outgoing. Rollie said, "How much do you think you can get out of that territory?"

Haynes thought 'I've got nothing to lose and they're going to find out anyway," so he said, "I don't know about one million of this or one million of that, all I'm worried about is who's going to pay for this dinner because all I've got left in my pocket is $22."

Atkinson took his glasses off, put the palm of his hand under his forehead and started laughing hysterically, "Not another one!" he said.

Haynes turned toward Rollie and Ron Clark and said, "What the hell is all that about?" When he saw they were laughing, he decided to laugh as well but didn't know why. He found out later that although Baldor did not have many territory representatives at that point, the ones they did have were a bunch of eccentric characters, all with different personalities. The kind of rebellious guys that probably wouldn't succeed very well anywhere else. But Rollie encouraged people to challenge him legitimately and had already entrenched a culture and policies that would last for decades, even as the company got bigger.

Haynes' comment had obviously taken away any remaining tension and formality. Clark got up to use the restaurant telephone. (At that time, cell phones were still a figment of someone's imagination.) When he came back to the table, reported that the Ramada Inn was all booked. "The only room left is at the Stonewall Jackson Hotel," He said.

"Dapper Dan" Atkinson's head perked up and said, "Jesus, Ron, the Stonewall Jackson Hotel?!?"

"It's the only game in town so you and David will have to stay in the same room."

Haynes said, "I'm just glad to have a roof over my head. Maybe I can use half of my $22 to pay for part of the room." Rollie put his fist down on the table and started laughing. Fred could only manage part of a grin. "Do they have double beds?" he asked.

"Don't worry, Fred, I'm not gay," Haynes replied.

Rollie picked up the check and they headed for the Stonewall Jackson Hotel, which had features that matched its name. The next morning, Fred woke Haynes up because Ron Clark was already waiting to take them to the office.

The first thing Haynes noticed about Rollie's office was the large glass window that looked out at the whole sales department so that he could see everybody and everything going on. He didn't do it to be imperialistic. He just liked being part of the action. He didn't care much for status or decor. Behind his desk were shelves full of paper files. His desk looked equally disorganized. Haynes looked out through the window into the salesroom and noticed four guys sitting around a large circular desk. On top of the desk was what looked like a circular Card-X and he noticed one of the men pull out a card, write something on it, and put it back in place. "What's that thing over there with the four guys?" he asked Rollie.

"That's our inventory control and stock motor order desk. Those four guys take orders from customers, remove the cards, write down the number of motors to be shipped and the available number left, then put the cards back in their place. They are also responsible for our own inventory control. "

One of the four caught Haynes' attention. He was a tall slim fellow who was leaning backwards in his swivel chair with his cowboy boots up on the desk, a phone in one ear and twisting elastic around with his other hand. Haynes liked the laid-back atmosphere.

Rollie said, "Would you mind showing me your air ticket?"

"No, not at all," said Haynes.

Rollie took a quick look at it and handed it back to him, then escorted him down the hallway to a conference room where Ron Clark was waiting.

They all sat down and Rollie got right to it. "How much business do you think you can do in the first year?" he asked Haynes.

"Well you told me last night that you were not doing very much, but I really don't have any idea, your company is not well-known where I come from."

"How about $100,000 forecast?" Rollie suggested.

"Well you haven't really decided whether you want me to represent you up there are not."

Rollie said, "Oh, we decided that last night. "

Haynes chuckled and said, "Well you have had more experience than me in dealing with new territory managers and you obviously know the market size, so it sounds reasonable to me."

Then Rollie said something very interesting. He said, "This is not a quota, this is a forecast."

Haynes said, "Understood."

About that time the guy at the desk with cowboy boots walked in and handed Rollie an envelope. Rollie said, "David, this is John McFarland. He works on the order desk we were talking about in my office."

McFarland was in his early 20's and had black hair and a mustache. He looked in good shape as most guys in their early 20's do. He looked very confident and comfortable with himself. After an exchange of pleasantries, McFarland left the office and Rollie slipped an envelope across the desk toward Haynes. "We want to make sure you get home, so here's a check for your airfare."

The cheque was for $323.23. Haynes was dumbfounded again. "This will be considerably more in Canadian money," he said.

"It would probably cost more to rectify," Rollie said.

A few minutes later another young man named Marty Goloski entered the room and dropped some green papers in front of Rollie. "When did you receive this?" he asked Goloski.

"Yesterday," Goloski said.

Rollie looked at Haynes and said, "It seems this your lucky day."

"Why?" Haynes asked.

"We received a couple of orders from these people yesterday. Do you know these companies?" Rollie asked, sliding the papers to Haynes.

The papers were order confirmations. Haynes said yes.

"Did you have anything to do with these orders?"

Haynes said, "No sir."

Rollie said, "Well, since we decided we want you to represent us up there yesterday, and the order came in yesterday, I guess we will have to pay you the commission when they are shipped. You should take copies with you. "

Haynes was dumfounded again. He thanked Rollie and Ron Clarke and spent the rest of the day being introduced around and taking a plant tour. When he eventually went through those green copies, he saw that the orders totaled over $30,000 U.S. That would give him over $1500 in commission. My god, he thought, if it had not been for Wilma. Two days of divine intervention in a row.

When Haynes got back to Montreal, one of the first things he did was meet with Wilma to give her a full report on what happened and to thank her, and of course, to repay the money.

Twenty five years later, Haynes threw the 25th anniversary party for his company Cirtcele-Tronic at the Helene du Champlain restaurant, a classy place on St. Helens Island where the 1967 World's Fair was held. It was a grand occasion with about a hundred guests.

Haynes got up and told the story about Wilma and his two days in Fort Smith. His friend Richard Rogers had come up from Greensboro for the occasion. Rogers never really believed the Wilma story, but now he was to meet her in person.

When David finished his story, he asked Wilma to come to the podium and said, "This is the person that paid for my air ticket."

Wilma leaned into the mic and said, "And when he got back, he paid me every cent and David has been a success ever since."

People applauded and Wilma started to leave, but Haynes grabbed the inside of her arm like she had grabbed his at the airport. "You come back here," he said. "You know in life, Wilma, what goes around comes around," and then he handed her an envelope. "This is what comes around, it's my thanks to you because god knows what would have happened if I hadn't caught that flight."

She opened up the envelope and stood there in shock. She was staring at a check for $3123.23. After Wilma had gathered herself, tears in her eyes she said, "I helped you just one time, and now you're doing the same for me because I'm writing a book about my experiences at Air Canada and I need to buy a computer."

Everyone in the place was on their feet. Haynes loved win-win deals, and this was one of those times. It was a wonderful night.

Ten years later Haynes was devastated when he was informed that Wilma had been killed instantly in a head-on car wreck

Sitting in the Washington bound Air Force jet, his wandering mind slipped back to Rollie. He was thinking about how much he learned from this icon. His first year's sales were $103,000, almost exactly what Rollie had predicted. Every meeting that Haynes went to hosted by Rollie was like going to a real-world business school. He was consistent and steady. He prospered and so did all the rest of them because of him.

At one point, Rollie decided to have new computerized machines installed in one of the factories. All of a sudden, product quality declined, and Rollie wanted to know why. He found out to his surprise that the problem was, a lot of the people working in the plant were illiterate. Instead of firing these people, he went out and found a literacy professor from one of the local universities, turned the company cafeteria into a schoolroom and told the employees that they would have to attend the school on their own time. One of the impressive things about it was that he was very careful not to embarrass anyone. The program was a great success, so successful that then Governor Clinton made him commissioner of business education for the state of Arkansas.

Rollie never cared about how much money franchise managers made. Commission checks reflected how much business they were bringing to the company which was in parallel with how hard they worked. It was a smart policy. There was lots of incentive and the company did not have to bother with payroll, insurance, warehousing, and all those other expenses and the outside employees that go with them.

Haynes recalled one of those few times Rollie was having some difficulty getting a point across to him, so he said, "10-4 David," and Haynes, knowing that it wasn't working, said "10-2 and a ½, Boss."

Rollie laughed and moved on, but he never forgot, and from that point on, every October 4 Haynes would get a phone call at his office from Rollie saying, "Hi David! It's 10-4 day!" even after he retired.

He got the news about his mentor on February 5, 2006, his birthday. He was on vacation in Florida when his phone rang. On the other end was his partner. "David, I've got some bad news. Mr. Boreham died earlier today. Mrs. Boreham has been looking for you and wants you to call her right away."

Haynes was devastated. He took about 15 minutes to gather himself before calling Judy Boreham, who was Rollie's second wife. Haynes liked her a lot and they had gotten along since day one. She had taken good care of Rollie. Haynes called and Judy answered the phone. She said with a voice stumbling with emotion, "Could you please come to Fort Smith as soon as possible? I need to talk to you."

Haynes arrived at Fort Smith late afternoon and checked into the Holiday Inn downtown. Judy sent her son Bill to pick him up at the hotel and bring him to her house. Judy was of slim build, like someone who did a lot of running, although she didn't, but she played a lot of tennis. She was attractive even without a lot of makeup. She was highly intelligent and she didn't gloat about it.

She gave him a big hug as soon as she opened her front door and introduced him to the people in the room he didn't know. There were Rollie's two daughters with their husbands and his grandchildren, along with Judy's son. Everyone sat down at the dining room table. After a while he realized that he was the only one there who was not a family member.

Judy was very sharp and gave him the 'come into the kitchen' signal. Before he had a chance to say anything she said, "I think you must be wondering why you are here."

Haynes said, "Well there must be some other people coming."

"No," Judy said.

"Why did you ask me?"

Her response was something that shook Haynes to the core. "Because your relationship with my husband was pure. Rollie adored you, David, and I know you felt the same way about him. You stayed in constant touch with him even after he retired and he loved that."

"I didn't know it was like that, Judy," he said.

"Well, you know that Rollie was a little reserved about those kinds of things."

Haynes was sitting at the kitchen table and he could hardly contain himself when Judy dropped another bomb. "You better get yourself together, because I would like you to deliver a eulogy at the funeral."

Haynes hung around for a little while and then Judy's son Bill drove him back to the hotel. He had not been in his room for more than 10 minutes when his phone rang. It was a voice he did not recognize.

"David, this is Chloe Delbigio." Chloe was the wife of Ron Delbigio, who was a Baldor representative from Manitoba. Chloe was one of those women that everyone liked. She was bubbly, charming and totally inoffensive, but not someone Haynes thought to be highly perceptive of certain things.

She continued, "I knew you'd be in Fort Smith today and I phoned three or four hotels and finally found you. You must be devastated."

Haynes didn't have a chance to speak as she continued. "I saw it. Every time you walked into a room, Rollie would light up like a Christmas tree. I just wanted to call you and tell you I was thinking about you."

At this point in Haynes' life, not very much surprised him. What surprised him now was the source. What kind of a person would go to all this trouble to find him? What a wonderful gesture. Chloe Delbigio was the last person he thought would notice something like that. How stupid of me, he thought.

Haynes said, "I guess you know I've had a big day," and told her about his visit to Rollie's house earlier and what he had to do. She gave him a boost and said, "Don't worry, David, knowing you, you will do a great job with the eulogy."

Haynes stayed up most of the night in his hotel room, crunching up paper and throwing it on the floor and starting over again until he was satisfied with his eulogy. He went over to Baldor's corporate headquarters to his friend John McFarland's office. John had made the climb. He was now chairman of the board of the $1 billion dollar company. What a legacy for John and Rollie. When Ron Clark had left Baldor years ago, Haynes and the rest of the Canadian representatives pushed Rollie to make John manager in charge of Canadian sales, and he eventually did. McFarland was smart, had a likable personality and was intellectually nimble. You could take him anywhere into any situation. The customers loved him. It was a no-brainer. He was on his way to the top. He and David had spent a lot of time together, in Montreal, Fort Smith and god knows how many other places over the years. They were good friends.

It was now 34 years since Haynes had seen McFarland through Rollie's office glass window. John's secretary was gracious enough to type up Haynes' notes. McFarland also had to deliver a eulogy. Haynes was nervous, so he practiced his eulogy over and over. He didn't want to lose control of his emotions at the church.

Rollie's church in downtown Fort Smith was a solid brick and stone structure. When Haynes arrived it was already packed to overflowing, with the excess people seated in adjoining buildings and with still more people on the street. TV monitors had been placed in some of these locations. Haynes stopped for a moment to contemplate the scene. It made him think about his own church, the Crystal Cathedral in Garden Grove, California. He seldom visited in real life but always watched the televised services. Robert Schuller's Crystal Cathedral had eventually gone bankrupt, and was sold to the Catholic Church. Haynes thought the main problem may have been nepotism, but in any case, Schuller's sermons had helped Haynes become a better person over the years. These days he watched Joyce Meyer, TD Jakes, Joel Olstein, and Dr. James Merritt when he got the chance.

McFarland's eulogy was poignant and funny. He talked a lot about Rollie's financial fingerprint on universities and hospitals around Arkansas.

Haynes focused on Rollie the character and got a lot of laughs. He talked about a hypothetical football team called the Baldor Bullets which was coached by Rollie Lombardi, and how Rollie who was now in the Arkansas business Hall of Fame along with Sam Wallman and the like, had led a bunch of contrarians from last to first in the electric motor business against General Electric and other powerful companies. He finished with, "How can I forget him, he died on my birthday."

His mentor was gone from this planet but Haynes had had over 30 years of watching authentic dynamic leadership up close.

CHAPTER 7

ARRIVING IN WASHINGTON

—⚛—

TUESDAY, November 11, 2014, Washington – early evening

Now Daul was reducing power somewhat and the nose was falling forward, so Haynes knew they were starting their descent into Washington. From the jump seat, he could see the stadium where the Washington Redskins play, with the Capitol Building and the White House off in the distance.

Then they were on the final descent into Andrews Air Force Base. Daul made a nice smooth landing and they taxied into an open area away from the buildings, and parked beside a black limousine that looked like a Lincoln, with a uniformed military person standing beside it. Daul shut down the engines and went through his shutdown checklist, then the three of them made their way to the exit and Haynes moved sideways to allow Daul to pass so that he could open the doors. Daul went down the steps onto the tarmac, shook hands with the uniformed driver and exchanged a few words while Haynes was descending the stairs with his baggage. The driver looked a bit like Daul. His military hat was pulled down low on his forehead. His military garb looked Air Force as well. By now, Haynes was at the bottom of the steps and the driver stuck out his hand and said, "Welcome to Washington, Mr. Haynes. My name is Lieutenant Anderson. Please let me take your bags."

He started to put Haynes' bags in the front seat but Haynes said, "You mind if I ride with you up front?"

Anderson said, "Sure why not," and put Haynes bags in the back. Daul and Richards were standing behind Haynes and he turned and shook hands with both men, saying, "I hope you guys are going to fly me home because I don't feel much like walking."

Daul said, "It would be my pleasure but as you know I just follow orders."

Haynes said, "Well, I don't follow orders anymore so maybe I could make a request to be sure that it is you guys to fly me home."

Lieutenant Anderson was holding the car door open and Haynes got in. He waved goodbye to Daul and Richards as they headed towards a gate manned by a couple of military personnel. Haynes was apprehensive but loving every minute of this because he loved being around military people. Being a history reader, he knew of the sacrifices being made by these folks – both men and women – to preserve our freedom. He would sometimes get emotional watching military people talking about their experiences. He was proud of his son Colin for his service in the US military both in Korea and Iraq. It gave him a good feeling to know that he was contributing annually to the Wounded Warriors Fund.

Haynes realized this was the first time he had come to the U.S. without clearing customs. "May I ask you where I'm going?" he asked Anderson.

"We are going to Blair House, across from the White House."

"Isn't that where some president stayed while renovations were going on in the White House?"

Anderson turned briefly and looked at Haynes, a little surprised. "I don't know, Sir."

Haynes did not want to embarrass him so he just said, "I'm not sure either. I just thought I might've heard that somewhere."

To his surprise, activity on the streets on the drive to Blair House appeared to be normal, despite everything going on. There were cars in the street, people walking on the sidewalks, and the occasional bus. Anderson answered his cell phone and said only, "We are 10 minutes away," before he hung up.

The limo pulled up in front of Blair House. There were reporters, some armed with cameras, waiting in front. Haynes got out into a barrage of camera flashes. Anderson said, "I can take care of your bags sir, General McCormick is waiting for you inside."

Haynes said, "What the hell do they want my picture for?"

Anderson replied, "They have been photographing everyone coming in all afternoon."

By now it was close to 8.30 p.m. A military officer opened the front door of Blair House and there was General McCormick to greet him. "Hello David," said McCormick, "It's been a while."

Haynes replied, "Sure has. Looks like you have your hands full, General."

McCormick said, "How was your trip?"

"Very enjoyable," said Haynes. "Guys like me don't get an opportunity to fly in an Air Force jet very often."

McCormick said, "Come with me. I need to brief you as to what we would like you to do."

McCormick and Haynes went into a small room and sat down. McCormick asked if he would like something to eat.

Haynes said, "A simple sandwich and a soft drink would be fine." McCormick picked up the phone and ordered something for both of them.

McCormick got right down to it. "We have a group of people in the conference room waiting for you. Did you see the news conference on TV this afternoon?"

"Yes, I did."

McCormick said, "Some of the people you're going to meet are the same folks you saw in the news conference. I want you to give a presentation on what you think is wrong with America and what you would do to try and fix it. I know that you can do this without notes because you did it with me and Peter Turner in Florida."

Haynes noted that he did not mention Stamp's name or the golf course. He didn't know whether this was intentional but he did notice. McCormick continued, "Just do it basically the way you did it with us in Florida, with special emphasis on your 'American Functional Charter.'"

By this time Haynes' sandwich had arrived and McCormick was having a cup of coffee. Things were moving so quickly that Haynes did not even have time to ask, "Why me?"

He finished his sandwich and they went down the hall. When they entered the conference room Haynes found a large number of people standing around in conversation. He saw Peter Turner and Bill Simmons. Haynes wasn't really sure if he should walk over to Peter and act like he knew him, so he waited for Peter to approach him. Peter introduced himself, and Haynes realized that he had taken the right approach. Haynes was introduced to most of the participants in the room and they all took their seats. Haynes was seated between McCormick and Simmons at the end of the long oval table. The noise in the room subsided and McCormick gave Haynes the nod. He stood up and said, "Good evening ladies and gentlemen. I have been asked to deliver a presentation for which I had not really prepared myself, but General McCormick seems to have great confidence in my off-the-cuff skills."

CHAPTER 8

THE PRESENTATION

—m—

TUESDAY, November 11, 2014, evening

Haynes had been thinking about these ideas for so many years, that once he was seated in the conference room, the words came naturally. "There is a reason why the American people are divided. It's a little more complicated than this, but basically Americans fall into three basic categories. There are the people on the left that include socialists and liberals with a few communists in the mix. On the other side are conservatives, libertarians and a few extreme right wingers in that mix. The third is a group of Americans really not attached to any ideology who want their leaders to use common sense and do what works. The first two categories are commonly defined in terms of red and blue states.

"Theoretically, if there were no federal government, the people would be represented by state legislatures only. What would be going on in neighboring states would not be of any great concern because those neighboring states would not be imposing their own policies on them. But we do have a federal central government and it does impose its will universally across America. Sometimes we have a President and a congress that represent the views of blue states and sometimes we have a President and a congress that represent the views of the red states, which creates division as well as hatred from whichever side is not in power at the time."

Haynes was noticing that he was using the word "we" instead of the "you" that would be expected coming from a Canadian. But he didn't think that his audience was really concerned at this point about semantics.

He continued. "People in America do not want the federal government imposing its will universally, or at least they want to limit this. Conservative people do not want socialists and liberals imposing their will through the federal government, nor do liberals and socialists want conservatives imposing their will on them through the federal government. My idea is to limit these resentments and inefficiencies to a minimum so that the people in states functioning under goofy state governments do not impose their policies through elected federal political officials that share their views and so end up imposing some of these policies on the other states.

"None of this is totally the fault of anyone in these parties. It is the fault of a Constitution run amok. I believe that the framers never intended for the federal government to be out of control and become way too large. This union was started by 13 colonies or states. Obviously they formed a federation for some very simple reasons. And if we put some thought into the realities of that time in history, we can make a pretty good guess what those reasons were, reasons that are equally important today. I think we can agree they formed a federation of the following reasons:

1. To be able to travel anywhere in America without borders or checkpoints
2. Freedom to conduct commerce or business anywhere in America without tariffs or restrictions
3. Use of the a single currency universally in America
4. One official language
5. To install universal rights and privileges
6. A military to protect them from foreign intervention
7. Being able to move to and live in any state

"The problem is that over the years, the federal government has slowly but surely taken over jurisdiction in areas where it does not belong. This has created a monster out of control and an inefficient central government that has created unnecessary divisions, resentments and political battles on both sides of the political spectrum. Just go on the internet and punch up 'Federal Agencies'. That scary list is endless.

"We would care for each other more if we had control over things that are close to us. We don't ask our neighbors to grow the grass in the same way we do. We respect the differences in our neighbor's tastes. Good neighbors don't insist the person next door grow his grass the same way we do. That ticks people off.

"One senator, congressman and president after another has come to Washington to make big changes. But the only thing that has really happened was to make the federal government bigger. You could be the greatest manager, organizer or administrator on this planet and it is still not possible for a reasonable number of people to manage. Government is so big it has become totally unmanageable. It's out of control and feeds on itself. So it's not really totally the fault of the congress or the president or the voters. The fault is in the structure, the Constitution.

"If things continue on this way you will see a steady decline in America. You will have some well-managed states that will be fed up and want to separate from the union and the bottom line is that America will no longer be able to defend itself.

"That phrase, 'strong federal or central government,' is an oxymoron. American citizens will have a stronger attachment to their country when they have more control over local affairs.

"Since the Constitution is currently suspended, you have a great opportunity to set America on a positive path for the next 200 years.

"Gentlemen, you need to have a new constitutional amendment.

He reached into his bag and pulled out his documents.

AMERICAN FUNCTIONAL CHARTER

"What will this do? It will define clearly, in simple English, what the responsibilities are for federal and state governments. The basis of this charter will be to define these autonomies from the bottom up.

This charter will divide responsibilities into three categories:
1. State only
2. Shared
3. Federal only

" 'State only' means that only the states will execute these functions or run these departments.

" 'Shared' means that a current department or function could be subdivided and separated to become the exclusive domains of the different level of government.

" 'Federal Only' means that the federal government alone will execute these functions.

"A classic example of Shared would be transportation. The FAA and aviation would be federal only. Local trucking licenses etc. would be state only. The following is how it should be set up.

ADMINISTERED BY STATES ONLY:
1. Education
2. Municipal affairs
3. Social welfare
4. Housing
5. Natural resources
6. Employment and manpower/labor
7. Health & human services [including Medicare/Medicaid, etc...]
8. Unemployment insurance/ transferable
9. Wages

SHARED:
1. Communications
2. Agriculture

3. Taxation & revenue
4. Environment
5. Justice
6. Fisheries
7. Transportation
8. Energy
9. National parks
10. Native affairs
11. Commerce
12. Lands
13. Arts

ADMINISTERED BY FEDERAL ONLY:
1. Defense/military
2. Customs and tariffs
3. Central bank
4. Monetary policy
5. Foreign affairs
6. Basic human rights and freedoms
7. Supreme Court/ federal courts
8. National sports/ Olympics, etc...
9. National police/ FBI
10. Trade and trade negotiation
11. Treasury
12. Homeland security
13. Veterans affairs
14. Banks & financial institutions
15. Immigration
16. External trade & commerce / exports / imports
17. Space
18. Food & drug safety

"Where the word ONLY is applied means that that government ONLY has the sole jurisdiction over that department or function. No other government can collect taxes or distribute money or services for that particular jurisdiction, directly or indirectly, unless requested by the states.

How will this be administered? By a commission called "The American Functional Charter Commission.'

"This commission would be made up of 51 members. There would be one member from every state, selected by the governor of each state, and one from the federal government selected by the president will automatically become chairman.

They would serve 6-year terms. The only exception would be for the first group of commissioners. There will be 25 that will serve four years instead of six, and the balance of 25 will serve six years only. This can be decided by pulling papers out of a hat at the first meeting, so that 25 members will stay for 4 years and 25 will stay on for six years. The reason is we don't want a wholesale exit of all members at the end of every six years. We would need to leave 25 commissioners so that the new 25 coming in can be brought up to speed by experienced people to ensure continuity. After the first term, all commissioners will serve six years. The federal commissioner will serve six years from the start.

Haynes went on to explain that a constitutional mandate would be established for this commission. The mandate will be established by negotiators for the state and federal levels selected to establish the exact content of the American Functional Charter. The mandate for commissioner's decisions or rulings will be based on the following principles:

1. The functions of government will be structured from the bottom up, to be closest to the individuals they serve wherever possible, not from the top down.
2. Does a particular function or department have national implications? If it does, then it must be made either the exclusive responsibility of the federal government or a shared responsibility. (The FAA and aviation would be a classic case of national implications.

If the state can handle the administration of any function or department within its state borders, it should be a state responsibility only. It could be possible that states could negotiate arrangements with adjacent states concerning matters that don't extend past other neighboring states, such as watersheds.

3. Where the word ONLY is applied, it means that that government ONLY has the sole jurisdiction over the department, function or jurisdiction. No other government can collect taxes; distribute money or services for that particular jurisdiction directly or indirectly unless both parties agree. The same would apply for the subdivisions of the shared section of the charter.
4. The committee will have exclusive jurisdiction to rule on applications for interstate or state-on-state disputes relating to the charter.
5. The committee's rulings cannot be appealed until four years after the date of the ruling. After every four years, governments can apply for another ruling.
6. The Congress, the Senate, the President, the Supreme Court, state legislatures or anybody else would not have any jurisdiction over this commission. The commission is entirely autonomous with regard to the charter.
7. The federal Congress, the Senate, the President and state legislators cannot pass legislation to establish any new departments or agencies without making an application and getting a ruling from the committee. If an attempt is made to pass such legislation, the committee may rule arbitrarily that these new departments or functions are unconstitutional for that level of government to manage. The reason for this is that some functions cannot be foreseen. For example, who in 18th century would have thought we needed a FAA?
8. Applications to the committee by federal and state governments will have to be heard. Citizens or citizen committees will also have the right to make applications, but the committee will have the right to reject or refuse to hear applications from individual citizens.

8a. The committee would also be granted exclusive responsibility to hear citizens' applications for rulings on private property or private domain confiscations by governments and to decide whether this is justified for the greater good and if so what would be a fair settlement. The Supreme Court would no longer have any authority over private property seizures, nor would any other courts. Private property is at the core of freedom and democracy. Rulings would have to be rendered within 60 days from the date of the application by statute. No longer would citizens have to wait years for a Supreme Court judgment. Justice delayed is justice denied. This committee would have no official holidays. They would have to be available for meetings 12 months a year if necessary to make rulings in a timely way. Backlogs like we see currently with the Supreme Court will not be tolerated under the rules of the charter. Backlogs have become an internalized cancer at the Supreme Court.
9. The chairman will be responsible for scheduling meetings. These meetings can be conducted over the internet or in person. The committee must make its rulings within two months (60 days) of the date of the application.
10. The committee may rule, where there is duplication of departments or functions between the federal and state governments, and designate the responsibility solely to one level of government or the other.
11. Any state or the federal government can appeal any regulation imposed on state or federal rights under the charter. The Supreme Court would have no jurisdiction here.
12. The committee may, from time to time, allow more than one state to negotiate a settlement of jurisdiction as long as the function does not extend past those neighboring states. This could be the case for things like dams. New dams would be part of the committee's jurisdiction.

The committee will make all decisions with consideration for the bottom up principle. First priority will always be given to the smallest autonomous jurisdiction, starting with the individual.

- Country [last]
- State
- County
- Town or city
- Individual's property
- Individual's family
- Individual [first]

All this would have to be accomplished before the new president takes office after the 2016 election. Does anyone have any questions?"

Former FBI director Simmons said, "It all seems very clear, Mr. Haynes. So what other things would you do to improve the situation?"

Haynes said, "Well, I have quite a list. Are you sure you want me to get into this now?"

Everyone at the table leaned forward with enthusiasm, and Peter Turner said "Do you have that part of your list? Maybe everyone could have a copy."

Within minutes, everyone had a copy of Haynes' numbered list. "Okay, so let's start with the first one," Haynes said, and started reading.

1. Health and national security - there will be no more 'Yeah but this' and 'yeah but that' concerning Ebola. So let's keep it real simple, anyone coming from a country where there are Ebola outbreaks is barred from entering the United States. Why would any clear-thinking person want to endanger America with an epidemic?
2. Abolish the Affordable Health Care Act and move health to exclusive state responsibility under the charter umbrella.
3. Implement tort reform to reduce medical costs.
4. Allow insurance companies to operate anywhere in America, in fact, as part of the Functional Charter, make it a rule that all business and commerce can operate anywhere in the country.
5. Impose term limits for senators, congressmen and congresswomen. Congressmen and women will serve 4-year terms instead of

the present two years; some elected during presidential elections and some during mid terms. The reason for this is that right now, Congress people spend too much time raising money for elections and not enough time serving the people, and this solution does not remove the mid-term elections 'so called' protest vote.

6. Introduce a line item veto for the president.
7. Give congress the right to appoint special prosecutors and have the right to reject the President's selection for Attorney General and pick their own candidate (the framers attempted to balance out power in Washington to prevent having an imperial President but they got one anyway protected by an Attorney General. This would prevent this kind of thing from happening.)
8. Seal the southern border tight by whatever means necessary [using the Australian Model] any new illegals deported immediately no lawyers, no hearings. You're out now.
9. Start hunting down folks with overstayed visas and deport them.
10. Deport immediately - criminals, anyone arrested and charged or anyone with a previous criminal record domestic or foreign.
11. When the aforementioned items are accomplished and things settle down, deal with the illegals that are here.
12. Reform social security. The politicians have stolen the people's money by dumping it into the federal deficit. A separate agency will administer the fund and keep it away from the hands of politicians. Actuarial calculations can be done to prove that if Social Security investments were handled like normal portfolios they would be more than twice the size of their present value, despite occasional downturns in the markets. Also if these Social Security payments were put in a separate fund, the money would be safe from an irresponsible central government and its politicians. What the federal government has done with the Social Security Fund makes Bernie Madoff look like child's play.
13. Introduce Herman Raines's 999 tax program. Only I would call it the 9999 program - Corporate tax, personal income tax, capital

gains tax and a goods and services taxes, which we can call the GST for short.
14. A 50 plus one senate vote to pass bills.
15. Keep control of the internet in the United States. We invented it, we keep it.
16. NASA to coordinate with private companies to re-establish visits to outer space from United States territory.
17. Get the Keystone Pipeline started immediately.
18. Get a program started to export natural gas.
19. Work with the automobile companies to start to introduce natural gas engines.
20. See what it would take to get natural gas stations commonplace in America.
21. Cancel immediately all non-essential federal regulations. Federal agencies will have to resubmit for approval any future regulations through the congress, starting immediately with what they perceive as essential. The ones not included would be the FAA and the FDA for now. These can be reviewed later. This is the Contrarian Approach. The people's representatives no longer have to waste their time going through volumes and volumes of mostly useless regulations. The bureaucracy would be forced to resubmit all regulations to the congress only to approve or disapprove. The President or federal bureaucrats will have no authority to impose or change any new regulations without congressional consent. A constitutional amendment will have to be passed ensuring that this will be the method used to introduce any new regulations by agencies. A people's regulation ombudsman should be appointed for individual's complaints and appeals.
22. Cut government waste and duplication which represents billions of dollars.
23. Appoint a serious and experienced businessman to re-energize American manufacturing, to have jurisdiction over tariffs and to review existing trade treaties to make it easy for American companies to bring their financial assets back to America and incentives

to rejuvenate manufacturing. This person is to meet with representatives of small business to discuss what can be done to turn small business loose and get the government off the back of the most important job creators in America, this could jump start the economy. All we have now is an anti-business administration that runs around discouraging tourism in Las Vegas, stating "You didn't build that" as if business people didn't build businesses and create jobs. These kinds of things are so stupid that they are indefensible, this is not Russia, this is the United States.

What is required is a leader who is not ideological, a leader who wants to do only what is practical and what works regardless of ideology.

I would respectfully like everyone to listen very carefully to what I'm about to say. Probably the most important threat to America and the world today is Islamic terrorism. I am frightened not so much by the terrorists but by the free world's approach to this threat. There is something wrong with America's approach to threats today, compared to a classic example of how America used to do it right. When the Japanese attacked Pearl Harbor and over 2,000 of our military personnel were killed, President Roosevelt immediately declared war on Japan with his famous speech to the Congress. Three thousand people were killed on 9/11 by Islamic jihadists who were allowed to roam freely around America and use our own laws against us. America has still not declared war on Islamic jihadists. Isn't there something wrong here? Presently, it is well known that Moslem religious leaders are preaching hatred, violence and sabotage toward any non Muslims who don't agree with their views. There have also been reports of weapons training by radical Muslims on private property in America. This is another classic case of our enemies using America's laws such as property rights and the second amendment against us. President Roosevelt would have never allowed Japanese religious leaders to preach subversion. And he certainly would have had any Japanese doing weapons training on private property arrested immediately. So why are we allowing this behavior to go unchecked? You know what happens to sports teams that sit on a lead. More often than not, they lose. Right now, America is sitting on a lead, hoping the other team won't score. We need to be proactive."

Simmons asked, "So how would you handle it?"

"In my opinion what is required is an immediate declaration of war against Islamic terrorists and in that declaration, special powers for the President and the FBI to deal with this domestic and international threat. A few of those special powers should be to bar any Muslims from visiting the US without special visas. And special powers of arrest and deportation of Muslims involved in subversion. President Roosevelt didn't allow this kind of thing to go on so why should you? Criminal charges would be laid against anyone trying to impose sharia law or any other non US law in the United States."

"What do you do if Muslims doing weapon training have American passports?"

"Have their passports revoked and deport them immediately."

Peter Turner said, "Well, you've certainly made your views on Islamic terrorism crystal clear. What about some of your other suggestions? The 9999 program represents quite a drop in the present tax rates?"

Haynes said, "It's a contradiction but for some strange reason when tax rates drop revenue increases. This has been statistically documented in the past. Note the 9999 program is 9% for each of the tax categories. Also presently there is no national sales tax this could close the gap and possibly exceed present revenues."

Question: "What if 9999 proves to be not enough?"

Haynes said, "Well, we would go to 10 10 10 10 once we've completed the eradication of government waste. That would still be well below the present rates."

Then came a question that surprised Haynes. It was again from Simmons. "If you were President, who would you appoint as your chief of staff?"

Without hesitation Haynes said, "Rodrick Giani, former mayor of New York."

Simmons said, "That was fast."

Haynes said, "It's a no-brainer. The guy has been one of the most effective leaders in the country. He's not afraid to pick strong, effective people to work around him and he knows how to get things done."

Simmons said, "Thank you very much for your ideas. Would you mind stepping out of the room for a little while? Our group needs to have some discussion."

Haynes was not even out of the door when he heard the high pitch of conversation breaking out. Now he understood why Churchill liked to drink so much.

He had been escorted out of the chamber and so asked his escort if he could get a vodka and orange. He wanted to call Sonja but didn't think it the appropriate time. Someone brought him a nice large vodka and orange with lots of ice. He hadn't noticed but it was now past 10.30 p.m. He sat sipping on his vodka until past 11 o'clock, when a military officer came in and said, "They would like you back in the conference room."

Haynes took his seat between Simmons and McCormick again. Simmons said, "I suppose you've been wondering what's been going on for the last hour or so."

Haynes said, "I wouldn't be human if I didn't."

Simmons said, "We were discussing the idea of giving you an important job with our government," and before Haynes had a chance to say anything, Simmons went on. "We have done an extensive background check on you, which was mostly very positive except you seem to have had a lot of women in your history and if you are in a heavy job for our government, we wouldn't want that to be a liability."

Silence swept over the room. Everyone was looking at Haynes.

Haynes had a flair for the dramatic. He let the silence sit for a minute while he smiled and even chuckled a little, and soon, some others at the table began to smile and chuckle along. Then he said, "Yeah. I like women. In fact some of my closest friends are women. My intimate relations I believe have been voluntary from both sides and at appropriate times."

Haynes looked directly at Simmons and said, "Whatever my social activities might have been, they are all behind me now because I have met the love of my life and believe me, her relationship with me is completely voluntary and appropriate, as I'm sure you already know. Any position that I might consider that would have me separated from her, I would not be able to take. I don't like it when she's not around." Then Haynes looked again at Simmons and said, "Let's see if your intelligence folks are any good. What's her name?"

Simmons seemed to lighten up. Maybe for some reason he saw things going his way. He smiled and said, "Sonja Martinez."

Haynes smiled again and said, "Well that's good. I hope the intelligence stays consistently accurate. We don't want to be acting militarily with bad intelligence."

The whole room started to laugh. Then Haynes looked at Simmons again and said, "Did your research on Ms. Martinez meet with your approval?"

Simmons said, "Very much so, in fact if a woman of her stature is with you, you can't be all that bad." Again, there was laughter through the room, Haynes leading it.

Haynes was beginning to feel more relaxed but that wasn't going to last long after he asked Simmons his next question. "What is it that you want me to do?"

Simmons hesitated and looked around the room. His glance stopped at General Jim McCormick and stayed there for a brief moment. McCormick looked to his left and right and then back to Simmons and nodded. Simmons turned back to Haynes and said, "We want you to be the Administrator of the executive branch of our government."

Haynes fell back in his chair and said, "Well, what will be the Administrator's responsibilities and who would I report to?"

"Well," said Simmons, "It will work this way. We will be watching you but basically you will become the de facto president until the next presidential elections in 2016. So now you understand why we want you to behave yourself and why we are very pleased that you will be with and stay with Miss Martinez."

Haynes sat there in shock.

Then Simmons said, "You understand that everyone at the table is at risk if this whole thing comes unglued, and if you accept this challenge you also will be at risk. You are also probably wondering why we would choose a foreigner for this position. We wanted a citizen of a country with compatible values to our own, and Canada is one of those countries. Our goal with this choice is to confirm to the public that we don't intend to extend this situation past the 2016 elections. If we had chosen an American, especially a military American, it would look like this situation could be indefinite. And we definitely have no intention of extending it beyond the 2016 elections.

"Also, all of us here realize that it's very important to have a civilian administration to make the changes needed over the next two years. We need the American people to believe that we are serious about conducting elections as normal in 2016. Do you think that you can accomplish the goals that you just laid out before us this evening, between now and 2016?"

Haynes sat back in his chair. By now he had gathered himself because this was not the first time he had been slapped behind the head in church, so to speak. He did not even ask, "Why me?" because he knew they already knew everything about him, including the hair on his ass. Haynes said, "What do you intend to do with the President, the Vice President and the other people under house arrest?" This was critical for Haynes because he did not want to be involved in any possible harm done to these people, like what happened to Allende in Chile and the Czar's family in Russia.

Simmons said, "They will remain under house arrest for the time being, but no harm will come to any of them, or their families."

Haynes looked at Simmons firmly and said, "I want this in writing and I want everyone at this table to sign, otherwise I will not accept this position. It's not their fault. These people were nominated and hired by too many American voters for positions they were not qualified for."

Simmons glanced at McCormick and got another nod, so he looked at Haynes and said, "No problem, we can do that."

Haynes figured that if the answer had taken any longer, it would have been an indication that they weren't sure about harm coming to those under house arrest. Besides, it would reassure the American people to know that such a document was signed. So he looked around the table and said, "Okay, I can accept this position, but if any harm other than house arrest comes to these people, I will be out of here faster than a speeding bullet. This is a great opportunity to fix America for the next 200 years. Let's not screw it up."

Then he added, "Can we take a break and get to know each other a little bit? And then we can maybe sit down and figure out the where, who, what and when? The 'where' being where am I going to work and it's not going to be the Oval Office and that should become public. The 'who' is who is going to be in the administration? The 'what' is what are we are going to do and in what order of priority, and the 'when' is when for all the above?

"I am sure you gentlemen have some ideas about who you want to serve in specific posts. I know who I want in some places and in others I'm open to suggestion. May I assume that I can get fast congressional support for the measures that we would like to take since the Republicans have won both the Congress and the Senate? If we don't get timely congressional support, I assume that we will arbitrarily move forward with our changes anyway since the Constitution is suspended."

McCormick interrupted and said, "Our most important priority is to get a team together ASAP to present this to the American people. That team has to be a confidence booster because we also have to reopen the American markets as soon as possible."

Haynes looked at McCormick and said, "I agree. Let's stay focused on that for now, but we need to have a travel ban on visitors coming from West African countries due to Ebola."

McCormick replied, "We have already started implementing this as we speak."

Haynes said, "What about the CDC director?"

McCormick replied, "He will remain in his post but he will report directly to Lt. General Russell Larocque."

Haynes said, "Isn't he one of the heroes of the Katrina floods in New Orleans?"

"That's him," said McCormick.

"Good," said Haynes. "We won't have to worry about any dolling around." Haynes stood up and shook Simmons and McCormick's hands while they said "Congratulations, Mr. Administrator."

Haynes put his hand on Simmons lower arm and said, "Thank you, Bill, and let's be successful." Then he realized he would have to repeat this with all the rest of the people in the room, so he started making the rounds. Everyone seemed enthusiastic about the monumental decision they had just made.

CHAPTER 9

THE PLANNING MEETING; A NEW DIRECTION FOR AMERICA

—⚏—

WEDNESDAY, November 12, 2014, 1:30 a.m.

On his way out of the conference room Haynes cornered Bill Simmons and said, "Bill, can you find me some kind of personal assistant to help me out with things?"

Simmons said, "Absolutely, let me make a call."

Haynes left the get-together before anyone else to gather himself and find a room to make some notes for himself. A little after 1:00 a.m. there was a knock on the door, which he'd left slightly open. Haynes said, "Come in."

The woman who entered looked to be in her late 30's. She was smartly dressed in slightly flared dress pants and a jacket, with an off-white shirt underneath. Her hair was short, dark and combed straight back. She was solidly built at 5' 8" and was carrying a small brief case. As he was getting to his feet, she reached out to shake his hand and said, "Hi. My name is Jeannie Flett. Mr. Simmons told me you might need some help."

"You've got that right! Would you like to sit down?"

"Yes, thank you. Now, what can I do for you?"

Haynes thought, "You might start by not looking so good," quickly followed by, "that Simmons guy must have a sense of humor." But instead he said, "I hope you don't find this too miniscule, but I need you to take some notes."

Haynes thought she might be a plant by McCormick and Simmons to keep track of what he was doing, but he didn't care; he really had nothing to hide. The only thing he wanted was someone who could pull the trigger and get things done, especially things he might not have thought of.

She said, "Not at all," as she reached into her briefcase and whipped out a small computer.

Haynes, who was sitting there with a pencil and pad, thought how much times had changed. "I'm going to have to read these notes. How am I going to read them on that thing?" he asked her.

"No problem, I can print them out for you."

They sat there for a while going through a list of items and Haynes had the list printed. Then he asked Flett to find Simmons and tell him he was ready to meet again in the conference room.

Slowly everybody found their way back to the conference table. Haynes said, "I would first like to give you some idea about my management style. I will quote something from President Reagan: 'I've been criticized for what some people call a 'hands off' management style. But the criticism has come from people who don't understand how we operate. I don't believe a chief executive should supervise every detail of what goes on in his organization. He or she should set broad policy and general ground rules, tell people what he wants them to do, then let them do it. He should make himself available so that if there is a problem, policies can be fine tuned, but I don't think he should peer constantly over the shoulders of those in charge of a project and tell them every few minutes what to do. That's the cornerstone of good management; set clear goals and appoint good people to help you achieve them. Don't interfere, but if somebody drops the ball, intervene and make a change.' "

"So number one: I need an office to work out of at the White House.

"Number two: I need someone to make arrangements for Gianni to be here yesterday.

"Number three: I want John McFarland, ex Chairman of the board of the Baldor Electric Company, to be the new commerce secretary. Please make arrangements for John to be here in the morning. Here are his coordinates. The Baldor Electric Company has a corporate jet. You may have to contact their chairman so that they can make arrangements for transporting John to Washington.

"Number four: Can there be such a thing as an assistant administrator? Someone acceptable to you who could take my place if I get hit by a train? My recommendation would be Giani. This committee may want to take this under consideration because it is not an immediate priority." Haynes just realized that he had somehow named this group 'The Committee.'

"Number five: I want to fire the serving Secretary of State and replace him with Oliver West." Haynes knew that this would be a controversial choice for a lot of people but probably not the military folks. Haynes knew that West had an extensive knowledge of the world and a very good understanding of the hotspots and the players. West was aggressive and a patriot. This would send out a message that they were not messing around. The real bonus was West's charming savoir-faire which suited the position, combined with extensive military experience, which Haynes considered a valuable asset for a secretary of state. Haynes noticed some eyebrows going up but didn't get any objections. Maybe his choice was a pleasant surprise for many in the room.

"Number six: I want to fire the secretary of defense and replace him with Jim McCormick." Haynes knew that he had to appoint someone sitting at the table to this position and he knew that McCormick was tough but not some Dr. Strangelove.

"Number seven: I want also to replace the secretary of homeland security and appoint a new Attorney General. I'm going to solicit Gianni's suggestions on this if it's okay with you.

"Number eight: I want that director of the IRS, Mr. Cover-up Magoo, fired ASAP. I would like Herman Raines to replace him.

"Number nine: I have no quarrel with the present FBI director but I would like you, Bill, back in your position at the FBI. I want someone the American people can trust.

"Number 10: One of those little things, but symbolic. I would like to have the Churchill bust put back in the White House.

"Number 11: I can't remember the name of the former chairman of Shell Oil. He always impressed me when I saw him being interviewed and I think he's someone I can work with. Can someone please find his name and coordinates and if there is no objection I would like to offer him the job as energy secretary. I think this man will put America first, and not big oil.

Number 12: I would like to ask Henry Rawlston to come back as treasury secretary for a couple of years. We need to restore confidence.

Number 13: I want the Fort Hood terrorist attack designated as just that, a terrorist attack. People in this administration are going to use the word terrorist as part of our vocabulary. I am going to fire the first person that says 'workplace violence' as a replacement for terrorism. Subsequently I want the victims and their families of the Fort Hood massacre financially compensated. We should never be treating people that serve their country in this manner. This whole mess is a disgrace to men and women in uniform. I also don't want anything swept under the rug for political or any other reason concerning the hearing of that soldier we just got back from Taliban custody. Let the evidence go wherever it leads, whether he is a deserter and cost the unnecessary lives of other soldiers trying to rescue him, or whether he is not a deserter.

"Number 14: I want to ask KT McFadden to be my foreign affairs advisor.

"Number 15: I want a pardon issued for the writer D'Souza, who wrote the book America. In my opinion he made an honest mistake. The charges against him were excessive and politically motivated.

"Number 16: I'd like to get John Bolton back at the UN for two years.

"Number 17: I would like to talk to Art Leever as possible budget director.

"Number 18: I would like to talk to Dr. Ben Carson for Health and Human Services Secretary. I would like to encourage him to prepare the agency for closure and the transfer of health and human services to states' control under the new functional charter.

"Number 19: I would like to talk to Thomas Sowell to become a special advisor to the administrator.

"Number 20: I would like politically motivated prosecutions of former CIA agents dropped immediately.

"Number 21: I need suggestions on who should head up the remaining following agencies - secretary of the interior, secretary of agriculture, housing, transportation and education.

"Number 22: I need to meet with our top military people tomorrow on an urgent matter.

"Number 23: Scrap the Affordable Care Act. That word affordable drives me crazy. Costs are rising like a speeding bullet and already insured folks are losing their coverage.

"Number 24: One thing I want to make clear, I am not going to be talking about abortion, gay rights, drugs or any of this other social stuff. We will leave that for the next president. Right now we have bigger fish to fry." Haynes knew that this was the way that the Conservative Canadian Prime Minister stayed out of trouble. It would be good advice for republican candidates running for president in the next election – stay away from social issues, no matter what you believe. Let their opponents beat those issues to death. Their own plates would be full with more important issues like the economy and the Jihadists.

"Can someone please tell me what is going to happen with the existing White House staff? Let's face it, most of these people are going to be hostile, so I definitely need some help as to how to proceed with this. Maybe I should wait till Gianni arrives tonight. In the meantime maybe someone can make arrangements for a working office and one for Gianni next to mine."

Haynes was getting tired and so was everybody else, so he suggested that he needed some rest. Haynes had noticed Jeannie Flett taking notes throughout the meeting so he asked Simmons if she could be his personal assistant for a while.

Simmons replied, "That's fine with me."

Haynes apologized to McCormick for suggesting that he should become Secretary of Defense in such an open forum, but explained that he had wanted to see the reaction from the other people at the table. Their body language had been very positive. "So I assume, General, that you have no problem assuming this position."

McCormick replied, "I am honored to be the new Secretary of Defense."

Haynes asked McCormick if he could meet with him and the three other military officers along with the new appointed Secretary of State at 7 o'clock the next morning at the White House.

McCormick nodded and said, "That will be fine."

Simmons said to Haynes, "Someone will escort you to a place in the building where you can sleep this evening. Or, more like this morning."

The phone rang at Bernard Goldstein's home in Florida late that evening. On the other end of the line was Jeannie Flett. She asked him if he could come to Washington as soon as possible. Goldstein asked what for. She replied, "The new Administrator needs some advice concerning a press secretary."

Goldstein replied, "Why can't we do that on the phone?"

Flett replied, "The Administrator and Rod Giani want to speak to you personally because they're going to need a lot of help right now with the media and they would like to have you around to help."

Goldstein still had the curiosity of a reporter so he asked, "Who is the new Administrator?"

"His name is David Haynes," said Flett.

"Who the hell is David Haynes?"

"Come up here and find out for yourself."

"I'll have to make some travel arrangements."

Flett said, "We have a plane waiting for you for a private flight to Washington as soon as you are ready. We would like you to leave as soon as you possibly can. We need you here early tomorrow."

Goldstein replied, "What the hell is going on up there, anyway?"

Flett replied, "Get yourself over to the private aircraft FBO at Miami international." Flett gave Goldstein the name of the two pilots along with the chief pilot's phone number. Flett said, "Bring enough clothes; you might need to stay a little while. When you arrive you will be driven to Blair House."

Goldstein, overwhelmed by his own curiosity, said, "Okay, I'll be at the airport in a couple of hours."

WEDNESDAY, November 12, 2014, 2:00 a.m.

The phone rang at the McFarland residence at 2:00 in the morning. Jeannie Flett brought McFarland up to date on the events of the previous day and told McFarland that there was someone waiting for him at the reserve base in Fort Smith to fly him to Washington. He asked to speak to Haynes but she told him he was fast asleep and that he would be pleased to see him sometime tomorrow. McFarland got the name of his contact at the base and while he packed, he explained to his wife that he had to leave immediately.

Flett located Oliver West and arranged for him to have a breakfast meeting with Haynes.

Herman Raines was also informed and had agreed to be in Washington the next day.

KT McFadden was also contacted, but said she could not make it to the 7 o'clock meeting.

Rodrick Giani was on his way from New York.

WEDNESDAY November 12, 2014, 5:45 a.m.

Jeannie Flett rang Haynes' room phone at 5.45 a.m. "Mr. Administrator, it's time to get up. Bernard Goldstein arrived early this morning and you have a breakfast meeting with Oliver West."

Haynes was not much of a morning man but now he had to learn. "Make sure Bernic Goldstein is in the meeting with Oliver West," he said. He was downstairs by 6:15 a.m. and found Flett, Oliver West and Bernard Goldstein sitting at a dining room table over their coffee. Haynes smiled, walked over to West and said, "Well, well, I know who this is! Thanks for coming, Oliver."

Then Haynes walked over to Goldstein and said, "Thanks for getting here so quickly. Would you mind sitting in on this meeting and afterwards we can have a conversation concerning how you may be able to help us?"

They sat down and Haynes said, "You know, Oliver, I've always been impressed with your analysis and perspective on what is going on around the world. The mainstream media tried to unfairly portray you as a cowboy and they will probably continue to do so. That's just what they do if they don't agree with someone. I just want you to know I don't give a damn what they think. I'm sure Jeannie here has briefed you on why you're here so I will make it official. I want you to be our next Secretary of State. I believe that you will be one of the best Secretary of States this country's ever had."

Goldstein was watching with amazement. West dipped his head and didn't say anything for a minute. Haynes was reading his mind. West had taken a hit for the team during the Reagan administration and this was his redemption. Haynes placed his hand on top of West's arm and said, "Oliver, you've come a long way since the 1980s and you're exactly what your country needs at this time. Will you please accept this position?"

West looked up and said, "Yes, sir."

Haynes said, "Please don't call me sir."

And West said, "Yes sir." again.

Haynes started laughing and was joined by the others. West's conversation was engaging and charming, but Haynes knew there was a toughness there; a perfect combination for his new position. Haynes enjoyed the conversation very much. He loved being around these soldiers of liberty. He wanted to ask West about the Contra deal but decided to leave it for another time, especially with a former reporter in the room. They got up from the table and walked out to the foyer where Flett introduced him to the two Secret Service agents, Caesar Alzani and Terry Riley, who had been assigned to him. This is when Haynes realized that he was going to be somewhat of a prisoner in this job. His life would never be the same. He looked at Oliver and said, "Oliver, let's take a walk over to the White

House. Those press people don't know who I am, but when they see you it's going to drive them crazy with curiosity."

They were escorted by Alzani, Riley, Jeannie Flett and Goldstein, followed by a group of reporters. Haynes thought, "There's not that many of them here. I guess it's too early for them to get up." They entered the main foyer and down a hallway to an office. Jeannie Flett asked Haynes if it would be suitable. Haynes said it was fine, he was never interested in playing office musical chairs. He peeked into the office but then noticed Rodrick Giani coming down the hall. Giani was well dressed in a blue suit; all of a sudden Haynes realized that he was only wearing pants and a shirt. In any case, he was very relieved to see Giani, walked towards and him shook his hand, saying, "Am I ever happy to see you!"

With Jeannie Flett, Oliver West and now possibly Giani and Goldstein, he was starting to build a team. It was critical for Haynes to have Giani as his Chief of Staff. Giani was known all over America as one of the heroes of 9/11 along with being an extremely effective mayor of New York. "How should I address you, Mr. Mayor, or Rodrick?"

Giani smiled and said, "Just call me Rod."

Giani looked over at West and Goldstein and said, "Oliver, how are you doing?" He greeted Goldstein in much the same manner. West and Giani exchanged pleasantries and then Haynes asked West and Goldstein to stand by with Jeannie while he had a conversation with Rod.

They settled into Haynes' new office and Haynes asked Giani if he had been brought up to speed concerning yesterday's meeting. Giani replied that he had been fully briefed by Miss Efficiency, Jeannie Flett. Then he said, "What's Oliver doing here?"

Haynes said, "You just met our next Secretary of State." Giani sat back in the couch with a grin on his face. Haynes said, "Have you got a problem with that?"

Giani said, "Well you must've had a good reason. I'll have to digest that, it's an unusual choice. The media is going to have a field day with that one."

Haynes said, "The mainstream media has a field day with anyone who doesn't agree with their point of view, especially ones that have worked as Fox contributors. But it seems to me, I've seen you frequently on Fox news."

"Touché," Giani said.

Then Haynes said that he would be very disappointed if Giani did not accept the position of White House Chief of Staff.

Giani said, "I really don't know much about you, so I'm not really totally comfortable with doing this under the present circumstances."

Haynes said 'Let's just try it out for a couple of days and then we can talk again, but right now in about 10 minutes we have a meeting with General McCormick, other military officers and the newly appointed Secretary of State. I would like you to attend. Is that okay?"

Giani replied, "Okay."

"Are McCormick and his people here yet?" he asked Jeannie.

She replied, "Yes, they're all waiting for you in the situation room."

Haynes took Jeannie aside and said, "Please bring Goldstein up-to-date on what is happening, especially concerning who we are talking to about cabinet posts. And ask him how we should handle it with the press. It will give him something to do until we finish the meeting."

CHAPTER 10

THE PROBLEM IN THE MIDDLE EAST

—⚊⚋⚊—

WEDNESDAY, November 12, 2014, 7:00 a.m.

HAYNES BARELY HAD TIME TO catch his breath before Riley of the Secret Service escorted him, along with Giani and West, to the Situation Room. Haynes' ID had not yet been confirmed so they had to get someone else to open the door. When Haynes entered the room everyone stood up. Haynes was embarrassed and said, "Please don't do that, please sit down. I guess all of you know Rodrick Giani, and our new Secretary of State." He noticed that Simmons was also in the room.

Haynes sat down and made sure that Rod and Oliver had the seats on either side of him. "Oliver West has accepted the position of Secretary of State," he said.

This was not a big surprise to anyone because Haynes had already expressed his desire the night before to have Oliver on board.

Haynes then said, "I trust that there will be no leaks from this meeting. Now, how many allies do we have in the Middle East? One is obviously Israel, but we have another one and we're missing the boat with it. That country, and I emphasize Country, is the endgame. That country is Kurdistan. Most of those Arab Muslims over there don't like us, including the ones in the Gulf who put up with us for security reasons. I really don't care if they like us or not but from this day on, they're going to start to respect us.

"This is what I want to do. I want the new Secretary of State, West, to fly to meet with the Kurdistan leaders and their people to discuss a security relationship with the United States. The reason for this arrangement is twofold. We need to have an operational military base in the region on friendly turf so we can respond quickly to any more Jihadist threats. I don't really care that much about what those idiots in Baghdad think about it. We went over there and shed a lot of blood to liberate them from that psychopath killer Saddam and they showed their appreciation by trying to kill us. Those Shia Iraqis snubbed their noses at us by letting Bagdadi, that terrorist enemy of America, out of prison. Does anybody remember his comments on his way out of prison? 'See you in New York!' Well I've got news. We are going to be proactive and see him or any of his friends in their own backyard in Iraq or Syria.

"Those people can't organize their way out of a wet paper bag and they don't deserve, by their behavior, to have us show any further concern for their country. Since we left, the whole place is coming unglued. Anyone with half a brain knew the Iraq Muslim Arabs were going to screw everything up. Instead of moving all troops out of Iraq we should have sent a residual force of 10,000 or more to Kurdistan to protect people who want peace and to modernize. It does not take rocket science to understand that the Kurds and other minorities have no cultural parallels with these jihadists.

"The endgame is that if this arrangement can be implemented, the United States will recognize Kurdistan as an independent state with only their northern borders defined. Their southern borders will be defined by what ends up happening in the south. We may have to move the Kurds' southern border further south than it is right now for security reasons. I want the Secretary of State to tell the Kurds that we are prepared to equip and modernize their military and sign a treaty to protect their sovereignty.

"I want to keep this meeting quiet for the time being. And you, Mr. Secretary, may want to go to Israel to make it appear your trip was a visit to them. We may also want to explore the possibility of having some kind of a military base in Israel as well. The whole idea of this is very simple and it has become clear in the last number of years that when the American sheriff is out of town all the psychopathic dictators and jihadists start running amok and threatening our freedom and security; which is a vital American interest. It is also a vital interest to free people everywhere. I want to keep these people in check in their own backyard before they come to ours. I want to make it clear that I don't give a shit if they like us or not but from now on they will respect us and the world will be a safer place for people and countries that want peace and freedom. I would like General McCormick, now Secretary of Defense, and a couple of other military officers to accompany the Secretary to Kurdistan. The Kurds will get the message that we are serious and Jim and his team can discuss with the Kurds what will be required concerning military assets for their security and possible offensive strategies southbound if necessary."

General McCormack then said, "What do you mean by southbound?"

Haynes said, "I don't want those brutal jihadist bastards cutting heads off anywhere close to the Kurdistan border or to have access to the oilfields that fund their operations. We need a buffer zone for now between the north and south for security. That zone can be determined by activity on the ground. If those morons in the south ever get their shit together, a new border line can be negotiated with the Kurds and if they don't want to negotiate we can set our own line. I want the military to know that this time they won't be fighting in vain. We won't be leaving Kurdistan. Our base will be permanent. The Secretary and General McCormick can work out the details of what will be required and report back so we can take it to the next level. I also need to know where those oil fields are. It's time for somebody other than the US taxpayer to pay for this.

"Absolutely no press on this trip. While you are in Israel you can slip away to Kurdistan and have your meetings. Make it so that it appears that you are conducting meetings with the Israelis while you are in Kurdistan. I would like you to leave right after the news conference introducing the new cabinet any questions?

"What about the Turks?" said McCormick.

Haynes replied, "For some reason those Turks are not helping. They are allowing those jihadists to pass through their country unabated. The Turks are a member of NATO. Can someone find out and explain to me what the hell is going on over there? Is it because they just elected a sharia law-sympathetic government or what?

"We can define more clearly how to proceed when you return from your trip. Please remember secrecy is of the utmost. One thing for sure, I absolutely want General Trais to lead any forces we install in Kurdistan. I think you should bring General Trais along, Mr. Secretary," Haynes told West. "You need to be careful that you don't inform anyone at your State Department of your visit to Kurdistan. There are going to be a lot of folks over there who will not be very happy with the fact that you are now Secretary of State. And while you are at it, fire those press spokesmen and women at your State Department.

"There is one more serious national security situation that has to be addressed. I share Bill Simmons' concerns with regards to Muslim extremists on our home turf. We have to address this as soon as possible. If we are not careful, the advocates of political correctness will do us in. The only way to deal with this is to bypass our own laws that extremists are using to their advantage against us, such as private property rights and the second amendment.

I propose that number one, we put Bill Simmons immediately back in charge of the FBI. Number 2, Congress must pass a declaration of war against Muslim Islamic terrorism both internationally and domestically. This declaration has to give the administration broad powers to deal with this threat.

Number 3, Bill, I would like you to be in charge of a task force comprised of assets from the FBI and the military to prepare for a single one-day assault on all domestic jihadist training bases. I want all these people arrested and detained at undisclosed locations. We need to document them so that they can be identified if they ever try to reenter the United States. We also have to make lists of their family members, their private property and financial assets and find out their countries of origin. The next step will be deportation or criminal charges. All passports will be revoked.

"If some of their countries of origin will not accept them, they can be flown to Kurdistan and driven to southern Iraq or Syria where they can feel more at home.

"The next thing we need to do is to arrest and detain any Muslim cleric preaching sedition against the United States and have him arrested and deported.

"Any of the remaining Muslims practicing sharia law will be given the same treatment. No courts, no lawyers. In the meantime, we have to prepare the immigration services as soon as possible to set up a system to prevent anyone from a Muslim country or Muslims from any other country from entering the United States without a very special visa. Muslim American citizens that have left the country and want to return must receive a clearance stamp at the nearest American embassy. We are not going to allow what has been happening in Europe to happen here. Would President Roosevelt have allowed Japanese immigration during World War II?"

Haynes looked around and everyone in the room looked shocked, but were nodding their heads in agreement.

"Does anyone have an objection to Peter Turner being the point man for the military to coordinate with Director Simmons on the operation to shut down the Muslim Islamic training camps in the US?" No one did, so Haynes next question was how long Simmons thought he needed before he could launch the operation.

Simmons and Turner glanced at each other and then Simmons said, "Two months."

"Bill, there is an outfit called ClarionProject.org. You might want to have a meeting with them to compare your intelligence on the training camps. You might be surprised. Your go-to guy at Clarion should be Ryan Mauro."

The meeting started to break up and General McCormick came over to Haynes and said, "It's about time this happened."

"Thank you, General."

CHAPTER 11

PICKING THE RIGHT PEOPLE

—⚏—

WEDNESDAY, November 2014, 7:40 a.m.

Haynes, Giani and West went back to Haynes' new office and Haynes said, "By the way Jeannie, can you find out where the Churchill bust is?"

Giani took a seat and said, "I have to tell you that I agree with everything that happened down there and I think you can use some help, so I will take the position as Chief of Staff."

"Wow, thank you very much," Haynes said, standing up to shake Giani's hand. "I think they've already made arrangements for your office next door. Maybe you can take care of some of these things: I need your recommendation for secretary of homeland security. I know that since 9/11 you have had lots of experience dealing with security people."

Without hesitation Giani said, "I think Ray Kyling would be good for the job."

Haynes said, "Okay, why don't you contact him and see what happens. I also need your recommendations for secretaries of the interior, agriculture, housing, transportation and education. Try to find women for all these positions. At the same time we need tough folks that might have to kick some ass and close down some of these agencies or transfer them to state control under the new Functional Charter umbrella."

Giani said, "What the hell is that?"

Haynes said, "We can get into that later. Why don't you start with that lady who was chairman of Hewlett-Packard. Also we need to make some decisions as to what we are going to do with staffing this place. I am sure there are a lot of people in here who are going to be hostile, useless ideologues, etcetera. We need to get the people who think this way out of the building."

Giani said, "I think I've got enough on my plate for today."

Haynes noticed that Jeannie Flett was starting to get herself set up on the other side of his office and Goldstein was sitting taking notes. Haynes signaled Goldstein to come in, and said, "Jeannie, do you think you can get hold of Henry Rawlston, former secretary of the treasury, and get him in here? Also try to find the former Shell Oil President John Hoffman and get him in here as well. Hoffman is now a member of the United States Energy Security Council." Haynes thought that Hoffman was an affable individual who could fit in really well around the White House. "Do you know if John McFarland has arrived yet?"

She said, "Yes, he's on his way over now."

Haynes said, "Great, make sure that Rod is close by so I can introduce him to John. Where's Bill Simmons off to?"

She said, "He's still with the Secretary of State and General McCormick."

Haynes then said, "Has Herman Raines arrived in town?"

She said, "Yes, he's on his way over."

"Please tell Simmons I would like to have him around when Herman Raines arrives."

Now it was time to talk to Goldstein. Haynes thanked him again for coming on such short notice. He then said, "Can you help us in the next little while with the press? It is critical that the proper information gets out at the appropriate time and we need a professional like yourself to take care of it. Could you help us out at least for the short-term? Primarily we need to instill confidence in the American people and what you do will be critical to that success."

Goldstein said, "These are very unusual circumstances."

"Well, Bernard," said Haynes, "you already know that we have been assured that elections will take place in 2016. We need you to give us suggestions as to when and how to handle the media. Can you help us?"

Goldstein replied, "Yes, on the short-term but I can't guarantee that I'll stay around for two years."

Haynes said, "Thank you, because the short-term is the only thing that counts right now. We need you to hang around until things quiet down and get back to being relatively normal."

Haynes then called in Jeannie and said, "Bernie has agreed to help us with the media. Can you arrange an office for him and make sure that he is kept up-to-date on an hourly basis on everything going on around here."

Haynes went back to his chair to make a phone call, but he had to call Jeannie back into his office and ask her how the damn thing worked. "Just press nine, then the area code and the number and if it's long distance press one, the area code and the number." She then said, "Do you know what the Secret Service has designated as your codename?"

Haynes said, "No I don't."

Flett said, "It's Freedom."

Haynes said, "I like that."

Haynes called Sonja in Florida. Sonja always had to know all the details of everything and when it was from her side she told you the history of the world so to speak. Haynes told her, "Sorry sweetie, but I don't have time to get into all the details but you need to pack up everything for a long stay and get up here to Washington." There had been no point in trying to get her on Goldberg's plane last night. She was scared shitless of traveling in smaller planes.

WEDNESDAY November 12, 2014, 8:45 a.m.

Haynes hung up the phone and a minute later someone appeared at the doorway. "Well, well, well, what do we have here?" It was a face that Haynes was anxious to see. It was his old, nearly lifelong friend, John McFarland.

Haynes stood up and greeted McFarland and then they sat down on the couch in the corner. Haynes said, "You must be tired."

McFarland said, "Probably not as tired as you."

Haynes spent about 15 minutes describing what had happened thus far, complete with as much detail as he could. Then he asked Flett to get Giani to join them. Giani was one of McFarland's heroes and he was very pleased to meet him. Haynes knew that having Giani in the meeting would serve as a great incentive for McFarland to accept the position, so Haynes got down to the nitty-gritty. "John, we have a number of objectives. Number one, we want to revitalize American manufacturing. Number two we would like to bring assets of American companies back home; we need to establish incentives for them to do that. Number three, we will have to find a way to get the Chinese to allow their currency to trade on the open market and if not we will probably have to get estimates as to what their currency would be worth as if it were trading on the open market and set tariffs accordingly. We need to re-examine our import tariff situation and find some sense of fair play with regard to our exports-imports with major trading countries outside of NAFTA. Most important of all, we need to revitalize small business in the country.

"So John, we would like you to be our next Secretary of Commerce. I know there will be a lot of other things you would have to do in this position but do you think that the goals I have just mentioned are sensible?"

McFarland did not look surprised. He had probably already been tipped off as to why he was in Washington. "Yeah, these are sensible goals but if I accept the position, will I have to go through those damn congressional vettings?"

Haynes said, "There are so many things we haven't thought about and that's one of them. Under the present circumstances we are just going to have to bypass vetting and just stick you in now as Secretary of Commerce and we will let them yell and scream. We haven't got time to mess around with these things. Besides, for the most part, all this vetting discourages competent people from serving in government. Anyone who has got it on in the backseat of a car when they were 20 years old doesn't even bother to apply."

They all laughed.

McFarland said, "You know, I don't have any political experience."

Haynes said, "That's an asset and besides you're not an ideologue. You came from nothing and became chairman of the board of a large manufacturing company and earned it each step of the way. Your decisions were based on what works and not ideology. So just do the same thing, the only difference being that instead of doing it for shareholders you will be doing it for the American people."

McFarland said, "Okay. I'll do it."

Haynes said, "John, you know what the goals are but how you accomplish them is up to you. We're just setting out the agenda of 'What,' the 'How' will be mostly up to you; just like the old days. Just be careful to remind yourself that you are now in government and please keep Rod and me in the loop for things that you think we need to know. You have great instincts and I'm sure you'll know as time goes by what those things should be."

They all stood up, shook hands and Haynes brought McFarland out to Flett's desk. Haynes said, "Jeannie has arranged for your transportation to the Commerce Department and there will be deputies waiting to receive you and to show you around, complete with your new office.

"And if you don't mind John, I would like you to stay at Blair House with me until you get settled in and maybe you can join Rod and me for dinner this evening." Haynes added, "What is Kim going to do? You are going to need a tank to drag her away from those two new baby grandchildren."

McFarland said, "Well, we'll just have to take one day at a time and get it all sorted out."

Haynes said to Flett, "Please make arrangements for John to have transportation when he needs it to return to Fort Smith."

McFarland nodded said, "Thanks." Flett escorted him out through the main foyer to a limo waiting to drive him to the Department of Commerce.

WEDNESDAY, November 12, 2014, 9:05 a.m.

Haynes noticed a tall, imposing man with a familiar smile near Flett's desk. It was Herman Raines, a very successful African-American leader in the food business. Haynes liked his 999 tax idea. "Bill, I think you should hang around for my meeting with Herman. You are probably going to have to escort him over to the IRS building tomorrow while you are firing that arrogant cover-up specialist director and escorting him out of the building."

Bill and Raines came into Haynes' office, and Giani also joined them. They sat down on the couch in the corner and Haynes said, "Well, Herman, I guess you are wondering what you're doing here."

Raines nodded and said, "Yes."

Haynes said, "Well, Herman, we would like you to head up the IRS and clean out that mess over there. We need you to serve your country for at least the next two years, how about it?"

"What would be my directive?" said Raines.

"Just like I said, Herman, I want you to work with the new Attorney General and clean up that mess over there. I want a major investigation and let the trail fall wherever it goes. We need all segments of the American population to have confidence that the IRS is not some political extension of Washington that singles out certain groups of individuals that don't agree with their philosophy – you know the drill. If you accept this position, tomorrow morning the FBI is going to escort the present director out of the building and the new Attorney General is going to lay criminal charges against anyone involved in illegal behavior. I would also like you to work with Steve Forrest to formulate a plan to introduce your 999 tax program. When he was running for president years back, Forrest introduced a flat tax program as part of his platform. Our tax program will be called 9999 - one category for personal tax, capital gains tax, corporate tax, and a goods and services tax, or GST. It should be simple; whatever you make, you pay 9% with minimal deductions. The corporate taxes are a little more complicated. You'll probably have to work out something with regard to what they can and cannot write off before taxable income. I would like you to work with Steve, who doesn't even know yet that we're asking him to do this, and develop a plan. I will contact Steve today and if he accepts to work with you on this we will have you contact him. I thought your idea was a great one and now you can have an opportunity to execute it. How about it?"

Raines looked at Haynes and smiled. "But I'm going to have to get vetted."

Haynes said, "I just went through the same discussion with our new Secretary of Commerce, John McFarland. I'm telling you what I told him, we haven't got time to mess around. We've got two years and we are not going to waste our time with vetting, okay? If you accept, you can join Bill and the FBI over at the IRS headquarters tomorrow and get underway."

"Okay, I'm in," Raines said.

Haynes replied, "By the way Herman, please get rid of that horrible federal death tax, and you might want to consider having people file their income taxes on their birthdays which would ease the workload on the tax department and have even flows of revenue for businesses participating in filing taxes throughout the year. Businesses already file their taxes based on their corporate calendar year. Unincorporated businesses should file their taxes like everybody else based on the owner's birthday."

They all stood up and shook hands and Haynes thought, "Great, another hole filled." Haynes said, "Good luck Herman, Bill will fill you in with all the particulars."

WEDNESDAY, November 12, 2014, 9:45 a.m.

Jeannie knocked at Haynes' door and said, "I found out where the Churchill bust is."

Haynes said, "Where is that?"

She said, "It's at the residence of the British ambassador in Washington."

Haynes said, "Give someone a call and say we would be honored and privileged to have it restored to the White House."

Jeannie said, "Okay, and by the way, John Hoffman, former president of Shell Oil, will be here tomorrow."

Giani came into Haynes' office and said, "Ray Kyling will be dropping in this afternoon. He's already accepted the offer to be Secretary of Homeland Security."

Haynes said, "That's great, he has a good reputation and a lot of practical experience after 9/11. I'd love to meet him."

Now Haynes asked Jeannie to send a note to McCormick to remind him that he wanted something done about the Fort Hood victims. He asked that it be declared a terrorist act and to have the victims' families compensated. For the life of him, Haynes could not understand why it was not called a terrorist act. Then he stepped into Giani's office and said, "How about Congressman Downy for Attorney General?"

Giani said, "That would be a great choice but Downy is strictly by the book, believes in the law and the Constitution and right now the Constitution is suspended."

Haynes said, "Why don't we run it by him, do you know him?"

Giani said, "Reasonably well."

Haynes said, "Why don't you make the call."

"Okay."

More and more every hour, Haynes was coming to really appreciate Flett's efficiency. She had all her ducks in a row and had great timing as to when she should pull the trigger. She had already made arrangements for Henry Rawlston, former treasury secretary, to be in the White House this afternoon. There was a great deal of outstanding controversy about whether or not he and the former Fed chairman did the right thing by bailing out the banks during the end of the Bush administration. Rawlston had to make decisions contrary to his lifelong belief of no bailouts. Haynes believed, like Rawlston, that under the particular circumstances of that perfect financial storm, Rawlston had had no choice – especially after the last shoe fell when he heard that AIG had insured the banks against losses they incurred for mortgages, which would have driven AIG into bankruptcy and would have caused a domino effect on financial institutions not only in America but throughout the world. Anyone who doesn't believe that just needed to watch the documentary movie, "Too Big to Fail." Haynes figured that even if only part of that movie was true, it would have been an international catastrophe. When anyone disagreed with Haynes' point of view on this subject he would simply say, "Would you like to go back and find out?" This was the safe play. Taking a risk on the alternative was a no-brainer. But the psychological pressure on Rawlston and the Fed chairman must have been overwhelming. Haynes was convinced, despite his own beliefs against bailouts, that Rawlston saved the financial community even if the banks didn't deserve it. He was looking forward to meeting him.

Flett said, "What are you going to do about accrediting and receiving new ambassadors?"

Haynes said, "What's that all about?"

She said, "Presidents normally receive and accredit new ambassadors."

Haynes said, "Well I'm not the President, so why don't you give these duties to the Attorney General or the leader of the House of Representatives or someone; I really don't want to be bothered with these kinds of things if possible. We need to keep on trucking and setting up the team so that we can have a news conference and lay it all out to the people and the sooner we do that, the better."

Flett said, "Okay, I'll take care of it."

WEDNESDAY November 12, 2014, 10:05 a.m.

Giani came in and said, "I have Ray Kyling in my office."

Haynes went in and introduced himself to Kyling. He said, "I am very grateful that you decided to join the team. Your experienced reputation precedes you."

Kyling was 50ish, about 5 foot 10, medium build, average looking with short brown hair and penetrating eyes. Haynes take-away from their conversation was that he was a no-nonsense, well-organized individual, and he felt good about having him there.

Haynes felt sure that jihadists had made their way across the southern border undetected and that a lot of them were now in the country. He made it clear to Kyling that he wanted him to make it a top priority to work with the FBI and other security people to track these jihadists down. "The other ones I want to start to keep track of are Moslem jihadists with American passports. We need to screen these people, especially when they're re-entering the United States."

Kyling said, "They're going to accuse us of racial profiling."

Haynes replied, "I don't know about you, but I am sick and tired of this political correctness, 99% of these terrorists are Muslim and I repeat TERRORISTS because that is a word that is going to be used around here with more frequency. Did you see any Swedes, Chinese, Japanese,

Russians, Hispanics, etcetera on those planes on 9/11? To a man, they were Muslim terrorists, so yeah, Ray, that's mainly where we concentrate our efforts. That doesn't mean that we don't keep our eyes open for domestic terrorists but for the most part these people will be Muslim. So to hell with this politically correct garbage and pass that message on down the line. The idea is to keep Americans safe and if that's what it takes, that's what we need to do. That way we don't get distracted. Bill Simmons is going back to the FBI, and is coordinating a secret operation to deal with domestic jihadists. The Director will brief you on the operation and explain how you can help bring it to a successful conclusion."

Kyling looked a little stunned at Haynes' directness.

"Another big threat we have are those jihadists trying to come into America through our open southern border. I am sure there are a lot of them already here. This is a very complicated subject so let's keep it simple. The first thing and the only thing we need to work on in this regard is sealing the borders tighter than Toby's ass; that includes the overstayed visas. Anybody found with an overstayed visa should be deported immediately. If you are asked what you are going to do with the rest of it, such as 'what we are going to do with illegals already here?' just say 'we don't know yet' except for illegals with criminal records. Another thing I want you to enforce is that any police officer or their supervisors that do not turn over an illegal with a criminal record irrespective of state law especially in states like California – will be guilty of a criminal offence. I'm sick and tired of seeing police officers and citizens being murdered by illegals. Some of them are deported and re-enter the country multiple times because our borders are not secured as a result of a lawless administration. Right now we are going to be almost exclusively concentrating on sealing the border, mostly for security reasons, and we will stay focused on this until securing the borders is complete. I'm tired of having our border enforcement people dragged into court like a bunch of criminals and illegal aliens being treated like heroes. We need to be working closely with governors of the southern border states to establish cooperative goals and procedures. Do you have any problems with this approach?"

"No," said Kyling.

WEDNESDAY, November 12, 2014, 10:45 a.m.

Now Haynes was anxiously waiting for the arrival of Henry Rawlston. He was brought into Haynes' office by Flett. Rawlston was surprisingly tall. Haynes had only seen him on television. Haynes was a little intimidated, not only because of who he really was but because he had a demeanor of superiority, which was probably exactly what was needed in a treasury secretary. Giani had joined them on the couch. Haynes and Giani were already becoming familiar with each other's body language, so when Haynes looked at Giani, Giani realized that he was going to do most of the talking.

He did quite a sales job. The first thing he did was to reassure Rawlston, as they had done with all the others, that elections would take place as scheduled in 2016. Giani wanted to make sure that Rawlston was on the lookout for any problems before they got started, but at least this time his job would be relatively easier because he knew by experience what the trouble signs might be.

Haynes was glad that Giani was there because he didn't think that he would take the position if he were there with Haynes alone. He was aware that Rawlston was glancing at him with an expression that said "who the hell is this guy anyway?" So he tried to give the impression that they really needed his help which was probably not far off. It was a relief when he agreed to come on board.

It would be a confidence booster for the domestic and international financial community. Haynes asked Rawlston for his ideas on what to do with Fannie May and Freddie Mac, adding that he wanted to get the government out of the business of doing business.

Haynes then looked at Giani and said, "Rod, we are way behind schedule and the markets are starting to become anxious, to say the least. Will you both excuse me for a minute?" He went out to Jeannie's office and asked her to get Bernie Goldstein down to his office immediately.

When he returned, he looked at Rawlston and said, "Mr. Secretary, would you have a problem going into the pressroom with Bernie Goldstein to give in impromptu press conference?"

Rawlston said, "What is it exactly that you want me to say?"

Haynes said, "Bernie is on his way down and then we can discuss that."

When Goldstein arrived, Haynes brought him up to date on Rawlston before he said, "We need to get the markets open ASAP and re-establish confidence."

Then he turned back to Rawlston's question. "First, you will be introduced by Goldstein as our new Secretary of the Treasury. The country is anxiously waiting to find out what is really happening and the markets have been closed for a few days. What the country needs more than anything right now is a boost of confidence. I think it goes without saying that your prestige and reputation can provide reassurance and confidence to the financial markets and the American people.

"Act like you are really taking charge of the situation, which is the truth. Stand up there with confidence and say, 'I will be calling the Presidents of all exchanges after this press conference instructing them to open the markets after the new cabinet is introduced.' Also, you can say that the new Administrator and the Chief of Staff's first priority is to reassure markets and Americans that things will be moving forward very shortly in a positive manner and that this new administration will be business friendly; especially to small business. The private sector are the ones who will create all the new jobs required, especially small business. Henry, you have seen the list of cabinet picks and advisors so you know how to elaborate on that. The message is, 'relax, everything is going to be just fine.' Just go out there and tell the truth as you've seen it."

Rawlston smiled at Haynes and said, "Okay, I've got it."

Haynes turned to Goldstein. "Okay, Bernie, you know the drill. Let's get the Secretary over to the pressroom and do it. Rod and I will be anxiously watching. After you're done, make a bunch of phone calls to your contacts and come back and tell Rod and me what the feedback was. Markets are still open in Asia so we'll see what happens after you've spoken and answered questions."

Haynes was always amazed at the speed at which information is transmitted all over the world. In this case it would probably be a great advantage.

The last meeting of the morning was with Arthur Leever. Leever had been in the Reagan administration and was a colorful character. Haynes had never met him but he had seen him on TV on many occasions. Haynes loved to be around these "loose as a goose" positive characters and Leever was not about to let him down. This was one guy that Haynes wanted on the team big-time.

Jeannie Flett didn't have to be told about timing or anything else. She had arranged for Leever to be waiting for the end of the Rawlston meeting so that Leever would be able to talk to Rawlston. Rawlston had already been given a heads up and asked to tell Leever to give the administration a hand. Rawlston and Leever already knew each other and exchanged a few pleasantries before Rawlston finished by saying, "These guys need your help."

Then Leever and Haynes sat down for a chat, Giani joining them. Haynes gave Giani 'the look' so again he did most of the talking, concluding by saying that they needed him to be budget director. And the fact was, they needed him badly, not only because he was competent but also to send a signal to the financial community that they were getting strong experienced people on our team. Leever gave them a story about how he didn't know how to disengage from his present work commitments but you could see that he was tempted by the feeling he got from the pace of the action within these walls. You could sense that he wanted to be a part of it.

CHAPTER 12

REASSURING THE MARKETS

—m—

WEDNESDAY, November 12, 2014, 12:15 p.m.

H AYNES NOTICED THE TIME, so he said, "Arthur, would you mind if we just took a minute to watch the press conference with Rawlston?" Then he stuck his head out the door and told Jeannie to monitor the Asian markets.

The TV screen showed Goldstein and Rawlston together. Goldstein was saying, "Ladies and Gentlemen, I would like to introduce you to the new administration's selection for secretary of the treasury and former secretary of the treasury, Henry Rawlston." Goldstein continued, "Secretary Rawlston will make a statement and then take questions."

Rawlston took the mic and said, "Ladies and Gentlemen, like most Americans and people around the world I was, to say the least, very concerned about recent events and existing circumstances. I can tell you as of this moment that I am no longer concerned and to the contrary, I am very comfortable, optimistic and confident after my meeting with the new Administrator and the Chief of Staff. They have assured me that for the next two years, the emphasis will be on energizing the economy and making changes in the Constitution so that future presidents, senators and congressmen will operate under a constitutional umbrella with clarity. The team that is being assembled and almost complete is impressive and experienced. I feel very comfortable and positive about our future. I, along with all the other incoming secretaries, have been assured that there will be elections as scheduled in 2016. After this press conference I will be contacting the presidents of all American markets to reopen their exchanges as soon as the new cabinet is introduced. When this new administration has finished assembling their team, my peers and I will be presented to the American people in the next few days. Now I can take a couple of questions."

The press corps was clamoring for attention and almost simultaneously screaming questions at Rawlston. Rawlston did not flinch. He had been there before under severe pressure. This time it was a walk in the park. He pointed at the White House correspondent from NBC. Question, "What is the new Administrator or President like?"

Rawlston was not expecting a question like that. He replied, "You know, that's a good question because I was thinking exactly the same thing before I came to the meeting. First of all he is not occupying the Oval Office. He and his Chief of Staff have simple offices in the West Wing. He made it clear that he didn't want to be called President. My first impression was that he was extremely relaxed and confident, considering what he's dealing with. The atmosphere was very relaxed. He was very easy to talk to and seemed to understand everything that was going on and at the same time he was tough and decisive. His knowledge of all the nuances of America and its players is surprising, in fact if you didn't know it you would've thought that he was an American and I found myself talking to him that way. Just the choices that he has made for his cabinet will tell you a lot about where he is coming from and what he plans to do. I believe that the American people are going to like him."

Question, "What do you think the markets are going to do when they open?"

Rawlston said, "The markets are all about business and jobs. When David Haynes presents his cabinet and some of his plans, the business community as a whole and especially small business is going to get a shot in the arm which results in more jobs, so I am confident that the markets will interpret things this way and that we will experience a rally."

Goldstein figured that this was enough to say for now, so he raised his hand and escorted Rawlston from the room.

Haynes and Giani were still watching and Haynes said, "Wow, I love a great professional."

Leever smiled and said, "Yeah, he did a great job."

Now Haynes and Giani went back to work on Leever, who hadn't really committed to stay as yet. Leever chuckled and said, "You guys set me up to be here right at this moment."

Haynes and Giani looked at each other and started chuckling as well. "I guess that shows you how badly we need you around here," Haynes admitted.

Leever said that he would need at least 10 days before he could show up, but he would. Leever was the one who had come up with the theory that lowering taxes led to a revenue increase. This had proven to be the case. He was another solid appointment.

Haynes didn't know a whole lot about the federal budget. His philosophy had always been to hire strong experienced people in a field and give them the responsibility and authority to do the job. At just that moment, Jeannie put her head in the office door and said excitedly, "The Asian markets are rallying!"

Haynes jumped to his feet, high fived Giani and said, "Way to go, Henry."

Jeannie said, "Mr. Rawlston is coming down the hallway."

Giani and Haynes stepped out to greet him. Haynes' face showed enthusiasm and relief. "Way to go Henry. What a great job. The Asian markets are already rebounding." Giani and Leever also shook Rawlston's hand with enthusiasm.

Rawlston turned to Leever. "Are you coming on board?"

Leever responded, "Yes I'm going to have to, because this is just too exciting to miss."

"Why don't you guys leave the building together?" Haynes said. "There's going to be a huge press scrum out there so Henry, why don't you just say that Arthur has decided to take the job as budget director. That way will get a double whammy boost of confidence out there."

Haynes then turned to Jeannie and said, "Phone Goldstein and tell him to press leak that Rawlston will be leaving by the main gate."

WEDNESDAY, November 12, 2014, 1:05 p.m.

Jeannie dropped in and said, "Maybe you should get something to eat."

Haynes said, "Yeah, I think I'll go down to the kitchen and sit down there with the boys and girls and have a good BLT sandwich and chocolate milk if they have any." Haynes was absolutely astonished by the size of the White House kitchen. He introduced himself around and they made him his favorite bacon cheese and tomato sandwich, toasted, with lettuce and mayonnaise. They didn't have any chocolate milk but they used a malt formula with white milk, which was okay for now.

WEDNESDAY, November 12, 2014, 2:00 p.m.

After Haynes returned from the kitchen he went to Jeannie and said, "What's up next?"

She said, "You have John Hoffman, former president of Shell Oil at 3 p.m. KT McFadden, Bill Carson and Jerry Bolton tomorrow."

"I think I am going to need more time with these folks, especially Bill Carson concerning health and welfare," he told her. Haynes was fascinated by Carson's intellect and knew the conversation was going to be engaging and informative.

"Rod has Denise Florio coming in for education and is also going to take care of Interior, Agriculture, Housing and Transportation."

Haynes said, "I hope most of his proposals are women."

Flett said, "I think he got the memo."

By this time Rawlston and Leever were just outside the main gate surrounded by press, and giving a walking press conference to generate more confidence. One reporter asked Leever, "What were you doing in the White House?"

Rawlston replied for him. "Meeting the new Budget Director," he said. At that point, they found themselves a taxi to escape the mayhem.

Haynes walked into Giani's office and asked him to join him and McFarland for dinner. "Looks like you've decided to hang around for a while, Rod."

Rod looked up from his desk and said, "It kind of looks that way, doesn't it."

Haynes said, "Thanks, Mr. Chief of Staff."

Rod smiled and said, "Okay, I don't know if I can join you guys tonight because I'm in the middle of straightening out all the staff problems. Do you have any suggestions?"

Haynes said, "They'll be working for you I'm sure; you know how to pick good strong people that believe in what and how we are doing things."

Haynes answer was related to an experience he had had while he was in business. There was this guy called Steve Brown who came to a meeting as a speaker and one of the things that he remembered to this day was Brown saying, "If somebody brings a monkey into your office, make sure they leave with it." Staffing was one monkey that Haynes did not want to deal with so he left it to Rod. It was true that these people were principally going to work for the Chief of Staff. Hopefully tomorrow they would be finished with selecting all the Secretaries and the rest of the team. They needed to hold the press conference to introduce the new administration soon.

"My biggest concern right now," said Giani, "is Kirk Downy."

Haynes said, "Why?"

"It's the same as I explained to you before," said Rod. "So what I did was, I called him and asked him for a suggestion as to who he would think would make a good Attorney General."

Haynes said, "What did he say? Did he bite?"

Rod said, "No, he said he would get back to me. So I guess we'll just have to see what happens."

Haynes said, "I have a suggestion, why don't you tell him since we're operating under emergency measures that if he becomes Attorney General he can keep his congressional seat and we want him to lead investigations and prosecutions at the IRS."

Rod said, "That's good. That could work."

Haynes said, "By the way I'd like to just say hello to Florio tomorrow."

Rod said, "That'll be fine."

Haynes went back to his office and contemplated his moves so far. He thought the people that he had selected were culturally compatible and this was very important for internal communications, which would make the administration more effective. He had been updated on Hoffman's background and had pretty much assured himself that Hoffman was not only competent but a good American patriot. Hoffman was now founder and CEO of an organization called Citizens for Affordable Energy, with an influential and impressive membership. The support of such people could be very positive.

Jeannie came in and said, "Mr. Hoffman is here."

Haynes got up to greet him. Hoffman looked relaxed and confident, as Haynes had expected. They went back into Haynes' office and sat on the couch. Haynes said, "I guess you're wondering why you're here."

Hoffman said, "I assume it's because you need some advice on energy."

Haynes said, "Yes, sir, and I would like to ask you some questions."

Hoffman said, "Shoot."

Haynes said, "Do you agree that we need to get the Keystone pipeline started now?"

Hoffman replied, "Yes."

Haynes said, "How about infrastructure for natural gas exports?"

Hoffman replied, "Yes, absolutely."

Haynes said, "How about natural gas into auto engines?"

Hoffman said, "Yes, but that will take a lot more time." Hoffman continued. "T-bone Pickens has started setting up liquefied natural gas stations, primarily in the west, for trucks that have natural gas engines. I think it's a good idea."

Haynes was satisfied with his answers. He said, "What would be your opinion of having a former oilman as Energy Secretary?"

Hoffman said, "That would depend on who that would be. Some are strictly into oil profits and shareholders and some have concern for things overall in America."

Haynes said, "Since you are the founder and CEO of Citizens for Affordable Energy the latter would apply to you."

Hoffman said, "I think that would be true. But I don't think you asked me to come all this way just to ask me these questions. It seems to me that you have a good understanding of what needs to be done."

Haynes said, "I also have a good understanding of who I need to do it. I'm asking you to accept the position as our next Secretary of Energy." Haynes explained who he already had on board, and said that Hoffman would be a great addition to the team. He sensed Hoffman's hesitation, so he continued, "John, we are only going to need you to be here for a couple of years. I am sure that you can get someone to fill in at your foundation and you are not going to be vetted by the Congress. This would be a great opportunity for you to implement some of the things that your foundation has been advocating. I haven't even looked at an alternative for this position. The circumstances that we are in until 2016 will allow you to implement things faster than any other energy secretary in history and right now energy is a huge deal for America's future." Hoffman was still sitting there. Haynes said, "Why don't we go to Rod Giani's office next door and you can have a chat with him."

Haynes got up and went to Rod's office, knocked and entered. Giani was just finishing up with Denise Florio, former chairman of the board of Hewlett-Packard. Rod said, "Meet our new Secretary of Education."

"Wonderful!" Haynes said, "If we can implement our new American Functional Charter, hopefully you will be our last Secretary of Education."

"That would be a great question on Jeopardy," Florio said.

Haynes was thinking that if Hoffman saw these two now on board, it might well help him make a decision. So he said, "Why don't you all come next door to my office? I am trying to talk Hoffman into becoming Energy Secretary and for some reason he's not committing."

Haynes told Florio that he appreciated her taking this position and explained how he wanted education out of the federal domain, and for the next two years he wanted her to prepare for a transfer of all education matters to the states. She said she was very enthusiastic about doing this because she agreed completely with the strategy. He left her with Jeannie Flett and made the necessary arrangements for her arrival at the education department.

He told Jeannie that he was going to take a walk around the building and to let him know when Rod was through with Hoffman. He had been so busy he hadn't had a chance to explore the White House. He asked Secret Service agent Riley to escort him. He wanted to see the Oval Office and the residence. Riley and Haynes made a little tour for about 30 minutes and then he noticed Riley listening to his headset. "Giani needs you back down at your office," he said.

When Haynes arrived, Rod had a big grin on his face and said, "Shake hands with our new Secretary of Energy. "

Haynes clasped his hands together loudly and said a big "yes," then walked over and shook Hoffman's hand, "I don't know what kind of a deal this is for you, but it's a huge deal for us. We are happy you have accepted this. Thank you."

Hoffman smiled and said, "Well I need a couple weeks to clean things up over at my foundation."

"Before that we're having a press gathering to introduce our new team," Haynes said. "We would really like you to be there for that."

"Let me know and I'll be here," Hoffman said. Jeannie Flett escorted him to a waiting limo while Haynes and Giani were high-fiving. This was a huge appointment. They were both convinced that they had found the right guy.

WEDNESDAY, November 12, 2014, 7:00 p.m.

That evening, John McFarland joined Haynes for dinner at the White House. They sat for a couple of hours over some red wine, agreeing on most issues and disagreeing on a few. They had done the same thing many times in the past and were very familiar with each other's positions. They reminisced over the last thirty years and even phoned an old friend and colleague, Julian Kessler, in Florida and did the 'guess where we are' routine. John was excited and enthusiastic about his new challenges and Haynes was happy to have him nearby as he trusted him unconditionally and knew that he would be a great communicator with and for the business community, since business and commerce were his forte.

THURSDAY, November 13, 2014, 8:00 a.m.

Outside his doorway, Haynes could see Dr. Bill Carson chatting with Jeannie Flett, so he dodged into Giani's office and asked if he wanted to join the meeting with Carson. Giani said, "I'm swamped. Why don't you just take care of it and we can have a brief chat before he leaves."

Like Herman Raines, Carson was an African-American. He was tall, wiry and wore glasses. His voice was soft and fluid but firm. When Haynes introduced himself, he noted that Carson's stature was a little more imposing than it appeared on TV. Carson was intellectually brilliant and a very successful brain surgeon. He had drawn national attention when he criticized the President of the United States in a speech at the National Prayer Breakfast. He had done it with a lot of class, which couldn't have been easy to do when the President was sitting a few feet away.

Haynes knew a lot about the Canadian medical system and its history, and was looking forward to a good discussion. "Dr. Carson," Haynes said, "I would like to give you a general history of the Canadian medical system.

"The system was started by a province, what you know in America as a state. That province was Saskatchewan. The premier – or as you call them in the US, governor – of that province was a socialist named Tommy Douglas. He introduced a state-wide medicare system for the province of Saskatchewan; there were no insurance companies involved. The system was administered by the provincial government, the equivalent of a US state government. There was 100% participation by provincial residents. Payroll taxes were used to pay the costs. I don't know the total financial cost of the system at the time. The system was similar to what Governor Ruby did in Massachusetts only the mechanics were a lot different. In 1966, Canada's central government decided to horn in on Saskatchewan and make the province's basic system national or universal. Canada's population at the time was around 20 million, about half the population of California today.

"I think you know what happens when central governments start these large programs; they become out of control financially and impossible to manage logistically. Again, the national system was financed by payroll taxes. Participants used what was equivalent to a credit card and called a Medicare Card. One hundred percent of the cost was paid by the central government. After quite a few years the central government decided that the system would be better managed by the individual provinces. However, they forced the provinces to operate under the rules of a federal law that was passed by the central government. In other words, the provinces had no flexibility to try to introduce new rules for their own structures. Among other things, private clinics were not permitted.

"Over time, some of the provinces got fed up with the restrictions of the federal law and said the hell with it. They began to make changes they thought were appropriate for their own province. The different provinces made different changes, but one of the most significant was allowing private clinics to open. Private clinics are now flourishing, so that anyone who doesn't want to wait six or seven months for a colonoscopy, for example, can go to a private clinic and pay 500 bucks to get it done immediately. The same applies for hip replacements, knee replacements and so on. The benefit is that it takes people who want to pay out of the government-financed line for these procedures; that cuts down somewhat on waiting times.

"My point is that now the Canadian medical system is operating reasonably well and improving all the time. The doctors are paid by the provincial departments of health, according to fees that are negotiated by the medical association and the departments of health together. The doctors association basically functions as a quasi union. Doctors can also work for private clinics if they wish to opt out of the public system. The hospitals are owned and financed by the government but each one is administered by its own in-house management team.

"Yes, we have our horror stories just as you have yours. Neither system is perfect. But one thing is for sure - if you have an emergency under the Canadian system you will be taken care of immediately. You are looking at one of the people who benefited. I checked into a local hospital at 9 o'clock in the morning diagnosed with a heart attack. I was rushed by ambulance to a specialist hospital and by 2 o'clock that afternoon I was lying in the intensive care ward recovering, with two new stents in my heart. All I needed to show anybody during the whole process was my Medicare card, and it was paid for by payroll deductions.

"So some of the people in the US media that bloviate about the Canadian Medicare system don't have a clue what they're talking about. It has taken Canada 60 years of changes to get to this point and the morons who passed the Affordable Health Care Act thought it could be done in a short period of time and be workable with one central government in control for 350 million people.

"I am a very conservative person when it comes to fiscal matters and I believe in a strong military to protect the American people and others around the world who desire to be free. However, when it comes to the health of the American people I believe that it would be better if everyone was covered. But that should not be imposed and operated by some incompetent central bureaucracy. Under my new proposal, which is called the American Functional Charter, states would have the sole responsibility for health care, and I want this as part of a new constitutional amendment. The citizens in each one of those states can vote for whatever plan is proposed to them in state elections. We can transfer over to the states whatever they have in place now and they can modify or adjust things the way they see fit. I want the Federal Government out of the health business. I want to scrap the so-called Affordable Health Care Act soon. It will create chaos in the short term but it has to be done.

"And this will be a major undertaking for the new Secretary of Health, whose job will hopefully, under the future American Functional Charter, become extinct at the federal level. So now I think you understand why you are here. There is only one area in which there is no flexibility, and that is that health is going to be transferred to state control. The central mentality of 'one size fits all' is not workable. As former governor of New Mexico Gary Ronson pointed out on many occasions, it is much more efficient to have 50 little fiefdoms tweaking and improving their systems as they learn from each other rather than having one fits all Czaristic, inefficient approach."

Carson finally interrupted Haynes. "If I am here because you want me to be the Secretary of Health, I have to tell you I'm sorry but I won't be able to accept the offer despite how tempting."

Haynes said, "Well I guess you can't run for president while you're Health and Human Services Secretary."

"As of now," said Carson, "it's an option and that option would not be available if I took this position."

Haynes said, "I understand. But could you be available for consultation and advice from time to time? You have a lot of experience and ideas with regard to the medical profession."

Carson said, "Yes, if I can give you any advice in the future I would be pleased to do so."

"Then I have a couple of personal requests. The first is related to my opinion that the most discriminated people in the United States in the present era are black conservatives, especially black conservative women. They are vilified even by their own community. I am planning to have, as the first social evening at the White House, an evening entitled "Black Conservative Night." It will be an evening to celebrate the success of these individuals and to be a positive example to the rest of the black community. Race baiters, socialists and liberals will not be welcome. Could you help me with this by providing me with a list of people that would fall into this category?"

Carson replied, "Yes, I can provide you with names that would qualify under your description."

Haynes said, "That would be very much appreciated and of course you would be one of the primary invitees."

"Well, I would hope so."

"The second request concerns a book called Flood Your Body with Oxygen, by Ed McCabe. It advocates the use of oxygen and ozone to cure various health issues. The grand-daddy treatment is called the

Recirculatory Hemoperfusion Ozone Delivery System. It's similar to kidney dialysis. Blood is taken from the body and passed through a machine that injects ozone into the blood and then returns it to the body. To me, ozone and oxygen are basically harmless entities. I would like to know why doctors who have advocated this treatment are discriminated against and why this procedure is not approved in the United States. Could you do me a favor and send me a report or analysis as to why this is the case? I can give you Mr. McCabe's phone number if you wish to discuss it with him."

Haynes was disappointed he wouldn't have Carson on his team, but realized he couldn't win them all. Then it hit him. That guy Gary Ronson was a pitbull. As governor of New Mexico he was the all-time world veto champion, had cut spending and all the rest of it. He also built and ran a very successful construction business in New Mexico so he was extremely competent. He ran for president but the American people either did not know him or if they did, they probably did not understand him.

THURSDAY, November 13, 2014, 10:00 a.m.

Haynes walked into Giani's office after Carson left and said, "He declined the offer."

"Why?"

Haynes said, "I think he's running for President."

Rod nodded and said, "Yeah."

"How about Gary Ronson?" Haynes suggested.

Rod said, "He's a libertarian and a little out there."

"Some of his ideas are perceived that way but that doesn't necessarily mean that all of them are wrong. Besides, he was a very successful two-term governor of New Mexico."

"He's admitted to smoking marijuana," Rod said.

"So has Clinton and over 100 million other Americans," Haynes said. "This health thing is going to take a tough, determined, organized and experienced person and he seems to be on board with decentralizing health to the states. I'm going to give him a call."

When Haynes left Giani's office, he told Jeannie Flett to find Ronson and get him in the next day if possible. "Also try to get Doug Snow in here tomorrow as well," he said.

THURSDAY, November 13, 2014, 10:15 a.m.

Now it was now time to meet with KT McFadden. She had served in three previous administrations under Nixon, Ford and Reagan and was an expert in national security matters. By the time she came into Haynes' office, she had been briefed on the cabinet appointments already made. McFadden was attractive and youthful looking. Haynes had learned that KT stood for Kathleen Troia, so he said, "Should I call you Kathleen?"

McFadden smiled and said, "KT would be fine." Her demeanor was firm but charming and she exuded a relaxing confidence. McFadden had been around the Washington block and was very experienced. Haynes felt she would fit very well into the culture of the team he was attempting to build. They had a good discussion about the current situation in the world, but he didn't feel that it was yet time to inform her that West and McCormick were going to Kurdistan. Instead he got straight to the point. "KT, we would like you to be our National Security Advisor."

She smiled and said, "I prefer to hear you leave the word 'our' out of it, and just say 'my' national security advisor. In previous experience with the word 'our,' it means I have to deal with too many people and too many opinions, so I hope you understand that if I take this position, I report to you."

"Yeah, I like your definition better," he replied with a grin. "But I do have a chief of staff."

McFadden said, "I think I understand the role of the chief of staff and how to conduct myself but I still report to you."

"I got it and that's the way it shall be," Haynes said. "I hope you understand that this position will be only until the swearing-in of the new president."

McFadden said, "You just answered my last question. If you are not committed to a 2016 presidential election, I couldn't take the position."

"I've made it clear to every potential cabinet member that elections will be held in 2016, and also that the politicians under house arrest would not be harmed in any way," Haynes said. "Having you here would make me feel a lot more comfortable. We desperately need experienced people like you to serve, so I take it that you accept the position?"

"Yes."

With a large smile on his face, Haynes shook her hand and kissed her on both cheeks. He was very comfortable around strong, competent women. He just generally liked women, period. As he escorted her out, he said "Jeannie, meet our new National Security Advisor. KT, Jeannie will take care of getting you settled in and any other arrangements you might need."

THURSDAY, November 13, 2014, 11:00 a.m.

Haynes noticed former UN Ambassador Jerry Bolan chatting with Rod in the hallway, and then watched as KT made her way over to them. She and Bolan had served together in previous administrations. Bolan's signature mustache and his hair combed flat over the side of his forehead made him unmistakable. Haynes waited for Rod, Bolan and KT to finish. He needed their conversation to run its course. It would give Bolan an incentive to go back to the UN as his ambassador for a couple years. Bolan was a no-nonsense, tough, brilliant individual.

Eventually, they noticed Haynes' presence and introductions were made before they convened in Rod's office. The conversation focused on policy and Bolan realized that there was no personal conflict with Haynes on the direction to take, so he accepted the ambassadorship.

After Bolan left, it occurred to Haynes that Bob Rails was going to be pissed that he was stealing some of his best Fox News contributors. The mainstream media was also going to have a field day with it. Of course the mainstream media would never report that Fox News had an extensive list of socialist and liberal contributors or that they themselves have hardly any conservative contributors. Fox News was probably the only TV network where competent conservatives could get a media job.

THURSDAY November 13, 2014, 11:30 a.m.

Gary Ronson arrived early and Flett sent him to be briefed by Goldstein. Once he returned, Haynes reminded him that he had commented several times on how much more efficient health would be if it was decentralized to the states, so each state could take its own creative initiatives and pass them on to each other for improvements. Haynes knew that Ronson's theory would dovetail nicely into his American Functional Charter plan to decentralize the country into more efficient administrative health services regions.

He started by telling Ronson that he wanted to set up a situation where health matters could be transferred to the states, and that he needed to coordinate this with cooperative governors. Then Haynes got into the area where he knew there could be some disagreement. He told Ronson that he didn't like Medicare for this and Medicaid for that. There were just too many complicated bureaucracies and too much unnecessary overlap to administer all these different medical programs. He would prefer if Ronson would encourage the states to cover everybody under one umbrella. Haynes continued, "This would require mandatory 100% participation by everyone in the state, and it might have to be imposed on everyone that they must contribute. However, I do not wish to force the states to implement such a program. I wish to encourage them to do it."

Ronson replied, "I'm not so keen on forcing people into buying things they don't want to buy."

Haynes replied, "I understand that and I am a free enterprise capitalist just like you. But in this case I believe an exception has to be made for all state residents to have coverage. Right now you have a semi-socialistic medical system anyway. People who can't afford it don't pay, so the domino effect kicks in. Hospitals raise their prices to cover the losses, and as a result, insurance companies have to raise their rates; in effect people with insurance are paying for everybody else.

"The largest part of a doctor's expenses is insurance because there is no tort reform. Because there is no tort reform, doctors order unnecessary tests, etcetera, to cover their asses. All of which again increases the cost back to the states. Coverage can be provided by insurance companies or by the state government's payroll taxes. The advantage of payroll taxes is that it simplifies everything for businesses, and the net result is that they are then able to hire more people and expand their business.

"What our job should be is to encourage some kind of a system that gives 100% coverage and that everyone, including young people, has to participate in it. Instead of having Medicare, Medicaid and all the rest of the Caids, along with those excessive bureaucracies that go with each one of them, we will have 100% coverage for everybody.

"Believe me, I have witnessed 60 years of trial and error in Canada and at the end of day you need 100 per cent participation. I believe it will be up to the voters in each state to decide to vote for someone who implements full participation. Some states may want to implement a 100% universal program that will supersede Medicaid and Medicare, etcetera. Other states may choose not to. How we transfer the administration and the cost of Medicare and Medicaid to a state that only wants to maintain the status quo is a question I don't know the answer to yet. But I believe all states will eventually come around. All we need is a couple of success stories from states using a universal system, and the rest will follow.

"I am sure you can find a way to make this work but the core has to be that the federal government will transfer all health and welfare responsibilities to the states. This is a huge undertaking but your background tells me you can handle this. In the short term I want you to scrap the Affordable Health Care Act. Next to National Security, this is the most important post in the government. We will try and do this through Congress and if we can't, we will do it anyway. This is going to cause a great deal of disruption and confusion in the short term and we will need a temporary bridge solution until a new system can be implemented. You understand you are going to be attacked by the AARP, the left wing media and all kinds of special interest lobbyists. You are going to have a target on your back. Your agency is the one I will be watching most closely. We are going to pass tort reform. The insurance burden on doctors is ridiculous. It increases the cost of health care dramatically. If states want to participate in the American Functional Charter they will have to stop using draconian measures to prevent companies from doing business in their states, especially insurance companies. Also since the federal agency will be shut down, I want to make sure that the states understand that we would expect them to offer positions to the former federal employees first. You may want to consider offering to pay for moving costs for former federal employees at the agency."

Ronson said, "You're talking to me like I'm already the Secretary of Health and Human Services."

Haynes smiled. "I would like to appoint you. Will you accept? You will have a wide mandate to implement everything we just discussed."

"Yes, Okay."

"Gary, I'm really only concerned with the what. The how is your own management style which I really don't want to interfere with. But may I make a suggestion?"

"Sure, why not."

"Well, I think you should take some of the very best people you can find over at that agency and divide them into groups, each with a leader and each with so many states to coordinate with. You may want to give maybe five states to each team or however you want to structure it. It's just a suggestion."

Ronson replied, "Sounds like a good one to me."

Jeannie Flett immediately began to arrange for his arrival at Health and Human Services. Haynes went into Giani's office and said, "Well Rod, we only have one big one left and that's the Attorney General; any news from Downey?"

Rod said, "Yeah, I brought him over for dinner last night, told him who we had appointed so far and all the rest of it. He reluctantly accepted and said he would try it for a while and if it went well he would give up his congressional seat and if it didn't, he would resign and go back to being a congressman."

Haynes said, "What exactly did he mean by if it didn't; why would that be?"

"One reason is probably because he hasn't met you yet," Giani said. "I gave him an example of where we probably would not want him to apply the law."

Haynes said, "What example?"

"Kyling has already been talking to governors along the Mexican border and they want authorization to ask for citizenship papers. I explained to Downey that we only have two years and so there are certain laws we don't have the luxury of applying." Giani continued, "You know, it's probably better that way because he can keep some of our people's excesses in check."

Haynes said, "Yeah, that makes a lot of sense. So he's on board based on let's try it for a while."

Giani said, "That's about it."

Haynes said, "Okay. Are we ready to go with the press conference?"

Giani said, "Yep, let's get the process started."

Haynes said, "I'll go talk to Goldstein after I get a sandwich. I like Saturday because it will give an opportunity for our new people to be on the Sunday news programs and Rawlston can announce that the markets will be open on Monday morning. We can't do it tomorrow. We still need to talk to some more people and Sunday's not much different than Saturday and the markets have to open Monday morning since the new cabinet will have to be here on Saturday. Why don't we have our White House reception for everyone on Friday night?"

Giani replied, "I guess we don't have a choice."

CHAPTER 13

PREPARING THE PRESS CONFERENCE

—☰—

THURSDAY November 13, 2014, 2:00 p.m.

HAYNES WAS IN GOLDSTEIN'S OFFICE, discussing the what, when, who, where and how. The "what" and the "who" would be the introduction of the new cabinet and advisers. The "when" would be sometime Saturday. The "where" should be in the White House, but in what room? They decided the East Room. It had the atmosphere for this kind of thing. They chose the morning because they needed to get it done before the afternoon football games and now they were down to the "how." Goldstein suggested that they erect seating for each one of the new cabinet members and advisors and that there should be two rows, the second one higher than the first so that they would be very visible to cameras and the media. Haynes said, "I think we need some members of the military there as well."

Goldstein said, "Why?"

Haynes said, "Well, I think it's important to let the country know that they are allowing and encouraging a civilian administration."

"That makes sense." said Goldstein. "Have you discussed this with McCormick?"

Haynes replied, "Yes, in fact McCormick even suggested they not even be introduced, to give them an even lower profile. McCormick told me they will just kind of sit there."

Goldstein said, "But McCormick has a cabinet post."

Haynes said, "Well, he will be introduced like everyone else and sit with the rest of the civilian cabinet members dressed in his civvies. That will reflect what really is, which is that McCormick is working together with a group of civilian cabinet members."

"Where are we going to put the rest of the military brass?"

Haynes said, "Put them on the left side of the standing microphone so that they can be separated from the civilian cabinet."

Then Goldstein said, "How and who is going to introduce the cabinet?"

Haynes said, "How about putting a standing microphone on the left of the cabinet members' seats so that you can introduce the cabinet?"

Goldstein said, "A press secretary shouldn't be doing that."

Haynes said, "Why not?"

Goldstein said, "That's not what press secretaries do."

Haynes said, "You are a part of this team and you can do whatever you need to do to advance our objectives."

Goldstein said, "Well okay, but how am I going to introduce them? Should I do them one at a time or have them sitting in the room when the press comes in or what?"

Haynes said, "How about if we keep them all outside the room and have all the chairs empty when the press come in and then you can address the cameras and the media and introduce the cabinet members and advisors one at a time."

Goldstein said, "I think we should leave Giani for last and then he can introduce you. I know that you can make a statement but are you prepared to answer questions? This is not familiar territory for you, Mr. Administrator."

"I think I can handle it, however, I will be watching you for a signal to knock it off before I get myself into doo-doo. From now on we could call it the doo-doo signal."

Goldstein said, "Okay. That's basically it, I can take care of the rest."

"What's the rest?"

Goldstein said, "I am going to have press kits prepared on the people in the cabinet and their backgrounds. That of course will include you."

Haynes said, "Do you have to put my educational background in there?"

Goldstein said, "They are going to find out anyway, aren't they?"

Haynes said, "Well a lot of these people are going to think – what the hell is this guy with a grade eight education doing here?"

"So far at least, the people around here think you are doing great, and that includes me."

Haynes said "Thank you" and left the rest of the arrangements to his press secretary. He was not surprised when Jeannie Flett told him she had been sure the press conference would be in the next two days, so she had already made arrangements for any cabinet members or advisers still out of town to arrive beforehand. Some were bringing their spouses and families. Haynes said, "Since we're holding the press conference late Saturday morning, maybe you can arrange an informal White House dinner for everyone tomorrow night, Friday night."

"Taken care of," said Flett. "Also, Mr. McFarland called and said that his wife joined him in Washington and Mrs. Giani is also here."

"Great," Haynes said. "That will give everyone a chance to lighten up a little."

"I have a little surprise for you." said Jeannie, "Sonja is over at Blair House. She didn't want to surprise you here because she thought you would be too busy. And the Press Secretary needs to see you again," she added, passing Goldstein on her way out the door.

Goldstein said, "I am going to have each reporter wear a large ID tag. How would you like to just come in and casually mix with them before we let them into the East Room? It will give them a chance to get to know you a little. But I will make sure they know that you will not answer any questions and if they try to turn it into a scrum, you'll be gone."

"Sounds great," said Haynes. "That's my kind of thing. Who's making the table arrangements for dinner Friday?"

"Jeannie Flett."

"Perfect," said Haynes.

Haynes checked into Flett's office later and said, "Have you finished the seating arrangements for tonight?"

Flett said, "Almost."

Haynes replied, "I want to invite Steve Forrest and his wife and have them sit with Herman Raines. Who is at my table?"

Flett said, "Who do you want?"

"Kim and John McFarland, the Downeys, the Leevers and invite Bill O'Leary, have him seated beside Sonja. I want Downy beside me. Why don't you invite some old veterans . . . Kissinger and the like. Oh, and Ronald Stamp. Make sure he doesn't sit with any of the military people." Haynes did not want to take a chance on phoning Stamp, so this would be a good opportunity to talk to him without it looking too conspicuous. Haynes added, "Jeannie, I hope we are going to have real music and not a bunch of noise."

"You will be pleasantly surprised."

By now Haynes was getting anxious to see Sonja, so he told Jeannie he was going to go over to Blair House. He found her in his room. They embraced and held each other for a little bit and then they sat down and talked about everything that had been happening. He told her about Friday evening's dinner. Haynes was crazy about her and was grateful she would be there with him.

FRIDAY, November 14, 2014, 9:00 a.m.

Now that Sonja was there, Haynes finally had a good night's sleep. The next morning he had Terry Riley give her the grand tour of the White House while he got ready to meet Doug Snow. Snow was a Democrat but not an ideologue. He was the kind a guy who wanted to do what worked. Haynes did not know what exactly he wanted Snow to do in the administration, but he knew he wanted to have him around. Maybe he could use him as an advisor and as liaison with the Democrats in the Congress. Snow was a straightforward, intense, honest, no-nonsense kind of a guy that did not toe any party line. Jeannie brought him into Haynes' office and Haynes tried to strike up a conversation, but sensed that Snow was uncomfortable, so he asked, "What's the matter?"

Snow replied, "I am not really comfortable with this whole situation. Are you?"

"No, not really. But on the other hand, yes, because we have the next two years to achieve great things and to set America on a new course for at least another 200 years. If you are not comfortable with that, maybe you should be around to keep us in check. It looks like we are going to be around for another two years so it would probably be better for you to be on the inside looking out rather than the outside looking in."

"What is it that you want me to do?"

"Well," Haynes said, "I would like you to be an advisor, for starters."

After they chatted for a while, Snow said, "I would like to talk to Giani."

"I'll go and get him."

Snow said, "I would like to talk to him alone if you don't mind."

Haynes said, "I understand," and escorted Snow into Giani's office.

Snow stayed with Giani until after 10:00 a.m. In the meantime Sonja had finished her tour with Riley and asked Haynes if he had a suit for the evening.

"I brought the tan suit," he said.

"You can't wear that thing to the reception!"

"Well," he said, "I don't have time to go get another suit."

She said, "I'll take care of it. I'll bring the tan suit to a men's store and have them match the size in blue and get some decent shirts and ties." She touched base with Jeannie before she went back over to Blair House.

Jeannie came in a few minutes later and before she had a chance to say a word, Haynes said, "I know. General Martinez has spoken."

Just then, Giani came in with Snow and said, "Doug has decided to join us."

"Wonderful," said Haynes. They talked for 10 minutes and then Snow and Haynes asked Jeannie to get Snow an office close to his and Rod's. Since his major interviews were now completed, Haynes spent the rest of Friday preparing a strategy for how to implement his American Functional Charter. He decided that he would need ten teams each handling five states, with a leader for each team. His plan was to have Congress introduce a constitutional amendment for the Charter but at the beginning, only involving the "States Only" section and the "Federal Only" section, since these were relatively straightforward to get agreement on. Later they would proceed to the more complicated "Shared" section of the charter. He knew that before he even attempted this, he would need to have a new set of Senate rules established by a constitutional amendment that could not be changed by whatever party was in power. It would include a 50+1 vote for all votes across the board, including constitutional amendments. He would prefer to do it that way but if not he would move forward anyway. He realized that maybe this was something Snow could help him with. Doug Snow was respected on both sides of the aisle.

CHAPTER 14

THE FIRST WHITE HOUSE EVENING

—w—

FRIDAY, November 15, 2014

By 6:30 p.m. Sonja and Haynes in his new dark blue suit found their way down to the lobby at Blair House. His Secret Service man, Terry Riley, was waiting for him. Haynes said, "We want to walk over to the White House."

Riley said, "No sir, I don't think that will be possible."

Haynes said, "Why not?"

"Well, whether you like it or not," said Riley, "you have become too important. We will drive you." Standing behind Riley was a redheaded female about 5'8' with short hair. Riley said, "Miss Martinez, we understand you are going to be here for quite some time so we have assigned Agent Brahim to head up your security detail."

Sonja looked quizzically at David and said, "I thought I had seen everything."

At the White House, Jeannie Flett was waiting to escort them to the East Room. Haynes asked, "Is everyone there yet?"

"No."

"How many are missing?"

"I don't really know," Flett said.

"Then we'll wait down in my office until we find out. I want to be almost the last to arrive."

Jeannie said, "But we've set up a reception line for you to meet all the guests!"

"I'd rather not do that. It would make me look like some damn king. Let's just let Sonja and me enter the room and start talking to people. I will make sure that I talk to everyone before we sit down and eat."

Then he turned to Sonja and said, "When we get there we will stay together for a minute or two to make sure everyone knows who you are, because I'm sure they will all be looking, and then you can break away from me and start chatting with folks. You know what a charmer you are, baby. You did it to me."

A little while later Jeannie put her head in David's office and said "Okay, we can go now." The door to the East Room was open and they walked straight in. David spotted McCormick immediately and went over. "Good evening Jim, I would like you to meet Sonja Martinez."

McCormick introduced them to his wife and it went on like that for a while with various people until Haynes spotted Caroline Dever. Caroline was married to one of Haynes very closest friends, Kenneth Dever of Nashville. He felt a rush of adrenaline and excused himself from the group he was talking to. Just then, Caroline turned and saw him coming. They gave each other a big hug and before he could get a chance to ask where Kenneth was, he felt a tap on his shoulder and he turned and there was his dear old buddy, looming over him like a lanky super-animated scarecrow. He could adjust his behavior to suit any occasion, from formal to ridiculous, but behind his demeanor lay a steel-trap brain. They hugged and he lifted his finger towards McFarland to acknowledge that he knew McFarland had orchestrated all this. Then he turned and saw another bunch of his old Baldor buddies and the same thing repeated itself. The Kirkpatricks from Dallas, the Cowerns from Connecticut, the Kesslers from Tampa, the Richards from Los Angeles, Rick and Sharon Rogers from Greensboro and by some stroke of luck, Ron and Chloe DelBigio from Winnipeg, who just happened to be in Washington at the time.

Flett was watching from nearby and she made her way over to Haynes and said, "No, no, no. The table arrangements have already been made and you have to sit at your table. You have all night to talk to your friends."

When all the greetings were over, Haynes rounded up Doug Snow and introduced him to Rick Rogers and Kenneth Dever. Haynes said, "Doug, Jeannie has arranged for you to sit at the same table as Kenneth and Rick."

Snow said "That'll be fine."

After cocktails everyone proceeded to their designated tables. O'Leary was petitioning Sonja for the first TV interview with Haynes. Haynes and the new Attorney General were getting along just fine. The food and the wine were excellent, and the atmosphere made it easy to get along with everyone. And then Sonja noticed that no one was dancing to the band so she took David's hand and dragged him onto the dance floor. She was an excellent dancer and finally some of the others got up on the floor and the place started to boogie a little bit.

Rod got up and thanked everyone for accepting to serve the country and asked Haynes to say a few words. He kept his comments brief: "We all believe in democracy. What we do in the next two years to set up this country for the next 200 years to continue democratic and free enterprise principles will be truly historic." Haynes got a polite round of applause and sat down.

CHAPTER 15

THE PRESS CONFERENCE

—⚏—

SATURDAY, November 15, 2014

WORKERS WERE IN THE PROCESS of preparing the East Room, a grand setting for a historic press conference. Seats were placed at the front for the new cabinet and the advisors to the new Administrator, arranged so that the second row would be slightly higher than the first, for the benefit of the photographers. To the left of the microphone where Haynes would make his speech were seats for senior military officers.

Press Secretary Bernard Goldstein was outside the room briefing the media, and information kits were being passed out with the names of the new cabinet and advisors along with background information on the new Administrator, who was probably the only individual that the media was not already familiar with. The place was a madhouse of voices and reporters anxiously combing through the pages of their press kits.

When Goldstein stepped in front of a microphone, questions came flying from all directions. Fortunately, Goldstein had been very well briefed on all aspects of the last few days. "I am going to take simple questions, but I am going to take them one at a time and I am going to be the one to point to the questioner," he said.

Before Goldstein had an opportunity to point to anyone, the reporter from NBC shouted "Where are the President and the Vice President?"

The room went quiet as Goldstein replied, "I don't know. I have been assured that wherever they are, they are safe and secure and as comfortable as possible, and that will continue to be the situation. I would not have taken this job if it were otherwise."

Goldstein then pointed to ABC's White House correspondent, who asked, "What guarantees do you or any of us have that that this is the case?"

Goldstein answered, "I have the word of people with flawless reputations who participated in this change of our government and I am satisfied with that."

ABC's guy followed up. "Are you satisfied with the present status quo?"

Goldstein replied, "No and yes. No because the Constitution is suspended and to say the least there is a great deal of anxiety, not only in America but around the world, which is reflected by foreign stock markets. Yes, because in the next two years there will be serious additions made to the Constitution that will chart a course for America for the next 200 years. These changes would not be possible under normal operating circumstances. You will also see in your kits, and in a few minutes in reality, that very solid and experienced cabinet members and advisors have been selected to guide and run the country for the next two years, and that the Administrator and the military are firmly committed to a presidential and congressional election in 2016. That was one of the conditions on which I would accept this post.

"I am not going to take any more questions for the time being. Mr. Haynes will be arriving in a minute or so. He is not going to take any questions at this time. His goal is for you all to get to know each other a little better informally. He will answer questions after the new cabinet is introduced in the East Room."

When Haynes arrived he was immediately surrounded by reporters. Some insisted on throwing questions at him, which he ignored, smiling. He kept introducing himself to everyone in sight for about 15 minutes, which felt like an eternity, before he finally escaped from the room. Now Goldstein took over and said, "I would like us all to proceed in an orderly fashion into the East Room, without a stampede if possible. The cabinet, advisers, senior military officers and new Administrator are waiting to be introduced."

SATURDAY, November 15, 2014, 10:30 a.m.

The doors were opened, but 'orderly' was not happening. Some of the reporters were squeezing themselves between the door sentries in a scene that reminded Haynes of the Three Stooges. Although the reporters chairs were clearly marked with their IDs, some of them just sat anywhere they wished. Finally after they were all inside, although some were some still standing, Goldstein worked his way to the microphone and asked the reporters to settle down and find their seats. The room was abuzz and cameras were flashing in the direction of the empty seats for the new cabinet and advisors. Goldstein allowed this to continue for a couple of minutes before saying, "Ladies and gentlemen, may I have your attention please. I would like to introduce America's new Cabinet and advisors." He started with the new Secretary of State. Oliver West entered the room and the place started buzzing again as Oliver calmly took his seat in the middle of the first row. Goldstein continued with the rest of the cabinet and significant White House staff and advisers, until they were all seated.

O'Leary was anchoring the coverage for his network. Haynes knew that he was tough but fair and he had an advantage over the others because he had been the only media participant at the White House dinner the night before, so had had a chance to grasp the whole picture. He didn't particularly like the situation but at the same time he realized that Haynes and Giani had put together an experienced and professional team that wanted to do what worked. His report was a combination of optimism about the new team and caution concerning whether the results for the American people would be positive. He figured it could not be any worse than what had been in place. O'Leary had a huge TV audience but Haynes knew that it was not so much the quantity of his audience as the quality; they were well-informed Americans who watched him every night. These were the people that Haynes needed on his side.

It was time for Goldstein to introduce Giani. The one thing that Haynes had emphasized to everyone was to make the most of every chance they got to emphasize that there would be an election in 2016. Giani did exactly that, and also gave an overview of the actions that would be taken to move forward. He congratulated the new Administrator for his actions so far, including the quality of the people that had been selected. Finally, he said, "Ladies and gentlemen, I would like to introduce you to the new Administrator of the executive branch of the United States government, Mr. David Haynes."

Haynes and Giani had already discussed emphasizing that he was the Administrator of the executive branch and not the whole government, so as to not let the Congress feel left out. There was a slight delay and then Haynes entered the room and walked directly over to Rawlston. Rawlston stood up and shook his hand. Haynes leaned over and whispered in Rawlston's ear, "Henry, you need to speak after me and tell everyone that the markets will be opening on Monday morning. Just give everyone a confidence booster." Rawlston nodded yes and Haynes continued over to the microphone. There was only slight applause, mostly coming from the cabinet and the military officers. Haynes stood for a moment waiting for complete silence, and the sudden dead quiet in the room made him feel for a second like Tiger Woods about to make a putt on the 18th for a win.

Then he began, "Leadership is not about me. Leadership is about knowing what you don't know and what you are not sure of. When you understand that, you engage strong, competent people that know what they're doing in their areas of expertise and you let them do their jobs and not be intimidated when they get in your face concerning disagreements. Real leaders set the tone and direction and then they let a strong team execute the plan. Real leaders are not on an ego trip. I think that America will get the message that for starters, we have set the tone and direction and chosen strong people to execute well-intended measures that will benefit all Americans.

This House does not belong to any of its occupants, it belongs to the American people. If the occupant is going to respect the American people then the choice of people who visit this house is of symbolic importance. As long as I am here, we will make our best attempt at not allowing any race-baiting extortionists, individuals purposely trying to divide the American people or organizations camouflaging their intent such as CAIR.

"A lot of young Americans that were 18 years old six years ago are now 24. They think the economy that we are experiencing is normal because they haven't really experienced anything else. Recovery times from previous recessions have been pretty much consistent, and the middle and working classes have recovered along with it. This one, unfortunately, has not been that way. Wages have not kept pace with any form of recovery. We plan to change that starting now, because America is only strong when it has a vibrant middle working class.

"We plan to make new additions to the Constitution that will allow America to function in the most efficient way on the planet by bringing functional government closer to the people it serves.

"Our military defenses have been reduced to dangerous levels. We plan to change that starting now. We will no longer give advance warning to the killer fanatics and Muslim jihadist terrorists in the world about what we are going to do. When American interests are threatened, we are just going to act and let them know later. We will be proactive. Being weak is the most dangerous of scenarios. Dangerous despots run amok and innocent people end up dead. A strong America will calm things down in the world. Ladies and gentlemen, we are sending out the message that America, the freedom beacon of the world, is back."

Haynes pushed back from the microphone indicating that he was done. The cabinet, advisers, military and some of the congressional people in attendance exploded onto their feet in rambunctious applause. Haynes' head dropped. He was overcome with emotion, mostly because of the intensity of the last number of days. He looked up and spotted Sonja who was on her feet applauding with the rest. He blew her a kiss and she blew one back.

After things died down Haynes again stepped up to the mike and said, "I can take some questions now." Haynes had already prepared himself for hostile questions from some of the media. He had written down a bunch of those questions in anticipation and was ready at least for the ones that he had anticipated. He thought to himself, "I'll get those ideologues at CSNBC out of the way first." So he pointed his finger at the reporter better known as Thrill Up His Leg. George Dicky stood up and said, "What makes you think that a person with an eighth grade education is qualified to run this country?"

Haynes stared him down and said, "Philippians 4-13."

Dicky said "What does that mean?"

Haynes responded, "That's for me to know and you to find out."

Then Haynes pointed to O'Leary. O'Leary asked "What are you going to do about the borders, mainly the southern border?"

Haynes replied, "Ray Kyling and I have discussed this and agreed that the border has to be sealed tight ASAP by whatever means necessary and instead of being hostile and not following the law as was the case in the past, we will work closely with the governors and officials of the states on the Mexican border in particular. We are also going to be looking aggressively for people with overstayed visas. We are going to install rigid rules concerning these visas so that they are adhered to. Any illegal immigrant with a criminal record will be deported immediately, no lawyers, no hearings, none of that. They are not going to get a chance to recommit crimes if we can help it. Private citizens and police officers have been murdered by illegal criminals who have been deported and re-entered the country more than once. This is treacherous and illegal behavior by our own government. The president's first sworn job description is to defend American citizens.

"Those are the three things that we will concentrate our efforts on now. What's the point of having all these rigid screening checks at normal border crossings when all a bad guy has to do is enter the USA via the Mexican border without detection? One time I was given a hard time by U.S. Customs and I was thinking, what's the point? While you are questioning me, hundreds of people including some very dangerous individuals have just crossed the Mexican border undetected. To stop a dam from leaking we must plug all the holes. Americans are going to wake up when they find out that some terrorist act has been committed by someone not even Mexican who just walked across the porous Mexican border. This is no longer an illegal immigration problem, it's a security problem."

O'Leary followed up with, "What are you going to do with the folks already here?"

Haynes said, "As I said Bill, we will have to deal with all that later. Right now we're going to do one thing at a time. Everything else will have to wait. We will stay focused on the three items I just mentioned for now."

The next question was, "What are you going to do about Iraq and Syria?"

Haynes replied, "As I said in my comments, we are not going to telegraph what our intentions are to anybody. Hopefully, there will be no leaks in this area but I promise you we will be proactive. However, I can promise you one thing – we are going to throw out that ridiculous CIA and State Department politically correct talking points manual that says we don't use the word jihadist. Terrorists and jihadists are words that will be commonplace in this administration's vocabulary, something that the American people have not heard for six years. If it swims like a duck, quacks like a duck and looks like a duck, it's a duck."

Next question, "Where is the President?"

Haynes replied, "I don't know and if I did I wouldn't tell you anyway. All I can tell you is that he and his family are comfortable and secure and will stay that way until further notice. I have a promise in writing to that effect from those responsible, and I made it clear that I would not accept this position if this was not the case. He's probably near a golf course enjoying a round a golf, which is exactly what I'd be doing if I were him."

Next question, "Are your new nominees going to be vetted by the Congress?"

"No" said Haynes. "We have only two years until the 2016 elections and we're not going to waste time on things that consume just that, time. Good competent people are not interested in sitting in front of a bunch of congressmen describing the color of their underwear."

"What about Iran?"

Haynes replied, "Iran is an enemy of the United States and all peaceful nations. They sponsor terrorism in Lebanon, Palestine and other regions.

Negotiations with those thugs are over. We are going to go back to our allies and attempt to renew the embargo against Iran. If we can't get our allies on board, the United States will act alone. All those Iranian mullahs want to do is kill anybody who doesn't agree with them. They have to understand that nuclear is a two-way street. They are now carrying a nuclear sign on their backs. Any form of a nuclear explosion or dirty bomb that happens in the West, we will turn Iran into the dark side of the moon. The repercussions will be a hundred-fold."

"Do you intend to invade Iran to eliminate their nuclear development sites?"

Haynes replied, "All options are on the table."

Haynes looked over at Goldstein, who gave him the hand across the throat doo-doo signal. Haynes immediately changed course and said, "Ladies and gentlemen I would like to introduce our new – I guess I shouldn't say new, I should say re-new – Secretary of the Treasury, a man the world financial community is very familiar with, Mr. Henry Rawlston."

Rawlston approached and Haynes shook Rawlston's hand with enthusiasm before turning to the microphone. Suddenly Haynes realized that they had overlooked a place for him to sit so he headed for a seat next to Sonja, who was right beside the press corps. He noticed that the TV cameras had tracked him and lingered on the two of them for an instant. He decided that was a good thing because she was a lot better looking than he was. He sat down next to her and she whispered, "You did great, baby."

Rawlston started by saying that the whole cabinet was very enthusiastic about the future. He promised the creation of solid new non-governmental jobs. "They will be created by the private sector, mostly by small businesses, because this administration will be business friendly – especially to small business. We will assure domestic and international financial markets not by our words but by our deeds and our results. I will be talking to all chairmen of American stock markets today to ask them to reopen on Monday morning as usual. America's socialist experimental nightmare is over."

Haynes twisted in his chair. He thought the last sentence of Rawlston's comments had been a little aggressive but it was the truth and that's not a bad thing. It would be a signal that the administration was not fooling around and the country was moving forward.

After Rawlston finished, everyone in the room stood up and started to mingle. A crowd of press surrounded Haynes, some of them still firing questions. Haynes said, "Guys, guys, guys, I just wanted to say hello." At that point Goldstein stepped in and escorted him and Sonja out of the room. Haynes spotted Rawlston on his way out and said, "Henry, I would like you to go up to New York and stand on that podium at the New York Stock Exchange for the opening."

Rawlston said "Sounds fine to me. I'll make arrangements this afternoon."

CHAPTER 16

THE MEXICO PROBLEM

—⚏—

SATURDAY, November 15, 2014, 12:00 p.m.

HAYNES HAD ALREADY ARRANGED WITH Jeannie Flett to have the Mexican ambassador over at 1:00 p.m. He was angry about the situation of a Marine who had accidentally got himself into the wrong lane with no reverse course at the Mexican border. It was an honest mistake that other folks had made before. All the marine had wanted to do was to turn around and re-enter the US; unfortunately he had some weapons in the back of his truck which were legal in the US but not in Mexico. Haynes was also angry that the previous administration had made no real attempt to get him out. He thought this was probably because of Chambers' real feelings on guns, revealed during an election campaign when he had said that some Americans were too fond of their religion and their guns. It showed that he had little regard for those kinds of Americans and thought the soldier in question probably deserved what he got. The Mexicans had been holding the marine in a Mexican prison for months. They put on a charade by parading him back and forth to their corrupt kangaroo courts, humiliating not only him, but Americans as well. Haynes had had enough.

Before he met with the Mexican Ambassador, he expressed his feelings on the topic to Ray Kyling and Rod over lunch. They agreed with his feelings but not necessarily the approach he would take with the Mexican ambassador.

Haynes did not, as a rule, want to work out of the Oval Office, but felt that for this meeting it was necessary to make sure the Mexicans knew who was in charge. After Jeannie Flett escorted Ambassador Suarez and his assistant in, Haynes greeted him with a very severe look and asked Suarez to tell his assistant to leave. Then he said, "Your government has been humiliating the United States for some time now and you have been successful."

"What do you mean?"

"I mean the American soldier that you have been holding for just too damn long. You people have been parading him back-and-forth from his prison cell to the courts of your so-called justice system just to humiliate the United States."

"Why would we want to humiliate a friend?"

"Don't give me that stuff, Ambassador. Friends don't do that to each other."

Suarez said, "He broke Mexican law."

"Technically yes." said Haynes, "But you know very well in this case there should be an exception. You claim that Mexico is a friend of the USA. Friends do not behave this way and we interpret this as hostile."

"We have no intention of humiliating the United States."

"Perceptions are real and the perception of us Americans is that you are not only humiliating us but enjoying every minute of it."

"I assure you… What do I call you, Mr. Administrator? That is not our intention." Then Suarez made a big mistake. He said, "Mr. Administrator, you just said 'us Americans.' You are not American."

Haynes' face turned red and he said, "Yeah, but I'm not some corrupt Mexican official either. Furthermore your President has been running around making comments like he is some kind of de facto President of the United States and encouraging illegal immigration into our country. This does not sound like a damn friend to me, so let's cut through the crap. Unlike you folks, I'm not here to try and intimidate the President of Mexico so I will give you a gracious way out. Mr. Kyling, Mr. Giani and I are the only three people in the administration that know about this discussion and it will stay that way for now. I'm not asking you, I'm telling you to tell your President that if our guy is not released by 8 p.m. on November 24, next Monday, it's going to get real ugly."

Haynes continued, "I have two options. One is to thank the Mexican President for his compassion in releasing our soldier. The second one you don't even want to know about, but I assure you we will execute it and you are not going to like it. You are not dealing with some Chicken Chamberlain, that British appeaser who gave up Czechoslovakia to Hitler and still ended up in a war. You are dealing with me and I assure you that I will do what I say. The details of this meeting will not go public so long as we have our guy back by 8 p.m. next Monday. That gives you plenty of time to parade him back to your courts to have him released."

Suarez said "That was going to happen anyway."

"Well, that's a wonderful thing, Mr. Ambassador," said Haynes. "I guess this meeting was not really necessary." Haynes stood up to indicate that the meeting was over and said, "Mr. Ambassador, thank you for coming over, have a nice weekend." Suarez looked a little shaken, probably because he was not sure quite how he was going to relay this unusual meeting to his superiors.

After he was gone, Giani said to Haynes, "So much for your diplomatic training."

Haynes said, "I am beginning to understand that not having any is probably an asset."

Kyling asked, "What do you think they'll do?"

Haynes said, "I don't know, but his last comment about being about to release him anyway might be an indication."

Kyling said, "Why 8 p.m. on Monday?"

"I want you to inform border protection at the crossing south of San Diego to start to rearrange the crossing in some way that will indicate that we are readying the border for heavy delays by Saturday. Mexican border officials will relay back to the boys in Mexico City that there is something unusual happening and I think they will get the message."

Kyling said, "What if that doesn't work?"

Haynes said, "We will have to back up traffic all the way to Mexico City. And I mean it. Ray, you better work out some other options just in case, like US checks going to Mexico don't get processed or something like that."

SATURDAY, November 15 - 1.40 p.m.

Haynes' only remaining meeting was with Doug Snow, who was waiting for him near Jeannie's desk. They went into Haynes' office and Haynes said, "You know Doug, I would have wanted you around here anyway but the fact that you are a Democrat who believes in doing what works could be a great asset to our efforts with the American Functional Charter and the Congress.

"Are you saying that you want me to be a liaison with the Democratic Congress?"

Haynes replied, "No, I want you to be a liaison with everyone over there."

"How do you know that the Republican members will trust me?"

Haynes said, "Because they have seen you criticize Democrats and Republicans alike and they know that you're not an ideologue."

Snow said, "I can give it a try but if I run into any difficulty I am coming to you."

"That's only part of it.," said Haynes. "Would you be interested in helping us by heading up my efforts to make this Functional Charter a reality?"

Snow said something interesting. "I would prefer to call it the Separation of Powers Act."

"Interesting," said Haynes. "Maybe we can add that in small print under the big title of American Functional Charter. So will you help us?"

Snow replied, "Sounds like it would be very challenging and historic."

Haynes yelled out the door to Jeannie, "What's Goldstein doing now?"

She replied, "He's in the press room doing a briefing."

Haynes said, "Send him a note that Doug and I will be coming over there to announce his appointment heading up our efforts with the AFC. Tell Goldstein that I will make the announcement in the press room." Haynes turned to Snow and said, "You know Doug, this is the first time I've used letters to describe the American Functional Charter."

"It's probably going to become commonplace," Snow replied.

They both headed over to wait outside the pressroom. Goldstein spotted them and came out to see what was up. "I got your note. What's going on?" he asked.

Haynes said, "Just go out there and tell them that the Administrator has an appointment to announce."

Haynes went straight to the microphone with Doug beside him and said, "Ladies and gentlemen, I'm very pleased to announce that Mr. Doug Snow will become point man for our efforts on the American Functional Charter – or as he likes to call it, the Separation of Powers Act. To make things easier in the future, I will be referring to it as the AFC. Doug's second job will be to liaise with the Congress."

Then Doug took the mic.

The first question to him was, "How do you expect to get along with this administration?"

Doug said, "Very well, and I'm looking forward to the very historic challenges ahead. I am delighted to have the full support of the Administrator to do it."

Haynes and Snow headed back to Haynes' office. Haynes said, "Doug, I would like you to contact each of the 50 governors and maybe even Puerto Rico to assess their feelings about the AFC. I think you should select team liaison leaders to handle five states each. Encourage the governors to hire their own liaison people to interact with ours. I don't want just guys as team leaders, find some women to be part of this team. These people need to be smart and experienced, but most of all enthusiastic about what we are doing. I think that you should handle the Congress concerning the AFC, but the first thing we need to do is to get the Senate to either change their rules or pass a constitutional amendment so that that 50+1 votes will pass any legislation in the future. Otherwise we will have gridlock and then we will have to do it without them, which I want desperately to avoid, so we have to get this done first."

Snow said, "Sounds like a good approach but let me think about it for a while."

Haynes said, "I would like to bring former speaker Goodrich on as an advisor to the administration, but mostly to give you some help with certain reluctant members of Congress. What did you think of those two guys you had dinner with last night?"

Doug said, "Yeah, they were all really nice and they had a lot of stories about you."

Haynes said, "I bet they did, but the two guys I'm interested in are Rogers and Dever."

"Oh those two," said Doug. "They were both a lot of fun and really smart guys."

Haynes said, "How smart do you really think they are?"

"They both have camouflaged brilliance," said Snow. "I could see it."

"Well, Doug," said Haynes, "This is my idea. Why don't you interview Kenneth and Rick to be team leaders for the AFC? Rick could handle the southeastern states and Kenneth could do the mid-southern states from Alabama to Texas."

Snow grinned. "You set me up on Friday night, didn't you?"

"Well, yeah, just a little bit."

Snow said, "Mr. Administrator, this is serious politics. Those two are fun and brilliant but don't you think they're a little bit off the wall for this?"

"Well," said Haynes, "so am I, but I'm here aren't I?"

"Touché," said Snow.

"Plus you are going to need all the help you can get and these two can be your eyes and ears," Haynes said.

"Eyes and ears for you or for me?"

"To be honest, for both of us," Haynes replied.

You know these people and you trust them, but you don't know me that well."

"I know all I need to know, Doug, and I trust you just as much as those two and I've known them for 30 years. They are going to help you more than you realize right now."

Snow said, "Are you ordering me to hire them?"

"No I am not, but I am completely convinced that they will be great assets, mostly for you. And I think you already know your job will be a lot more fun. If you decide to go with this and if you have any problems keeping a handle on things just tell me, and I will intervene, okay?"

"Okay," said Snow

"I'll talk to them," Haynes said, "I believe they're going to be in town until Monday. More than anything else, these team leaders are going to need people skills and negotiating skills. These two guys have street smarts. It doesn't matter whether or not they're talking to presidents or hobos, they can shift gears lightening fast."

After Snow returned to his office, Giani came in and said, "David, am I your chief of staff?"

Haynes looked at him with confusion. "Yes. Why?"

"Well if I am and you want me to be effective, you need to run things like this Snow decision past me before you implement them. It's not that I disagree with what you've just done, but sometimes there are other implications that you may not be aware of. Besides, you need a break."

Haynes said, "I'm sorry; I forgot one of my very first principles. Don't give someone responsibility without the authority. I'll try not to let it happen again."

"Look David, you've done a hell of a lot in a very short period of time. You have accomplished the biggest part of your job. We have nearly all the team assembled and now it's just a question of managing things. We have acquired very experienced people. Now, let's just let them do their jobs. There really isn't much for you to do today or tomorrow, so I'll give you a job. Why don't you go and spend the rest of the day with Sonja and tomorrow morning you can watch the Sunday morning shows starring Rawlston, Kyling, McFarland and Ronson."

"You see, there you go," said Haynes. "You arranged all this without running it by me."

They both laughed and Giani said, 'Yeah, but you gave me the responsibility and the authority. That's what you hired me for."

Haynes was tired and he knew it. But he realized so was everybody else. He went out to Jeannie and told her he was going over to Blair house to rest, hopefully until Monday, and that he wanted her to get some rest as well. "Just leave," he told her.

Jeannie said, "Well, I have other things to do today but barring anything unexpected I will take tomorrow off. May I make a suggestion? Why don't you and Sonja go up to Camp David until Monday morning?"

"Wow!" said David, "I never thought of that. How can that be arranged?"

"Rod has already taken care of it."

"I guess he's exercising his authority," Haynes smiled. "I would like to bring John and Kim McFarland with us."

Flett said, "You can't because McFarland is appearing on Face the Nation tomorrow morning."

"Well then, fly them both up there after he's finished his TV appearance."

"Okay," Flett said, "I'll take care of it."

CHAPTER 17

CAMP DAVID AND THE KURDS

—⚭—

SATURDAY, November 15, 2014, 3:05 p.m.

Haynes headed over to Blair house where Sonja was waiting. He said, "Sweetie, I've got a surprise for you."

"What would that be?"

"How would you like to go to Camp David for the rest of the weekend?"

"Oh my god," she said, "that would be wonderful. Besides, you need to get away."

They packed up their bags and were driven back over to the White House lawn where the helicopter was waiting. Military guys were saluting him so he instinctively saluted back, then took a few minutes with each Marine to chat before they boarded. He asked the pilots questions about the control panel and then they rotated off the lawn and headed up to Camp David, about 20 minutes away.

Camp David is located in wooded hills about 62 miles northeast of Washington near Thurmont, Maryland. As soon as Haynes saw the place, he felt at home. The compound was very country style and laid-back. They entered the main cabin and Haynes was amazed how country normal it was, not opulent at all. It was a very inviting relaxing atmosphere, which was something he loved.

David and Sonja spent the rest of Saturday afternoon calling friends and relatives. Sonja was big on family even though she didn't have children of her own. She was on the phone yapping excitedly in Spanish with her Cuban-American relatives in South Florida. Haynes called his brother Russell in

Canada and other family members. Almost all of them wanted to come visit the White House, and Haynes explained that he didn't know when that could happen. All of a sudden he felt a wave of panic when he realized that his family members were suddenly vulnerable. He summoned Riley and said, "God, Terry, I forgot about my family in all the chaos."

Riley said, "We have already taken care of Colin in Phoenix and we are making arrangements as we speak with the RCMP in Canada for your children and your brother."

"Okay, but Colin didn't mention anything about the Secret Service."

"We just started to make arrangements for that yesterday and we will be talking to him tomorrow."

"Good."

SATURDAY, November 15, 2014, 6:45 p.m.

Jeannie Flett never missed a beat, as Haynes discovered at dinner time when Riley knocked on the door at about 6:45 p.m. and said "Dinner is ready in the dining room."

Suspecting nothing, they followed him. Riley opened the door and a gang of people all screamed 'Surprise." It was all of his old Baldor buddies, even the McFarlands, who would be flown back on Sunday in time for John's appearance on Face the Nation. He had been regretting that he did not have much time to talk to his friends at the Friday evening White House dinner, but Jeannie had arranged for every single one to be driven up to Camp David. Haynes headed straight for Chloe DelBigio and gave her a big hug. He had never forgotten her phone call to his hotel room after his mentor Rollie Boreham died. It was a wonderful evening full of old stories and reminiscing, exactly what David and Sonja needed.

When everyone was finally heading off to get a good night's sleep, Haynes cornered McFarland, Dever and Rogers and took them into the sitting room. He had not had time to talk to John about what he was about to propose to Dever and Rogers. He got straight to the point. "You two are both retired. How would you like to get back in the saddle working for the administration?"

Dever turned serious, as he always did when things got that way, and stumbled his first words as he always did. "Weeeelll, David, what do you want us to do?"

Haynes explained the plan for the AFC and told them the plan he had recommended to Doug Snow, adding that he had been careful not to shove the two of them down Snow's throat. So he asked them to sell themselves to Snow because he really needed them around so he would have feedback from more than one person as to how things were progressing. "He knows you guys are going to communicate with me from time to time, so you have to make sure that he understands that you are working for and with him."

Rick looked towards Dever and then said, "Okay, we will talk to him on Monday."

Then John McFarland interjected, "You both understand the way this works. David cannot force Snow to hire you. You will just have to do what we've always done. Sell it."

SUNDAY, November 16, 2014, 10:15 a.m.

David and Sonja got a good night's sleep and did not wake up until 10:15 Sunday morning. By that time everyone had left, Dever and Rogers catching a lift on the flight Flett had arranged so McFarland could make his television appearance. Snow met with the two and found out that under formal business conditions, both Rogers and Dever were very serious and competent. He called Haynes afterwards at Camp David and said, "You're right, I wish I could find eight more just like them."

Haynes said, "Well why don't you ask them to help you do that."

"I already have."

"Great, you have dug the first hole for the foundation."

Director Simmons called next and said he was planning to get Herman Raines installed at the IRS first thing Monday morning. He said that he had been tipped off that the present IRS director was planning to lock himself in his office and make a scene, claiming that the new administration had no authority to fire him.

Haynes said, "Make sure you get some people over there before he arrives and have that cover-up king Mr. Magoo escorted out of the building." Haynes added, "I already discussed with the Attorney General at dinner Friday night the need to be very aggressive in pursuing criminal charges against anyone involved in targeted audits and conspiracy to cover them up. No one, I don't care if they're liberal, conservative, libertarian or communist, should be directly targeted for their ideas, beliefs or opinions. We have to send a message that anyone participating in this is going to end up in jail."

After the call, Haynes flipped on the TV to catch McFarland being interviewed. McFarland didn't need any talking points, he was a pro. Any small businessman watching was going to be energized by his remarks. John was really smart. He indicated that there would eventually be a credible, workable solution that would relieve a lot of the burden regarding employee healthcare. Small businesses had been cutting back or not hiring new employees because of the excessive cost and regulation of the health care burdens imposed on them by the Affordable Health Care Act, and McFarland understood that confidence was a huge factor for the small business community.

All the other Sunday morning TV appearances went very well. Haynes was confident that they had given the American people the impression that things were under control and the country was moving in a positive direction.

Meanwhile, Oliver West and McCormick had arrived in Kurdistan and were in intense negotiations with Kurd officials. Oliver called Haynes on a secure phone and reported that it didn't take the Kurds long to accept the proposals and conditions the Americans had laid out. "They told me to send their regards and appreciation to you." Then Oliver gave him a recap of the agreement.

"1. In exchange for a permanent military base located there, we will recognize Kurdistan as an independent country.
"2. We will train and equip their military with whatever is required.
"3. They will share oil revenues with the United States to cover the cost of our military there.

"4. When ready, Kurdish and United States forces will move south and west to retake the oilfields and cut off the jihadists' money supply, and transfer possession of the oilfields to Kurdistan.

"5. Kurdish and US forces will seize a strip of territory in northern Syria all the way to the ocean between Syria and Turkey. This will provide a supply line and also cut off the jihadist's access to Turkey. They have been using Turkey as a transit point for fighters and equipment into Syria. The Turks have been looking the other way because they want Syria's Hassad regime gone.

"6. All other options will remain open after these goals are accomplished."

When he had finished, Haynes said, "Good job, Oliver, I think it's a great plan."

Then McCormick got on and said that he wanted to bring some Kurd officials back with them to Washington to finalize the details of the new agreement.

"That's okay, but please make sure that no one sees them," Haynes said. He realized that the deal was pretty much a no-brainer for the Kurds; they had wanted their own country ever since he could remember. It was also a no-brainer for America because besides Israel, Kurdistan was practically the only place in the region that shared American values. A US presence there would calm things down and save a lot of innocent lives. He had to be very careful with Turkey's reaction. There has been, to say the least, friction between Turkey and the Kurds for years.

McCormick said, "This should have been done a long time ago."

"True, but there's no point in going there. It's like after a car accident – what if, what if, what if I had only turned right or left. That kind of thing is not going to change any of the existing circumstances. The car is still banged up. Let's not look back and let's move on from here. The blame thing is a total waste of time. They have been blaming Bush for six years and where has that got us? If our opponents want to practice it, that's their problem. We need to start getting our people in there as soon as possible after this agreement is signed. How long do you think it's going to take to train a Kurd Army?"

McCormick replied, "About six months."

Haynes said, "I was in boot camp and that only took two months so let's set a target of three months max."

McCormick said, "It's probably better if we discuss that when we get back."

Haynes said, "Okay. And congratulations."

"Thank you, Mr. Administrator."

MONDAY, November 17, 2014, 9:15 a.m.

When Haynes got back to the White House Monday morning, Jeannie told him that the Mexican President wanted to talk to him.

"Fine," said Haynes, "set up the call."

About 15 minutes later, Haynes pushed the button on his speakerphone, which he had finally figured out how to operate, and said, "Good morning, Mr. President."

President Fernandez said, "Good morning to you, Sir." He continued, "I'm not sure who I'm really supposed to talk to up there."

Haynes responded, "I'm sure you watched the Saturday press conference introducing our new cabinet and you are now talking to the person in charge."

"Very well," said Fernandez and launched into a 10 minute monologue about how the US was interfering in Mexico's internal affairs and justice system, etcetera. Haynes was thinking how much these Hispanic leaders loved to talk. In his opinion, most of them didn't do much else, especially in countries like Mexico where corruption was rampant. So Haynes just sat there patiently listening to the diatribe, rolling his eyes and silently moving his mouth in harmony with Fernandez. After Fernandez seemed to be done talking, Haynes let silence prevail for about 10 seconds. Finally Fernandez asked, "Are you still there?"

Haynes said, "Yes Sir, I am. Are you done?"

"Yes," Fernandez said, sounding perplexed.

"Mr. President, I will keep my comments short and sweet. America has been sending truckloads of money to your country over the years to prop up Mexico because you guys down there can't get your act together. You have been humiliating the country you call 'your friend' by parading our innocent Marine back and forth to that kangaroo court. My comments to you, Sir, are – 8:00 p.m. Monday the 24th of November. Mr. President, you have yourself a nice day." And Haynes hung up the phone.

Fernandez had just found out that his ambassador was not exaggerating when he had reported the tone and content of his meeting with Haynes at the White House.

David went into Rod's office and brought him up-to-date on his conversation with Fernandez. Then he asked, "What are we going to do about the Labor Relations Board?"

"I haven't really thought about that one," said Giani.

"Well," said Haynes, "there are five members on that board and almost all of them are extreme leftists. We need to get it balanced up to two business members, two labor members and one perceived independent. Business people are the ones that create the jobs. Government rules regarding union applications for unionizing companies are now heavily slanted on the side of the unions. We need more balance. Probably we should work with the Speaker and the Senate leader to see if can work on some names."

Haynes then went over to Goldstein's office to watch the opening of the stock exchange on the business channels. Goldstein had a huge smile on his face. "The futures are not too bad, considering the situation," he said. Reports were coming in on American companies that were listed on foreign exchanges and had taken a hit. Almost all of them were making a recovery.

Now Rawlston appeared on the screen, ringing the bell for the opening of the New York exchange. Traders on the floor below were applauding wildly. The Dow opened down over 300 points from when the market had shut down last week. Haynes thought this was very good considering that the world markets that had stayed open had taken huge hits. He decided to go back to his office and wait for the markets to equalize or sort themselves out.

MONDAY, November 17, 2014, 11:30 a.m.

Haynes called McCormick, McFadden, West and the CIA director to a meeting at the White House. He had questions for the CIA director about what they were doing about the terrorists who had killed the ambassador and three other Americans in Libya. The new CIA director said they were being tracked down, but he didn't say it with much enthusiasm.

Haynes made it clear that he wanted to aggressively track down as many of them as possible. "We don't want those people to think they can sit around a hotel room in Libya after they've killed four Americans," Haynes said. "And if you capture some of these folks, don't bring them to America or Guantanamo Bay. They don't observe the Geneva Convention when they conduct war and terrorism and in this case we're not going to either."

MONDAY, November 17, 2014, 1:30 p.m.

Jeannie Flett and Giani met in Haynes' office to discuss how they were going to track the progress of the administration. Haynes gave them an example of how he wanted it done. He brought out an 8 x 11 sheet of paper and showed them how, for instance, they would track Doug Snow's progress with the American Functional Charter.

Title/American Functional Charter Progress
Stage 1 / Divisions of State and Federal Only Items -Timelines

1. Selection of the remaining eight team leaders.
2. Track governors' selections of their liaison people.
3. Preliminary meetings with the state representatives to find out what objections there are and try to get them resolved.
4. Governors' summit with the Administrator and all their teams and congressional leaders.
5. Pressure to get states that have refused to attend. (Note: if they don't we are not wasting time. We will move forward without them.)

6. Congressional constitutional amendment for stage 1.
7. State approval for stage 1.

Haynes said, "I want one of these drawn up for all of the cabinet members and advisors. The three of us will monitor and coordinate the progress made or not made. We can have another meeting for review as soon as this is completed and then send them on to cabinet members and advisors and they can complete the timelines and return the copies."

MONDAY, November 17, 2014, 4:30 p.m.

The Dow opened 710 points down from its last close the week before and after a wild ride finished down 205 points. Haynes considered this very good considering recent events and the fact that it had started the day down over 710 points. He took it as a sign of recovery, and telephoned Rawlston to congratulate him. Rawlston's opinion was that the markets would stay flat for a little bit in a wait-and-see environment.

CHAPTER 18

RUSSIA REARS ITS HEAD

MONDAY, November 17, 2014, 5:00 p.m.

KT McFADDEN CAME INTO HAYNES' office and said, "I didn't want to trouble you with this before because I know you have been overwhelmed with matters, but now this is becoming urgent. The Russians have amassed troops, tanks, and armor in Eastern Ukraine. It appears as though they are planning to overrun the country."

Haynes slammed his fist down on the desk. "That's what happens when you have a bunch of Chicken Chamberlains running Western democracies, especially in America. They think by kissing that little Hitler Stalin Putin's ass it will make the world safer. Now it's clear to everyone that this kind of approach makes the world more dangerous.

"Okay, KT, let's start with this; you need to get the word out there that I am some kind of super right-wing militarist nut case. If nothing else, it will get Putin thinking twice about what he is doing. Get hold of Oliver and McCormick and bring them up-to-date. Then I need you to tell Oliver to visit Poland, Hungary, the Czech Republic and one of the Baltic States as soon as he has finished with the Kurd thing. I want Oliver to make arrangements with the Czechs to install those nuclear weapons that we planned to put in there years ago as soon as possible, and to make it public that these weapons will be aimed at both Iran and Russia so that Putin will understand that we are not screwing around.

"After that I want him to fly to Germany, because it's one of the three biggest members of NATO. Tell them in no uncertain terms that this is their Europe, not ours, and if they're not prepared to man up and defend it, don't expect us to do any different. We need mostly European NATO troops to move their locations at least as far as the Eastern sectors of Poland and Hungary. We need to contact the French President, the English Prime Minister, the German Chancellor and the top NATO commander to have an emergency summit with Oliver in Germany. The objective is to make it clear that we are united and any further Russian aggression will not go unchecked. I want this announced at an emergency summit and I want them, at the end, to be standing in front of cameras looking united. Tell all these European socialists that they have to start manning up because the United States is no longer going to be alone defending their freedom, whatever is left of it. Ask Oliver if he would like the former Secretary of Defence to accompany him. Since the schedule is real tight he may want Leo Fennett to take his place in one of those countries after he has briefed him.

"At the right time, I want the Press Secretary to announce Oliver's visit and stress that the administration is not going to allow a repeat of 1939 by letting that little Stalin run amok; we've seen that movie before. Again at the right time, I will go before the microphones in the pressroom and announce that the Cold War has returned with a vengeance and that the Russians can no longer be trusted and are dangerous evil aggressors. I will state that they have broken their commitment not to interfere in or invade the Ukraine in exchange for the Ukraine removing nuclear weapons from its territory, just like Hitler did in the 1930s. Maybe the timing should be right after Oliver gets back from Europe.

"Russians will no longer be able to visit the USA without special visas. This is not going to make some of the Russian elite very happy with Putin. Many of them have property in the USA, especially in South Florida."

TUESDAY, November 18, 2014, 11.05 a.m.

Haynes received his first reply concerning his mandate to cabinet secretaries to make spending cuts channeled through Levers budget committee.

This one came from Lever himself. He wanted to eliminate the penny and change the nickel. He said each penny cost 1.06 cents to produce and too many end up in coin collection jars in American homes. The nickel also cost more than its value to produce. He produced staggering cost-saving examples that would save the Mint and taxpayers billions. His proposal was first to eliminate the penny. He would stop producing pennies immediately. Give everyone a year to cash pennies in. After that they would be worthless. Second was to use the same metal material used to make pennies to produce five cent pieces in the same size and format that would result in the cost of this new so-called nickel become less than its street value.

He was also looking into cost savings feasibility if any to replace the dollar bill with a coin. All this was already in place in many countries around the world. Haynes thought it was a great idea and gave the go-ahead for the ONE and FIVE cent pieces.

TUESDAY, November 18, 2014, 11:30 a.m.

Haynes had asked Flett to organize a lunch meeting with the congressional majority leaders so he could get a feel for their reactions to the administration's plans. Besides Haynes, McFarland, Florio, Giani and Hoffman were there.

It became clear that the congressional folks liked having a say concerning new Attorney Generals. They also liked that the onus would be on the federal bureaucracies and agencies to resubmit any new regulations through Congress. They liked the idea that the ball was in the bureaucrats' court, so that they would not themselves have to try and decipher unnecessary regulations, which could take years and years while the bureaucrats stonewalled them.

But they were a little nervous about the outright closure of federal departments like education, health and human services, housing and labor. They were worried about having too many federal employees out on the street. Haynes dampened their concern somewhat by saying that the administration was encouraging the states to give employment priority to former federal employees who were willing to relocate from Washington.

The minority leaders didn't show up for the meeting. The new minority leaders - who Haynes described as Stonewall Henry Weed and his left coast counterpart Nellie Rossi – were ranting and raving that the whole thing was illegal and they didn't consider Haynes or the new cabinet legitimate. This was fine with the people in the new administration because they didn't really want to deal with them anyway. They were rigid ideologues and would only waste time. The administration would try to communicate with moderate Democrats who wanted the country to progress.

Haynes thought that Senate rules were goofy anyway and never could understand how Senator Weed could prevent proposed legislation from coming to the Senate floor. In any case, the administration could now use some of these rules to its advantage.

A few of the new Senators elect were at the meeting. Senator Tim Coleman was also there. He was an expert on government waste, and had catalogued where it all went. Congressman Paul Wright also came. Haynes appreciated that he had more experience and was more knowledgeable than anyone in Congress about the details of the federal budget. Haynes made sure that his new budget director Leever became well acquainted with Coleman and Wright. He wanted the three of them to work closely together to eliminate government duplication and waste.

Everyone at the meeting agreed to change the Senate rules to a 50+1 vote majority and to make it permanent; this item would be included in the first constitutional amendment proposal. No one stated but it was made clear indirectly that if there was no cooperation on these principal proposals, the administration would move unilaterally to put them into place.

Now it was crunch time. Haynes addressed the Speaker and said, "I want the house to pass a declaration of war against jihadist terrorists." He reiterated, "Make it clear who this war is against in the declaration - Islamic Jihadist Terrorists. We are not fighting a specific country or any specific army therefore rules of the Geneva convention in this case don't apply. Make sure that the declaration states FOREIGN and DOMESTIC. It doesn't have to be complicated. And I believe it should be at the very least for six years. I don't think anyone can argue that we have been at war with these people since 9/11. It is time that we have an official declaration by the Congress. The administration needs to react quickly to any threats and would appreciate the support of the Congress."

Haynes knew that according to the Constitution, the newly elected senators would not be taking their seats before noon of January 3, 2015. Since the Speaker already had a majority, he asked him to pass the legislation before the Thanksgiving break and not forward it to the Senate until January 4, 2015 when the new majority would be seated. The Speaker did not commit. He said he was personally in favor of it but would have to convene with his caucus and other members.

Haynes insisted that the declaration should contain broad emergency powers to address the domestic threat from jihadists within US borders, including the right to revoke passports, and arrest and deport.

Haynes also insisted that they have a bill passed and ready to be forwarded to the Senate the week of January 3rd restoring the military budget to at least what the present administration perceived was adequate for national security requirements. McCormick's deputies had prepared a detailed list of appropriations the military required immediately. The Speaker said he was in favor but would have to look at the details in the report.

Haynes repeated several times that they had opportunities available for the next two years and they didn't have time to waste on prolonged debates if it made more sense to move.

Haynes did not want to discuss Social Security matters at the meeting, especially since it would probably remain in the federal domain. They had enough on their plate for the short-term. The meeting was productive and went past 3 o'clock in the afternoon. The administration had prepared its proposals well and now the ball was in the congressional court. Haynes again insisted that he expected them to move quickly. The Speaker said he thought he could pass the military appropriations bill before the Thanksgiving break, but the AFC constitutional amendment would have to wait until after Thanksgiving.

What Haynes didn't know was that McCormick had a long-term strategy. He had already talked to the Speaker and they had agreed that they would slip something hardly noticeable into the first constitutional bill, stating that a person did not have to be born in the USA to become President. This would be a one-time only resolution with a time limitation expiring in January of 2017, the same day a new president would be sworn in.

TUESDAY, November 18, 2014, 2:00 p.m.

Fortunately for the interim administration, the Chamber of Commerce was holding its annual meeting in Washington, DC at the Marriott that week. This gathering of companies both small and large had the ability to influence the success of the interim government in several areas. Secretary of Commerce McFarland requested the opportunity to speak to the group and make them aware of the economic direction of the interim government. His goal was to help everyone become comfortable enough with the new policies being implemented that they would start investing in the United States, something that they had been unwilling to do over the previous six years. This was also a great opportunity to get feedback on the upcoming changes and additional ideas.

After a nice introduction including being referred to as "one of us" because of a career culminating as chairman of the board of a large industrial company, McFarland took the podium.

"Good afternoon, everyone. Thank you so much for the opportunity to address this important group of businessmen and businesswomen who can have such a big impact on the prosperity of our country. I, like the new Administrator, like to listen more than talk, so my comments will be short and to the point to allow plenty of time for your feedback and comments.

"Your interim government has established a number of key goals to promote the success and prosperity of the private sector. We believe that your success will lead to millions of new jobs and great new innovations. We have a short period of two years to implement our new strategy. We hope you will believe in what we are doing and not take a wait-and-see attitude. We are in a hurry to get this country on the right track and ask you to move quickly with us.

"An important part of our strategy is to get people back to work in the private sector and not in government. We want smaller, more effective government and we believe that the new American Functional Charter, or AFC, will accomplish this. When Americans have jobs they feel better about themselves, become customers, are less of a burden on government budgets, and become positive role models for the younger generation. We have begun to put policies in place to make the USA the best place in the world to do business. We want this to be the best place to manufacture, the best place to invent, and the best place to start or headquarter a company. We will move quickly, in the next month, to reform the tax code for companies. It will be simplified and rates will be reduced so companies from all over the world will look to our country as the best place to do business.

"All regulatory agencies except for the FAA and the FDA are canceled effective as of now. That would include the NLRB. New IRS tax laws will supersede any preceding tax laws. If government bureaucrats think there are essential regulations that need to be reinstated, they must be passed by the Congress."

Then McFarland said something unusual. "If some federal government inspector enters your premises to harass you, just remind him or her that all federal government regulations with the exception of the aforementioned are no longer in effect, and have them gently but firmly escorted off your property."

The crowd jumped to their feet and applauded.

"Incentives for USA companies to export to other countries will be implemented where they do not violate free trade agreements. Our goal is fair trade. We will begin immediately negotiating new free trade agreements with our trading partners. We will also begin implementing fair trade policies. If a country inhibits the importation of our products, they will be met with the same treatment here. Fair and free trade is the goal. We will not take advantage of others or allow ourselves to be taken advantage of. Currency manipulation will not be tolerated and will be reflected by tariff rates. Currency values must be established by the free market. We believe our policies will promote the creation of millions of jobs in the USA. We believe our policies will drive an improved economy globally and will be the roadmap for other countries whose people seek better job conditions and prosperity for themselves. We believe our policies will result in lower government deficits. We believe our policies will promote better environmental policies and practices globally. In short, we believe these policies will help create a better world for us all. Thank you for your attention, and so now let's open things up to your ideas, questions and thoughts."

The room was buzzing with hope and enthusiasm for the administration's new initiatives. McFarland's speech was sunshine and a breath of fresh air and the opposite of the anti-business rhetoric that they had been hearing for the last six years.

McFarland's biggest challenge was answering their questions concerning the health care burden on businesses. The business community agreed unanimously that the Affordable Health Care Act was a job killer. Business people were spending their time, if not cutting back employees, then cutting back hours to get around the Act's rules.

McFarland informed the group that the Act would be scrapped totally and that the AFC charter would be implemented as soon as possible; the effect would be to decentralize health care to the states. McFarland admitted that there would be some confusion in the interim but tried to assure them that the new administration was moving as quickly as possible to bring clarity to healthcare so that businesses would know what they were dealing with and be able to move forward. He pointed out that former governor Ronson had a reputation for toughness and no nonsense. He said he was very aware of the negative impact that the current situation was having on jobs. "Initiatives are underway as we speak to rectify this as soon as possible," he concluded.

WEDNESDAY, November 19, 2014, 10:00 a.m.

Rogers and Dever had stayed on in Washington and were working in a corner office at the White House. This morning, Haynes had scheduled a meeting with the two as well as Snow and Giani. Snow had made fast progress; he had already assembled the 10 teams that would be responsible for negotiating the American Functional Charter, each team dealing with five states. He had the ten teams laid out on separate pages of a flip chart at the front of the room.

Team One, including North and South Carolina, Georgia, Florida and Alabama, would be led by Rogers. Dever had Team Two, with Tennessee, Arkansas, Mississippi, Louisiana and Texas. The next eight pages showed the remaining 40 states broken into groups of five, but none of these had yet been assigned team leaders.

"Very impressive." said Haynes. "When are you going to get the rest of the team leaders on board?"

Snow replied, "Hopefully by next week."

Then Dever said, "Rick and I have already contacted all the governors in our states. Doug has agreed that Rick will operate out of Greensboro and I will operate out of Nashville. By the way, David, are we on the government payroll and if so how do we get paid?"

Haynes sat back in his chair and smiled, "I've never really thought about that until now. I don't have a clue, but I'll find out. But, on another note, who is going to liaise with Capitol Hill?"

Doug said, "I'll take care of that."

Haynes said, "I've received a proposal from our legal people on the wording of the constitutional amendment with regard to the AFC. Jesus, Doug, they sent me a book and I don't know what language it's in. They say it's in English. I can't understand a damn thing. Tell these overeducated morons that I'm stupid and I don't understand what they're writing so have them write it in simple English so I and the rest of the American people can understand it. Right now it's written so that down the road lawyers can sit and argue over what's in it. If they're so damn smart and well-educated no one should have to argue about what's in it! Besides, the Congress and the Senate will spend endless hours debating the language, which is another waste of time. It's hard enough to spend time debating over a one or two page document. So I have reduced all this bullshit down to one piece of paper."

Haynes passed out the sheet to everyone. "It starts off with the 'The American Functional Charter Constitutional Amendment.'

"The purpose of this amendment is to clearly define and separate governmental/departmental and agency responsibilities by two levels of government, the federal government and the state governments. The first part of the amendment defines sole responsibility for each level of government by using the word ONLY. The word ONLY as referred to in this charter means that only one level of government has the sole autonomy to manage the departments or agencies listed below."

The rest of Haynes' page had a line down the middle. On the left, under the heading 'Federal Only,' was a list of the sole responsibilities of the federal government, as he had proposed in previous meetings. On the right was 'State Only,' with a list of the sole responsibilities for state governments. "Tell these people if they can't write this stuff in plain English, we will get someone who can."

WEDNESDAY, November 19, 2014, 1:30 p.m.

After lunch, Haynes called Henry Rawlston and Giani into his office. Haynes wanted Rawlston to gather a team of negotiators to sell the post office to private enterprise. "The most likely buyers would be UPS, Federal Express or similar companies," he said. He said he would like to sell the post office to big corporations involved in the delivery business.

Haynes also told Rawlston that the government needed to get rid of Fannie Mae and Freddie Mac and get mortgages back where they belonged, in the private sector. There was a perception in America that the banks were responsible for the fiscal disaster in 2008. Haynes thought that the primary culprit was government involvement in something that should be the responsibility of the private sector. The primary blame belonged to the government, which had set up conditions for the private sector to run amok. He believed the government should be responsible only for making and enforcing the umbrella laws regulating the operation of banks and investment houses.

Then he gave Rawlston another suggestion, aware that it would possibly be perceived as way out there. He wanted Rawlston to investigate the possibility of having the FDIC, the federal watchdog for financial institutions, run by a private company under the direction of the Treasury Secretary. As far as he was concerned, the FDIC was just a bunch of incompetent bureaucrats that had allowed Bernie Madoff and people of his ilk to commit criminal acts and steal investors' money right out from under their noses; they had been warned by outsiders on many occasions and failed to do anything. There were reports of employees at that agency watching pornography on their computers and remaining on the government payrolls. This would never be tolerated in the private sector.

THURSDAY, November 20, 2014, 9:00 a.m.

Haynes had had dinner with Rogers and Dever on Wednesday evening and the two were now headed back to Greensboro and Nashville to get the constitutional effort underway. He was now in a meeting with Giani and some interns. They wanted him to look over a two-page document that would be presented to the Speaker of the House, Snow and the Senate Leader. Haynes read it, eliminated a few clauses and made some corrections. Then he looked at the interns and said, "Did any of you guys ever see the movie *Three Days of the Condor?*"

Only one had seen it, so he said, "Do you remember the scene between Cliff Robertson and John Houseman, who was playing the head of the CIA in the movie? They were sitting waiting for the Condor to call, with computers all around them reflecting the complexity of the modern era and Robertson said, 'You were in the intelligence network during the Second World War before it became the CIA. You must miss that?'

Houseman looked at him and said, 'What I miss is the clarity'."

Haynes let that sink in for a second, and then said, "A lot more of these papers will have to be written before we are done, so let's try and do it with clarity, shall we? This new one you have written I think is very good."

CHAPTER 19

REPORT FROM THE MIDEAST AND OTHER HOTSPOTS

THURSDAY, November 20, 2014, 11:00 a.m.

McCORMICK WAS FINALLY BACK FROM his Mideast trip so KT McFadden, Giani and Haynes took the helicopter over to the Pentagon to have a luncheon meeting with him and some Kurdish representatives. Haynes did not want the Kurds spotted anywhere near the White House for now.

A couple of the Kurds spoke English, but they had brought along translators too. McCormick laid out the proposed agreement. He had a version in English and one in Kurdish. The agreement covered the basic points McCormick had described.

1. The Kurds would allow a permanent American military base within their territory.
2. In exchange for the base, America would recognize Kurdistan as an independent country.
3. The US would station about 10,000 military personnel in the country, and would also install an Air Force base.
4. Americans would train and equip a new Kurdish military. The training target deadline was two to three months. The Kurds would eventually pay for the military equipment.
5. The northern border between what are now Iraq and the Kurdish territory will be defined as the new Kurdistan border.

6. A joint Kurd, American military offensive will be launched southbound to occupy some of the oilfields to take away funding from the Moslem jihadists. Oil revenues would now be Kurdistan's, a percentage of which would be used to pay for the presence of the American military base.
7. A corridor between northern Syria and the Turkish border will be occupied by American and Kurdish forces to cut off any access by the jihadists to Turkey. Supplies and recruits will not be able to enter Syria or Iraq from Turkey. This corridor will extend all the way to the water on the west to give the Kurds sea access and the corridor could be used for a future pipeline.
8. Modifications to this agreement could be made from time to time if both parties agreed.

Haynes, Giani and McFadden read the agreement carefully and Haynes said, "This looks very good, Jim."

"It's what you asked for and a little bit more, Mr. Administrator. We are all ready to sign," McCormick said, holding out a pen.

Arrangements had already been made to fly the Kurds back home along with a group of American military officers to start preparations based on the agreement they had just signed.

"The Turks are going to yell and scream," McFadden observed.

"So be it," said Haynes. "They were not being that helpful; they were allowing jihadists to pass through their country into Syria." As far as Haynes was concerned the Turks weren't much different from the Pakistanis.

After the meeting, Haynes cornered Oliver West and asked him, "What are we going to do about that Pakistani Doctor that helped us get bin Laden? Dr. Shakil Afridi is rotting in a Pakistani prison for helping us and we are, doing practically nothing to get him out."

West replied, "I have been so busy, I haven't given it much thought."

Haynes said "Bribe somebody, pay somebody, do something to get Dr. Afridi and his family out of there. If that doesn't work then threaten to cut off American aid." Haynes continued, "Why don't you contact Leo Fennet and send him to Europe as a special emissary to the Secretary of State?

Fennet is well respected by the Europeans and we need to get this missile treaty back in place and get weapons in the hands of the Ukrainians."

Oliver looked at Haynes and said, "Yeah, good idea, I'm going to need some high-level help."

Haynes then approached General McCormick and said, "Jim, I'm curious. What's the deal with the football?" He had noticed McCormick had the famous briefcase containing the nuclear trigger codes in case of a nuclear war. It normally accompanied the president everywhere he went.

McCormick replied, "I've got it and I intend to keep it for the time being."

That was fine with Haynes. He really didn't want the responsibility anyway, and besides McCormick was a highly responsible individual and understood the implications far better than Haynes.

McCormick said, "I've contacted the families of some of the victims of the Fort Hood massacre and informed them that we are changing the designation to a terrorist attack and they will be eligible for compensation."

"Good." said Haynes. "I don't want to ever hear that damn workplace violence thing again."

When Haynes returned to the White House he told Jeannie Flett to add the Pakistani doctor's release to Oliver West's list of goals. Flett said that the Attorney General had called to confirm that all federal charges had been dropped against the author of *America*, Mr. D'Souza, and that he was reviewing charges against former CIA agents. Further, he and McCormick had agreed that the Fort Hood Massacre would now be formally labeled a terrorist attack.

FRIDAY, November 21, 2014, 10:00 a.m.

Next was Haynes' meeting with David Rockman, who had served as budget director in previous administrations. Haynes wanted Rockman to do an analysis of Social Security. As far as Haynes was concerned, the people's money was being swallowed up and disappearing into a hole called the federal budget. He wanted Rockman to do several things.

1. An actuarial analysis of what the total value of the Social Security fund would be if it had been invested in a combination of bonds, market funds and other investments – like a normal, relatively conservative portfolio – and kept in a separate fund away from politicians and the government.
2. Determine the present value of the Social Security fund that had been swallowed up by a practically bankrupt federal government. Haynes wanted to know how much the government owed the Social Security fund.
3. Provide a report on how the government had mismanaged the fund.
4. Assess how an increase in the retirement age would change the composition of the fund.
5. Appraise the successful Social Security plans of some countries such as Chile and Singapore.

"Once we have your report, we can see if the AARP and similar organizations have the balls to print an article on it," Haynes said. "We will need this kind of information to sell it to the American people."

Homeland Security Secretary Kyling phoned Haynes just before lunch to inform him that physical readjustments were being made at the Mexican border crossing south of San Diego. He reported that they were using a large crane to move cement pylons into position so that they would dramatically slow processing volume. "The Mexicans asked the customs director at the border crossing what we were doing and he told them it was none of their business," he said. Kyling said the crane stood out like a sore thumb so the Mexicans couldn't miss that something was up.

David had lunch with Rod so they could bring each other up-to-date and then Haynes and Sonja headed up to Camp David for the weekend.

SATURDAY, November 22, 2014, 10:10 p.m.

Haynes was sitting in the main cabin at Camp David, thinking about one of his favorite presidents, Jack Kennedy. It was on this day in 1963 that Kennedy was assassinated. Anyone who was of age then still remembers where they were when they heard the news, and Haynes had vivid memories of that day. He had been working at a flight simulator factory in Montreal. His thoughts were interrupted when he was asked if he could take a phone call from the Mexican Ambassador. "What can I do for you today, Mr. Ambassador?"

Ambassador Suarez said, "We have been receiving reports that there is some activity taking place at the border crossing south of San Diego. It appears as though you are planning to slow down or block the crossing completely. Does this have anything to do with our discussion last week?"

"Mr. Ambassador," said Haynes, "I indicated to you in that meeting that I had two options. One was to congratulate President Fernandez or the Mexican courts for having released our Marine. As far as I'm concerned you have had more than ample time to get something done that should have been done long ago. You also indicated in our meeting at the White House that you were planning to release him anyway. I am not looking forward to exercising the second option, so please don't put me in a position where I have to. As for us, Mr. Ambassador, our position is set. Now Sir, I am asking, what are your courts or your government going to do?"

Suarez said, "Will you be available to receive another phone call today?"

"I will be looking forward to any further communication today." Haynes put emphasis on the word today.

SATURDAY, November 22, 2014, 2:35 p.m.

Suarez called back an hour later. "Mr. Administrator, we have communicated with the judge in this case, and it seems he is prepared to pardon the Marine in question on the basis that his act was not intentional. It appears that he will be back in court on Monday or the latest Tuesday and it is possible that our courts may want to release him, but that of course will be up to the judge."

Haynes laughed to himself but kept his voice serious. "You really can't interfere with your courts. You must let your justice system run its course.

I am sure that your government and ours would like to see all this come to a happy conclusion." Haynes continued, "I will be in the White House swimming pool at 8:30 Wednesday morning on November 26. What will you be doing, Mr. Ambassador?"

"I will be having a peaceful breakfast with my family."

Haynes said, "I'm sure that your government encourages you to have peaceful breakfasts with your family. Thank you for calling, Mr. Ambassador." Haynes felt like his diplomatic nuance was improving. He had given them a way out to allow them to save face and had compromised by extending the deadline to Wednesday.

Haynes immediately called Ray Kyling and told him to halt any further movement at the border but to leave the crane where it is.

MONDAY, November 24, 2014, 11:36 a.m.

Energy Secretary Hoffman was holding a press conference to announce that the US would finally be moving ahead with the Keystone pipeline. He also announced that hearings and negotiations would start as soon as possible to set up an infrastructure for the export of liquid natural gas. Relief would also be forthcoming for the coal companies, which had already made great progress in cleaning up their industry. Hoffman stressed that the US needed to utilize all forms of energy for the short and medium terms to keep costs in check for the American people. He also stressed that emphasis would be put on environmentally friendly sources of energy and that it was even possible to improve their outputs.

MONDAY, November 24, 2014, 9:30 a.m. Pacific Time

The Monday television reports showed US Marine Sergeant Bristol being driven to another court hearing. Forty minutes later, Sgt. Bristol's Mexican defense attorney announced that the judge had decided the Sergeant's actions at the Mexican border had been unintentional and had shown leniency. He sentenced him to time served and released him into the custody of his attorney, who delivered him to US officials.

An hour later, Press Secretary Goldstein reported the news to the media and thanked the Mexican court system and President Fernandez for bringing the incident to an end and allowing Sergeant Bristol to be reunited with his family. Mexican Ambassador Suarez dropped by the White House for lunch with Haynes. This time the meeting was more relaxed and they talked mostly about golf.

TUESDAY, November 25, 2014

Early afternoon in Germany, Oliver and the Supreme Commander of NATO Forces in Europe gave a news conference in Bonn, announcing that Russian aggression against any NATO country would be interpreted as an attack on all NATO members. Haynes watched the conference from Washington, and was pleased to see the presence of heads of state from France, Germany and Britain, a show of unity that would send a message to 'Little Stalin.'

When the news conference was over, Haynes made his own announcement from the pressroom. The Cold War with Russia had resumed with abandon, he said, as a result of Little's Stalin's behavior. He emphasized the 'Little Stalin.' He wanted to make it clear that Putin had not kept his word on the Ukraine and could no longer be trusted. As a result, all treaties with Russia were in jeopardy. Then he addressed what he hoped would be the Russian people directly. He told them that their elitist leaders were nothing but a bunch of thugs stealing their money and it was time for them to wake up and get rid of them. Haynes made sure that his tone and his body language showed that the West was now united and would act if necessary to defend European freedom.

Haynes knew that a two-by-four to the head was the only thing that the oppressionist Russian leaders would understand. He recalled how the Russians had bribed the referees to call penalties on Canada's national hockey team during the 1972 Russia/Canada hockey series. They had also arranged to have the phones ring in the players' rooms at all hours of the night to disrupt their sleep. The communists had absolutely no sense of fair play.

Within minutes of his comments, the Russian ambassador called to try to arrange a meeting with Haynes. He was informed that Haynes was too busy organizing the deployment of NATO forces in Europe.

TUESDAY, November 25, 2014 - Washington

The House of Representatives passed the administration's military appropriations bill with very few changes to McCormick's original proposal. It also passed a declaration of war against jihadist terrorists. Neither bill was forwarded to the Senate just yet. Both the House Majority leader and Haynes knew that if they were forwarded, Stonewall Weed would refuse to bring them to a vote. Weed was known around Washington as the roach motel – bills came in but never got out. They would wait until January 5, 2015, the first working Monday after all members of the new Senate majority officially took their seats. But at least the administration now had approval of the House.

THURSDAY, November 27, 2014, 4:00 p.m.

McCormick called Haynes to report that there were now 3,000 military personnel in Kurdistan setting up the infrastructure to support 10,000 more. Meanwhile, the Air Force had begun construction of their air base. He also reported that the Kurds had made an unusual move in openly requesting that their military be put under the command of US forces.

Despite some objections, Haynes had allowed the director of the Department of Veterans Affairs to stay on, even though he had been appointed by the previous administration. Haynes felt he was trying his best do a good job, especially as he had just announced that veterans would be issued vouchers so that they could use non-VA hospitals for treatment – a temporary measure to get rid of the logjam until the VA got its act together.

Haynes called the VA director to make him understand that the Constitution was suspended and as far as Haynes was concerned, so were any work-related arrangements with VA employees. Therefore it was completely unacceptable that incompetent employees – or as the director put it, employees who had violated the VA's values – were on paid leave at the same time as some veterans were experiencing long delays in treatment. Haynes told him to fire anyone in this category immediately. "If they don't like it, let them stand in line and sue just like the veterans had to stand in line," he said. "The one thing I am not going to tolerate is the mistreatment of our veteran heroes, period!" The Director could tell that Haynes was sincerely very angry, but at least he had the support of the Administrator concerning firings.

While he was on a roll, Haynes told Flett to inform all agencies that anyone on paid leave for wrongdoing was to be terminated immediately with no paid leave.

TUESDAY, December 2, 2014, 8:00 a.m.

McCormick asked Haynes, Giani, West, General Trais, McFadden and other military planners to meet him in the situation room to plan the action for Kurdistan. He said they would be ready to go sometime in mid-January. Haynes asked, "How many Moslem jihadists do you think there are in Syria and Iraq?"

"We are not really sure," said McCormick, "but estimates are somewhere in the area of 10,000."

West intervened, "From the reports I've been getting it could be anywhere up to 30,000."

Haynes said, "It looks like there is really no way of knowing exactly how many we're facing, so why don't we just assume 40,000 to be on the safe side."

McCormick said, "That is going to change the plan dramatically."

"We have to rethink what our objectives are here," said Haynes. "I know my first instinct was to secure a Kurd base and an ally and then move south to the oilfields to redefine Kurdistan's new borders. On second thought, these jihadists are increasing their numbers dramatically and we cannot just leave them there slaughtering innocent people and free to develop a caliphate or a country that will turn into a terrorist training ground. If we don't clean them out now, we will be fighting them in that area for the next 50 years. America has been fighting these half wars since Truman fired MacArthur in Korea and left a brutal dictator in place in northern Korea. Now the North Koreans have been suffering and starving to death for over 50 years. And they have nuclear weapons. If we are going to do this, I personally don't want it to be a half war. We need to retake Iraq and occupy parts of northern Syria and this time we're going to stay."

There was a brief silence and then McCormick said to the room, "Would you excuse us for a minute, I need to have a conversation with the Administrator outside."

McCormick brought Trais with him. McCormick said, "When did you come to these conclusions concerning expanding the war further south than the oilfields?"

"Actually, since yesterday when I knew this planning meeting was going to happen."

"Well," McCormick said "You could have given me a heads' up."

"Sorry," said Haynes, "It wasn't intentional."

"I understand," said McCormick, "and I don't necessarily disagree with the plan. Half measures are not going to work with these fanatics. What I need to know from you, Mr. Administrator, is what is going to happen when this battle is over? What do you want to do?"

Haynes said, "The Sunnis and Shias are never going to get along, so what I would like to do is put a line across southern Iraq to separate the south, which is Shia country, from the middle section, which is predominantly Sunni. And then another line further north to separate the Sunnis from the Kurds. The north will become Kurdistan. And this time we are going to stay there in Kurdistan, close to any potential trouble, until we are absolutely 100% sure that the place is stable. We will leave a permanent military base in Kurdistan. I wouldn't say this 'would have, could have, should have' stuff in public but we should have never left Iraq in the first place. But let's not waste our time with that, we have to deal with the situation as it exists right now. Let's also make it clear that any Iranian military presence including advisors any place in Iraq will be dealt with militarily. Any loss of American life resulting from actions relating to Iran, they are going to lose an installation in their own country. I've had enough of those terrorists from Iran indirectly killing our people."

Haynes looked at Trais and said, "What do you think General? You know the place like the back of your hand."

Trais said, "Well, I probably would not have agreed with this two years ago but if we leave Iraq in one piece, the secular divisions will continue. If the Sunnis and the Shias have control of their own territories it will relieve a lot of the tension and disputes. The problem I see is that there will be some Shias left living in Sunni territory and vice versa. And what about the Turks?"

Haynes replied, "Their objectives are different than ours. They do not want the establishment of a Kurdish state. If they were encouraged to enter the fray, that means they will be going into northern Syria and maybe even parts of Kurdistan. With them there, it would be hard for us to establish the corridor between Turkey and Syria to the Mediterranean that has to become part of the new Kurdistan. Where we are in agreement with the Turks is they want to get rid of Hassad and the jihadists. But getting the Turks involved would create more problems than it's worth. Besides, for a so-called ally, they have not really been very helpful. They didn't even let us use their country for a staging ground for the first invasion of Iraq."

McCormick said, "Maybe we should adjourn the meeting and reassess the situation and the plan, then reconvene next Tuesday."

"Jim, why don't we go back inside and you will announce this meeting is terminated and that we have to make adjustments to the plan," agreed Haynes, wanting to make sure McCormick did not lose face.

THURSDAY, December 4, 2014, 9:15 a.m.

Haynes heard from Doug Snow that he now had all his ten team leaders in place to start negotiations with the states on the AFC.

FRIDAY, December 5, 2014, 8:00 a.m.

The meeting on Kurdistan and Iraq reconvened earlier than planned, with Haynes, Giani, West, Mcfadden, McCormick, Trais and the military planners all in attendance. This time Trais would present the new plan. By now West, Giani and Haynes had managed, with Oliver's approval, to convince former Secretary of Defense Leo Fennet to get back in the saddle as European and NATO liaison. Leo had the respect of the US's NATO allies in Europe and had been an asset at the European Summit. His job would be to continue to make sure that European NATO allies followed through on their military commitments.

Trais was now personally confident that the US was committed to the entire plan all the way through to keeping some forces in Iraq for the duration. One hand would not be tied behind his back as it had been before. His mandate was clear, the plan was clear and he could proceed with confidence.

Trais said, "I am very pleased that General McCormick has asked me to be the commander of this operation. We think the best approach is to divide our strategy in two. The first is to execute our original plan to expand Kurd territory further south. Our second objectives are northern Syria and Iraq. The reason for this," said Trais, "is that we don't yet have enough forces to achieve our second objective but we will have enough to achieve the first by January 21, when we will have 20,000 US troops and 8,000 Kurd troops. We will need time to increase these numbers before we can proceed to the second objective. Our first objective will be called Operation Leatherneck. I am not going to go into extreme detail here but I will lay out our basic plan and objectives.

"Number one: we will attack south from Kurdistan and completely surround the Syrian town of Kobani. Two: Kurd forces will enter Kobani, with air support, and annihilate the jihadists in the city while forces surrounding the city will cut off their escape. Three: the night before, we will drop Special Forces in and around the nearest oil fields south of Kurdistan. Their objective will be to gain control of the oilfields, intact if possible. We will have oilfield fire control specialists on the ready in Kurdistan in case they might set fire to them as Saddam did in Kuwait.

"Step four: As soon as the battles for control of the oilfields commence, we will send helicopters in with reinforcements to join the battle. We want to take them by surprise. Sending helicopters south too early would tip the defenders off that we are coming so we will send in helicopter reinforcements only after the battles start. Five: a tank and armored brigade will move westbound and surround the city of Mosul.

"Six: The remaining forces will push south from the Syrian border across to the Iranian border at a fast rate to relieve our special forces who by now, we hope, will be occupying the oilfields and surrounding areas. Seven: We will surround the cities of Kirkuk and Tikrit in the south. How we clear the cities of jihadists will be determined after an analysis of what we are faced with in each case. We will take our time and develop a plan for each case.

"Phase eight of Operation Leatherneck will be to clean up and rid the new occupied territory of jihadists. Eventually we will have to occupy a corridor between the Turkish border and northern Syria all the way to the Mediterranean, which will become new Kurd territory.

"The second part of the plan will be called Operation Retake. As step one, we will increase our strength up to 50,000 including coalition partners. We think the Kurds by then will have 10,000 of their own people trained and ready to go. Two: We will reinforce our newly occupied areas in the north along the line just south of Tikrit.

"As step three," Trais continued, "I will seek to contact the Sunni leaders that I know personally to see if they are interested in helping rid their territory of jihadists. I will make it clear to the Sunnis that the line just south of Tikrit will be the new territorial border for the new country of Kurdistan. I will explain how we are prepared to establish a Sunni country and a Shia country in the South. I will tell the Sunnis that we are not really all that concerned about what the Shias think because they have set up this situation by practically excluding Sunni participation in the new Iraqi government; plus the Shias are aligned with Iran, which is our enemy and an enemy of the Sunnis.

"There will be no great urgency in launching Operation Retake. It may not even be necessary. That will depend on how quickly the territory taken is rid of jihadists and stability is restored. We'll wait and see, mainly to see how the Sunnis react.

"Secretary West has agreed that right after our launch of phase one of Operation Leatherneck, he will visit various Arab countries in the Middle East to try to convince them to persuade Hassad to leave Syria. He does not want to do that any sooner for fear that some of them will tip off the opposition of our forthcoming offensive. If Hassad leaves, then our coalition forces can move in and finally provide Syria was some peace and stability. If not, we will move anyway because we do not want to leave any place for these jihadists to escape to and start up again – at least not in this region. Are there any questions?"

"Will you take part in the political negotiations with Iraqi factions? You, General, have extensive contacts on both sides."

"If I am given authorization," replied Trais.

Haynes glanced to his right at McCormick, then back to Trais and said, "You will have it, General. More than that, I would like you to head up these negotiations."

Haynes added, "We don't really want to reload Guantánamo Bay with more prisoners. All these jihadists want to do is to kill anybody that does not agree with their twisted definition of the Koran, and that includes a lot of fellow Moslems and it certainly includes all of us. We are not going to change their minds or convert them so just kill those butchers of babies and innocent people and the rest you can turn over to the Kurds.

"And General Trais, I want you to listen very carefully to what I am saying here. When we left Iraq with no residual forces, we left military equipment in the hands of the mostly Shia Iraqi Army. When faced with the jihadist threat, they ran like a bunch of chickens and left the military hardware in the hands of the jihadists. If and when the Sunnis decide they want to fight, tanks and heavy armor will not be part of the equipment we supply them. I would like the CIA officer in charge of terrorist interrogations during the Bush administration to join you in Kurdistan and head up the interrogation team. We need to be keeping a lookout for any of these captured jihadists carrying foreign passports, especially US passports. They should be turned over to the CIA." Haynes then whispered to McCormick who was sitting beside him, "General McCormick, why don't you tell the room it's a go."

FRIDAY, December 5, 2014, 1:30 p.m.

Haynes, West, McFadden and Fennet were on a secure phone with Canada's Prime Minister Harris. The Canadians had endured two terrorist attacks in the month of October. The first one was in Quebec, where a domestic jihadist sympathizer had run over two Canadian soldiers, killing one. He was subsequently shot and killed by police officers. The second attack took place in the Canadian capital. A soldier was killed at the War Memorial just outside the Parliament Buildings and a few minutes later, the shooter was shot to death inside Parliament by the House Sergeant at Arms. Haynes noticed that the Canadians weren't referring to these acts as 'workplace violence' but labeled them immediately as terrorist acts.

Canadian leaders had apparently figured out that appeasing jihadists did not make them immune to attacks. Haynes figured the Canadians would now be more than willing to provide military help for the upcoming military action in Kurdistan. Prime Minister Harris said he would be pleased to receive Special Envoy Fennet the following week.

CHAPTER 20

BLACK CONSERVATIVE NIGHT

—⚇—

SATURDAY, December 6, 2014

Haynes and Sonja were in their room at Blair house, dressing for the gala night for Black Conservatives. Haynes had been offered the use of the residence at the White House, but had refused. He did not feel comfortable with the idea although he could not articulate why. Maybe he was waiting for some signal from the American people that he was doing a good job? Maybe then. He remembered the words Rollie had placed in Baldor's annual report to shareholders: "We are only as good as perceived by our customers." Haynes knew he was only going to be as good as the majority of American citizens perceived him to be.

He had extended a special invitation to his nearly lifelong friend John Michel and his wife Jane. They were not exactly conservatives but Haynes wanted all his buddies with him on this particular evening. John was now an American citizen transplanted from Montreal. Jane was an African American and a successful patent attorney. John was in his mid 70s but looked like 50. The guy never seemed to age. He had always looked basically the same. Jane always looked elegant and was consistently soft-spoken and extremely polite.

Haynes' brother Russell with his wife, Pearl, were visiting from Canada. Russell did not have any idea what his brother was going to say later that evening. Sliding on his tuxedo jacket, Haynes noticed that Sonja looked absolutely magnificent in a long stone-studded dark blue jacket that complimented her curly blonde hair. The front of the jacket had a deep vee that tastefully revealed her cleavage and was cinched with a wide belt. The jacket extended below her hips over flared pants that could have been taken for a dress. "You look nervous," she said as she adjusted his bowtie.

"I am. What I'm going to say this evening is going to surprise everyone in the room except for maybe you, John and Jane."

Sonja said, "What do you mean?"

"You just have to wait and see."

They found Jane and John Michel and his brother Russell and his wife at the entrance of Blair House. Haynes couldn't remember ever seeing Michel in a tuxedo, although he doubted John had ever seen him in one either. "You look like a damn penguin," he told him.

John fired back, "You don't look any better."

Then John and Kim McFarland showed up and Haynes introduced them to the others. Haynes was going to sit at the same table with Charles Layne. Haynes wanted Layne to be the keynote speaker and introduce him.

Again, Jeannie Flett had wanted to have a reception line set up for him and Sonja to greet all the guests, and again Haynes refused. He said he just wanted to enter the room so that he and Sonja could start talking to everyone during the cocktail hour. As soon as they entered, Haynes spotted Thomas Sowell and Jason Riley. Sowell was an eloquent spokesman for conservative values. Riley was the author of the book *Stop Helping Us*. After a brief exchange with the two, he spotted Angela McLain. Angela was charming, articulate and knockdown gorgeous. She told him what a great idea she thought this evening was. Haynes felt comfortable talking to Angela and wanted it to continue but he knew he had to move on.

Haynes was beaming. The place was full of successful African-Americans. The atmosphere was electric and they all seemed to be enjoying themselves immensely. It made him feel really good.

The all African-American orchestra was led by Winston Marshall, great musician and world ambassador for American music. Everyone finally found their way to their tables and dinner was served. The Laynes, Michels and Haynes' brother Russell were at his table. John Michel and Russell had been friends since their professional football days with the

Canadian Football League's Saskatchewan Roughriders, playing with the likes of Cookie Gillcrest, who eventually ended up being a star running back with the Buffalo Bills.

Now that dessert and coffee were being served it was time for Charles Layne to speak. Layne spent most of his talk explaining how progressives and their policies had stymied the progress of black people. He ended his remarks by stating that being a black conservative was a lonely profession but thanks to David Haynes' idea to have an evening like this, he wasn't feeling quite as lonely. Layne had asked Haynes earlier how he should introduce him. He replied "Just introduce me as David Haynes."

At the microphone, Haynes said, "Ladies and gentlemen, the people here this evening are probably one of the most discriminated against groups in America. You are shunned as practically traitors and Uncle Toms by an extremely high percentage of your own African-American community. Especially vilified are black women conservatives. The mainstream media almost makes it seem as if you are not allowed to be black and conservative at the same time. The truth is, whether these folks like it or not, you are shining examples of what can be achieved in America if you want to work hard and be positive. I wanted this evening to be a celebration of your success and for you all to serve as an example for young up-and-coming African Americans, so go back out there and continue to encourage the possibilities available to young people in America."

He got an enthusiastic round of applause, but Haynes was feeling emotional and nervous. "I guess you are all wondering what this white guy is doing at an event like this." He hesitated and then started to tell them about a ship's manifest showing that on November 14, 1912, a 19-year-old young man named Otto and his 11-year-old sister Ursula boarded a ship called the *SS Korona* in Barbados that was sailing to New York. They had found their way to Barbados from the island of St. Vincent.

"Why this young man was bringing his 11-year-old sister with him on a voyage like this is a mystery. They arrived at Ellis Island on November 24, 1912. The hand-written immigration form from that day shows them as having $30 in cash and the destination of the 19-year-old was his brother

Wilfred's home in Brooklyn, New York. Somehow Ursula ended up living in the Carolinas.

"Later documents showed that Otto crossed the Canadian border at Rouses Point, New York, in February 1916. He eventually joined the Canadian Army and was shipped off to Europe to crawl around the trenches at Vimy Ridge in that dirty First World War. Fortunately he returned to his new home safe and eventually, later in life, started a family.

"He had two sons. His second son was born when Otto was in his early 50s. He never really said much about his past and his sons only found out in 2014, after digging through archives in Ottawa, that they had two uncles and an aunt named Ursula.

"On Otto's army enlistment form was a line beside his name for complexion, where someone had written the word 'dark.' "

Haynes was now trying to gather himself and he stumbled over his next words. "His full name was Otto Irwin Haynes. He was my father."

There was a hush of sighs and some of the ladies had their hands over their mouths. When Haynes left the microphone, the place stayed dead quiet until Charles Layne jumped to his feet and started applauding. Then the rest of the place exploded. Haynes headed for his brother Russell and the two embraced and patted each other. They both had tears in their eyes. Then Sonja gave him a big hug and a kiss. Charles Layne came over and shook his hand along with everyone else at his table. John and Jane Michel also gave their friend David a big hug. Finally things calmed down and they all sat down again to enjoy their dessert. Afterwards Haynes made the rounds of the tables and there was a lot of high-fiving and great exchanges with everyone.

MONDAY, December 8, 2014, 12:15 p.m.

A crate was unloaded at a side entrance of the White House and rolled on a dolly to the East Room. The Administrator made his way down to watch it being dismantled. Screws from the base and support clips were removed and the cover was lifted from the base and voila, there it was. The Churchill Bust was finally back at the White House.

At 2:00 p.m. Haynes welcomed the British ambassador and various media into the East Room for the official ceremony to mark Winston's return. He thanked the Ambassador and the British people for being gracious enough to return the bust to the White House. He also pointed out that the White House and everything in it was the property of the people of the United States and not the personal property of any president.

FRIDAY, December 12, 2014, 9:00 a.m.

Special envoy Fennet had returned from his trip to Canada to report that the Canadians would participate in the forthcoming hostilities in Kurdistan. Having a major NATO player on board was a huge boost to the administration. Fennet would now head off to Europe with a high-ranking Canadian military officer to try to enlist other NATO members. While there, he would also hold discussions concerning reactivating missile defenses in Europe, which the previous administration had canceled.

CHAPTER 21

THE NEW TAX PLAN

—⋙—

MONDAY, December 15, 2014, 9:30 a.m.

IRS DIRECTOR HERMAN RAINES WASTED no time after moving into his new office. He had already worked out his tax plans and held meetings with key congressional staffers concerning the details of his 9999 plan. He proposed a Goods and Services Tax which would apply to goods and services including utilities and gasoline. There would be no consumer sales tax on food purchases or medical services. Purchases of items like toothpaste, light bulbs or non-food products would be taxed at food stores. The Goods and Services Tax is a pretty straight forward formula; businesses pay a 9% tax on goods and services they purchase. When they sell their products to the next level they collect 9% from their customers and so on until the end user pays 9%. Companies only have to calculate the difference between the tax they paid out and what they received and send that to the government. If a company's purchases represented $100 plus $ 9.00 GST and its sales represented $ 200.00 plus GST of $18.00, the company would simply send the government $9.00 – the difference between the tax paid on purchases and the tax collected on sales, along with a Goods and Service Tax report filed every quarter, or four times a year.

Now Raines was about the present his tax plan while standing beside Steve Forest. This was a symbol of redemption for Forest who had proposed a flat tax plan when he had run for President years earlier. Forest had been ridiculed on CBS News by a reporter with a liberal bias. Bernard Goldberg was also a CBS reporter at the time, and was dismayed by the unprofessionalism of the report, so he wrote an OpEd piece in a New York financial paper that exposed the liberal bias of CBS News. CBS management benched Goldberg to his desk and eventually he left CBS for good. Subsequently, Goldberg wrote a book called Bias, exposing multiple examples of how the news media in general exercises a liberal bias.

Raines was waving a single sheet of paper in the air. Copies had already been passed out to the assembled media. "This form is called the PI form, meaning personal tax for individual taxpayers. It uses a flat tax formula. As you can see, there is one line where the individual states their gross income before payroll deductions, and a second line where they enter their total payroll deductions as deducted by their employer. The form does not require these deductions to be itemized because they will differ from state to state. The deductions amount simply reflects the allowable deductions already deducted from their paycheck. These payroll deductions will be limited to medical insurance, workman's compensation and social security. The virtue of this approach is that there is a single line for reporting net income after payroll deductions.

"The fourth line is for net income multiplied by 9%. If you made $100 in net income, you will enter $9 on the fourth line.

"The employer will be responsible for preparing three copies of a simple slip stating how much money has been sent to the government – one for the employer, one for the government and one for the employee or unincorporated business owner. The fifth and final line has two boxes, for outstanding payment owing or refund. Using the hundred dollar income example above, if the employer sent $10 over the year to the government then the taxpayer would fill in the refund square for $1. In most cases the employer will be accurate and this amount will be zero, but if your employer sent the government $8 for some reason, your outstanding payment would be $1.

"I have also given you copies of a second proposed form called the P2 form. This form would be for unemployed or retired individuals. The only difference between the PI form and the P2 form is that there is a two-line section after gross revenue where the taxpayer will list the simple approved deductions that employers normally handle for their employees, for medical insurance and social security. Taxpayers will attach their receipts.

"Taxpayers earning less than $50,000 will pay a graduated tax as follows:

"Earners of net income less than $20,000 will pay a 3% flat tax.

"Net income of less than $30,000 will be taxed at 4%.

"Net income under $40,000 will be taxed at 6% tax.

"Net Income under$50,000 will be taxed at 7%.

"Any net income of over $50,000 will be taxed at 9%.

"In the past," said Raines, "all tax filings have been packed into a mad scramble in the month of April; that will now come to an end. Individuals will file their taxes 60 days after the last day of their birthday month. If your birthday is November 1, then your tax year will end on the last day of November and your filing deadline will be 60 days after that. This will provide a nice even tax flow. The only exception will be in the first year of the new system. For the first year, starting on May 31, the fiscal year for anyone with a May birth date will end on May 31. People with a May birth date will have 60 days from the last day of May to file for a fiscal period of five months, covering January 1 to May 31. Anyone with a June birth date would file 60 days after the last day of June and report for a fiscal period of six months from Jan 1 through the end of June. The same procedure will apply for every subsequent birth month until the 12 month cycle has ended.

After that everyone will file for 12 month periods. This same system will apply to unincorporated business owners filling under B2 and CG-PI. Business owners and operators of investment houses would have to adjust the issuing of government tax slips confirming income according to the employee's or investor's birth date."

Then Raines held up another form for capital gains. "This is the CG-PI. The PI stands for personal income. This tax form is for individuals that have a combination of capital gains, interest, dividends, and other personal income. There is a line across the middle of the page separating the two categories. The upper section says CG in large print, and this is where capital gains, interest and dividends are reported. Below the black horizontal line is the PI heading. This second part is the same as the individual PI form for personal income only." Raines had copies of this form passed out to the media.

He said, "A high percentage of people accumulating capital gains, etcetera are older Americans. They are going to get a break and this will encourage more investment. This form has several lines. The first line is for dividend income, which is pretty straightforward. The second one is interest income. The third one is capital gains on stocks, which is reported only when a stock is sold. If you bought a stock for $100 and sold it for $200 you would simply pay 9% of the difference, or gain. The fourth line is for OTHER, or income that does not fall into the above three categories.

"Brokers and investment houses will issue information slips to investors listing their dividends, interest and capital gains. The second part, Personal Income, will be filled out the same way as the individual PI form. The individual only has to provide the numbers from their confirmed income slips onto their one-page tax form, add the total for CG and PI and send in the check. If individuals have only capital gains to report and no other personal income, they simply check off the box for NONE in the PI section. Basically, taxpayers just need to use the one page form that applies to them.

"Businesses would be a little more complicated. We have divided this category into two, with separate forms for each. The form called the B1 is for normal businesses with employees, incorporated or unincorporated. The B2 form is for self-employed unincorporated individuals with allowable expense deductions and no employees. A separate list of allowable expenses is attached.

"The first category, B1 businesses, will be expected to file and submit employee payroll taxes and taxes on business profits every quarter. They will be allowed to continue their normal deductions as currently and will pay 9% of their net income after expenses. The B2 category will file once a year according to the same schedule as individual taxpayers. The B2 form also contains a capital gains section on the reverse side. If there is no capital gain income, these taxpayers will just check off the last box as 'none.'

"These new rules will eliminate any IRS filing regulations relative to the number of employees or number of hours worked. All other IRS regulations are terminated. If the IRS has overlooked a regulation that would make things even simpler, this can be done with Congressional approval only. Senate and Presidential approval is not required.

"This new system will mean that, with a few exceptions, the US will have the lowest corporate tax rate in the world.

"Over the coming year, we will review and readjust the definition of legitimate expenses for businesses. The standard ones will be capital equipment investments, salaries, utilities, state and local taxes, etcetera. The more contentious ones will be the calculations of old and new inventory, etcetera."

Raines continued, "We have set up a website with clear categories for individual and businesses. If you click on the category applicable to you or your business, you will find simple explanations concerning how the system will work. You may also print out these instructions or copies of the tax forms. These new rules will be effective January 1, 2015. Businesses will have to adjust their computers to conform to these new rules. If this cannot be done in the remaining days of this year then we expect businesses will record this data by hand until their computer programs have been updated.

"There is one brutal tax that will be eliminated effective Jan 1. 2015; it is the estate tax, better known as the death tax. We are concerned about farmers, ranchers, small property owners and small businesses that have this unfair burden loaded on their backs. We are still looking at whether this tax will be applied to the super wealthy, but even if it is reinstated for this group, the super wealthy, it should be marginal. Our department is presently looking at solutions for the people in the middle and lower income classes who have been brutalized and burdened by the tax system. We are presently looking at some way that in certain cases, we can refund death taxes that have been collected. There are some farmers, ranchers and private property owners that have been taxed for more than the value that their deceased relatives paid for their property, unused useless equipment or outrageous assessment values, etcetera; this is unfair. Effective January 1, 2015, no one will have to pay any further death taxes. And we are presently working on an arrangement where in certain cases any death taxes that have been – and I am going to use the word 'stolen' – can be repaid with interest to the taxpayer by deferring their future taxes until the slate is wiped clean. This will be done on a case by case basis. Any questions?"

"Please elaborate on this repayment plan."

"Well it would kind of work this way. If someone has paid a total of $100 in death taxes as of January 1, 2015, the government has to pay back the taxpayer that $100. So if that taxpayer owes the government $500 in taxes for 2015, he will be given a credit of $100 plus interest. Therefore that taxpayer would owe the federal government $400 minus back interest."

"How far back in time will this go?"

"As I said, this will be done on a case by case basis where fairness will favour the taxpayer until the last death tax payer's application is closed."

Second question: "Won't this benefit the rich?"

Raines replied, "This will benefit everyone across the board. Socialists love to talk percentages. They don't like talking dollars because dollars show that people earning higher incomes pay more tax in pure dollars. For example if someone makes $100,000 a year after allowable deductions, under our new program that person will pay $9,000 in tax. A person earning $500,000 a year will pay $45,000 tax and they will no longer have all these fancy deductions, so therefore the person making $500,000 a year is paying five times more in real dollars than the person making $100,000 a year. There is an incentive here for people on the bottom of the ladder to climb further up or to the top without being penalized."

Next question: "What about the mortgage tax deduction?"

"There are no other deductions for individuals. We have already lowered the tax rate by a significant amount. Allowing additional deductions would lead to the slow, gradual creep back to where we are now with a mountain-high stack of tax regulations that can be debated by tax lawyers and accountants because it's not clear to them either. The idea is to maintain a simple approach that the average citizen perceives as understandable and fair. Our government is only as good as perceived by American citizens.

"I am going to make a prediction. Washington will be flooded very soon by lobbyists representing tax lawyers, accountants, tax processing firms and other special interests. My advice to them is don't waste your time. This system is going into effect on January 1 no matter what, and we will let the American people know which one of their representatives opposes it. My personal opinion is that anyone who opposes this in principle represents special interests and not the voters who put them there."

Next question: "When will the Congress pass these new rules?"

"We are hoping that these will get passed before the end of the year. The Congress has a lot on its plate but these rules will go into effect in any case on January 1, 2015. The leadership in both houses have agreed, after negotiation, that these new laws I presented today are basically what will be in the new legislation."

Next question: "What makes you think that tax revenues will increase with these measures?"

Herman answered: "First of all, historically speaking, revenues have increased when tax rates are lowered. It's counterintuitive, but this is what has happened in the past. Even President Kennedy lowered taxes. Let me give you an example. If a corporation pays lower taxes, its profits will increase. When a corporation's profits increase they tend to invest more in infrastructure for growth. These purchases are taxed. Secondly, dividends to shareholders will be much higher. These new higher dividends provide more income for people and are also taxed under the capital gains section. What do people do when they have more income? They go out and buy things that generate more sales taxes and so on and so on. Instead of the tax cycle deteriorating it is energized."

Next question: "How will this affect unemployment, if at all?"

Raines replied, "That's a terrific question. My conversation with the Administrator the other day was exactly about that. He is going to measure any recovery by the following.

1. Reduction in the official unemployment rate.
2. Re-entry into the workforce of people that have dropped out and are not included in the so-called official unemployment rate.
3. When improvement is shown in the two previous examples, the final measurement will be an increase in wages and take-home pay as a result of employer competition for labor. People who had no choice but to accept lower paying jobs to stay employed will have options to return to the income level they had previously, because they will now be in demand by employers. This will also create a jobs vacuum for people one rung below to fill. All boats big and small will rise, so to speak.
4. The granddaddy indicator will be inflation. Inflation usually comes as a result of a hot economy with low unemployment. That indicator will be apparent when the Fed starts making noises that they are becoming concerned with inflation. Then we will know that we have turned the corner."

"How is the GST going to affect federal revenue?"

Raines said, "We estimate the tax will generate about $200 billion plus. Some of this will come from the underground cash-paid part of the economy. Now people dealing in cash will have to pay 9% on their material purchases for contracts and the like. The thing that the Administrator and I are concerned about is when the political types see more funds coming, some of them are going to want to spend it. We want to change that mindset, we intend to use a percentage of these funds to pay interest and reduce the deficit as well, along with reduced spending; some of which comes from senator Colman's waste list. We want the narrative to change from TAX AND SPEND to CUT AND REDUCE DEBT."

That night on Fox News, a commentator summed up the day's groundbreaking news conference with the following remarks: "The thing about Herman is that he has done all these things in the business sector and understood the details of filing business and private taxes. He has plenty of hands-on experience in the real world and knew this stuff like the back of his hand. He didn't have to go to school to learn all these things. He knew exactly what to do; he was a professional, experienced person and not some theoretical bureaucrat. Herman has two simple philosophies; you are either part of the solution or part of the problem. If you are part of the problem you wouldn't hang around very long."

TUESDAY, December 16, 2014, 10:00 a.m.

Late Tuesday morning, the CIA director phoned Haynes to report that US Special Forces had conducted an operation in Libya and captured two terrorists, who were being taken to a destroyer off the Mediterranean coast. Haynes said "As I told you before, we don't need any media coverage on this. The time for tipping off the rest of the world as to what we are doing is over. The fewer people that know about this, the better."

THURSDAY, December 18, 2014, 8:30 a.m.

When Haynes arrived in the conference room Thursday morning, he found McFarland, Giani and Ronson already there, along with the House Speaker, Senate Leader, the two minority leaders, members of the relevant health committees, and various representatives and senators. He was a little surprised to see McFarland, but then realized that the solution to the health issue would provide a lot of clarity for the business community.

Haynes began the conversation by saying, "Ladies and Gentlemen, the American people need a Christmas gift. Secretary Ronson is going to lay out a health proposal, which I think is absolutely innovative and brilliant.

Ronson distributed folders to everyone in the room and began his presentation pretty much the same as at the previous meeting with the Administrator two days before. He pointed out that preparation for the state trials in the selected states was going to start right after New Year. The trials themselves would launch on July 1. Ronson continued, "What I want done is described in detail in the folders you just received, but these are the main points:

1. We would like to have the bill scrapping the Affordable Health Care Act passed by the middle of January, 2015.
2. We need a tort reform passed with a provision that if states pass their own tort reform laws down the road they will supercede federal tort reform law.
3. Arrange for the agency that provides unemployment insurance to have 5% deducted from unemployment insurance checks to cover these people's health insurance in the two trial states only for now.
4. Direct federal funding will cease as of the official start date estimated at July 1st 2015. By then, people should have a single state medical ID card for coverage.
5. The federal government will fund the trials based on the amounts the trial states expended on Medicare, Medicaid, etcetera in 2014. The trial states will receive 25% of these federal funds at the beginning of every quarter commencing July 1, 2015.
6. If these trials are successful, federal funding or subsidies will eventually end. We want these programs to stand on their own.
7. States want a constitutional amendment passed preventing lawsuits aimed at overriding laws pertaining to state health care. They don't want some zealous lawyers causing a good state health care act to come unglued over technical glitches in the law."

After Ronson's report, there was a lot of discussion to try to clarify some of the issues. A number of ideological and pro big government Democratic senators and congressmen objected to the transfer of a federal domain to the states, and so did some of the Republicans. Haynes did not bother trying to appeal to their common sense, but he did ask, "Do any of you know how much fraud is involved in these large uncontrollable federal programs? Independent smaller state programs will eliminate a lot of this fraud, plus be more efficient and closer to the people they serve."

CHAPTER 22

THE KIDNAPPING

—⚏—

MONDAY, January 5, 2015, 8:15 a.m.

Businessman Eric Craig had just got into his car on a quiet Georgetown street in Washington when he noticed a dark vehicle double parked about a block ahead. Someone was standing beside the car smoking a cigarette. Craig was in the security business and naturally observant of things around him. "Asshole thinks he owns the road," he muttered, and then rechecked his briefcase to make sure that he had not forgotten files for his next meeting.

When he looked up again and was just about to turn on the ignition, he saw a man descending the staircase from the townhouse beside the double-parked vehicle. At the same moment, a dark van came screaming to a halt beside the double parked car and four men wearing hoods and brandishing weapons jumped out. They grabbed the man smoking a cigarette and the second gentlemen who had just stepped off the stairs onto the sidewalk. The back doors of the van flew open and Craig could see another hooded individual inside the van. He was putting down something that looked like a police scanner. The assailants had already pulled hoods over the heads of the two men and now they threw them roughly into the back of the van, slammed the doors shut, and then quickly stepped back into the side doors.

As soon as the van sped off, Craig pulled out of his parking spot and followed the van from a careful distance. He dialed 911 on his hands-free phone. The 911 operator came on and Craig started to describe what had happened and what he was now doing.

"Can you tell me what intersection you are approaching?" the operator asked him.

Craig gave her the information and added, "They looked very dangerous to me. I don't think you should send marked police cars with sirens blaring. Can you get a helicopter in the air and tell the cops not to use regular police channels? They are probably being monitored."

The 911 operator said, "I don't know about that, sir."

Craig raised his voice and said, "Are you listening to me? I'm in the security business and one of those guys had a scanner so you tell the cops to use some other form of communication. Do you understand?"

"Yes sir, I'll pass that on."

After a brief delay, the operator came back on and said, "Give me a full description of the van and of your automobile and update me on your location."

Craig did all that. He was getting anxious because now there was more traffic and he didn't want to lose the van. He had been trailing it for about 10 minutes but hadn't dared to get close enough to get the license plate.

Two minutes later the operator said, "You are being overtaken by a 4-door green Ford sedan with an African-American officer driving. He is going to give you a thumbs-up signal and you are going to make the first right turn and stay double parked with your flashers on. The officer will continue to follow the van. A police vehicle will be at your position as soon as possible to take down details."

The driver of the unmarked Ford was Officer Michael Herman. There were two other unmarked vehicles right behind him. It appeared to Herman that the van was heading for a section of town filled with warehousing and light industry. He used his cell phone to call the traffic helicopter that had been pressed into service while the police department scrambled to get one of their own into the air. The traffic helicopter was relaying info back and forth to the station.

When the van turned into a quiet industrial side street, Officer Herman was right behind. "Don't turn off after them, you don't want to spook them. We'll tell you where they stop," Herman was told.

The traffic helicopter watched the van drive to a low gray building and through the automatic doors.

Officer Herman went down the next street a couple of blocks and parked behind the building directly across from where the van had entered, which happened to be the business office of a distribution company. He called headquarters with his location.

Meanwhile the helicopter was circling nearby, trying not to be noticed but making sure that no one exited the building from another door. At headquarters, preparations were being made to insert special squads into the buildings surrounding the warehouse.

By now a police car had arrived at Craig's location. The most important information he had was that there were five men involved, and maybe a sixth if there had been a driver waiting behind the wheel while the kidnapping occurred.

Headquarters learned that the building had been rented to an unincorporated company called Asian Distribution. The building's owner admitted under duress that he had accepted cash from an individual for a six month rental, and hadn't asked any questions.

MONDAY, January 5, 2015, 9:30 a.m.

The meeting with McCormick, McFadden, Giani and Kyling was about to start and Giani hadn't turned up. Jeannie Flett told Haynes, "Rod called in to say he was going to make some phone calls from his home. He should be here shortly."

Haynes decided to start without him, but a half hour later, Giani had still not shown up so Haynes postponed the rest of the meeting and went back to his office. A few minutes later, Jeannie put through a phone call, and he heard a voice say, "This is FBI Director Simmons."

Haynes found this strange because Simmons normally called himself Bill. "Is your chief of staff there?"

Haynes replied, "No, he didn't show up for a meeting this morning."

"Then I believe I have some bad news. It's possible Rod was kidnapped this morning."

Haynes nearly dropped the phone. "How the hell is that possible? What about his security?"

"He only had one guy on detail and it appears that he has been kidnapped as well."

Haynes told Simmons to hang on a minute, and then yelled out to Jeannie's office, "Tell Kyling and McCormick not to leave the building and find a place for us to have a conference call with the FBI director. He's on the line now."

Jeannie shouted back, "Just use the speakerphone in your office!" She tracked down Kyling and McCormick, who were still waiting at the entrance for their vehicles, and escorted them quickly into Haynes' office.

Haynes turned on the speakerphone and said, "Bill, tell us everything you know." Simmons recapped the basic details and then said, "We're tracking cell phone use in the building. There have been several calls made from a rented cell phone to a phone number in area code 510, which is in San Francisco. We are trying to track down where the cell phone was rented and who the number in San Francisco belongs to."

McCormick said "Can't you track the location of the cell phone in San Francisco?"

"Right now it's turned off," said Simmons.

"Has Mrs. Giani been informed?" Haynes asked.

"Yes," said Simmons. "There are a couple of female officers with her right now."

McCormick said, "Sooner or later we are going to have to enter that building. I think this is a job for Navy SEALs."

"How long are we going to be able to keep this out of the media?" asked Haynes.

Simmons replied, "I don't really know."

MONDAY, January 5, 2015, 12:30 p.m.

Just after noon, a courier company delivered an envelope to a local TV station. It was from a group calling itself the American Liberation Army, claiming they had kidnapped Chief of Staff Giani. They threatened that he would be executed if the President was not returned to Washington within 24 hours.

Haynes put McCormick in charge of the kidnapping crisis. McCormick was running everything from a White House conference room, with Simmons at his side. When the news editor at the TV station contacted the FBI, he was told to sit on the story for 30 minutes. After some heated discussion, McCormick asked Simmons to call the TV station and tell them to broadcast the message from the kidnappers, along with the fact that the FBI had absolutely no leads except for finding Giani's car double-parked in front of his town house at 1:00 p.m. McCormick of course had known about the vehicle some time ago but needed to make it appear that they only found the abandoned car after the courier had delivered the envelope. He didn't need to tip the kidnappers off.

In the meantime navy officers were working with the building owner to get a detailed plan of every square corner of the warehouse. They assumed that the kidnappers were holding Giani and operating out of the first floor of a three-story building, because the only bathrooms were there. The building was old and some of the staircases were made of wood. They were trying to figure out how to get SEALs onto the roof and into the third floor undetected. There were reports coming back from spotters in nearby buildings that the kidnappers had a lookout walking around the roof every hour or so, exiting from a small dome-like section sticking out of the roof.

MONDAY, January 5, 2015, 3:03 p.m. - Washington

The FBI got its first break when the San Francisco phone dialed the number in the hostage building. The phone stayed on long enough for the San Francisco FBI office to track its location to an address in the suburbs that turned out to be the home of Edward Wilson. Wilson was arrested back in the early 70s, along with his wife and various other people, for committing terrorist acts in various parts of America. He managed to get off on a technicality and eventually a university in California had hired him to teach political science. Wilson's wife served time for related charges.

The FBI's theory now was that either Wilson remained part of a sleeper cell ever since, or he remained a left-wing fanatic who became enraged over recent events in Washington and decided to act.

2:00 p.m. - San Francisco

The FBI sent a SWAT team to surround the Wilson home and used a man dressed as a courier to ring the doorbell. When Wilson answered the door, he was pulled out into the arms of two members of the SWAT team. The rest entered the house and found his wife in the kitchen. She started to scream and yell and they got her on the ground and then into the police wagon with her husband. McCormick's instructions were to bring them to a building where CIA officers were waiting. Simmons warned McCormick that Wilson would get off again because his rights were being violated. McCormick shot back, "I don't give a shit about his rights. I'm only concerned about rescuing Giani and his security."

2:40 p.m.

CIA officers had Wilson sitting in chair with his hands cuffed behind his back. His wife was similarly cuffed just down the hallway, and since she had been screaming 'fascists' at the officers for a steady half hour, they had eventually just taped her mouth shut.

A CIA officer put his face up close to Wilson's and said, "I guess you're wondering why you are here and not at some police department where you can have your rights read and call a lawyer. You are going to tell us everything we need to know."

"I'm not going to tell you squat," Wilson said. He refused to cooperate under a barrage of questions to determine who else was involved in the kidnapping. Finally the CIA officer nodded towards someone in the doorway of the room and 30 seconds later the tape was ripped off his wife's mouth. Then came a blood curdling scream. Wilson looked clearly shaken. The officer said, "We're not screwing around with you; if we have to we will kill her and drop her into San Francisco Bay. Right now we don't have to answer to anyone."

Wilson could hear his wife crying in the other room and then it went silent again as the tape was replaced. Wilson said, "You can't treat us this way."

"This is a lot better treatment than the people you and your outfit were responsible for murdering back in the 70s," the agent said.

After more uncomfortable persuasion Wilson decided to answer their questions. He described two Iranians who had come across the Mexican border into the US years earlier. They had embedded themselves into American society and were being financed by Iranian security. The other three members of the cell were domestic left-wing extremists. One of them was single and the other two had families in Greensboro, North Carolina.

The agents knew that sooner or later there are going to have to put Wilson on his phone with the leader of the terrorist cell at the warehouse in Washington. So they told him that if Giani was killed, they were going to blow his wife's brains out.

Now at least they knew that there were five and not six in the warehouse. This was critical information for the SEALs. Wilson also told the agents that his next call was not expected until 8:00 p.m. Washington time. So McCormick decided he would not use Wilson to telephone the kidnappers for fear he might try to tip them off. Instead, he ordered in the SEALs.

7:00 p.m. - Washington

The SEALs waited for darkness to make their way to the top of an adjacent building. They watched as, right on schedule, one of the kidnappers did his patrol of the roof, and as soon as he went back inside they made their move. Down below, a SEAL dressed as a trucker parked a truck rigged with a big plow tucked out of sight near the warehouse doors. One of the SEALs aimed a grappling hook and cable at a point on the warehouse roof as far from the domed entry as possible to mask the noise, and the group slipped silently across on pulley straps. By 7:35 p.m. there were 15 men on the roof. They waited patiently until almost 8:00, when one of the kidnappers exited from the rooftop door. He was grabbed from behind, an ether-soaked cloth placed over his mouth and out he went. He was stripped to his underwear. A SEAL with a similar build stripped off his own dark clothing and put on the kidnapper's clothes. Then he led the other SEALs into the building. Once they had scoured the third floor and found it empty, they continued down to the second. They moved slowly, and now, through the cracks between the old wooden planks, they could see four of the kidnappers sitting around a table not far from the automatic doors. There was some sort of electrical box with a large red button sitting on the table.

One of the kidnappers at the table looked up at the ceiling and yelled, "Is everything okay up there?"

"Yeah," one of the SEALs said and then immediately whispered "Go" into his headset. At almost the same moment, another SEAL noticed large blobs of something on the walls around them, connected to what looked like new wires.

Seconds later the truck came crashing through the garage door. The kidnappers hit the floor, knocking over the table, and reached for their weapons. SEALs came streaming between the truck and the wall, shielding behind the plow, while the SEALs upstairs poured down the stairway from above, all blasting at the four men on the floor. It was over in seconds.

Then the SEAL who had noticed the wired explosives shouted, "They pushed that red button, the building's going to blow!" The squad leader looked at the red button, and realized that either the kidnapper had not managed to hit it, or the explosives were on a timer. "Quick," he shouted, and led the way into an adjacent room, where they found Giani and his security man tied to chairs. Almost simultaneously the truck screeched backward out of the building. Another SEAL screamed into his headset for the two men who had remained on the roof to get off fast.

Two SEALs were trying to untie Giani but the squad leader screamed, "Forget that, pick up him and the chair and get him out the front door now!" The SEALs carrying Giani and his security guy made it about halfway across the street before the blast went off, knocking them to the ground. Up above, the third floor had exploded just as the two SEALs landed on the next-door roof.

In seconds, the men on the pavement picked themselves up, grabbed the two men tied to the chairs and headed up an alley as far as they could get from the warehouse before the second floor collapsed.

The roof of the adjacent building where the remaining SEALs were waiting was also on fire and nearing collapse. One SEAL managed to drag the pulley back across, burning his hands in the process, and then they used it to escape to the next building over, dragging the unconscious kidnapper with them, just as the third floor caved in.

Down below, one of the SEALs handed Giani a cell phone. "Call your wife," he said.

At the White House, McCormick was advised that Rod had been rescued. Haynes banged his fist down on the table and said, "Yes! I love those SEALs."

Wilson and his wife were flown the next day to Guantanamo Bay, where they were going to stay until further notice.

An investigation was launched into Wilson's phone records and email, and it was discovered that there had been a lot of communication with some media outlets and other agencies sponsored by Czech-born New York billionaire Tomas Tireza. Tireza had a reputation for trying to destabilize the currencies of certain countries in Europe and for promoting extreme left-wing causes in America through his media and political agencies and by financing candidates with socialist agendas. Tireza's outlets had been recently spouting negative things about the new administration and especially McCormick.

TUESDAY, January 6, 2015

When McCormick finished reading the FBI reports concerning Wilson's frequent contact with outlets sponsored by Tomas Tireza, he decided he'd had enough. He told FBI director Simmons to launch a full-out investigation into Tireza's activities. McCormick wanted him monitored 24/7. McCormick always suspected he was a European traitor transplanted to America. And every extreme left wing political candidate was kissing up to him because he sponsored a lot of their campaigns.

CHAPTER 23

PUBLIC PERCEPTIONS ABROAD AND AT HOME

—⚜—

WEDNESDAY, January 7, 2015

Jeannie Flett rang Blair House at 7:30 a.m. and told Haynes to turn on the television. Paris was on high alert while police searched for two masked terrorists screaming jihadist slogans who had massacred 12 journalists at a satirical newspaper and a police officer on the street outside. A third terrorist shot four people in a kosher grocery store in a Paris suburb. A Muslim employee of the grocery store, an immigrant from Africa, saved the lives of another dozen customers by hiding them in a walk-in fridge.

When Haynes finally got to the White House, his first question to Giani was, "Where did they get the weapons? Europe is in huge doo-doo with their Muslim populations. They make up ten percent of the population of France alone, and that share is growing rapidly because their families are larger than the average French family. If France lets this continue, Muslims will eventually make up the majority, and will start trying to introduce sharia law. This could possibly lead to a French civil war. There are already Muslim cantons all over France that are considered no-go zones for the police. So in other words, they are already operating little countries within French territory. We cannot allow the same thing to happen in America."

SUNDAY, January 11, 2015

Haynes had sent Oliver West to participate in the Unity March in Paris, although he felt the whole thing was a useless exercise unless the Europeans started to get brutal with their Muslim no-go zones. He was more anxious than ever for operations in Kurdistan to commence.

MONDAY, January 12, 2015, 9:00 a.m.

Treasury Secretary Rawlston invited bankers and other interested parties to a conference in Washington on the future of mortgages in the United States. The meetings stretched over two full days. The attendees were separated into groups of eight, with small and large banks in each. Rawlston asked each group of bankers to submit a list of ideas on how the government and its agencies could be removed from the mortgage business. This was to include Fannie Mae and Freddie Mac, but would not affect the implementation of banking regulations.

Rawlston felt that some good ideas were presented, which made for a good start. He asked each team to keep meeting over the internet, picking a spokesman for each team to provide liaison with someone at Treasury so that there would be an ongoing flow of new ideas. The goal was a second meeting where the strategy would be solidified.

MONDAY, January 12, 2015, 10:00 a.m.

Haynes asked the CIA director "Is it possible to shut down these jihadist terrorists' websites?"

The director said, "That's a great question, I don't really know."

"Well let's find out."

MONDAY, January 12, 2015, 1:00 p.m.

Most of the White House staff gathered in and around the White House entrance foyer to welcome back Rod Giani, who had taken a week off to recover from his ordeal. He was greeted with a resounding round of applause, handshaking and hugs. Haynes was hoping that his return was not too soon, but Rod was one tough dude. His absence had made it obvious, especially to Haynes, how valuable he really was.

TUESDAY, January 13, 2015

Haynes asked Giani, Commerce Secretary McFarland, Treasury Secretary Rawlston and the Majority Leaders of the House and the Senate to attend a White House meeting with the Chinese Ambassador. Haynes wanted to show him that America was speaking with one voice. He had prepared a list of issues to discuss. Haynes stressed that he wanted to have good trade relations with China but that it was not a one-way street. He had two main concerns:

1. The fact that the Chinese currency was not traded on international currency markets and was deliberately being kept low by China.
2. The deliberate and aggressive computer hacking of American computer systems supported by the Chinese government.

The Chinese Ambassador replied that China would not be dictated to concerning its currency policy. He also denied that the Chinese government was deliberately hacking American computers.

Haynes replied, "I have no illusions about being able to tell China what to do with its currency. On the other hand, China should not have any illusions about how the US will react to what it considers unfair trade relations. You, sir, can do what you want with your currency and we can do what we want," he said. "I guarantee you that if this very unfair situation with regard to your currency continues, there will be a response. I don't blame the Chinese Government for taking advantage of a situation that's our fault, not yours. However we don't intend to allow this situation to continue. Secretary McFarland gave you a head's up on the currency issue in his speech to the business community on November 18. We are going to take a reasonable amount of time to see what the Chinese Government will do and as I said we don't presume to dictate or to control any decisions the Chinese Government makes in its own interests. But we do have our own interests, and from this day on, we will be acting in our own interests.

"As for your denial regarding computer hacking, you know and we know exactly what is going on and if it continues it will have a negative impact on our future relations." Haynes had had personal experience in dealing with Chinese business people. They were always expounding on their cultural history. He knew that they could look you straight in the eye, smile and lie through their teeth while they were doing it. That was consistent with people brought up in an atmosphere of communism. Relations with these people had to be realistic. It was sad but Americans just had to understand that the Chinese wouldn't respect them any other way.

When the meeting was concluded Haynes told McFarland to give the Chinese 60 days to react and to gently remind the Ambassador a couple of times in the interim.

WEDNESDAY, January 14, 2015

Simmons called a meeting at the White House, with Turner, Kyling, McCormick, Giani, Simmons, West and Haynes and the CIA Director in attendance. He told Haynes, "Our plan is complete and we're ready to order FBI and military personnel into position around 22 moslem training camps across the country. We've also set up holding locations for everyone we capture, staffed with people ready to interrogate, profile, fingerprint, and trace and contact their family members. We're ready to move and just need you to give the okay. All we need is Senate approval for the declaration of war already passed by the House," he said.

THURSDAY, January 15, 2015

The Senate passed Raines' tax bill. It would come into effect retroactively to January 1, 2015.

The following day, the Senate passed a law outlawing the application of any laws beyond American law. This was directed principally at blocking any application of sharia law. Haynes felt bad that such a law was necessary, but it was the result of the lack of respect for American traditions among Muslims. If there had ever been another immigrant group making such a law necessary, he couldn't remember it.

FRIDAY, January 16, 2015

Press Secretary Goldstein called a meeting with Giani, Flett and Haynes. Goldstein expressed his concern that the press reports concerning the administration were escalating and becoming vicious – especially those from media outlets financed by Thomas Tireza. Most of the attacks were directed at Haynes. He felt that the situation was getting out of control and needed to be countered in some fashion.

Ideas were thrown and finally Flett suggested that maybe Haynes should be interviewed with someone sympathetic to the administration's effort.

"What good would that do?" Haynes said. "The people we need to talk to are the ones who are listening to the stations where all the criticism is coming from. I've already given this some thought. Jon Stewart has been mocking and making fun of me almost every night. He has called me a dictator and god knows what else. What is the size of his nightly audience and who are they?

Goldstein replied, "I think his audience is about 1.8 million every night and the viewers are mostly between 20 and 40 and left-leaning."

"I have a suggestion," said Haynes. "Since most of these attacks have been directed toward me, I guess I'm the logical one to counter them, not only on my behalf but on behalf of everyone in the administration."

"So I want to do the Stewart show sometime in the first two weeks of February. Some time on that same day I want to record an interview with O'Leary on Fox to be broadcast the day after Stewart's show." Haynes could not discuss the timing because of all the people at this meeting, only he and Giani knew about the Kurdistan campaign and that it would probably be completed sometime in early February.

"I'm going to go on that show and do something comical to confirm the things he's been saying about me but I'm not going to tell you what, because you guys will try to talk me out of it. For better or worse there is going to be a journalistic stampede to get copies of this for broadcast on other networks and his audience is going to think I'm cool and down to earth. It will also give O'Leary an opportunity to show some parts of the Stewart interview again on his program the following evening. O'Leary doesn't care if he's interviewing liberals, conservatives, libertarians or communists. His interviews are the same hard-hitting stuff for everyone and

I will be ready because I've got nothing to hide. The objective of that interview is to give the American people confidence that our administration has a plan and a group of highly professional American patriots to execute it. Even though they may not agree with everything we are doing, they're going to know that there is leadership in the executive branch."

Goldstein asked, "What the hell are you planning to do on the Stewart show?"

"That's for me to know and you to find out," replied Haynes. "What I would like you to do is to get preliminary confirmation that these interviews could be conducted sometime in the first two weeks of February. I can't tell you the whole story but I have to wait until a certain event in February is completed before I can do these interviews. Just tell them that we will give them a heads up to confirm the dates when the time gets closer."

When Haynes got back to his office he asked Jeannie Flett to find the most prestigious costume house in New York City, close to the television networks. Jeannie said, "May I ask why?"

Haynes replied, "No you may not. Just get me a contact and a phone number."

Flett returned a couple of hours later with a phone number and a contact. Haynes had the White House switchboard make the call and found himself on the phone with a gentleman by the name of Allen Diamond. Diamond said, "Am I really talking to David Haynes?" in a kind of New York, Jewish twang.

Haynes replied, "Yes. If you want to confirm that you can call back the White House and ask for me."

Diamond said, "Okay, I'll bite. What is it that I can do for you?"

Haynes said, "Can you be trusted to keep your mouth shut and that includes your wife and friends?"

Diamond replied, "Yes Sir."

Haynes told him he was going to go on the Stewart Show and explained exactly what he wanted him to do. When Haynes was done Diamond was laughing hysterically. "Are you serious, are you really going to do this?"

"Yes but it will only be a complete success if you keep this just between us, understand?"

"Yes sir," said Diamond.

"How much is this going to cost?" said Haynes.

"Between five and seven hundred dollars," said Diamond.

"I'll tell you what," said Haynes, "let's make a deal. You are going to charge me squat in exchange for us spending some personal time together and for me saying, on the Stewart Show, who is responsible. That advertising will be worth a lot more than seven hundred bucks."

"That's a deal," said Diamond.

Haynes said, "Call my assistant Jeannie Flett when you have everything ready but don't tell her what it is. No one here has a clue."

"Got, it," said Diamond.

MONDAY, January 19, 2015

Haynes met with Giani and McFarland to discuss the post office, which had been bleeding taxpayers' money for years. It was now obvious that electronic email, bank transfers and the like were impacting the letter delivery component. Slowly but surely, the younger generation was going to make letter delivery practically extinct. It was time to sell the post office and everybody knew it. The problem was that the post office is a tradition in America, especially in rural areas. So the process would be a huge undertaking.

McFarland had extensive experience in mergers and takeovers and was the right man to organize such a gigantic undertaking. There were only three logical buyers for the post office – the two biggest package delivery companies in the United States, and one foreign-based. But there was going to be a problem for the buyers with regard to union benefits and pensions. McFarland had already been informed that some kind of an arrangement needed to be made with the unions. If the unions tried to prevent the sale by demanding unreasonable payouts or transfer agreements, the only other option was to bankrupt the post office and move forward with a clean slate, or close it and sell the assets.

TUESDAY, January 20, 2015

The Senate passed the bill scrapping the Affordable Health Care Act and approved the state trials along with the requested provisions.

Finally the administration had a clear answer for the longstanding question "What is your alternative to the Affordable Health Care Act?" Now Ronson could get to work trying to get as many states as possible to pass their own state healthcare laws, which would make it easier to pass the toughest part of the AFC – the transfer of health and human services to the states. If Ronson could get more than half the states started on this path, there would be no turning back.

WEDNESDAY, January 21, 2015, 12:30 a.m. Washington Time

Haynes, Giani, McFadden, West and McCormick were in the situation room getting set to launch Operation Leatherneck. Special envoy Fennet was in Bonn. It had taken almost three months to build the base infrastructures, train and equip the new Kurdistan Army and move more than 20,000 American and coalition military personnel into Kurdistan, 15,000 more than they had originally planned. The offensive was set to launch at 1:00 a.m. Washington time.

Haynes was nervous with anticipation and feeling he'd rather be suited up over there than sitting here. He would have liked to be the one breaking down the door to capture some of those jihadist bastards that cut innocent people's heads off.

When 1:00 a.m. passed, they all waited in silence for the first reports of activity. Haynes finally left the room because he couldn't stand any more of the tension. He told Riley to let him know when the first reports started coming in. At 2:30, word came that US forces had surrounded Kobani. By 4 a.m., after heavy fighting, US forces had occupied one oilfield north of Mosul. The jihadists had set two other oil fields on fire but the Special Forces had secured the perimeters. There was still fighting going on at the other oil fields but reports were that it was just a matter of time before they were taken.

The northwest-bound force was heading for the Mediterranean just south of the Turkish border. The left flank of this force veered southwest to rendezvous with the rapidly advancing main force on their eastern flank and meet up with the Special Forces still trying to take the remaining oilfields. By 5:30 Special Forces Commander Colonel Menendez reported that they had secured all oilfields in the area, with only seven wounded and no casualties. Helicopters were being dispatched to get the wounded out and to temporarily reinforce the Special Forces. Menendez was desperately waiting for the southbound main force to relieve him.

In Kobani, there was heavy fighting between the Kurd forces and jihadists inside the city. US spotters fighting alongside the Kurds were providing bombing locations to jet fighters overhead. There were also some Marine gunships in action. This time there was no press anywhere near the action and it would be difficult for any reporters to slip into Kobani since the place was surrounded.

MONDAY, February 2, 2015, 10:00 a.m.

Monday morning, McCormick gave a press conference at the Pentagon to announce that the US had achieved its objectives. A team was currently attempting to put out the fire at one of the oilfields and forces were still mopping up pockets of resistance. He thanked the Kurds for their enthusiastic participation and said that they had routed the jihadists in Kobani. McCormick reiterated that the US would maintain a permanent base in Kurdistan to prevent any further threats to the Kurds and Turkey. He knew that this would anger the Turks, but considering their previous behavior and lack of support, they had it coming. The Turks had allowed jihadist recruits to pass through their country and let jihadist-controlled contraband oil flow through Turkey in the other direction. Turkish tanks and infantry had parked on the Turkish border in plain sight of Kobani and did nothing while the jihadists routed and slaughtered innocent people, mostly Syrian Kurds in that city.

McCormick was asked the usual post-battle questions, and finally, "What are you going to do now, General?"

McCormick responded, "Nothing. We have achieved our objectives." The administration was not going to tip off anyone that the second phase,

Operation Take Back, would soon be underway. They wanted the jihadists to think that this was the end of the offensive.

MONDAY, February 2, 2015, 1:00 p.m.

Goldstein confirmed that the Stewart and O'Leary interviews had been arranged for Wednesday, February 11, 2015. He could tape his interview with O'Leary earlier in the day for broadcast on Thursday evening and do the Daily Show on Wednesday night.

TUESDAY, February 3, 2015

The Attorney General held an afternoon press conference announcing that 12 former IRS officials had been arrested and charged with various offenses ranging from conspiracy to deliberately targeting individual Americans, groups and businesses, illegally distributing private information to second parties, and illegally soliciting information against IRS regulations, among other things. As the Administrator had directed, none of these people would receive paid administrative leave.

WEDNESDAY, February 4, 2015

The new majority Senate elected in November was now seated and passed the declaration of war against jihadist terrorists that the Congress had passed earlier. It granted broad powers to the administration, as Haynes had requested. On the same day, Haynes picked up the phone and gave Simmons the go-ahead for the raids on the American jihadist training camps.

THURSDAY, February 5, 2015, 10:00 a.m.

Haynes understood from day one that confidence in American leadership had to be reestablished to get the allies to come along in the fight against the jihadist and Russian aggression.

He had just completed telephone discussions on secure phones with the president of Egypt and the king of Jordan. Secret meetings had been conducted with both countries regarding a plan to reestablish normality in the region. Both leaders now understood as a result of the Kurdish campaign that America meant business and would follow-up through with commitments. The morning telephone conversation with these two leaders established the plan. Haynes congratulated the President of Egypt for his courageous address to a Egyptian mullah's to stop the teaching of jihadism in mosques, schools or anywhere else.

1. The United States would supply the weapons required for Jordan and Egypt to move forward.
2. Arms would be supplied to legitimate Libyan government forces to fight the jihadists within Libya. Egypt would decide what would be required and to whom arms would be distributed.
3. If Egypt decided to back up the peaceful Libyan government with an invasion they would be assisted by American air power.
4. The King and the president agreed to try and enlist the participation from other Arab states in the region except for Iran.
5. Jordan and Egypt agreed to try and coax president Hassad into leaving Syria and to join the Americans to somehow get the Syrian army and the original Syrian fighters to join forces to rid Syria of Islamic jihadists.
6. Jordan and Egypt agreed to remain in Syria after hostilities ceased to bring order back to the country until a new peaceful government can be reestablished.
7. The Americans insisted and got agreement on the separation of Iraq into three states. Kurdistan in the north, Sunnis in the middle and the Shia in the south.
8. The details of objectives in military planning would be kept out of the media. The only thing that would be publicized would be that they were united in the defeat of extreme jihadists and this would be culminated by a visit later in the day by the ambassadors from both countries in front of the media to show solidarity.

The ambassador from Egypt and Jordan were now present in the White House and now sitting on each side of Haynes. Flashbulbs and cameras were popping. The ambassadors and Haynes had their hands piled up in the center of to show solidarity for the media and the world to see.

Haynes made a short statement to blunt any further questions concerning the details of the plan. He said we are united in this effort and we are not tipping anyone off with regard to what the plan is. The objective is to rid the Middle East of these extremists. The two ambassadors concurred and they did not take any further questions.

Privately the Egyptian president had had enough of the jihadists. They had recently beheaded 21 Christian Egyptian citizens on a beach in Libya. His plan was now to arm the military of the peace seeking Libyan government based in Tripoli. When the arming was completed they planned a joint operation complete with American air cover and ground spotters to launch an all-out offensive starting with the Libyans moving East and the Egyptians Army moving west into Libya to squeeze and annihilate the jihadists or any other paramilitary groups.

SATURDAY, February 7, 2015 - Hancock, New York

In Hancock New York, about 145 miles northwest of New York City, FBI and Special Forces surrounded the 30-acre property of Islamberg and were closing in on foot. They timed their arrival to coincide with the dawn cross-country march of the latest trainees. As the raiders came out of the woods, about 40 dark-clothed individuals dropped their weapons and ran for the woods the other side of the path, straight into the arms of the waiting FBI agents.

Soon the 40 of them, almost half of them women, hands handcuffed behind their backs, were loaded into unmarked vans and driven to a holding centre in an old warehouse, where a very organized team of interrogators was waiting.

The first young man taken into the interrogation room immediately announced that he was an American citizen and demanded to call his lawyer.

"Not this time, buddy," came the response. "This is a new day in America."

The same scene was playing out across the country, in abandoned school houses and warehouses that the FBI had commandeered for the operation. By mid afternoon, nearly 400 of 732 detainees had been processed and the decisions were starting to be made about ultimate destinations of those captured in the raids. One thing remained clear, not one would remain in America.

TUESDAY, February 10, 2015, 10:00 a.m. - Washington

Haynes was anxious to get his security briefing out of the way before his 10:00 meeting, which he expected would be exciting. He was going to meet with three of his heroes. One was Elon Musk, president of Tesla and manufacturer of a 100 percent electric car. Musk also owned a space company which NASA had contracted to send their rockets into orbit. Musk had made a truckload of money from selling his internet company. He could have just drifted off to enjoy life without ever working again, but he risked all on these two enterprises and nearly went bust doing it. He was the entrepreneur's entrepreneur.

Bert Rutan was a world renowned aircraft designer. He was best known for his Cunard designed aircraft which has the elevator in the front instead of the back, making these airplanes instantly recognizable. He was also responsible for using carbon fiber for the construction of airplanes. He proved that carbon fiber designs are lighter, stronger, and allow for smoother airflow, which increases speed and efficiency. It was now commonly used by large manufacturers like Boeing. His aircraft had broken international flight records and he and Richard Branson, Haynes' third guest, had teamed up to develop an airplane that could go into outer space and return intact.

Finally the security briefers left and Haynes followed them out to greet Rutan, Branson and Musk, who had been waiting outside with Rod. They chatted in the Oval Office for several hours. Haynes wanted to know if Rutan still had the twin boomerang prototype he built a long time ago, and had a variety of questions for the three of them. In the meantime the Speaker of the House, the committee chairman responsible for funding space operations and the director of NASA were waiting outside. Haynes hadn't wanted them in the preliminary meeting for fear will that his three guests would speak less freely in their presence. All three had nearly gone bankrupt at some point because they were high risk individuals. They were also the kind of winners and inventors that America needed. Haynes was tired of all the government money wasted on losers. He was determined that if taxpayer money was used to assist development, it would go to winners like these three. The three had been given a heads up to bring him ideas for expanding their existing successful products and what they needed in terms of government assistance for research and development. Haynes was especially interested in Musk's rockets, because he wanted to stop using the Russians to get Americans into outer space. Haynes didn't care how much money they made doing it. It would still be a lot more cost-effective than some government-run bureaucratic project. Private enterprise always does it better.

Both Rutan and Musk had new ideas and concepts that they did not have the capital to pursue. Haynes was so fascinated that he spent another half hour quizzing them on the concepts. Rod was starting to tap his feet because people were waiting outside. Finally, Haynes asked the Speaker and the others waiting outside to join the meeting. Rutan and Musk went through their lists again along with the total amount they would need to design, develop and test prototypes.

After his three guests had left, Haynes told the Speaker and the Senate leader that it was time to start funding research and development for proven winners and that he wanted some of these projects funded as soon as possible, especially the one that would put space exploration back under US control.

WEDNESDAY, February 11, 2015, 9:00 a.m. - New York

David and Sonja had flown up to Manhattan the previous afternoon in a private Air Force jet. Haynes didn't like to use Air Force One, especially for these short trips. He also wanted to avoid columns of limousines disrupting traffic in New York or anywhere else; and besides he thought it was safer to travel in vehicles that looked like everyone else's.

Haynes was ready to make his way over to Allen Diamond's company, Costume Galore, which only a few blocks from his hotel. His Secret Service detail was going crazy because he insisted on walking. Diamond greeted him at the door, and Haynes' first thought was that people never look the same as what you imagine them from telephone conversations. Diamond was slightly balding with curly hair on the sides. He was slim and average height and in good shape for a man in his 60s. Diamond appeared nervous but was enthusiastic and excited at Haynes' arrival complete with his Secret Service entourage. Diamond was buzzing with nervous energy as he escorted Haynes into his costume warehouse.

"Well Allen," said Haynes, "do you have my stuff?"

Diamond chuckled and said, "Yeah, it's in the other room."

Haynes told Agent Riley to wait outside, while he entered the next room, which had walls but no ceiling. Riley could hear the two of them laughing and shuffling around on the other side of the wall and was wondering what was going on. Finally he shouted, "Is everything okay in there?"

Haynes replied, "Relax Terry, we will be out in a little bit."

Finally Haynes and Diamond came back out, wearing smiles like a couple of guys that had known each other for 25 years, carrying a huge duffel bag. Haynes handed it to Riley and said, "Make sure this is in the dressing room at the Daily Show." Haynes turned to Diamond and said, "Alan, I'll make sure that all this stuff is returned to you. You may want to hang onto it because it might have some historical value down the road." Then Haynes said, "Bring your wife to the White House sometime. Just call my assistant Jeannie Flett and she can make the arrangements."

In the meantime Riley was starting to open the zipper on the duffel bag. Haynes looked over and said, "Don't even think about it."

Riley said, "But Sir," and Haynes shot back, "But Sir nothing. Leave it closed."

The entourage left with the duffel bag strapped over the bewildered Riley's shoulder. Riley had arranged for a limo to be waiting outside Diamond's office to drive Haynes over to the Fox building for the O'Leary interview. Riley had had enough of walking around New York.

Haynes had left Sonja back at the hotel, one of the few times that he did not bring her with him. She would never understand what he was about to do and he didn't feel like explaining. Instead he made arrangements for her to go directly to the Fox building to watch his interview with O'Leary.

O'Leary gave Haynes a nice greeting. Haynes said, "Yeah, I know O'Leary, you're nice now but as soon as they turn that camera on you're going to turn into a pitbull."

O'Leary's questions were straightforward and so were Haynes' answers. On a couple of occasions O'Leary seemed genuinely surprised by Haynes' directness. Haynes had been watching O'Leary for years and understood his body language. He knew when O'Leary's back straightened and he leaned backwards in his chair, it meant he had heard something unexpected. Haynes thought the interview went extremely well.

Later it was time for the Daily Show. Haynes made arrangements for Sonja to be driven over a little later so that she would arrive just before he was being introduced. He didn't want her fretting. Stewart greeted Haynes and Riley, and shot a glance at the duffel bag Terry was carrying. After pleasantries, Haynes said, with a big smile on his face, "You're going to try and kick my ass tonight aren't you, Jon."

Stewart said, "Why don't we just make it fun and interesting."

"10-4," said Haynes.

Stewart explained how the segments of the show were run and said because of the unusual nature of Haynes' appearance the fact the he didn't know how long their discussion would take, Haynes would come on right after Stewart's opening monologue Then he asked, "What's in the bag?"

Haynes replied with a smile, "Weapons for the Secret Service."

Stewart replied, "I Hope you are not going to use them on me."

Haynes said, "Only if you don't behave yourself."

Haynes was shown to a dressing room down the hallway and Riley brought in the bag. Haynes said, "Well, Terry, I guess you can open it now and lay everything out neatly."

Riley pulled each piece out and then asked, "You're really not going to do this are you?"

Haynes shot back, "Damn right I am. Now if you could excuse me I need to get dressed."

At about 8:00 p.m., one of Stewart's assistants knocked on Haynes' dressing room door and said, "Sir you need to be standing near the studio door before you are introduced." When Haynes opened the door and the assistant nearly fell backwards. "Is that you?"

Haynes replied, "No, it's how your boss has been describing me the last couple of months."

They made their way to the studio entrance where Haynes could see Stewart giving his monologue while Haynes stood behind a small curtain.

Now it was time for the introduction. Stewart gave a sarcastic and yet very funny description of Haynes and said, "I'd like to introduce the AD MIN IS TRA TOR," dragging out the word. Haynes step out from behind the curtain and Stewart's jaw dropped. He started that silly chuckle of his and turned around and walked the other way, then turned again and started laughing some more in disbelief.

Haynes was wearing a full battle dress Army helmet with six stars across on the bottom front. Above the stars were painted white letters spelling out KILL WASHINGTON. His eyes were covered by a pair of aviator style sunglasses. He was wearing a false black mustache and an army jacket with polished brass buttons and a khaki shirt and tie underneath. There were six stars on each shoulder. His pants were khaki riding britches that bulged out stiffly from his hips to his knees. The bottom part of the trousers were tucked into a pair of high, well shined boots. He was wearing a General Patton style pearl handled pistol in a holster. The left side of his jacket was full of travel ribbons and the right side was covered with medals.

The audience was confused. Some were laughing and some were just sitting there.

Haynes approached the guest seat beside Stewart's desk and Stewart was still laughing. Then he stuck out his hand toward Haynes and Haynes raised his voice and said, "Sit down, I'm not shaking hands with someone who's been saying nasty things about me."

They both sat down. Haynes managed to keep a straight face while Stewart was still laughing. All of a sudden Haynes right arm started to go up and he began pushing it down with his left arm like Peter Sellers in the movie Dr. Strangelove, where Sellers played the German Nazi scientist.

Stewart said, "What's wrong with your arm?"

Haynes said with a fake accent, "I have to have an operation to keep my automatic arm from lifting. Dr. Strangelove was my uncle." By now the audience had caught on and there was a lot of laughter. Then Haynes said, "you must be wondering why I came out here like this?"

Stewart laughed and said, "I have no idea."

Haynes said, "Well, I just wanted to look the way you have been describing me for the last couple of months."

The cracks went back and forth for a bit and then Haynes said, "Do you mind if I take my helmet off? My empty head is taking a beating." He removed his helmet, his sunglasses and the mustache and then looked out at the audience and while still seated, opened his arms and said, "Well America, this is the real me, so why don't we all just lighten up?"

Haynes was pretty certain he had somewhat disarmed the audience not only in studio but those watching on TV. Now Stewart's questions became somewhat serious on a whole range of issues including the Kurdistan operation. One of Haynes' answers was, "If you think you're going to go around cutting off the heads of Americans without consequences, you've got another thought coming."

Stewart didn't agree with everything the administration was doing but at least now he was showing a little respect.

Sonja came out for the last few minutes of the interview. She was still in a bit of shock but even she started to laugh. Stewart asked if she had known Haynes was going to do any of this and she replied, "No way. I wouldn't have allowed it if I had known."

Haynes felt he had accomplished his limited goal. He showed that he was just down-to-earth like most folks, complete with a sense of humor, and wasn't the pariah some people thought he was. Meanwhile, the last part of the Stewart interview and the O'Leary interview to be shown the next day would show off his serious side.

Flett and Goldstein were freaking out at the White House but not Giani. He understood exactly what Haynes was trying to do.

David got a lecture from Sonja in the limousine all the way back to the hotel but at the same time she could not stop laughing. She was worried about how the interview was going to be received by the American public because they both knew it was likely to go viral on all the networks over the next few days.

Later that week, O'Leary did one of his private surveys on the public's reaction to both his interview and Haynes' appearance on Stewart's show. Some called the Daily Show appearance outrageous, but for the most part the reaction was very positive, especially among younger people.

CHAPTER 24

TAKING ON THE JIHADISTS AND OTHER THREATS

—☙—

FRIDAY, February 13, 2015, 9:00 a.m.

HAYNES HAD BEEN GETTING REPORTS that surveillance of domestic terrorists, most of them Muslim, was stretched to the limit. He had invited Nigel Forage, the United Kingdom Independent Party leader, to have lunch with him while he was in Washington on other matters. Forage had very strong views on the serious problems that England faced with regard to Muslim immigrants. Their discussion left Haynes even more committed to an idea that had been percolating for a while.

So after lunch, he called on Ray Kyling, director of homeland security. They both knew that the war in Kurdistan/Iraq was going to increase the risk of homeland attacks in the short-term. Now Haynes was about to do something that had not been done since the 1930's when the Congress barred further Japanese immigration to the United States. America had always been a country of immigrants, but the jihadists were forcing his hand. In any case, too many Muslims were not integrating very well into American culture. Too many were becoming disenfranchised and being manipulated by jihadist websites. Since he was now responsible for the security of American citizens, he was going to put Americans first. He told Kyling to refuse any citizenship applications from Muslim countries and Muslims living in non-Muslim countries. Visas would be required for these same groups to travel to America. An exception could be made for business people, diplomats and people known to Homeland Security as not a threat. There was no point in making a big public announcement about this because the left-wing media and their supporters would go crazy. But instinctively, Haynes knew he had the majority of the American people on his side on this matter.

Haynes went on to explain. "Ray," he said, "my old mentor used to like dividing things into categories and I think this is something that can be applied here. I think there are four categories of Muslims. The first group are those jihadists who want to kill everybody who is not a Muslim and even good Muslims that don't agree with their twisted definition of Islam. The second group are the ones who don't participate in terrorism and lead normal lives but at the same time are sending money to terrorist organizations and privately cheerleading the jihadists. The third group are just good people but unfortunately they are scared and intimidated by the other two groups, especially the jihadists, so they say nothing and don't report possible future criminal attacks or rhetoric in mosques encouraging terrorism. The fourth group is small but very significant; these are the Muslims in this country who do not try to change American culture and values, instead they adapt to our culture while still practicing their religion. They are bold and courageous speakers against the behaviour of the other three categories. Ayaan Hirsi Ali is a perfect example. The fact that she requires security to move around this country is a disgrace.

"But without more Muslims willing to speak out, you only need a small percentage of armed, intimidating people to eventually dominate the majority. It happened in Iraq where a small vicious minority took over the government. It happened in Germany in the 30s when the Nazis took over. It's kind of like a barrel of apples; there may be only two apples in the barrel that are rotten. If you don't get them out of the barrel in a timely way they will contaminate all the rest."

MONDAY, February 16, 2015, 9:00 a.m. - Kurdistan

The need for surprise in Operation Take Back was not as great as it had been for Operation Leatherneck, where the main purpose had been to prevent the jihadists from blowing up the oil wells.

The northern coalition forces surrounding Mosul and Tikrit started to move into both. A couple of thousand Special Forces paratroopers were dropped around the Baghdad airport and a number of C-150s were flown in filled with Marines and tanks. Within four hours they had seized the Baghdad airport and were now using it for a staging ground to assemble a major force to head north, where it would be joined by a fast-moving portion of the northern force moving south around the eastern flank of jihadist resistance to reinforce the forces at the airport. Then it was time to squeeze the jihadists between them and the remaining northern forces now heading south.

They had landed enough tanks and supplies at the airport that they could send a tank column into the green zone where the American Embassy was. The tanks and Marines would sit there until further notice.

The administration had decided that once the fighting had been reduced to small pockets, they would appoint a group of people to manage Iraq – this time under American supervision. There would be none of that nonsense where some new Iraqi administration was going to prosecute American soldiers that had sacrificed to put them there in the first place. A portion of oil revenues would be used to pay for the presence of the military and the rest would be used for infrastructure and kept out of the hands of corrupt officials. The Americans would limit their own movements and casualties. From this point on it would be the Iraqis who would take on the jihadi pockets of resistance and if that didn't work, things were going to get brutal. There would be no messing around this time and the Iranians were not going to have any influence. The Iranian border crossings into Iraq would be blocked. Only selected traffic would be allowed to leave and enter. There wasn't a living Iraqi who had experienced a real democracy. They had been living under brutal dictators and a few years of messed up secular leadership. Transition to a real fledgling democracy would take years, if not decades. In the meantime, the administration was not going to leave Iraq to the resurgence of a bunch of killer thugs influenced and supported by Iran. That would eventually threaten America, and America had to be proactive in defending itself. The administration's philosophy would be, "We don't care if they like us but they are going to respect our desire to have innocent people treated with dignity." The modern world was much too small to take any other approach.

This attitude formed the basis of a short address Haynes made to the American people on the evening of Tuesday, February 24. He started off by praising the professionalism and bravery of the men and women in the Armed Forces and singled out General Trais for his skill and innovative battle strategy.

TUESDAY, February 17, 2015

Haynes met with Giani and Kyling on the progress of border security, especially along the Mexican border. Kyling reported that good progress had been made on the super fence and he thought that for the most part it would be completed by the end of the year. Most important, Kyling had reorganized the patrolling and monitoring procedures of the border patrol. Coordination between federal and state law enforcement was now excellent.

Kyling also reported that deportations of illegals with criminal records had increased dramatically. What was making a huge difference was that anyone caught crossing the border was documented and fingerprinted and then immediately deported. They were told that if they tried to re-enter the United States they would be permanently barred from ever having a chance to obtain visas, green cards or citizenship. Kyling said that the word seemed to be getting out below the border and there was an obvious decline in illegal border crossing attempts. He also reported that a number of suspicious Muslim jihadist types were caught crossing and were being held in a special location for interrogation.

Haynes told Kyling that he wanted to know when he felt the border was fully secured or down to a trickle of illegals, so they could move to the next phase.

Governor Moonbeam, as Haynes described him, had called from California ranting and raving about Haynes' immigration efforts. Obviously, some of his Hispanic and extreme liberal voters wanted to allow the status quo to continue, allowing California to become a quasi

Mexican state. Interestingly enough, he was the only governor to call and complain.

Kyling reported that they had implemented new procedures for tracking visas, and had already tracked down some folks with overstayed visas. They were documented and fingerprinted in case they made further applications, and then deported.

"Sounds good," said Haynes, sliding a one page document toward Kyling. "Now I've got another project for you. We need to set up locations all over the country, but primarily in areas where illegal immigrants are located. These offices are to be staffed by government employees under the direction of your agency. Their function will be to document illegal aliens no matter where they're from. I want to make sure that the people staffing these offices are polite and courteous. Basically we need to know the following about everyone:

1. Normal things like their name, age, birthday, etcetera.
2. Country of origin/ previous address.
3. Employer.
4. Social security number / driver's license /green card if any.
5. How long have they been in the United States? We have got to be careful with this one because some of these folks are going to lie figuring that the longer they've been in the US, the better their chances to stay. You will probably need some proof like previous addresses, witnesses or employers and so on.
6. Do they have any family members in the US and which ones were born here?
7. Do they have a criminal record and if so from what country, under what circumstances?
8. You might want to use the Nexus program as an example and use retina scans for identification.
9. They can be given a plastic bar-coded ID card with their picture on it so if they are asked after the four-month registration period they will be safe from deportation until the next phase.

"I don't want to hire any new federal employees for this. Transfer people from existing agencies to get this done. We need to have enough of these offices so there won't be any huge lineups and delays. We need to have them up and running by October 1, 2015. We want to give these people four months to register so you have to know approximately how many and where they are and have enough offices up and running by October 1. Too many offices are better than not enough because we don't need excuses to extend this program because of delays in lines. Maybe you can come up with a name like National Non-citizen Identification Program or something like that. We need to have a good advertising program also, in Spanish, so that no one will have an excuse like "they didn't know." The advertising should start a month before, in September. After the end of the four-month registration period, any non-resident not registered will be deported immediately. The registration program will terminate January 31, 2016. If necessary it could be extended but not by a lot. If you can get these offices up and running before October 1, let me know and we can start the program earlier. Absolutely what we do not need is a computer screw-up like with the Affordable Health Care plan. I have worked with software designers before and the software for this is not complicated so let's just use real smart people that have small software offices that are not expensive. Governments tend to want to hire huge companies for this kind of thing but it's not necessary. Let's save the taxpayer's money. This program is going to have huge benefits. The biggest one is we are going to know how many of these folks are in the country."

Kyling said, "What are you going to do after the registration period is completed?"

"Good question," said Haynes. "I don't really know right now but we have lots of time to think about it. One thing for sure is we will know approximately how many people we're dealing with. Up until now no one has had a clue because of this loosey-goosey, unorganized approach."

Kyling next reported on the results of Haynes' instructions to ask certain Russian citizens to leave the USA. They had been informed that they could only re-enter with a visa, and most visas would allow them to stay in the USA for a maximum of one month. Any violation of the one month rule would result in their immediate expulsion and visas would no longer be issued to such violators. Government employees were told that if they were asked why these rules were being imposed, their reply was to be "Ask the Ukrainian president."

A lot of wealthy Russians now owned property in the United States and had some influence with the Russian hierarchy. As far as Haynes was concerned, these rules would stay in place until the Russians got out of the Ukraine.

THURSDAY, February 26, 2015, 5:45 p.m.

Military personnel grabbed Tomas Tireza outside his office in New York City and drove him to New Jersey's Teterboro airport where he was put on board a private Global Express jet and flown to Czechoslovakia. McCormick had already made arrangements with the Czech Government for his arrival. Later that evening, his wife was informed of what had occurred and told she was free to stay or to leave the country. Tireza's passport was seized and so were his American bank accounts. Mr. Tireza was no longer going to be able to finance what McCormick perceived to be his anti-American propaganda outlets. McCormick didn't want the domestic FBI involved. That would not be perceived well.

Haynes did not find out about any of this until later. McCormick was good that way. He took full responsibility for these kinds of things.

MONDAY, March 3, 2015

The FDA had finally approved one of Haynes' pet projects, the operational approval of oxygen and ozone-related clinics. He was really pleased about the approval of Recirculatory Hemoperfusion Ozone Delivery Systems, a procedure somewhat similar to kidney dialysis except that blood is removed from the body and ozone is inserted into the blood before it is returned to the body. Haynes was convinced that ozone was very effective for a multitude of ailments.

MONDAY, March 16, 2015

More than 60 days had passed since the meeting with the Chinese Ambassador and as both Haynes and McFarland had anticipated, the Chinese had done nothing about their currency. McFarland had been consulting with various currency traders and concluded that if traded on the open market, the yuan would be worth approximately 12% more than the Chinese fixed value cap.

The following day, the Chinese Ambassador was invited to the White House to meet with Giani, Haynes and McFarland. Haynes informed the Ambassador that starting May 1, tariffs on all Chinese products would increase at the rate of 1% a month over the next 12 months. "Because we have estimated that your currency is worth 12% more than the Chinese Government's fixed rate," he explained. He repeated that this was in contravention of fair rules of trade. "Your government has been getting away with this for years and it's time for a correction. You have been reminded on several occasions during the last 60 days that we expected the Chinese Government to do something about this so it would look like it was your idea. I guess you assumed that we were not serious. Now you know we are."

Haynes was very clear that if the Chinese took any action that the US considered retaliatory, the US would retaliate in kind and things could escalate out of control. That would be the choice of the Chinese Government. The administration had decided that a slow tariff increase of 1% a month would give businesses a chance to adjust their prices.

After the meeting, Haynes gave the Chinese a few days grace so if they changed their minds, it would look like their idea. There was nothing forthcoming from the Chinese, so on Wednesday McFarland announced the new tariffs at a press conference. On Wednesday, McFarland confirmed the new tariffs in a speech to a large business organization. He added that the commerce department set up a special section to receive complaints from American businesses, especially in the manufacturing sector where Chinese imports had unfairly damaged their business and led to the loss of American jobs. He added, "We will assess all this information and further measures may be required."

He verified that the Commerce Department was also working on an equivalent retaliation approach to trade relationships. If a particular country did not allow the import of American automobiles, the US would not allow importation of their automobiles and if they didn't sell automobiles it would find something else. If their import duties were 10% on certain products they would be 10% coming into the United States and so on.

Someone in the audience asked, "What do you think the Chinese will do with the American bonds they're holding?"

McFarland said, "They'll do what they have to do, but we are no longer going to have a gun held to our head. This administration is starting to get the budget under control and we are on our way to reducing the deficit. These deficits make America weak and this has to be reversed. This is going to be about Americans first."

WEDNESDAY, March 25, 2015

The Chinese announced that they would be putting even more restrictions on American companies based in China. Haynes was ready for this; he took to the microphones again and said that America would be increasing the tariffs on Chinese goods from 12% to 15% over the next 15 months starting May 1. "We have other measures waiting in the wings if necessary. The Chinese are not the only ones in Asia that America can buy products from," he said.

Haynes was getting phone calls from aircraft manufacturers and the like and he told them he wasn't backing off and they should pass this on to their Chinese customers. Haynes had already anticipated that the Chinese would threaten to cancel their contracts with American manufacturers as a pressure tactic.

WEDNESDAY, March 25, 2015

Most of the heavy fighting in Iraq was now over, although there were still pockets of trouble throughout the south of the country. The northern part, now under Kurdish and coalition control, was quiet. The Kurds still wanted to take the jihadists on anywhere they could find them and teamed up with willing Iraqi forces and even some British Gurkha troops. The Kurds were not only great fighters, they wanted revenge for the unspeakable atrocities committed by the jihadists against Iraqi and Kurdish Christians, good Muslims and anyone else who didn't agree with their insane ideology. The Kurds were leading the fight against pockets of resistance and didn't take many prisoners. The jihadists were finding out that hiding among civilians wasn't doing them much good either.

General Trais made it clear that anyone outside the police forces caught with a weapon of any kind would be arrested or shot on sight. The idea was to rid Iraq of weapons.

The Kurds were not stupid. Right after signing the agreement that America would recognize Kurdistan as an independent country in exchange for a military base, the Kurds hired election specialists from all over the free world. These consultants had been in the country for quite some time and prepared Kurdistan for a preliminary election for regional representatives and a president. Those delegates and the president would write a new constitution for Kurdistan. Finally, America would have a very valued new ally in the Middle East, along an operational military base. Maybe now the Iranians would think twice about developing nuclear weapons.

Behind the scenes, General Trais was in intense negotiations with the Sunni leadership. The goal was to draw the northern border for a new Sunni state. There were no Shias present at these negotiations. The Shias were going to get what was left in the south.

Trais was also preparing to take possession of a small territory between the southern Turkish border and Northern Syria, extending all the way to the Mediterranean, to provide the Kurds with a sea port along with a possible oil pipeline down the road. He was prepared to sit in the middle of Iraq, south of the new Kurd border, and put out fires when he could. But for the most part he would let the Iraqis battle it out while Kurdistan was flourishing in the North in peace and quiet. If moderate Shias and Sunnis wanted some help to remove some jihadists, the US would provide air support and on occasion maybe some ground troops. Haynes' opinion was that they would finally get tired of the chaos and agree to a division to establish two new countries for the Sunnis and Shias.

THURSDAY, April 2, 2015

Haynes attended a meeting with Snow and his AFC team leaders, including Rogers and Dever, to see how the AFC was progressing. Each member of each team, including the team leader, had been encouraged to become a specialist on one or another federal government agency. Rogers' specialty was health and human services and he made the first presentation. The perception of people that did not know him well was that Rogers didn't look very organized. In fact, he was one of the most organized people Haynes had ever met.

Rogers said, "The Health and Human Services Agency is supposed to transfer all health services to the states. However, my personal opinion is that there are several responsibilities that should be left in the hands of the federal government and within this agency." He passed out a paper giving a basic description of the departments within the Health and Human Services Agency as it stood. He said, "You can see that under the present system, the department's budget is around $940 billion and it has about 77,000 employees."

Rogers continued, "I have been in constant contact with the members of the other teams who have been focusing on Health and Human Services. We have coordinated our negotiations with all the states and have narrowed down how the responsibilities of this agency should be divided up from the state's point of view.

"The question came up as to whether departments not being transferred to state power should be moved to the Shared section of the Charter. However, the final consensus was that Health and Social Services should remain in the State Only section with the exception of the Centers for Disease Control, the Food and Drug Administration, and Indian Health. It was agreed that these three will fall under the Federal Only section.

"As the Administrator anticipated, there are ongoing negotiations regarding the short and long-term fiscal arrangements for the transfer of this agency. There are approximately 40,000 employees working for the three aforementioned sub departments. That means that there are going to be 37,000 people no longer required at the federal level. The state negotiators have unanimously agreed that these 37,000 people will be first in line to be employed by state governments if they want to relocate.

"We have now completed the first phase of the Federal Only side of these negotiations, and are ready for discussions on the State Only side."

Snow interjected, "One very interesting and unexpected thing happened. The governor of Louisiana suggested that if this new constitutional amendment was successful, which he hoped it was going to be, that the leader, being myself, and all team members be appointed as the first AFC Committee members. He felt that since they led these negotiations they would be the most competent to serve on the Committee, and would have the confidence of state and federal officials."

Haynes said, "I think that's a great idea. Let's see how we can work this into the initial amendment. I think the first thing we should do now is formalize these additions to the Federal Only part of the charter and submit them to the Senate and the Congress. I don't foresee them having a problem with retaining any of the powers listed in that section. After we have Congress' approval for what will remain in the federal domain, we can then submit the more controversial State Only agencies' responsibilities. This will take some serious negotiating. Let's take the Shared Section of the Charter to the states and see if we can get some consensus on those. The states can be negotiating the Shared part while the feds are still working on the State Only provisions. One step at a time is the process."

MONDAY, April 6, 2015

The following week, Snow presented the revised Federal Only part of the Charter to the Congressional leadership and the AFC committees. As discussed on November 11, the new version included a new item number 20 for the Centers for Disease Control. Snow commented that this was definitely a national issue and that the states agreed. Indian health was added under number 19, Native Affairs.

Snow said he didn't think there would be any issues with this modified and hopefully final Federal Only list. One of the participants immediately brought up the State Only part of the Charter. Snow answered that he wanted them to concentrate on the Federal Only list for the time being, and not muddy the waters by discussing another section of the Charter. His primary goal was to get the items on the present Federal Only list accepted.

After Snow's meeting with the Congressional people, Haynes told the press that the states had been very cooperative and accepted all the items on the Federal Only list. He expressed the wish that they would have the same cooperation on the remaining parts of the Charter. "This whole process is not about turf, it's about what's good for the American people," he said, adding that the administration was going to be extremely vigilant concerning elected officials who appeared to be doing things in their own self interest or on behalf of special interests. The current process was the most important since the one leading to the original Constitution. Elected officials could act on behalf of Americans and go down in history, or be part of the problem.

The Kurds and Americans decided to coordinate their announcements, so that Haynes would announce that the US was recognizing Kurdistan on the same day that the Kurds announced their preliminary election. The election was termed preliminary because its primary purpose was to elect a president and delegates from various areas in Kurdistan to write a constitution for the new Kurdistan. The election was scheduled for Monday, April 27. They gave themselves 12 months to complete the new constitution. Then they would go back to the people with a referendum on the new document. Three months after that there would be a general election to elect representatives to the new structure and also a president.

Secretary of State West went to Turkey the day before these announcements to give the Turks a head's up on the plan. He expected it to be an ugly meeting, and sure enough, the Turkish government and press immediately began calling the Americans traitors and threatening to leave NATO. West responded that leaving NATO would be a terrible idea. Turkey would be vulnerable to its neighbor, Russia. He also said that he didn't understand why they were so upset because there was a large Kurdish population in Turkey that was considered problematic by the Turks. They would probably want to leave Turkey peacefully to be part of the new Kurdistan. At the same time, Turkey would finally have a progressive and stable neighbor on its border.

WEDNESDAY, April 8, 2015

The last of the states approved the constitutional amendment passed by Congress for:

1. New and permanent Senate rules including the 50+1 vote proposal;
2. The right of the Congress to appoint special prosecutors;
3. The right of the House of Representatives to override the President's selection of Attorney General and vote their own selection into office. Only the President could fire an Attorney General.

MONDAY, April 13, 2015

In Hawaii, Chinese and American trade negotiators were trying to work out the trade impasse. The Chinese brought forward a proposal which was relayed to McFarland in Washington. McFarland found it totally insulting and a complete nonstarter. The Americans and Chinese were so far apart on a solution that the negotiations were called to a halt.

THURSDAY, April 16, 2015

The Congressional negotiating team told Snow that they were worried that the proposed future committee might move some of the sub agencies on the Federal Only list to state control. Snow pointed out that the states had already agreed that the Center for Disease Control should be added to the Federal Only section because it made sense – diseases spread beyond any given state. The committee's decision would be equally rational, he said. There could be further discussion on the committee's precise mandate, but in the meantime Snow wanted to know if they accepted the proposed contents of the Federal Only part of the Charter. This was pretty much a no-brainer and they unanimously accepted it.

Then Snow threw something at them that they didn't expect, a document explaining how the commission to oversee the charter was to be structured along with its mandate and a framework of guidelines for their decisions. "We want you to pass the first part of the amendment and include:

1. The Federal Only mandate you have accepted this morning:
2. The committee structure complete with its mandate."

The Speaker said, "We were not anticipating this."

Snow shot back, "Mr. Speaker, you've already accepted the Federal Only structure and it cannot be protected without the committee. We are going to need the committee's structure passed sooner or later so why not do it now? This should not be a problem because the House and the Senate have not signed off on the other two parts of the Charter anyway."

The Speaker looked toward the Senate leader and then looked back at Snow and said, "We will take this under advisement."

The Speaker looked at Haynes and asked, "What are you going to do if we can't get this passed?"

Haynes said, "I will just have to appeal to the common sense of the American people and hopefully they can persuade opposition to this to change."

The Speaker had no response to that. He had seen how effective Haynes had been so far with the American people, even on matters that would have been illegal under normal circumstances. Haynes' polling was high because the majority of Americans were getting off on watching him kick some ass. Americans were starting to feel good about their country again, and the economy was on the move.

The Speaker also knew that the communications department Haynes had set up at the White House would be pounding the constituents of any members who opposed what he perceived to be common-sense solutions. The department was already highly organized with contacts throughout the country that could flood any member's office with phone calls, letters and emails. As long as Haynes stayed popular, these members would have to be looking over their shoulders.

TUESDAY, April 28, 2015

The Kurd election results were now confirmed. They had elected their delegates and a new president, Kobani.

TUESDAY, May 5, 2015

The newly-elected Kurdish leader, President Kobani, came to Washington on an official state visit, complete with a state dinner at the White House. The event marked a huge win-win for both countries.

THURSDAY, May 7, 2015

Two days later, Haynes addressed the troops at Fort Hood, telling them, "You can now have confidence that your efforts in Iraq were not in vain, despite the stupidity of the Iraq pullout. Actually, in retrospect, the pullout from Iraq had benefits despite the horrible losses. We now have a new great ally in the state of Kurdistan, a new base, and we have you, the veterans of Iraq operations, to thank for it."

By the end of his speech, the entire audience was on its feet. This was the part of the job that Haynes loved, talking and mixing with these folks. He had brought along his son Colin who was also an Iraq veteran. He had also brought a special guest. "Ladies and Gentlemen, I would like to introduce the new President elect – and I stress elect – of Kurdistan, President Kobani."

The troops were on their feet again. Kobani was waving at the troops and they were applauding back. The new president seemed shaken and started to tear up. Haynes put his hand on his shoulder and Kobani turned and hugged him briefly. "Thank you," he said.

"Don't thank me, thank them," and Haynes pointed to the troops. Haynes' hand gesture didn't go unnoticed; the troops understood what the two men were saying and applauded even louder.

Kobani took to the microphone, and the area went dead quiet. "Sorry for my English, I thank David Haynes for bringing me here today to thank you from me and I bring message from my people, thank you for your sacrifice. Thank you, we won't forget you. Please come and visit Kurdistan."

The troops were still on their feet as Haynes and Kobani made their way off the podium to mix with the troops. The event was broadcast live on some US networks and in Kurdistan. From this point on, Americans and especially American veterans would be received in Kurdistan with open arms. Haynes remembered Robert Schuller's book Tough Minded Faith for Tender Hearted People. He had got tough right from the start and didn't let the Chicken Chamberlains alter his course. Today was the culmination.

On the plane back to Washington, Kobani asked Haynes what kind of a constitution he thought Kurdistan should have. Haynes said, "Pretty simple. I think the changes that we have made and are going to make will make the American Constitution the best in the world, bar none. The only difference is, you will have far fewer states and if I was you, I wouldn't have a Senate. A Senate like we have does not represent the population and if things are decentralized properly you don't need one."

"Why did you not do that here?" asked Kobani.

Haynes said, "There is a limit on what one can do with the entrenched status quo. The Senate was an invention of the founding fathers and has been institutionalized, or I would say actually psychologically internalized in the American psyche. The reason the Senate was created was because states that were not heavily populated were afraid of being dominated by more heavily populated states. So the framers decided to have two senators from every state no matter what their population was. But if you have power decentralized and closer to the people and not dominated by some wasteful over-bloated central government, then the need for a Senate is diminished."

Haynes continued, "Just remember a couple of things:

"1. Anything that you put in a constitution will take a crowbar to remove down the road.

"2. There is this myth out there, created by liberals and socialists, that would lead you to believe that a strong central government will be more efficient and makes the citizens feel more patriotic. This is absolute bullshit. When power is executed by political institutions closer to the people, those same people feel a stronger part of the whole and as a result are more patriotic. They tend to respect the differences of other people within their borders as long as things are not shoved down their throats by an over-centralized central government. They can make local decisions about things like education without interference. Outside interference creates resentments, especially when it comes from airheads in the academic world who have spent most of their lives not doing anything other than theorizing what they think is better for people. Good leaders in a free society respect the collective wisdom of the citizenry. The first and main purpose for a central government is to protect the country from the enemies of liberty. All things after that are not nearly as important.

"3. Remember that only a small percentage of the population are risk takers, dreamers of new inventions or other lofty things. This is just the way it is and will always be. For any country to be successful, its leaders have to recognize that these are the people that create real jobs rather than government wasteful jobs that suck taxpayers' money. If you restrict or put reins on these talented business people with stupid unnecessary regulations or dumb politicians that criticize their success, jobs and the economy will suffer and your country will become less competitive in the world."

CHAPTER 25

A SURPRISE FOR THE ADMINISTRATOR - AND FOR THE PRESIDENT

THURSDAY, May 14, 2015, 7:00 p.m.

A DINNER WAS SCHEDULED FOR 7:00 that evening. Haynes was under the impression it was to be a relatively modest social gathering of members of the cabinet and the administration and their families, so he was very surprised to see the Chief Justice in attendance.

For the last year, the Supreme Court had been operating pretty much as normal. Only on a few occasions had Haynes told his people to ignore decisions the Supreme Court rendered long before he arrived. Fortunately, even with the Constitution suspended, there were no decisions that would cause delays in the recovery or threaten security. So far Haynes had not been put into the situation of having to inform the Chief Justice that a particular recent decision would be ignored. The only real issue that Haynes had with the Supreme Court was with Justice Feinberg. As far as he was concerned she behaved more like a socialist legislator than a jurist.

At one point during dinner, Rod stood up and asked for everyone's attention. "We have just concluded the first six months of the Administrator's tenure," he said. "So, David, would you please come up and join me, we have a surprise for you." Giani was holding something in his hand that looked like a certificate or a diploma. "This is a document confirming you as a citizen of the United States," he said.

David was thrilled and surprised and his body language showed it.

Then Giani said, "I would like to ask the Chief Justice to come up and swear you in officially."

After the brief swearing-in routine, it was David's turn to say a few words. "I am very pleased to have this. I was afraid I might get deported because I have overstayed my visa." After the laughter quieted down Haynes said, "Thank you so very much."

On the way back to his seat he stopped and shook McCormick's hand. He had a gut feeling that this was part of some larger strategy of McCormick's. It was becoming more and more evident to Haynes that McCormick was behaving like MacArthur in Japan. He sensed that McCormick originally thought he would have to tightly control Haynes' actions. But Haynes was pushing the agenda faster than McCormick ever anticipated so he never really had to get on Haynes' case. Haynes and McCormick had some sort of wordless communication system. They both instinctively understood each other. McCormick had come to respect and understand Haynes' finely tuned instincts.

It started when Haynes appointed McCormick as Secretary of Defense. From the beginning, Haynes understood who was really running the show. He appointed McCormick as Defense Secretary before McCormick even had a chance to suggest that this was a position that he must have. Since then, McCormick's respect for Haynes had grown. David had exceeded his wildest expectations and McCormick knew that to dislodge him from his position now would cause all kinds of chaos. They both instinctively understood this without saying a word to each other. They were socially different but in the ways that counted, they were very much alike. And they watched each other's backs.

WEDNESDAY, May 20, 2015

The Libyan campaign had now started. Haynes was pleased that this was mostly an Egyptian and Libyan effort to rid Libya of the jihadists and paramilitary fighters. The Americans were on board with air cover and some ground spotter units as agreed. The Egyptian army entered Libya from the West led by an armored tank corps and the Libyan freedom Army now newly equipped started moving east from Tripoli. Both armies by now had good intelligence was aware of the opposition was located. The campaign lasted for about three weeks.

WEDNESDAY, June 5, 2015

The Senate passed the constitutional amendment for the Fedcral Only part of the American Functional Charter complete with the description of the mandate of the committee that would oversee it. This meant the AFC was one-third completed. Haynes and Snow knew that the states would approve it, so it was time to move on to the State Only section. The administration had planned one of its famous Gala evenings for the participants on Saturday evening because these social events showed appreciation for those who made a positive contribution to the process and created an atmosphere of enthusiasm to move forward.

Snow was not wasting any time. He introduced the second phase of negotiations for the State Only responsibilities of the charter. Haynes attended the meeting to try to gauge the mood. He knew there were a lot of members of Congress who wanted to retain big government, and this part of the charter transferred some agencies outright to the states and closed some departments. Some federal employees not hired by state agencies would get pink slips. "Let the games begin," he thought.

After the meeting, Haynes asked Snow, "Did you get the same feeling I got from their reaction?"

"I'm afraid so," said Snow.

"Well, Doug, it's just human nature not to want to give up turf. It's like a president of a company coming to a manager and saying 'I'm taking away some of your responsibilities and giving them to someone else.' In any case I anticipated this. Let's think like contrarians for now. Let's just keep negotiating with the states with regard to the State Only section. When we have agreement from the states, let's get them to pass it as if it has already been passed by the Congress and the Senate. After that, we will meet again with the Congressional people with the state ratifications in our hands. Forces in the Congress will try to delay us to death, hoping they can get past the 2016 elections and that with a new President, it will die a natural death.

"I guarantee you this is not going to happen. We are going to use our communications department to blast the constituencies of members conspiring to oppose this and after that I am going to go on national television to inform the American people what is happening. I will make sure that the name of every member opposing us appears on the screen while I am speaking. If that doesn't get them to move, then what I never wanted to do is going to happen. I will force closure and institute this constitutional amendment without them. There is no bloody way I'm going to let these people keep this over-bloated federal elephant intact."

THURSDAY, June 11, 2015

Haynes was now on the phone with the Egyptian president. Except for a few small skirmishes here and there it was now clear that the Libyan campaign had been successful. Haynes wanted to make it clear that the Egyptians needed to stay in Libya until it was sure that the Libyans could maintain control of the country and that there was no possibility of a jihadist resurgence. Haynes used the premature American military exit from Iraq as a classic example. He wanted to be sure that there would not be a repeat of the American mistake in Iraq.

THURSDAY, June 18, 2015

With the help of Sunni Iraqis, the Kurds and the coalition forces, the jihadists had finally been pushed out of Anbar province back into Syria. Now it was time to try to normalize the Syrian situation. Diplomatic pressure was being applied to persuade President Hassad to leave Syria. If he left, the Syrian army could be used to get rid of the jihadists left in the country since they would no longer have any allegiance to Hassad. The Syrian refugee problem was becoming critical and resources stretched to the limit, especially in Jordan.

WEDNESDAY, August 5, 2015

After months of negotiations, Secretary West had finally obtained the release of Dr. Afridi, who had been jailed by the Pakistanis for helping the Americans find Bin Laden. He was flown with his family to a German military base and a few days later would be flown to the United States. Secretary West asked Haynes to keep any meeting with Afridi very low-key and free of media. Embarrassing the Pakistanis was not a good idea and he didn't want to put a target on the backs of the doctor and his family.

So Haynes and West met with the doctor and his family in a private ceremony the following Saturday. West presented the family with honorary citizenship and American passports. Haynes made sure that the doctor would get housing and financial benefits for the same length of time that he had spent rotting in the Pakistani prison.

MONDAY, August 24, 2015

Homeland Security Secretary Kyling advised Haynes that the noncitizen registration offices would be operational by October 1, so Haynes announced the program on national television. He made it clear that there was no excuse for not registering, and that anyone who failed to register would be immediately deported – no lawyers, no hearings. He reminded noncitizens that state and federal law enforcement would have the right to ask for proof of citizenship after the registration period. Any business caught employing anyone without a registration card would be heavily fined. Haynes was not about to divulge what the plan was after the registration period except that anyone entering the country after January 31, 2016 would have to declare the length their visit.

TUESDAY, September 1, 2015

Rawlston's team concept had brought results and he hammered out an agreement in principle with most of the banking community. Mortgages in the hands of government agencies would be divided into regions, and banks closest to a particular mortgage address could bid to take it over. The target date for handover was April 2016, after which these agencies would be shut down and the federal government's involvement would be restricted to creating an umbrella of laws and rules under which banks, investment banks, mortgage companies and investment houses would operate.

FRIDAY, October 23, 2015

Coalition forces penetrated deep into Syria. The writing was on the wall for President Hassad. He was either going to be killed in Syria or live in one of the Gulf States. He also had his family to consider. So he finally decided to leave.

The following Sunday, Trais met with high-ranking Syrian military officers at a coalition base. Some of the original Syrian freedom fighters who had launched the uprising against Assad – before the jihadists came in to try to take their place – were in attendance. Trais needed the help of the Syrian army to finish the job in Syria. He knew they wouldn't cooperate unless they were guaranteed that there would be no war crimes charges against them when hostilities came to an end. He also needed the involvement of legitimate opposition forces to pave the way for a new beginning in Syria. Now the Syrian army and opposition forces would be fighting as one to rid Iraq of ISIS and restore normality to Syria.

MONDAY, October 27, 2015, 10:00 - Hawaii

President Chambers watched the television news report on Hassad's departure from his office in a villa the military had rented for his family on the Big Island of Hawaii. He loathed what the new administration had been doing. He had seen Haynes several times on television and felt like throwing a shoe at the TV set. The new administration had more or less implied that the carnage inflicted by the jihadists in Iraq and Kurdistan was a result of some of his decisions.

He had had months to contemplate and was coming to the conclusion that it was no longer possible for him to be reinstated as President. Although he had access to newspapers and television, he had no phone, so he sent for the Chief of Security, and told him that he wanted to use his cell phone to speak to General McCormick. Chambers asked McCormick when he was going to be reinstated. McCormick answered, "That is not a realistic question. You know that's not going to happen. But I'm sure that you already knew that before you called. So what is it that you really want, Mr. President?"

Chambers replied, "Well, since there is no chance for me to be reinstated I would like my house arrest ended."

McCormick had been preparing for this for quite some time. "Mr. President," he said, "I will send you a list of conditions that you will have to agree to and adhere to absolutely. I can tell you now that if you break even one, you will find yourself back in your present condition. You will have these conditions by tomorrow and after you have read them we can have another conversation."

WEDNESDAY, October 29, 2015, 9:00 a.m. - Hawaii

Chambers was permitted to read the conditions, but was not allowed to keep the list. McCormick wanted to avoid any chance that one day the President showed it around. It was a long list.

1. You must convince the Vice President to resign.
2. Once he has resigned, you can tender your own resignation.
3. You may not give any speeches or interviews or write articles of any political nature. If the media sticks a microphone in your face, your answer will be 'no comment.'
4. You may not associate with or contact any American radicals.
5. You will not travel outside the USA.
6. You will not be in possession of a US passport.
7. You will be able to live anywhere you like in America.
8. You will not conduct yourself in any way that could inflame the passions of some of the American people.
9. Before you resign you will sign a presidential pardon for everyone involved in your removal from office.
10. These conditions will remain in effect until the day after Inauguration Day in January 2017. After that you and your family will be able to renew your American passports and all other conditions will no longer be in effect.

11. You must agree to keep your Secret Service detail.
12. You will continue to receive your presidential salary until Inauguration Day in January 2017.
13. You and your family will be furnished with two limousines and chauffeurs wherever you decide to live in the USA.
14. All of the above conditions will also apply to Mrs. Chambers and your children.
15. You will also be entitled to your presidential pension just like any other former President.
16. You and Mrs. Chambers may not discuss any of the conditions in this agreement with anyone outside your family.
17. You and/or your wife may not attend any public social events, fundraisers or make speeches. You may attend private gatherings where there is no media. You must make it clear to the people inviting you to these private gatherings that there is to be no media; however, you must inform the Secret Service of these private invitations for their approval.
18. Any breach of these conditions and you will find yourself back in your present circumstances with more limited movement than before.
19. If we have overlooked any other reasonable conditions, they may be added later. You will contact General McCormick if you agree to these conditions. We will provide you with the phone number for the Vice President if you wish to proceed with this process.

Chambers studied the list for a bit and handed it back to the officer. "I need to discuss this with my wife and children. I will give you an answer tomorrow," he said. But knew that his children wouldn't take much convincing.

FRIDAY, October 31, 2015, 9:00 a.m. - Hawaii

Chambers called General McCormick first thing in the morning to tell him he agreed to the conditions. McCormick said, "You understand that before we can implement this agreement you must convince the Vice

President to resign? You don't have to explain the conditions; we will take care of that."

The President dialed the number he'd been given, and said "Hello James. Are you okay?"

Vice President Dryden had not talked to the President for over a year, and sounded very happy to hear his voice.

"I'm fine under the circumstances, and so is the family. How about you and where are you?"

"I can't tell you that," said the President. "But I've received an offer that will relieve me of my present circumstances." Chambers knew he was being listened to and was being careful not to use the term military house arrest. "I have accepted certain conditions because I have come to the conclusion that there is no way that I will be reinstated as President. You will be offered the same conditions yourself, but I have to tell you that one of them is that, like me, you would have to resign. But you will have to resign first for me to get out of my present circumstances. I am not telling you what decision you should make but my family also agrees that it would be fruitless not to accept the conditions."

Dryden promised to think about it and let him know the next day.

SATURDAY, November 1, 2015, 9:15 a.m. - Hawaii

The President heard from McCormick instead, who informed him that the Vice President had agreed to resign the next day. "Are you prepared to tender your resignation tomorrow as well?" he asked.

"Yes," said the President. "And then what will happen?"

"Where do you want to live?" said McCormick.

The President said, "We would like to go back to our home in St. Louis but still come here on vacation from time to time."

McCormick said, "If you tender your resignation tomorrow, you will be free to leave on Monday. But we have a request first."

The President's rolled his eyes.

McCormick said, "We want you to take your chauffeured limo into town and kind of parade yourself around. That will suck media from all over the world to the Big Island, but by that time you will be gone. In the meantime you can pack up your belongings. We will have a Global Express private jet ready to fly you direct to St. Louis. Please tell Mrs. Chambers that your home in St. Louis has been kept spick-and-span by government cleaning contractors. The aircraft will be at your disposal until January 2017. Please use discretion regarding its use. We do not want to be accused of any excesses. You show us a little respect and we will do the same for you."

The President replied with a strained "Thank you."

SUNDAY, November 2, 2015

After a year cooped up, the President was quite excited about doing what McCormick had asked. He and his family did some shopping and had lunch in town. By that time the local media were following them all over the place. Chambers made no comments other than to talk about how nice the weather was. By 3:00 p.m. the family had had enough, and got back in the limo. They were beginning to appreciate the solitude they'd enjoyed for the last year.

Chambers suspected that McCormick had a second reason for asking him to put himself on display – he would have to get re-acquainted with a life of severe scrutiny. He decided in the car that he would not be seen in public again before they got back to St. Louis. He wanted to be home before Thanksgiving.

Back at the villa, Chambers phoned McCormick and asked if he could arrange to get them off the island on Wednesday morning."

"Experiencing a little media madness, are you?" McCormick asked. "I'm already ahead of you, it's all arranged. The helicopter will be there early Wednesday morning."

The President had really never liked the military very much but he was beginning to appreciate McCormick's twisted sense of humor.

This was good, McCormick thought. He could now complete his plan prior to Thanksgiving. "The Secret Service guys will tell you about all the arrangements. Have a good trip, Mr. President and you enjoy your Thanksgiving."

WEDNESDAY, November 5, 2015, 8:00 a.m. - Hawaii

On the plane to St. Louis Chambers phoned Dryden and found out that he was on his way to Boston. They made arrangements to get together soon. On the Global Express, the former President was feeling like an important person again and was even being treated like one. When they arrived at their old house in St. Louis, they were amazed to find that not only was it spick-and-span, it had a lot of new amenities. Chambers wondered if they had bugged the place while they were at it.

THURSDAY, November 6, 2015, 9:00 a.m. - Washington

Now that McCormick had the resignations and the pardons he demanded, he was ready to execute the rest of his political plan. He arranged to meet with the House Speaker and the Senate Leader at restaurant private room at the Monocle at noon.

Once the Federal Only section of the AFC was passed by the House, the Senate and the required number of states, it would formally become a new amendment to the Constitution. And the Speaker had sneaked into the amendment a one-time, temporary provision that would allow the House of Representatives to select an American citizen who had not been born in the US to serve as President until inauguration day in January 2017, if the President and Vice President resigned. At lunch, the Speaker explained what he had done to McCormick. "I had the votes to get this done, and it was a no-brainer. The majority of the Congress likes what the Administrator is doing and they like him. His approval ratings are high and getting better, so to do anything else at this point would be extremely disruptive," he said.

THURSDAY, November 6, 2015, 7:00 p.m.

McCormick was having a working dinner at the White House that night with Haynes, Giani and Secretary of State West. He had already informed Rod and Oliver about his lunch with the House Speaker, and the three of them were waiting for Haynes to arrive.

When Haynes sat down, he immediately picked up on the strange expressions on their faces. "What's up with you guys tonight?" he asked.

McCormick figured he better get right to it. "The President and the Vice President have both tendered their resignations as of yesterday. A bill is going to be presented in the House of Representatives next week to have you sworn in as the next President of the United States."

Haynes didn't say a word for a little bit. Then he said, "Jesus, is this really necessary? I like being Mr. Administrator. I've been elected by nobody."

McCormick replied, "The same could be said for Gerald Ford and a bunch of others. Now, if this passes – and there's no reason for me to believe that it won't be – you will probably be sworn in by the end of next week, so you can fire me." Haynes erupted into laughter, but McCormick continued, "What we need you to tell us now is who you want for VP, so that you can both be sworn in at the same time."

Haynes didn't hesitate. "I want Rod, but I want him to stay on as Chief of Staff as well."

McCormick looked at Giani and said, "Well, Mr. Chief of Staff?"

Rod said "I am honored, but I'll have to give you my answer tomorrow. My wife would like to think she is part of this because as the Vice President's wife, she is going to be more involved in the administration."

McCormick said, "This is unprecedented in our history and the closest thing we have in the Constitution is amendment 20, the last part of section 3, which deals with presidential succession. So the Speaker has also submitted a letter to Congress abstaining from the line of succession."

In the meantime, Jeannie Flett went to Blair House to inform Sonja that David was going to be sworn in as the next President of the United States and she was going to become the First Lady even though they weren't married. By the time Haynes got back to Blair House, Sonja had been on the phone for over an hour, talking in Spanish with her family back in Florida. She was nervous and excited, although she had boasted to her sister, "Not bad for a Cuban refugee that came to America with her family at eight years old."

FRIDAY, November 7, 2015, 7:00 a.m.

While Haynes and McCormick waited for Giani to join them, McCormick asked, "What if Rod says no? Who do you want?"

"You," Haynes said.

"No. We can't have a former military officer serving as vice president under these circumstances. But I think you knew that. Nice try, though. Seriously, who would your other choice be?"

Haynes replied, "John McFarland."

Just then, Giani came in. "Well?" said Haynes.

Giani said "Okay, I'm in. I got the boss's approval."

TUESDAY, November 18, 2015, 3:00 p.m.

The House of Representatives passed the bill allowing David Haynes to be sworn in as the next President of the United States and Rodrick Giani as Vice President. The Senate passed it the next day and the swearing-in was set for 5:45 p.m. on Saturday, November 22, at the Capitol Building.

McCormick now completed the last stage of his grandiose plan. Bills passed by Congress and the Senate had been signed by Haynes, but only in his capacity as Administrator, so they all had to be signed again once he was sworn in, in case someone tried to overturn the legislative advances after the 2016 elections. Some lawyers and Supreme Court justices were already licking their chops at the possibility, but McCormick was not about to give up all the hard work done and the changes that had been made. He had a plan underway to make sure that the President elected in 2016 would reappoint him as Secretary of Defense. But he was also prepared to arrest any Supreme Court justice who tried to overturn the advances made over the two-year period. He would shut down the building if he had to, to prevent a return to pre-2014 conditions. He figured that after four more years as Secretary of Defense, the new changes would be entrenched, and that would take him into 2020. At that point, he could retire, because he didn't foresee any serious challenges to the changes once things were working smoothly.

SATURDAY, November 22, 2015, 10:00 a.m.

David and Sonja got up late and had a leisurely breakfast at Blair House. Then he went over to the White House to be briefed on his schedule of activities. There would be an inauguration gala at the White House Saturday evening, with his favorites Merle Maggart and Chris Boshee providing entertainment. His son Colin's grandmother Wilma and mother Lana would be there from Las Vegas, as well as his two children and other relatives from Canada and close friends from all over America. Sonja would have her sisters and some other family members there from Florida. Rod was having his gala at the Marriott. His guest list had become too large for the White House.

SATURDAY, November 22, 2015, 5:15 p.m.

At 5.15 p.m. the future Vice President's limo started out toward the Capitol Building. The Secret Service would not let him and Haynes ride together. Five minutes later Haynes' entourage followed Giani's. Haynes found it ironic that today was the anniversary of President Kennedy's assassination in 1963.

A reluctant Chief Justice was at the Capital to do the swearing-in. No doubt McCormick had read him the riot act – show up or else. After the swearing-in ceremony, Haynes entered the chamber for his speech, which lasted only about 25 minutes. He and Sonja were back at the White House by 7:00 p.m. He had insisted that there be no official table seating, as long as there were enough tables and chairs for all the guests. Buffets had been set up in several locations. It was all very relaxed and everyone sat where they felt like. Haynes and Sonja got up and danced to Merle's "Lady I Know You're Out There Somewhere But Our Paths May Never Cross." It was a laid-back evening and everyone seemed to enjoy themselves. David and Sonja finally left just after midnight. Tonight they were moving into the official residence and tomorrow Haynes' office would be oval and Rod would be in the office right next to him. Giani appointed Fennett as his deputy VP to take on some of the Vice Presidential responsibilities, so he could keep his post as Chief of Staff.

WEDNESDAY, December 2, 2015

In the Oval Office, Giani asked Haynes who he thought would win the Republican primary.

Haynes replied, "I don't know, but one thing for sure, is they have a great field of experienced candidates. But if Rubio doesn't win, and is not picked as a running mate, the winner is a moron. That's the huge mistake the last guy made. They lost Florida."

"Do you promise to keep what I am about to say between you and I?"

"Okay" Giani responded.

"There are some very experienced governors in the race with outstanding records, but one excels and stands out in a critical area. The likability or charisma factor. John Kasich from Ohio has that honest trustworthy down-to-earth charm that stimulates the likability instincts in people. This, along with his great balanced record as governor makes him more electable in a general election than his competitors. Plus he comes from Ohio, one of the must win states. I absolutely don't want to be perceived as taking sides so please keep this to yourself."

CHAPTER 26

WRAPPING UP THE AFC AND CUBA AS WELL

—⁂—

WEDNESDAY, January 13, 2016

In mid-January, Snow reminded Haynes that the State Only part of the AFC had been presented back on April 16th.

Haynes was surprised to realize that so much time had passed, and still Congress had not passed the State Only section. It looked like some of the Congressional people were dragging their feet hoping it would just go away. It was time for a meeting. He scheduled it for January 19.

TUESDAY, January 19, 2016

Knowing that he needed ammunition to get things moving on the State Only part of the AFC, Haynes brought Ronson into the meeting to give Congressional people a presentation on the health situation in the two trial states, New Mexico and Washington State. Both states had had good success with the new program and after the six-month trials, were ready to implement the health care program permanently. The most important part was that polls showed voter approval to be very high in both states.

Ronson now had seven more states ready embark on the program using the adjustments made in Washington and New Mexico as guidelines for their own programs. Haynes knew that healthcare was the most contentious part of the State Only section of the AFC. But the success of the two trial programs and the enrollment of seven more states created a new reality on the ground, especially with voters, that healthcare was slipping away from federal control to the control of individual states. Even big government proponents in Congress were beginning to realize that opposition to this was not going to be popular with the voters. The process was now irreversible.

Ronson concluded his presentation by saying, "Everything is moving forward and you folks are the only ones left. We need to get passage of this by April 1 this year."

THURSDAY, February 4, 2016

At the White House, there was a "come to Jesus" meeting with the congressional leadership, congressional committees, some congressmen and some Senators concerning the last phase of the noncitizen program. The presidential primary debates had already started and had been marked by fireworks from both sides over what the administration was doing and was going to do. The Democrats and the candidates running in the Democratic primary were going crazy. Haynes couldn't understand their reaction. "What's wrong with these people?" he wondered. "For the first time we're getting a grip on the problem and close to solving it. Are they simply in love with chaos? We're using a step-by-step organized program with targeted goals."

Haynes was more determined than ever to get the immigration plan finished before a new President was sworn in, in January 2017. He wanted to remove the statute that provided automatic citizenship for anyone born in the United States. Illegals were taking maximum advantage of this provision, which was never the intention. The administration's approach was to handle illegals on a case-by-case basis and although there was no specific timetable, the plan had a target of November 1, 2016. The process would continue until there was no one left on the list.

By the time of the White House meeting, the registration offices had been open since October 1, 2015. Each had an evaluation team sitting in the back with a list of criteria. Some of this process was going to be ugly and sometimes unfair, but it had to be completed to get America's immigration policy back to being law-based, orderly and normal.

1. Anyone illegal with a criminal record was to be deported immediately and not allowed to return. If they were caught back in the country they would be arrested charged and put in an American prison. The country didn't need any more dead police officers or citizens. Appeals could be made for the special consideration of people who had stayed out of trouble for some time, especially if they had families.
2. Families were defined as mother and father and their children. The Administration had defined two categories that would be given preference. The first was families with children born in the United States and with one or more family member employed. This group was sorted by additional priority as follows:
   A. If one of the family members owned a long-standing business with employees. Businesses recently formed for the purpose of getting preference would not be considered.
   B. The length of time already in the United States, with the longest given priority.
   C. One family member was a property owner.

This group was being granted a path to citizenship and government files updated to reflect that the process for these individuals was complete.

The second category was single individuals, who were judged on the same basic criteria as the 'family' category. Non-qualifiers had their ID privileges removed from the database and were given 30 days to leave the country. However, they were still listed in the government database if they wished to stand in line and apply for citizenship like anyone else. Once this particular process was completed, the US would revert to processing citizen applications as originally intended

There were heated debates for most of the day and the administration heard only a couple of minor constructive comments. The rest of it was all politics, ideology or some Hispanic members trying to support their own by any means necessary.

Haynes did not really say very much. He didn't have to because both Kyling and Giani had lost their patience and had had enough. Finally

Kyling said, "We will implement some of the constructive changes suggested. The rest of it is just political and ideological nonsense that leads us back to the status quo. We are going to get a handle on this thing once and for all and we are going to implement this program starting today, period."

A Hispanic Congressman from Chicago stood up and hurled some personal attacks at Kyling, who, red-faced, shot back, "You have been an obstructionist to a resolution for too long. All your so-called objections are just a camouflage for your real agenda, which is to maintain chaos to keep the borders open and prevent the return of normal, orderly, legally-based citizenship applications. This is no longer an option. This meeting is adjourned."

TUESDAY, March 3, 2016, 9:00 a.m.

Now that he was President, Haynes felt that it was time for him to address another constitutional amendment. This was one going to be difficult, and more so for the Senate. He invited the House Speaker, House Minority Leader Rossi, the Senate Leader and Senate Minority Leader Mason Weed. Haynes was not really looking forward to having the two minority leaders in the meeting but he had to try to convince them, even though he knew they would try to stonewall everything. But Haynes believed voters would perceive any opposition to these changes as pure self interest. He also invited Carolina Senator Tim Watt. Watt was a brilliantly articulate African-American and Haynes had met him at the black conservative night at the White House. They had hit it off and now his instincts told him Watt could be helpful.

Haynes made sure that he had a fat publicity budget and was using television and other media to expose and refute opposition to his reforms as being driven by self interest, special interests, blind ideology or lies and distortions. He put together a team in the White House just for this purpose, to respond to certain media agencies immediately at the local level where problem opposition members served. "Hit them where it counts, right in their own back yard where their voters are," was his directive, although he cautioned the group to be fair. Members of cabinet, White House staff, and members of Congress were encouraged to congratulate positive contributions that helped move things forward no matter what political persuasion they came from. The point man for this approach was the press secretary, who would say, for example "We would like to thank Senator X's positive opposition in pressing for these changes." Haynes wanted to make sure that positive contributions were known in member's districts as well, regardless of party. It had become part of the operational culture of the administration, and was evidently having an effect, moving some members from blind opposition to positive opposition. Except for, of course, some members from the left coast. Haynes was not about to give up on that region. He challenged his White House media group to use a common sense approach with the West Coast and the Northeast. "Use this logic. Get someone to look into a camera, explain what we are attempting to do, then explain the opposition to it. Then say, does this make any sense to you? If you can't sell it nobody's buying."

He proposed that members of congress be limited to serve three four-year terms, staggered to allow the tradition of midterm elections to continue. Senators would be limited to three six-year terms, staggered again to allow the continuation of midterm elections.

To try and get cooperation from existing members, Haynes had a pension package introduced that would be limited to existing members and would not be extended to future members of Congress or the Senate. This was kind of a carrot to try and get them to cooperate. Another carrot he proposed was that existing members be treated like brand-new members and be able to serve under the new rules starting from the date of their last re-election. In effect, this provided another set of three terms for existing members of the House and Senate.

The reasoning behind the four-year term was so that members of Congress would spend less time campaigning and so would not need as much money to finance re-election campaigns. Instead they could spend more time taking care of the people's interests.

Haynes asked for a bipartisan committee to establish fair, sensible rules – to be included in a constitutional amendment regarding the Senate – that would apply to any majority in power in the future and that could not be changed no matter who had a majority. He also insisted on the importance of the 50+1 vote. His reasoning was it was already difficult enough to pass legislation through three levels of government. Requiring more than 50+1 votes to pass anything in the Senate was raising the bar too high. The same amendment would include a line item veto for future presidents, which could only be overridden by two-thirds of the Senate.

The administration also included in this amendment the new rules for the introduction of any regulations, big or small. All federal agencies would have to submit any new regulations or the reinstatement of existing ones for the approval of Congress. This would be the exclusive domain of Congress, although Congress could invite affected parties to participate. Congress could, by majority vote, cancel any given regulation at any time. Provision would be made for the introduction of an Ombudsman's Office for citizen's complaints and the appeal of unfair, unreasonable, or excessive application of regulations. It also gave Congress the right to reject the President's choice for Attorney General, to vote for their choice from the President's slate of candidates for the position, or to propose and vote for their own selection. Congressional committees would also be given the authority to appoint special prosecutors. These prosecutors would be given subpoena authority.

THURSDAY, March 12, 2016

The Senate passed the immigration bill that would allow the administration to continue the direction it was on. Evaluations of illegals would continue until everyone that registered was completed. It would still be a lengthy process but now there was a clear path to completion.

TUESDAY, March 22, 2016

The Russians were on the move again in the Ukraine. It had become obvious that their goal was to retake control of that country, breaking the agreement they had made to honor Ukraine's boundaries in exchange for the removal of nuclear weapons there after the breakup of the Soviet

Union. The Russians had broken their treaty obligations and Haynes was determined not to honor any previous agreements with the Russians as a result.

The Russians had also resumed their menacing flights over Northern Europe and into the Atlantic close to North America, as they had done during the height of the Cold War. Haynes was getting nervous that the Russians would next try to reestablish their influence in Cuba, which could lead to a replay of the Cuban missile crisis.

The situation room was filled with military brass as Haynes pointed out that since the Russians were not honoring their treaties, any agreements with them were no longer in effect. "I don't know what their intentions are but we are not going to take any chances. We need to be proactive. Allowing the Russians to reestablish themselves in Cuba would be extremely dangerous. We need to invade Cuba and free the Cuban people from the Castro brothers. We need to let the Russians know we have our own sphere of influence.

"I need to have consensus for the invasion of Cuba at the earliest possible date. We need to use overwhelming force. I want a campaign that doesn't last any more than three to five days. And this discussion absolutely cannot leave this room," Haynes concluded.

At this point McCormick weighed in. "Why don't we draw up a contingency plan and reconvene in a couple weeks?"

WEDNESDAY, April 6, 2016

The term limit constitutional amendment with its riders was passed by the Senate and sent to the states.

MONDAY, April 11, 2016

The consensus at the second meeting on Cuba was for the invasion Haynes proposed, and that it needed to be carried out quickly before anyone got tipped off. The invasion date was set for Wednesday, June 1, 2016. McCormick planned to use 75,000 troops to invade the island from all sides. A second invasion by civilians would be required to help the Cubans reorganize their society. Medical equipment and other necessary supplies would be provided, and the military would implement a program to rid the island of all weapons.

TUESDAY, April 12, 2016

After a massive campaign from the administration's communications office and state governors, the Senate finally passed the State Only provision second part of the AFC constitutional amendment. It included a rider that disallowed any state from preventing legitimate businesses from operating in it. Another Saturday evening Gala would be held to celebrate the second part of this historic accomplishment.

Now they were two-thirds there with the project, with only the Shared provision left to be negotiated. Haynes realized that they probably would not be able to finish section three, the Shared part of the AFC, before his mandate ended the first week of January 2017. This part was particularly complex and lengthy because agencies would have to be subdivided and separated into Federal and State Only components.

Haynes knew that taking the same approach to the third and final part of the Shared section of the AFC could not be completed before he left office. So he made a personal request to the Speaker and the Senate Leader.

"You have been part of the most historic constitutional changes since the original documents. I think you both understand that the last part of the Shared section of the AFC cannot be completed before the next election and may be in jeopardy. I have a suggestion. The first of the AFC committee members come from the original team negotiators. You and I know they have diligently based their conclusions on the spirit of the AFC'S guidelines without bias and there is absolutely no reason for anyone involved intimately in this process to believe it will not continue this way.

"There may be a way to complete this process before our electoral mandates are finished. Why don't we just give an exclusive mandate or authorization to the committee members to complete the Shared section on their own, to become entrenched as part of the overall charter so that it cannot be overturned by state or federal legislators. If we attempt to do this ourselves there will be battles raging for years. Even the committee's completion process for the Shared section is going to extend beyond our mandates. Besides, the big advantage is there still will be the appeal process left as part of the Charter's mandate for later fine tuning. This is the only way I know to have this entrenched and completed so that it cannot be messed with except by the appeal process."

The Speaker and the Senate Leader exchanged glances. They had reluctantly gone along with this process at the beginning, but after participating all this time, the historic nature of the effort combined with the idea of their personal legacies had been internalized. This was now their baby, too. So there was no way they intended to leave the Charter unfinished before the next election. After some discussion the plan was approved and the path for the conclusion of the AFC was set in motion.

Haynes was elated. He had started this whole process alone and now he finally had an army of enthusiasts on board with him.

SUNDAY, May 1, 2016

Customs started the process of assessing Chinese imports the additional 1 percent. The Chinese were trying to apply pressure from as many angles as they could, but to no avail. The Yuan was trading at 0.16 to the US dollar. Now it was not only the Americans who were putting pressure on the Chinese to float their currency, other nations had joined them, as often happened when the US led the way. It was just a matter of time.

WEDNESDAY, June 1, 2016

The American Navy surrounded the island of Cuba before dawn. The first amphibious force landed at the Bay of Pigs, equipped with obsolete tanks with no ammunition. They set up a fake invasion force slightly inland, and then retired to their ships. Cuban forces took the bait and headed for the decoy. Late morning, the Americans landed a force on the coast near Cienfuegos and another to the west of the Bay of Pigs. As the Cuban troops moved closer to the Bay, the American forces closed in behind them and sealed them off between the Americans and the sea.

The strategy was designed to avoid as many casualties as possible. Cuban soldiers in training were given only one bullet each, because Castro didn't trust them. Now this would come back to haunt him, as American air traffic dropped thousands of pamphlets over the Cuban forces at the Bay of Pigs to tell them that the invaders had come in overwhelming force to liberate them from the Castro brothers, and did not intend to harm Cuban troops or the Cuban people. The leaflets mentioned that there were many Cuban Americans participating in the invasion, and that if soldiers surrendered they would come to no harm. Then the American forces sat tight and waited, hoping Cubans would understand that fighting was a hopeless option.

In other parts of the island, troops were dropped near key airports, and more troops and equipment were flown in at a rapid pace. And the Americans had been quietly reinforcing their troop numbers at Guantanamo Bay and by morning had taken by surprise and overpowered the Cuban guards overlooking the base. The American troops at Guantanamo Bay headed inland. So far, no one had been killed or injured.

By late morning pamphlets were dropped all over the island discouraging Cuban forces from engaging in a futile defense. Wherever American forces came close to the Cuban military, they tried to surround them and not engage. This was the advantage of using overwhelming force – there were enough troops for some to advance while leaving a solid force behind, so that the Cubans could not move in any direction.

On the southern peninsula, landings were taking place at Manzanillo and northeast of Pilon, just east of Guantanamo. The plan was to seal off this part of the peninsula, trapping any Cuban military located there. Meanwhile the force coming out of Guantanamo was moving west, joining up with the invading forces landed at Manzanillo. At its widest point, Cuba is only 100 miles across, and amphibious craft were also landing on the north side of the island and moving west. Other forces landed near Cienfuegos in the south, and yet another just north of Santa Clara, near the center of the island. These two groups would rendezvous to cut off that part of the island, and then part of the force would move east toward Havana while the other part headed west to squeeze any opposition and rendezvous with the forces coming from Guantanamo. All forces were directed to surround and not engage any Cuban military if possible. Once the airport west of Havana was taken, that part of the island was effectively cut off leaving no access to the rest of Cuba to the East.

Within 48 hours, the invasion was complete. There were still some Cuban forces that had not surrendered. Haynes told McCormick not to engage them unless their own forces were threatened. This was the advantage of using former General Powell's philosophy of overwhelming force. He wanted them to just sit there and wait it out to prevent unnecessary casualties.

Finally, Cuba would become a free country. The celebrations in Miami went on for days.

The State of Florida had a list of several thousand Spanish speakers, mostly of Cuban origin, willing to go in and document all Cuban citizens. Within the week, the passport office would be printing special Cuban passports to be issued to every Cuban citizen. Photo equipment and supplies required for the job would be shipped to Cuba.

Seizure of private property is one of communism's hallmarks, while private property ownership is the basic symbol of a free people. The US was anxious to restore this symbol of freedom. So the State Department was soliciting specialists to document property ownership in Cuba. One of the oldest and best organized of these agencies was the notarial network in the province of Quebec in Canada, and the State Department engaged it to register properties in Cuba back to private ownership.

Teams of retired businessman were flown in to Cuba as well. Their job was to assess businesses and get them back in the hands of private owners in some form or another. There was to be no wholesale grabbing of businesses by Castro's remaining sympathizers.

The political plan was to divide Cuba up into a number of autonomous states, each with a governor. There would be a central government but the opportunity for dictators to take over would be diminished. All this earned the attention of the thugs in Venezuela, who were eyeing the US action nervously.

A 55-foot sailboat was intercepted by an American military vessel between Cuba and the Cayman islands. There was a man and a woman on board, and a single crew member. The man, who said he was the boat's owner, was casually well-dressed and said he was on his way back to Venezuela. When asked to produce his passport, he replied that he had left it at his hotel in Cuba in his haste to avoid the invasion. The Americans started searching the tight quarters of the vessel and finally discovered another man huddled in the engine room. It was none other than Raul Castro. Apparently Fidel was just too ill to travel, and stayed on the island. The Americans told the man and his crew that they did not mean them any harm and ordered them to sail the boat back to Cuba. Castro was taken on board the American ship.

FRIDAY, June 3, 2016

The Federal Labor Board shut its doors for the last time. Under the State Only provisions of the AFC, labor was now a state-by-state responsibility.

THURSDAY, June 18, 2016

Final state approval for the term limit amendment, based on the principles discussed at the meeting of March 3, was passed and was now part of the Constitution.

The White House planned to celebrate with a grand Gala on Saturday, June 27. Haynes knew these get-togethers were a lot more than social. Not only did they give members of Congress and the administration the opportunity to celebrate what had been accomplished, but they made everyone feel like they were part of the process and promoted a positive atmosphere in the Washington political establishment. He made sure that Flett invited famous political veterans including former Speaker Goodrich and former Senator Runn.

CHAPTER 27

THE ADMINISTRATION'S LAST ACTS

—⚉—

MONDAY, August 3, 2016

Air Force One departed Andrews Air Force Base bound for London. On board were Sonja, Secretary West, the Leader of the Senate, Secretary McFarland, General McCormick, Rod Giani, Senator Maggi from Virginia who had just dethroned Senator Weed as Minority Leader and various Congressmen and Senators. The House Leader stayed behind for family reasons. Meetings were conducted with the Prime Minister and British officials and then it was on to Warsaw. Haynes was flown by helicopter to the eastern Polish border and inspected NATO troops, who were from various NATO countries. Then it was onto Bonn, Germany to meet with the Chancellor and thank her for her contribution to reinforcing NATO's presence closer to Ukraine and Russia. They didn't visit France because the French were still annoyed about Haynes' comment that it was "time for the Europeans to man up concerning the new threat from Russia's little Stalin, Putin." They made a quick visit to Latvia, one of the Baltic states right on the Russian border, before a final European stop in the Czech Republic to inspect the newly installed nuclear missiles that should have been there long ago.

WEDNESDAY, August 10, 2016

It was wheels down at the American Air Force Base outside of Erbil, Kurdistan. General Trais and President Kobani, recently re-elected, were waiting for Haynes and Sonja at the bottom of the stairway of Air Force

One. Haynes was thrilled to see General Trais, Canadian Prime Minister Harris who had contributed troops to the effort, and especially Kobani and Maggi. Their shared experience with the troops at Fort Hood was still fresh in their minds. President Haynes and his entourage had come to attend the official opening of the Kurdistan National Assembly on Wednesday.

The group proceeded down the red carpet and then came to attention while the Kurdistan military band played the American national anthem. There were throngs of Kurdish citizens waving Kurdish, American, British and Canadian flags. Haynes imagined they had to go through very stringent security to be there. Mrs. Kobani presented Sonja with a bouquet of flowers. President Kobani was beaming as he escorted Haynes, Trais, McCormick and West to work the crowds. Sonja had to give a continuous barrage of flowers to aides so she could shake hands with as many people as possible. She looked absolutely gorgeous.

Haynes decided to wade into the crowd. People with tears in their eyes were touching and grabbing him but not in an aggressive way. The same was happening to McCormick, West, Maggi and especially General Trais; everyone knew who he was. Maggi looked like he was enjoying himself. Maybe this would change some attitudes when he got back home. Prime Minister Harris was way on the other side working the crowds. McFarland had never experienced anything quite like this before and neither had Haynes. All of a sudden a man that looked to be in his 50s, with dark hair and wearing an ordinary shirt, caught Haynes' eye. The man had a gold cross hanging from his neck and tears falling from his face, his mouth stretched sideways with emotion. The President went over and hugged the man. He could feel him shaking, and stepped back, his hands still on the man's shoulders. The man looked up and said in broken English, "I lost some family members. Thank you for freeing us from those jihadist animals."

The Secret Service guys were going crazy and were trying to get the President back to the front of the crowd. Haynes turned to agent Riley and said, "I'm working all of this crowd, I don't care if it takes all afternoon. And get that man's name and coordinates."

Then he shouted at Trais: "Dismiss those marines over there and let them shake hands with the crowd as well, they're the ones who made all this possible, we didn't fire a damn shot." All this was captured by the television crews and broadcast back home.

Haynes thought, "My god, this must've been what it was like for soldiers entering liberated Paris in the 40s." This whole experience was the most rewarding the President had since day one. Being tough against criminal aggressors had paid off.

On Tuesday, Sonja was all over the TV screens. She had been a huge hit since they had arrived. Haynes remembered President Kennedy's remark about his trip to Paris. "I am the man who escorted Jacqueline Kennedy to Paris."

FRIDAY, August 12, 2016, 10:00 a.m. - Kurdistan

On Friday Haynes sat with Kobani at the new Kurdish legislature. The official ceremonies were almost completed and it was time for Haynes to speak. He got a rousing ovation and shouts of "bravo" from the audience. On his way to the podium he shook hands with the man with the cross whom he'd met at the airport; he had asked Kobani to make sure that the man was seated in the front row. He introduced General Trais and asked him to stand and take a bow.

The President asked for a moment of silence for civilian and military lives lost. He exchanged glances with the man with the cross and hoped it made him and others like him feel a little bit better. Then Haynes thanked the Kurdish and coalition troops for their bravery. He made reference to how historic this occasion was. He concluded by saying, "America now has a new friend in the Middle East. Long live Kurdistan."

Before the President left Kurdistan that afternoon, he planted another star on General Trais' shoulder.

THURSDAY, August 18, 2016

The third and last section of the AFC, the Shared section, was passed by the Senate. This allowed the AFC committee to complete the separation of powers for this section only. Since April, Snow had been working on the states to pass the section and he now had the required number of states on board to complete the process. The AFC was now going to become the law of the land.

Celebrations erupted in the White House. The President spent the best part of the day on the telephone with the Speaker and the Senate Leader and others who participated in the process. The President was relieved. The completion of the AFC was the domestic hallmark of his time in office.

SATURDAY, August 20, 2016

Anticipating the final passage of the AFC, the White House planned a large Gala on Saturday evening to celebrate this historic event. Governors from most of the states, Senate and House leaders, Senators and Congressmen, members of the White House staff and other special guests participated. It was one of those rare social events in Washington that was free of political agendas and full of celebration and appreciation for efforts made.

When the President introduced Snow he was given a standing ovation. Snow went on to introduce the team leaders and negotiators who were now the first members of the AFC Committee, while Snow was now the chairman. The President was very proud because his old buddies Dever and Rogers were among that group.

WEDNESDAY, October 10, 2016, 8:00 p.m.

Both political parties had picked their presidential candidates for the November 4 election. The final Presidential debate, between candidate Julia Hilton for the Democratic Party and John Kasich, Governor of Ohio, was held on the campus of Duke University in North Carolina. Nothing very significant had happened in the first debate. The candidates took their usual positions – the Democrats advocating big government and social programs, slamming the new tax system for being unfair and favoring the rich, etcetera, etcetera and etcetera. The Republican candidate used his economic record as governor as an example of what he would do as President and pushed the virtues of free enterprise, decentralization, a strong military and defending most of the goals accomplished in the last two years.

Everything was going pretty much as anticipated until it came time for each candidate to give their closing argument. The Republican Governor gave a brief presentation and then looked into the cameras and said, "I want you to listen very closely to what I'm about to say. Picture the scene at a hangar in Washington DC. There is a military honor guard and a podium with the President and Secretary of State, there are four flag-draped coffins of American heroes, an American Ambassador and three of his security detail. Family members of these four heroes assassinated by terrorist jihadists are present. The administration has refused to use the word terrorist in any of the descriptions of these events. The Secretary of State stood up and stated in front of the families and other people in attendance that this tragedy was a result of an offensive anti-Muslim video. She lied at this solemn event. Anyone who does this is not qualified to be President of anything, let alone President of the United States. But what difference does that make? Thank you."

A roar interrupted from supporters of the Governor.

FRIDAY, November 4, 2016

Governor Kasich won the Presidency and he and Senator Rubio were to be sworn in as President and Vice President in the first week of January.

WEDNESDAY, November 23, 2016

Burt Rutan and Musk had been pooling their resources to combine Musk's rocket designs and Rutan's aircraft designs to get into outer space. On this day they carried out the successful launch of a specially-designed spacecraft that used a multitask engine design that included ramjet to get them up to high altitude, at which point the same engine became a rocket. The hybrid engine was designed by a brilliant Canadian inventor by the name of Luc Laforest.

The craft also had a nose which would open up and retract, exposing a connection for the international space station. The purpose of the design was to change the traditional re-entry into the atmosphere from space. Musk's rockets were still being refined to be used as a secondary option. The entire enterprise was a triumph given that there had never been any backup for the now-retired space shuttle. Haynes phoned to congratulate them on their success, knowing full well it might never have happened without his decision to fund their research and development. Under NASA, it would have cost four times as much at least.

MONDAY, December 12, 2016

Energy Secretary Hoffman and Commerce Secretary McFarland christened a new natural gas export facility just outside Portland, Maine. All that was left under construction was the gas pipeline to the facility, so that the US could export natural gas to Europe at a lower cost than the Russians, which would be a huge boon to US exports.

FRIDAY, January 20, 2017

Governor Kasich was sworn in as a new President of the United States and Marco Rubio was sworn in a Vice President

David and Sonja boarded a helicopter and headed for Andrews Air Force Base, where they boarded the Vice President's aircraft for their flight to Miami. After an overnight in Miami, they boarded the aircraft again, this time with some of David's closest friends – including Secretary McFarland – in tow, as well as an entourage of Sonja's family.

They flew to Havana International Airport, where they were greeted by the newly elected Cuban president and driven in a motorcade to Havana. Crowds swarmed the Prado as they were driven to the Presidential Palace, and David and Sonja stood with their heads through the top of the limo waving back. At one point, their cavalcade slowed to a crawl, so, against Secret Service advice, David and Sonja decided to get out and walk for a little bit. But the adoring crowd mobbed them and swiftly surrounded by Secret Service and Cuban military they were escorted back to their vehicle. That night, there was a grand dinner at the Presidential Palace in their honor.

The next day they took a drive out of Havana, escorted by some military vehicles and the Secret Service, to a place on the coast that Sonja remembered from childhood. Ditching their security, they walked alone along the beach toward a secluded cove overlooking the sea. They sat there with arms around each other looking out over the ocean and David said, "Maybe I should buy this property and build us a beach house."

THE END

Made in the USA
Lexington, KY
31 October 2015